AMBASSADOR 4: COMING HOME

PATTY JANSEN

CAPRICORNICA PUBLICATIONS

GET FREE EBOOKS

Visit pattyjansen.com
or scan the QR code below with your phone to get four series starter
ebooks for free!

DID YOU KNOW?

Ambassador 4 is also available in audio. Click the image or visit https://pattyjansen.com to find out more.

1

———

THE MIDDLE OF the afternoon—that lazy, comfortable time after lunch when people more fortunate than I could afford to have naps—was not the ideal time to be catching up with administration. It was the time that I would normally go for a walk, find someone to visit or something to buy. But the neglect of my administration account for the past three weeks had exploded the list of exceedingly boring tasks that also happened to be important, such as to make sure my staff was paid.

And I was a little ashamed that I found it impossible to concentrate, my thoughts drifting off to more pressing issues such as Captain Luczon of the Aghyrian ship, who lodged in the apartment below mine and who had proven to be a little . . . difficult to deal with.

Who *had* to be dealt with—*after* I'd done the damned administration.

Someone knocked on the door.

I looked up from my reader. "Come in."

The door opened, briefly letting in a snatch of sound: a woman yelling at the top of her voice, somewhere in the hall, I judged, by the way the sound echoed.

My trusted member of staff Devlin slipped into the room.

The noise cut off when he shut the door behind him. He sat on the armrest of the chair opposite the desk, glancing over the various readers spread out before me, each with a different accountancy page displayed. He knew what I was doing. Respected it. It *needed* to be done.

"Is she still at it?" I asked him.

"Yup." He gave a lopsided smile, because, seriously, smiling was the only thing one could do besides hoping that this ordeal would soon be over, and Xinanu would go home and terrorise everyone there.

"What's she on about now?"

"Apparently, Eirani brought her yellow-coded breakfast and she spent most of the morning throwing up."

"Isn't that what most pregnant women do?"

Devlin shrugged. "You tell me, Muri. I wouldn't know."

"So what about this breakfast? Did she accidentally get Evi or Telaris' trays? Did they get their breakfast?"

"They did. They ate at the table." He grinned. "You have no sympathy for the poor woman, Muri."

"Not if she behaves like that."

He chuckled, and then his face turned serious. We all knew this episode would cause trouble somewhere down the line. We could laugh at Xinanu now, but we wouldn't laugh so much when she went home and her clan leaders heard her side of the story. I'd already suffered more run-ins with Delegate Ayanu than I cared to remember.

And then Devlin said, "I have a problem, Muri."

"*A* problem? I would love the luxury of having just *a* problem." Ever since we had returned from the Aghyrian ship with its captain, the problems that we hadn't solved before we left appeared to have bred in dark corners. They were swarming us like a herd of cockroaches: when you squished one, two new ones appeared.

"I think this may be the mother of all problems." His face was perfectly serious, but I didn't miss the playful look in his eyes.

I had often accused the local keihu people of being lazy, humourless bureaucrats, but like so many of my ill-informed snap judgements, I was quickly coming to re-evaluate that opinion. Even if keihu weren't blessed with the most attractive physique and their ways were unassuming, they were incredibly stubborn and could be funny if you took the time to pay attention to their dark, self-deprecating comments.

"Let's have this mother-of-all-problems, then."

"I've discovered why so many people have been angry at you."

"You mean any reason other than that I cleared out without notice, stayed away for three weeks and came back with someone who will change the course of history?"

"Other than that."

"It had better be something we can fix then."

"We can, but it's going to need some investment. The reason why you haven't responded to a lot of urgent correspondence is that you never got it. The hub storage is full."

I stared at him. "Is that all? Empty it."

"That's all very well, Muri, but what do I do with all the messages, materials and documents that people have sent you?"

"Isn't there some sort of backup running?" I didn't see why this was my problem. Information systems and communication was Devlin's job. Surely he could shift all that stuff elsewhere and allow the current space to be usable again? I didn't know anything about data systems. That's why I had him.

"There is a backup, and it works. And we use it all the time. It's just that I cannot back up things that haven't been dealt with."

Oh. Hell. "You mean . . . the storage has filled up in the space of those three weeks?"

He nodded. "And more is coming in every day. More than we can deal with. I'd apply for bigger storage, but I'm sure Delegate Namion would get upset because it will then be bigger than his storage."

And Delegate Namion could certainly not be allowed to get upset. I was tempted to roll my eyes, but Delegate Namion and whoever elected the doofus as Chief Delegate was another subject altogether. "Well, in that case . . . maybe we should try to direct some of the correspondence to Delegate Namion."

"We're already doing that, but we cannot stop people using your main address."

No, we couldn't. "What is it all about, anyway?"

"Your trip, the Aghyrians, any of your projects in the past. A long list of subjects."

"Who is it from?"

"All kinds of people. A lot of civilians. Individuals, smaller organisations, businesses. All kinds. From everywhere. *Gamra* worlds, non-*gamra* worlds, Indrahui, even."

"And why are they all writing to *me*? They should be writing to their own representatives."

"Yes. And some have. But the representatives cannot answer the questions, so they've sent them on to you."

"But why not Delegate Namion?"

"I've looked at it. A lot of messages ask quite detailed questions and I know I'm not supposed to comment on it, but I don't think Delegate Namion would have a clue how to reply to them."

Oh. Yes. I couldn't disagree with that. And ouch. And I still didn't understand why the assembly had chosen him to succeed Delegate Akhtari.

The little voice in my head said, *Then you should have been here, shouldn't you?* That was the story of my life in these last few days.

But I'd had no idea that using the Asto military's single-node exchange sling would lose us three weeks. Three weeks! The biggest chunk of time the regular Exchange system lost was about half a day on a transfer to Hedron.

I spread my hands. "All right. I will make a quick selection of the correspondence. I will probably authorise you to dump a huge lot of it in Delegate Namion's account. Then we'll clear it all out. And get more storage, anyway. We can't stop people sending us correspondence. If Delegate Namion complains, send him to me."

He nodded, looking happy. One of the rumours about me I'd heard in the corridors was that my staff liked to work for me because I would often do exactly as they'd hoped I would. Whatever that was supposed to mean.

Devlin opened the door, letting in another wave of yelling.

"Devlin, while you go past Nicha's room, do tell that woman to shut up."

"Uh-uh. Not doing that. I'd rather keep my head where it belongs, Muri."

I could understand that.

He shut the door. I ignored the sound of muffled yelling through the door and pulled my reader in front of me.

I hadn't accessed the correspondence directories since coming back, because I'd been too busy, and because I had relied on my staff to keep them under control and pass the important items to me, but I was horrified to see that Devlin had been right. Everything was full to capacity. Almost every directory had a time period of a few days this week when no messages had come in at all—probably bounced because there was no space, until the ones from yesterday and today, when the auto-backup had made some space because I had dealt with some correspondence.

The most recent ones that I had received were all high-priority correspondence, from the Aghyrian delegation whom I had abandoned without notice or from the Barresh council and various other people who had been upset with me not reacting to their correspondence because it wasn't getting to me. This included messages that should have been replied to with automated responses. For example, every three days a slew of authorities like the Barresh Council, the Pilot's Guild and a whole bunch of additional professional organisations would send me a message requesting updates on the negotiation process. My account would automatically send out this material from the relevant administration accounts where my staff kept recordings of meetings and tabulated the status of various negotiation processes.

When I left with Ezhya to go to the massive Aghyrian ship that the Asto military had cornered in a distant part of the galaxy, it was bad enough that I'd left the negotiations about the Aghyrian claim in limbo. My account had failed to send out updates to all the people who wanted them.

Bloody hell.

What a disaster. As if having the *zeyshi* Aghyrians walk out furious about a week after I disappeared wasn't enough. Fortunately, I had received their latest statement yesterday, because I don't think my system would have survived having it re-sent without scorch marks.

Three. Fucking. Weeks.

Thousands and thousands and thousands of messages.

With one tap of a button, I sorted everything according to the mandatory *gamra* priority levels. This system was only used within *gamra*, so any correspondence from outside automatically fell to the bottom of the priority scale, where, ironically enough, it was easiest to find.

As I scrolled to the top of the list, there were a couple of priority one messages, all of them from Ezhya Palayi's account.

That was weird.

Ezhya didn't use the *gamra* account. If he wanted to contact me, he would use the direct link through the Exchange which reached me through the hub, not via the *gamra* system. I opened the oldest message. It said,

Daddy tells me not to be upset that you left suddenly, but I cannot be 'not upset' when I am upset. You promised me that we would go to the beach if I did all my work. I finished all of it, and I even helped Eirani with her things. I know how to make bread and how to fold the laundry. I did everything she said, but I did not even get to see you before Daddy's guards came to take me home. It's so boring here. There is no one to talk to. I don't like my sister. She screams too much and my parents give her too much attention. They tell me I have to have more lessons, but my tutors are all boring old men. I understand that you're busy and that what happened is important for now. I would like to make a time that I can come back soon and you'll be able to teach me how to surf.

She used the Isla word for surf, with Isla characters.

I chuckled. At only eight years of age, that little rascal Raanu was fast starting to outsmart her father, learning how to use his top priority message privilege.

There were a couple more messages from her, each sent a day apart. None of them were identical.

Another said,

I got into an argument with my tutor today. He says that the *zeyshi* Aghyrians are nothing but opportunistic sleazebags taking advantage of a loophole in gamra law. I asked him has he seen how these people live, in holes in the ground, guarding the old treasures? I think they deserve better than what we have given them so far. I don't know. I could be made to agree that the Aghyrians in Barresh are sleazebags, although their sense of fashion is impeccable.

I laughed out loud at that one.

Another message said,

After you left, I was so bored I actually went to sit in the public gallery at the assembly meeting. I saw how they elected Delegate Namion. He got the votes basically because a lot of people hated Delegate Ayanu so much. I felt sorry for the poor guy who put his name in after the first round of voting. He seemed a decent sort, but by that time, the race was between Delegate Ayanu and Delegate Namion and he came in too late.

I laughed at that analysis, too. That "poor guy" had been Delegate Samarin of Miran, a very serious gentleman who would have had to be extremely stressed out by the situation to put his name forward. Its turbulent history notwithstanding, Miran was usually a quiet bystander in most conflicts, a major agricultural export powerhouse that saw no sense in upsetting too many of its customers.

Raanu had sent the last two messages this morning. The first one said,

I am very sorry to have bothered you. I should not have wasted your valuable time with my childish complaints.

Raanu Palayi

Hmm, that was oddly formal.

Coldi rarely signed their clan name, preferring to go by first name only—their first names were unique. A register was kept to let expectant parents see which names were available. A Coldi person would only sign with a clan name for very serious occasions.

The second message said,

Daddy made me write the previous message. He discovered that I'd been using this account, and he wanted me to apologise, although I'm not aware that I did anything wrong.

I laughed. The rascal.

Privately I was sure Ezhya was laughing as well. Raanu was every bit her father's daughter.

My good mood lasted until I saw that underneath the last message from Raanu, arrived barely an hour ago, was another priority one message from an unfamiliar account in the *gamra* security group.

What the hell? Why would security send me anything urgently?

I opened it up, feeling sick. It was bad enough that we'd had Tamerians running around the supposedly secure island, a fact which I didn't expect security to openly acknowledge. Was this about some other problem?

The message was very short. It said,

I heard you found it. Please confirm at your earliest opportunity and arrange a visit.

There was no name, but the location tracking showed that the message had been sent from a unit on the ground floor of my building.

I knew who was in that particular apartment. I guess I'd better inform *gamra* security that Captain Kando Luczon had been here less than a week and had already cracked their system.

Add that to the growing pile of disasters. No, actually, it was something I needed to address right now.

2

I **WOULD NORMALLY** have left the room in search of Thayu, but I was hesitant to brave the situation outside, so I sent her a message instead. She came into the room not much later, again letting in a wave of yelling.

"Seriously, does that woman ever get tired of it?"

Thayu shrugged while she sat down. "She's very stressed."

"Really? I hadn't noticed."

She gave me her famous cold dead fish look.

"What? She's been behaving terribly ever since we came back. I can't find any good excuse for it, especially not when most of the abuse is directed at Eirani and the staff who have been going out of their way—"

"It's not unusual for Coldi mothers to become extremely stressed just before the birth. Their bodies are telling them that they should seek safe places and make everything perfect before they go into labour."

Oh. Variation number six thousand and fifty-nine of putting my foot in it. Thayu had given birth. Thayu wanted another child. Despite having no love for Xinanu, Thayu understood what she was going through, about to bring a child into the world in an essentially hostile household.

I sighed. Boy, I was an arse. "Well then let's hope it all happens speedily and safely."

She looked out the window.

I sighed and put my hand over hers on her knee. She didn't respond at first, but then turned her hand palm up and squeezed.

"I'm sorry," I said. "I guess we're *all* stressed. We just seem to be going from monumental fuck-up to monumental fuck-up."

"What happened now?"

I showed her Kando Luczon's message.

Her eyes widened. "He broke into security?"

"It seems so."

"Have you let security know?"

"I will, unless something else fucks up in the next few minutes."

She was still frowning at the message. "What is this thing that we're supposed to have found?"

"He's talking about the location of the old ship that brought the first Aghyrian refugees here."

"Didn't they find it even before we left? I mean, we did go to that site on the other side of the island and people were walking around with scanners. And somebody's back wall had collapsed from the sound waves. We knew it was there."

"We knew where the wreck was likely to be. Apparently the Barresh historians have now uncovered the precise site. I saw it on the news channels yesterday."

"Oh. Would there be anything left of the ship for us to look at? I mean, it's been submerged in marshland all that time."

"I doubt much of the main structure of the ship will have survived, but something obviously has, because it responded to the signal that the main ship sent out."

"He seems really keen to see it."

"Yeah." The captain had asked to see the site of the ship as soon as we had told him that it was there.

"Wouldn't you be keen, in his situation?"

"Keen? I don't know. Would I be keen to see the site where people I knew and used to work with, or who were my friends, landed, spent the rest of their lives watching the ruin of our planet become enveloped in a cloud of dust? To know that those people died fifty thousand years ago while by some fluke of physics, I was still alive? I don't know how keen I'd be."

Thayu pressed her lips together. No, she couldn't have followed that train of thought.

Coldi were absolutely never sentimental about their roots or history. I had gotten the impression that the Aghyrians were a lot more like Earth people. Sometimes, they were disturbingly like humans, down to the nasty, vindictive streak.

Thayu gestured at the screen, which still displayed Kando Luczon's message from the security account. "So, do you want me to go to security and give them the bad news?"

"We'll go downstairs with a detour via security."

"Downstairs?"

"I have to address his questions. He came with us on the basis of our willingness to show him the old sites and ruins. Judging by his efforts, he's clearly getting impatient."

"I thought you were going to let him cool his heels after that assembly meeting."

I shuddered at the memory. I'd taken the captain to attend a plenary session. The assembly had honoured him by allowing him to use the title Primary Delegate.

And what had he done?

The speech he'd given had to go down as the single most offensive address ever held in the history of *gamra*. He'd called the Coldi a substitute race that could be retired now that the original inhabitants of Asto were back. He'd called all non-Coldi backwards because they couldn't possibly understand the intricacy of Aghyrian thoughts. He said that the very institution of *gamra* was an exercise in mediocrity because it would never be smarter than its dumbest member entity.

And so on and so forth.

Every time I thought we'd run out of toes that he could step on, he'd found another big foot of them. It was a wonder that he managed to get out of the building alive.

"I was going to let him cool his heels." Even if only for the reason that someone would pull a gun on him if he kept going this way, and I couldn't guarantee that this someone wouldn't be me. "But if he's getting into the security systems, we need another plan. When he goes back to that ship, we don't want him to do so with schematics of our entire security operation and goodness knows what else he can get his hands on if we don't keep him busy."

Thayu said, her voice low. "I don't understand why people are still talking about letting him return to the ship."

"You think he shouldn't?"

"Of course not. As soon as we allow him to go back, that ship will attack the military vessels that guard it. I do not particularly look forward to my father's sling being fired in anger."

No, having seen the equipment in question, I didn't, either. And of course I should have realised that, apart from a means of transportation, the military sling was also a weapon. "What if the ship wakes up and comes after the captain if he's not back by a certain time?"

"The military will destroy it."

I huffed. "You don't destroy something that old."

"That is the problem with *gamra* and this whole situation. People go stupid over this issue of preserving history at all costs. That's rubbish. If the ship is a threat, it should be addressed. People crawl at this man's feet not because of what he's said or done, but because of who he is. He knows that. The guy is arrogant enough to have had people crawl at his feet since he was born. People are hanging off his lips, watching his every move."

I was going to protest, but she was right as usual. In all truth we still knew little of the captain's motivations. I'd randomly selected his two companions for the sole reason of finding out what I could about the ship and its occupants. Better the devil you know, my mother used to say. But so far both companions had been quieter than the proverbial corpse.

"Don't trust him, Cory. This is the guy who refused to take on extra passengers in the days before the meteorite hit. How much effort would it have been to pick up a couple of thousand people from Asto? He could have dropped them on Ceren, if he was that concerned about the ecosystem of his ship."

"It was a long time ago—"

"It's the same guy. He's a first class arsehole. And he's had four hundred years' ship time to cultivate his arseholery. We need to make sure that we keep him harmless."

"That's what I'm doing. Keeping him busy with stuff that interests him. Make sure he keeps out of the fucking security systems." I spread my hands in frustration.

A deep silence followed my comment, in which the sound of the argument in the hall drifted through the door. Someone slammed a door, and opened it again, and Xinanu yelled, "Suit yourself!" Someone replied. I wasn't sure if it was Nicha, but I felt so incredibly sorry for him right now. Xinanu had torn a strip off him when he returned after three weeks.

"Seriously, Thay', is all we can do in this house lately yell at each other?"

"We do plenty of other things." She pulled me close and kissed me. For a moment, I hovered in blissful oblivion. Then she withdrew. "So. What's the plan?"

"Well, clearly the captain is getting bored, so I was going to visit him to see if we can go to the dig site and show him what we found. I have no doubt that he has a fair bit of information that historians would kill for."

"If they believe him." The impostor rumours were all still going strong.

Probably because they couldn't get their mind around how someone who left over fifty thousand years ago could still be alive today. Or if they believed that it might be possible because the ship had travelled at near lightspeed and there had been serious time dilation, they might have trouble believing that someone could live for four hundred years. "They will, once they hear his stories."

"I hope you're right," Thayu said.

Yes, I hoped so, too. If he got involved with the dig, that would alleviate my worries about what he might do when bored. "And we urgently have to notify security about this breach."

"Yes." And then she chuckled. "I can just about hear what Sheydu will say about it."

Sheydu rarely had a good word to say about *gamra* security. "I also need to do something about the hub storage situation."

She frowned at me.

"Apparently a lot of people have contacted me about the Aghyrian ship in preference to contacting Delegate Namion. Devlin came to tell me that the hub storage was full."

"Ah." A look of understanding came over her face. "I was wondering why I got these impatient messages about stuff that I never heard of before."

It affected all of us. I rose from my desk. "We better get dressed." I took my jacket from the cupboard.

"We're going out now?" Thayu asked. "Into town, I mean?"

"If the captain wants to come."

"All right." She pointed at the cupboard. "Gun. Armour."

I'd shut the cupboard door and now reopened it, heaving a sigh. I hated wearing the armour and preferred not to carry a gun; she knew that. I slipped my shirt off over my head and pulled on the armour. There was a mirror inside the cupboard to help me do up the clips at the sides. Thayu helped me with the back. Her hands were strong and warm and made short work of the clips. *Snap, snap, snap.* She squeezed my shoulder. I turned around and pulled her into a kiss. The armour had a rigid front plate that went down in a v-shape at the bottom to give maximum protection to my soft parts while still allowing me to walk. It was not designed for certain—um—bodily functions. Ow, it got really tight down there.

Thayu grinned.

"We need to give Menor a reply soon," I said.

Her expression sobered. "Do we? It's our decision whether we use him or not. I presume his seed remains well-preserved. He can give us some any time."

"Yes, but we should make that decision. I don't like keeping him hanging."

Thayu closed her eyes.

"It's all right by me, really." I'd said this many times before. I wasn't sure why she hesitated so much. Maybe because Coldi didn't have a strong culture of adoption. Children who grew up in someone else's household, say because both parents had died, were often deliberately made to feel inferior. Maybe it was that, and the fear that any child from Menor's seed would have curly hair. I said I didn't mind. After all, I had curly hair, but curly hair was a very serious matter for Coldi.

More and more I feared that we would not end up using Menor at all, and Thayu would either stay with me and grow increasingly unhappy or she would leave me for a man who could give her what she wanted. Maybe she felt even now that she had an obligation to me because I'd paid a huge sum of money to Taysha to sever his contract with her. Even if I got my money back.

Finding a donor had been my idea and my initiative. Sometimes I would catch her looking for pictures of her son, who no longer lived in the Inner Circle, because I'd shot his uncle and the family had been ousted in the reshuffle following the big shakeup of power at Asto's top.

We could adopt him, I'd said.

We could use Menor, I'd said.

I did *not* mind that the child wouldn't be mine, I'd said.

Her replies were always inconclusive.

But the issue would just not go away. She said she wanted *my* child, but if there was some sort of secret process that made it possible, no one had informed me.

The whole thing was starting to give me nightmares. Most of them had Thayu walking out on me, leaving me the compete and utter wreck I had been when Inanu left me.

Memories of that time were a very hairy place to be, one of drinking too much and standing on a rooftop overlooking Athens holding a bottle of zixas and thinking I might just skull the lot and be done with it.

Damn, my eyes clouded over just thinking about it.

And here we were once again just going about our daily business, ignoring the issue. Getting dressed and getting ready for all eventualities, as long as it didn't involve making a decision.

I wanted this solved, decided one way or another, but just like all the previous times, there was no time for an argument.

I went to the bedroom to put another shirt on, because the one I'd been wearing was too tight to be worn over body armour. The bracket with the gun went on my arm before putting the jacket over the top. This was not my *gamra* issue jacket but a security-style design with a lot of room in the upper sleeves so that one could retrieve the gun without taking off the jacket. Thayu had ordered it made recently, in *gamra* blue and all.

"Do you think Nich' should come?" I asked while inspecting myself in the mirror. I would normally ask Eirani to do my hair, but I didn't want to subject her once again to Xinanu's ire by making her walk past the room where Xinanu stayed.

"You still ask that question?"

"I guess that's a no?"

"Of course he should come. We're a complete association."

That balance between caring for one's family and extreme callousness towards them was one I'd probably never get right. I was sure that on Earth, any young man who left his highly pregnant partner in pre-birth distress over some routine job would get clobbered over the ears by her. I didn't comment further. I'd probably exhausted today's supply of get-out-of-jail cards for failing to understand.

We went into the hallway, where it had gone relatively silent. The door to Nicha's room was shut. Xinanu's voice drifted from within. She was crying.

I cringed and knocked. "Nich'?"

The door opened a moment later and Nicha appeared in the door opening, looking harassed and tired.

"We're going into town to take Captain Luczon to the dig site. I'm sorry if you don't want to—"

"Give me a moment to get ready."

He disappeared, leaving the door to the room open.

Xinanu sat on the couch by the window, her feet on a footstool. She wore a long dress of stretch fabric that sat snugly around her distended stomach.

She gave me a hard look. Her cheeks were wet with tears.

Like the stupid human I was, I felt like I had to say something. "I can ask the medico to come if you want."

"What would I need her for? What do you think I am?"

"That is not how you speak to your host," Thayu said, in a very snippy tone. "Even if he asks a question you don't like."

"Leave it, Thay'," Nicha said from somewhere inside the room.

"No, I will not leave it," Xinanu said. "He asks me a rude question. Am I supposed to simper just because he is in charge of paying the rent on this place?"

At the same time Nicha shouted, "Stop it, please," and Thayu said, "Yes, you should. Because you don't rule the world."

Before it could get any worse, Nicha scurried out of the room with his shirt half done up and carrying his armour and gun bracket. He slammed the door behind him.

Xinanu yelled through the door. "That's right! Leave me alone!"

Thayu pulled a face. "What a drama queen."

"Let's go," Nicha said. In all the time Xinanu had been in his room, I'd not heard him say one bad word about her. He surprised me sometimes.

While he put on his gear, I ducked into the hub, where Devlin greeted me with a lopsided smile, a small oasis of mirth of someone who understood how I felt.

"Can you tell our captain that we're coming to pick him up?" I asked. "And let the council know that we're coming to the dig site."

"I'm onto it."

"Also, Devlin, I've had a look at all the messages and shifted the ones that are of immediate importance to my personal work area. Of the rest, you can ask the office downstairs to sort it in rough categories. Anything to do with the assembly goes straight to Delegate Namion. I don't want to see it anymore. Everything else gets sorted into broad subjects. If it's easy to deal with, deal with it. Use my stamp file. Try to sort everything else into stuff with some kind of time limit and non-urgent messages. Send all the non-urgent stuff to Delegate Namion, too. Sort the urgent and semi-urgent messages and put in my work area the stuff that you think I should absolutely deal with soon."

He nodded. "Can I take time off from covering the negotiation?"

"The Aghyrian claim is dead, not that anyone has noticed yet, but I don't expect there to be a lot of work associated with it in the near future. Do whatever you need to keep yourself out of trouble until the bureaucracy catches up with the truth on that front."

"All right."

I returned to Thayu and Nicha, now both fully dressed and ready to go. Telaris at the door asked if he should come, but Thayu said it wouldn't be necessary.

We walked over the gallery to the part that went underneath the artificial waterfall to the other side of the atrium, where a set of stairs led down on the outside of the building.

The security station was in the space under the bottom of the staircase. Today, it was occupied by a single officer who sat yawning at his tiny workstation. The man was Damarcian and listened to my story with an expression of disinterest. He copied Kando Luczon's message to me with all the relevant details and assured me that he would raise it with his boss. When, he didn't say.

Oh well, at least if this all blew up, security couldn't use the argument that they knew nothing and no one had told them.

"You want to check on Xinanu?" I asked Nicha when we'd left the office and were underway to Kando Luczon's apartment.

"Not really." He sounded quite flippant.

"But what if she has the baby while we're gone?"

He and Thayu both frowned at me.

"Yes. What if?" Nicha said.

Thayu said, "Most Coldi children are born in the living rooms of their homes. Often the mother's friends are there, but there is not always time for them to come." Which, by the look on her face, there hadn't been for her.

"What if something goes wrong?"

"If it takes a long time, then the family gets a medico."

Nicha said, "You know how most Coldi are touchy when people remind them that they are 'only artefacts made by the Aghyrians'?"

Yes, they were frequently more than a little bit touchy about this. I'd never even heard Nicha says those words. Coldi found them deeply offensive.

"Well, in this case we're glad that we are just the way we are. Coldi women don't gamble their lives when they fall pregnant. Birth is nowhere near as hard as it is for your people or for Aghyrians."

So, I understood that they'd be happy for Xinanu to have the child by herself in Nicha's room while we were gone.

All right. Whatever. Who was I to argue with them anyway?

I was just a stupid human and I was not really feeling the vibe at the moment.

3

____

I N THE SHORT TIME that I'd dealt with him, I'd learned that Kando Luczon loved to keep people waiting. One day, when the many issues between us had been settled, I'd turn up really late and let him wait. I would put up some bugs so that I could see him looking out the window, opening the door and checking if I was there yet, doing everything to make sure that _he_ was not the one standing out here waiting, but sitting in the apartment and waiting nevertheless.

I doubted he'd learn anything or get the hint. It was immature and I'd probably never do it, but even thinking about it was fun.

I was lucky to be working with people who were least likely to play the coming late tactic. Coldi were always early because they had curious natures and hated the thought that they might miss out on something.

For now, the waiting was our job.

We did so on the ground floor of the atrium, leaning against the wall that surrounded the water basin at the bottom of the waterfall. The air here was cool, laden with droplets of water. The apartment that had been allocated to Kando Luczon and his two companions was on the ground floor, next to the ground floor of mine. It was a guest apartment and could be use by whoever needed it in our building. I wondered if he got hungry with the smell from our kitchen.

The covered courtyard with its trickling waterfall consisted of a central area with paving surrounded by a lush garden bed. We could see the front door of the apartment through a riot of bushes and vines and other potted greenery. It was still firmly shut.

Thayu rolled her eyes. "I'm thinking about how well this guy is going to get on with Ezhya, when they finally meet."

"Yeah," I said, and thought of the tense standoff around the Aghyrian ship that I'd helped resolve. "On the other hand, I'm not sure I want to know." Patience was not the Coldi's strong suit.

Nicha yawned. "Why are we going to this place in town? Do you actually have any new data on this dig?"

I said, "There was some news on the Barresh channel that the engineers managed to enclose the site by driving metal plates into the ground and sealing them, and have the pumps running full time to get the water out, so they can finally see the bottom and start digging. They found it easily enough. The captain saw the news coverage and now he wants to go there."

Nicha shrugged. "It's his right. You know I still can't quite comprehend that this guy saw that ship that they're digging up. Most of it will be so far decayed that it won't be more than a thin metal-rich layer in the soil. Imagine that. Going on a trip and coming back when all of this—" He gestured at the lush atrium. "—is buried under layers of mud, and some boorish folk have built ugly houses over the top. Imagine that."

"No thank you. Losing three weeks was bad enough." Losing fifty thousand years . . . I couldn't even begin to comprehend.

Thayu said, "Don't you two start as well. The man is an arsehole and the fact that he survived for whatever doesn't make him any less an arsehole. Everyone looking at him in awe makes him more of an arsehole."

Yes, but that didn't take away from the fact that he *was* special and I couldn't see how that could *not* affect the way we dealt with him.

Hmm, here was another assessment about the Coldi: their society might be highly structured, but in the scheme of things, the structure mattered more than the individuals who provided it. There were certain positions in the society, and it was important that those positions were filled. Who filled them was not so important. This contributed to the sense that Coldi lives were entirely disposable, because when a position became vacant, someone else would take it.

Coldi had trouble getting their minds around the occasional people, like Kando Luczon, who—arseholes or not—were entirely *not* disposable or replaceable. Did such key individuals even exist in Coldi history? Any people I knew who were true trailblazing exceptions who thought and acted outside the rigidity of Coldi society had moved elsewhere. They were people like Xiya Ezmi, the founder of Hedron and its incredible mining wealth. And Dosha Vonayi, brilliant scholar and mathematician, who lived in London.

We waited.

Nicha and Thayu were looking at something on Nicha's reader. Nicha had looked up the details that the Barresh Council had released about the dig site and he and Thayu were discussing the technical issues as they could deduce them from the images.

"It seems pretty stupid to do any of the excavation with heavy machinery," Thayu said. "These artefacts are usually extremely fragile. The soil is extremely soft. Why didn't they ask for an expert to come from Asto? We've been dealing with Aghyrian artefacts for thousands of years."

Of course it was a rhetorical question. Asking Asto to take part was akin to giving them part ownership of the process, and heaven forbid if that happened.

In fact, the whole ownership of the site and its associated history was still horribly muddled even if the Barresh Council was moving ahead with the excavation because they owned the land. Who had the first right to excavate this site? The original Aghyrians, who had no equipment or authority to do so, the Barresh Council, who had the equipment, was already digging and whose population was descended from the group of refugees that had come on the ship? Or the new Aghyrians, who were highly critical of the council's methods and who would, all facts considered, probably do the most professional job?

A door fell shut somewhere in the building, and finally there was activity at the ground floor unit. First out of the lush garden in between the square that surrounded the fountain and the apartment's door was Lilona Shrakar, a tall woman who looked like she was in her forties, but I'd been informed she was probably closer to sixty. I had learned that she had spent much of her life in stasis and was bound to the ship, whatever that was supposed to mean—I guessed it meant she was flight crew.

Then came the man himself: Captain Kando Luczon of the Aghyrian behemoth ship that still floated about in the middle of space with its huge crew in stasis, surrounded by an armada of ships from Asto's armed forces. Like all Aghyrians, he was extremely tall. He liked to wear flowing, loose garments, and with his long white hair he resembled a wizard from the books my mother had read to me while I was growing up in New Zealand.

The last one in the group was Tayron Kathraczi, a quiet young man about whom we had learned little but whose function seemed to be limited to bodyguard. From the way the captain treated him, he was definitely lower on the pecking order than Lilona.

Both the captain's companions acknowledged me with a nod of the head, but their master, as usual, did not greet me. I'd gotten to the point where I'd stopped being annoyed about this. There was so much more serious stuff to occupy me.

I explained to him where we were going. He merely nodded in a cold, professional manner, but asked no questions, not even about his message and whether I had received it.

It irritated me. This man irritated me with everything he did, from the way he moved to the way he looked at me and my association, or staff, or any one of the people dedicated to make his stay comfortable. He never thanked anyone or offered his help. He just assumed that stuff would appear and people would turn up.

I had tried to make excuses—that he'd been cut off from normal people for so long and that space was very lonely and even more so with all his crew in stasis and blah, blah, blah. But Thayu was right. The man was a first-class arsehole.

And I could think of a whole list of things I'd rather do than take him on an outing, and an even longer list of things I *should* be doing instead, like dealing with the correspondence.

We left the building and set off in the direction of the station on the other side of the island.

The main thoroughfare in that direction led from courtyard to courtyard bathed in the dappled shade of the giant trees that were coming into new leaves before the start of the wet season.

Various cricketlike creatures chirped in the branches. A soft breeze carried the ubiquitous scent of wet mud from the marshland, mingled with the smell of cooking, since it was almost lunchtime.

None of us said anything, because there was nothing to be said. I'd covered all the subjects relating to the Aghyrian history of Barresh. Anyway, he'd had plenty of time to read up on this subject himself, and by now probably knew a lot more about it than I did.

He wasn't sharing any of it.

He walked next to me like a silent ghost, with his two companions behind him. Thayu walked in front and Nicha bringing up the rear. They kept an eye on people we met and people who watched us from balconies or windows. We were a very odd and disharmonious group. Not a group at all, but two complete associations, each with a leader and two seconds. And the leaders barely tolerated each other and one pair of seconds did all the work while the other pair were passive. This situation would set Coldi teeth on edge.

Hell, it set *my* teeth on edge.

We were about to enter the underground passage that led to the station when Kando Luczon said to me, without preamble, "You have an interest in fertility."

It was not a question.

"Well, um . . ." What the hell? Hell, he *had* gotten into a lot more systems than just security.

He went on, "We designed the all-purpose colonising genome to be self-sustaining. Unlike ourselves, they do not interbreed."

By *all-purpose colonising genome* he meant Coldi, and he had so far refused to use that name. His every word seemed designed to throw barbs at those very Coldi people.

"We have noticed the lack of interbreeding." Why did I even discuss this with him? "But on the other hand, the Coldi sometimes do interbreed, on very rare occasions. The Barresh Aghyrians are descended from those rare occasions."

He snorted. "Throwbacks." Spoken with callous disdain.

I started wondering what Marin Federza would make of being called a throwback when I remembered how he had come to me, scared from having his apartment ransacked and then was shot at while in *my* apartment and, damn it, had I even seen him since I'd come back?

His position as the Trader Guild representative to *gamra* had been taken by a Kedrasi Trader, and in amongst the plentiful correspondence that had been waiting for me, I'd been informed that a woman

called Feylin Herza now spoke for the Barresh Aghyrians at the negotiations for the Aghyrian claim.

But no one had said anything about Federza.

Shit.

I struggled to maintain the conversation. "Those you call throwbacks are people with lives, and jobs and families. They work for the
community. They deserve to be treated with respect."

Kando Luczon went on, oblivious to my words. "Throwbacks were
possible because some mistakes were made when handling the
genome. The main perpetrator of these mistakes lends his name to
some of these throwbacks you have here."

Waller Herza, his enemy, the scientist who had developed the
Coldi. I understood that the Barresh Aghyrians had only started using
the Herza name recently.

"What you call throwbacks, we prefer to call people like everyone
else."

"The mistakes weaken the genome."

"Regardless of these supposed mistakes, the Coldi people have
done well enough for themselves." Coldi society was strong, mature,
with enormous depth of talent and determination. What did he mean
—weakens the genome?

He didn't reply, his standard reaction when the matter discussed
was beyond argument. I glanced at his two companions, but their
faces were as impassive and haughty as their master's. Sometimes I
wondered if they even listened.

Thayu shot me a sharp look. I might have pulled a face had Kando
Luczon not been with us. Seriously, it was not my idea to discuss the
subject of Coldi fertility in the company of a couple of Coldi people
and speak over their heads, all right?

We'd arrived on the platform where a good number of people
stood or sat on benches. The train was yet to arrive, but a screen on
the wall showed that it was not far off.

We waited.

I talked a bit about the location of the dig site, to fill the awkward
silence between us. It was talk for the sake of talk. He would have
read all of this already. He would probably tell me so soon, to shut me
up. Tayron had asked me two days ago why we talked so much, but I
couldn't go out with a bunch of companions who said absolutely

nothing to each other. Coldi didn't do that, keihu didn't do that. I knew of no people who did that.

All around us normal train platform life went on. People going to town for errands. Servants doing their daily trips. There was a mother with two young children, a rare sight on the island. People chatted, behaved *normally* while we stood in uncomfortable silence.

The train shot out of the tunnel with a whoosh of air. The silver and gold three-car vehicle came to a hissing halt at the platform. The doors opened.

Because the track ended here, the cabins emptied of people. There were not many, mainly local council people coming to meetings, I guessed, as well as some domestic staff who had been on errands into town.

We sat on two facing benches, Kando Luczon facing me with our companions on either side.

"About those mistakes in the all-purpose colonising genome," Kando Luczon continued the conversation that we had broken off when we got to the platform. He was good at drawing conversations out over a long time. His mind was like an elephant's: he never forgot.

From the corner of my eye, I noticed that the muscles in Thayu's arm tensed.

"We want to rectify them."

What? I almost burst out laughing, wanting to say: "Do you know that there are more than ten *billion* of those mistakes running around in the galaxy?" But at the same time, I sensed that I was finally getting somewhere, finally seeing a corner lifted of the blanket of mystery that covered the Aghyrian purpose. I simply asked, "Why?"

"Why?" Now he frowned at me. He didn't usually show emotion, so I also regarded his confusion as a step forward.

"I understand that you call the Coldi people . . . flawed, but they don't see it that way." I felt all hot saying that, keenly aware of the presence of Thayu and Nicha on either side of me. Of all the things I thought I'd be talking about . . .

"There are flaws," he said, his voice insistent. "They are the result of the incompetence of certain people."

"Don't we *all* have genetic flaws? Isn't that part of what makes us human?"

"They can be the perfect colonising genome after we fix the flaws."

"They're perfect enough. As I recall from the history of Asto, it took a very, very long time after the meteorite strike for the Coldi to rebuild. Most of the rebuilding has come in the last few hundred years. Civilisation and technological development has accelerated during that time. This is not something that was built into them and they were not given clear maps on how to develop technology. Civilisation is something that comes from within."

"They took it all from us and the blueprints we gave them. It's an outright shame that they took so long to act on the information. As for innovation: they may have added a few things, but it all comes from us."

At this point Thayu rose. "I'm not listening to this bullshit."

She had been sitting next to the window, so she climbed up on the bench and pushed herself behind me and Nicha and jumped into the aisle. She went to the back of the cabin and found another seat. I couldn't see her from where I was sitting.

To be perfectly honest I felt like joining her.

"Excuse me." Nicha rose and went after her. I could hear snatches of their conversation.

Thayu said, "No. I'm through with this. If this arsehole wants to insult people, let him reap the consequences. Someone will turn a gun on him and I won't be sorry."

Nicha replied again, trying to shush her up.

I faced my three Aghyrian travel companions in a moment of intense awkwardness. Kando Luczon raised his eyebrows.

He really did not get it, did he?

And I was utterly failing at making him see our side of the discussion. I'd tried to talk, but he didn't listen. I'd tried the *gamra* assembly meeting and what a disaster that had been.

But his presence here was on *my* invitation. Because I had, foolishly, believed that I could talk to him. Maybe I did need to be more blunt in my approach.

I took a deep breath, hesitated, sighed, and said, "The reality is that it makes matters very hard for me if you keep insulting people."

There. My heart was thudding.

"Insult?"

He met my eyes. Damn, he even had the gall to look affronted. "I was offering a great service to them. We have a full medical facility. We can fix genes."

"They don't want fixing."

"Don't want. . . ?"

"They're not broken. They're people."

"But what about the throwbacks?"

"They happen, especially in the Ezmi clan. They know why it happens now. Those people no longer suffer. They're happy. They even have children."

He was still looking at me with an expression of shock on his face.

"Really, there is nothing wrong with these people."

The captain's companion Tayron said, "They're too short, their eyesight is weak in the dark." I was surprised that he spoke up, because he rarely opened his mouth. His voice sounded just as haughty as that of his captain, only younger.

"Does poor night vision justify extensive medical procedures?"

"We could simply bring all the young women in and treat them," Kando Luczon said.

"*All* of them?" This conversation was getting increasingly absurd. Was *this* what they had come back for? Some misguided idea that the people they had created weren't perfect enough and that they should be grateful that they could be "fixed"?

I was glad that Thayu and Nicha weren't here to hear this.

I was meant to assist and protect this man, but I'd been proud when yesterday in the assembly meeting the new Barresh Aghyrian leader Feylin Herza had risen in the audience and had asked, "The story goes that when the meteorite was about to strike Asto, yours was one of the three ships that could evacuate people, yet you did not allow anyone on board, despite having room for thousands. Is that true?"

By the time she made that remark, Kando Luczon had upset so many people that a chorus of cheers had broken out.

And when the collective assembly had quietened down, Kando Luczon had said, "The story goes that it is now possible for people to visit Asto. Our measurements confirm this. Yet you maintain the restrictions. Are you going to prevent an old man from returning to his home before he dies?"

This remark led to more shouting.

I'd been sitting up there in my box cringing all the way, with all my staff and all their equipment ready to record, lobby and vote and *solve* this issue. To come to an agreement with this massive ship and where they could go. Where, possibly, the crew could settle, if they wanted. But the captain appeared only interested in causing as much offence as possible. Answering a blunt question with another blunt question. Come to think of it, had he *ever* answered any of our questions?

More evasive than a gamra diplomat was an expression in keihu. Kando Luczon took evasiveness to uncharted heights.

The train was slowing down and nerves returned. I hadn't heard back from the council about the visit. I hoped that, for once, something about Kando Luczon would click with some of the local people. All right, the man was no diplomat, but it would be awesome if he was an academic.

Outside the window Barresh's main island slid by, with its jumble of roofs of the stately old houses intermingled with spreading tree canopies. The western side contained the airport, the administrative centre and the houses of the well off. The eastern side of the island was more quiet and unassuming in nature. The houses were a lot closer together and people who lived here were the middle-class workers and well-off Pengali.

I leaned into the aisle so that I could see Thayu and Nicha in the next compartment. They were already on their feet ready to go. Above all, they remained professional. They removed themselves from situations where they might step out of line.

It would be nice if I could do the same.

The train slowed further while still being above the water and then slid into the station. The doors opened, letting in a waft of warm humid air. This station, on the southeastern line, was nothing more than a concrete platform raised over the water. It had a wide overhanging roof, so that passengers didn't get wet in the monsoonal rains, and a small shed that might contain maintenance equipment and an electrical substation.

A bridge connected the station to the land.

I'd been here not long before we went to the Aghyrian ship. Back then, it had been dark and we'd come from the land. Back then, there also hadn't been the giant white tent over a section of marshland, nor the shacks or digging machines that stood on the strip of dry land adjacent to the back walls of the yards that faced the marshlands.

"I assume that's it?" Kando Luczon said. He squinted into the light which was unusually bright because the sky was cloudless—almost unheard-of in Barresh.

When we came here before, we approached the station from the marshland and had to return to the main road to access the station bridge, but since that time the council had built a flight of stairs that led directly from the bridge to a timber walkway across the marsh, from the station to the white tent.

It was much more humid on the walkway than it had been on the platform, a reminder of the pressing heat of the monsoon that was to come.

There was a lot of activity at the white tent. The sides were open, and I could see people walking around on platforms inside.

We had barely covered half the distance to the tent when a couple of Barresh guards in black came in our direction.

One man called out, "Halt. This is a restricted site. What are you doing here?"

"I sent a message that we'd be coming." Certainly he would know who I was.

"I have not been informed about that. We can't have curious folk crowd around. We need space to work."

I couldn't see any curious folk other than ourselves. "Certainly you're familiar with this man here: Captain Kando Luczon of the Aghyrians. He is coming to have a look at the ship that carried his fellows here."

"Can I see your ID?" His face remained impassive.

I pulled out my pass, puzzled by this state of affairs. He took it from me and ran his scanner over it. He looked from the screen to my face and back again. His brown eyes were the only thing that moved. He was keihu, of the body type that was solid and short, with a course face. His nose had the characteristic longitudinal groove in the middle.

"Hmm." Then he held his hand out for Kando Luczon's pass.

The captain gave the pass he had received yesterday, frowning. The guard ran the scanner over that, too. His face remained unemotional as he gave both passes back.

I expected to be let through now, but he asked, "Do you have a permit to enter the site?"

"Well, nobody told me that we needed—"

"I need to see a permit."

"When did that come into force?"

"Since the dig started. We can't have sightseers trampling the site."

"That's all very well, but have you seen who this man is?"

The guard glanced at Kando Luczon, who glared back. To his credit, the guard didn't seem to be impressed by the captain's death stare. "Look, I don't really care who he is. He could be Asto's Chief Coordinator for all I know. I have orders, I'm afraid."

"Can I talk to your superior?"

"They're all at lunch."

That was Barresh in a nutshell. Anything important to be discussed? Everyone was at lunch. Not to mention that it was so late that lunch was in danger of bleeding into dinner. "When are they due back?"

He shrugged. "After lunch, I guess."

Ha, ha, ha.

"What's going on?" Kando Luczon asked. He had not yet developed the ability to understand keihu, but considering the Aghyrian aptitude for languages, I didn't expect that to take very long. Keihu was not a terribly complicated language either.

I translated for him. "He says we can't get in because we don't have permission."

"We don't need permission. I give permission. This is my ship." He pushed past the astonished guard and strode in large steps in the direction of the white tent.

"Hey, hey, sir." The guard ran after him, yelling in Coldi. "You can't just—"

"Yes I can. This is my ship."

Kando Luczon's legs were much longer than the guard's.

The guard had stopped his pursuit and was on his comm. A couple of men in council black came out of the tent. Guards, with guns clearly displayed on their belts. They blocked Kando Luczon's path. Even without the long white hair and flowing robe, he was impressive, at least a head taller than the guards, who were not short men.

I ran over the walkway.

When I reached the group, a guard was saying in heavily-accented Coldi, "Everyone who comes here must show their pass and must have been authorised by the council."

"Rubbish," Kando Luczon said.

"Those are our orders. Challenge them with the council if you must."

Another said, "We can't let anyone in the site. It's a very delicate site and we don't want people trampling over it."

"Rubbish, rubbish!"

I stepped between them, holding up my hands. "Calm down, calm down everyone. There must be some sort of misunderstanding. You know who this man is. Are you really telling me that the council has expressly forbidden him to enter the site?"

The guard turned his attention to me. "Not just him, just all people who don't work on the dig. The council says they will reveal the findings when it's all done."

I saw. This was about ownership of the process. I tried again. "But you know who he is, right?" One thing I'd understood about the Aghyrian ship people was that they had strong feelings about their home ships, which made sense seeing as they spent their entire lives on board.

"I don't care who he is, Delegate," the guard said. "Unless the council sends us an update with people allowed access, we won't let him in. We won't let you in. When the Chief Councillor comes, we won't let him in. When Ezhya Palayi comes, he won't get in."

I snorted. "Well, I'd like to see you get challenged on that last one, but I get the point, stupid as I think it is."

"Raise it with the council, sir."

"I will." Then I added in Coldi for the benefit of the captain, "We'll be taking this up with both the council and the general assembly."

"Do that," Kando Luczon said. "I'm looking forward to that discussion."

4

———————

SO IT SEEMED that this was determined to be one of those days that consisted of a long string of turds lined up in a row, waiting for me to stupidly blunder into them.

We could do nothing at the site except go back. I hadn't come because I'd thought there was an awful lot to see at the dig yet, but I'd assumed that those doing the excavation would be interested in the views and experiences of someone who had been alive at the time the ship landed here. I mean—which archaeologist on Earth would refuse the assistance of a real live ancient Egyptian while studying the pharaohs' graves?

I couldn't believe that the historians themselves would refuse this assistance, but clearly the Barresh council was assuming ownership of the dig to the point of excluding everyone.

Stupid councillors with their stupid egos.

Meanwhile, what was I going to do with this man who was getting increasingly antsy, who was extremely smart, who had aims we could only guess and commanded technology we had never seen?

We made our way back to the station in a brooding silence.

"It strikes me that your current council is none too smart," Luczon said once we sat in the train.

Well, that was stating the obvious. It wasn't *my* council either. I wanted nothing more to do with those self-important idiots.

"I'm sorry. I honestly have no idea what is going on here." At the first chance I got, I was going to find a higher authority to override them, although I realised that would be hard.

The silence continued. Clearly, *he* was unimpressed. With the council. With me.

When we reached the *gamra* island, Kando Luczon and his two silent companions went back to their apartment—goodness knew what sort of mischief they'd get up to there—and we went upstairs.

Evi stood at the door; and at my questioning if anything had happened, he said that no, it hadn't.

He was right. It was blissfully quiet in the apartment. The hall was empty, the corridor was empty, and from somewhere within came the usual sounds: Devlin talking in a quiet voice in the hub, Eirani singing while bringing around the clean laundry.

Hopefully, Xinanu had gone to sleep. Nicha went to his room, and with a bit of luck, he could do so without setting her off again.

I went into the office where the first thing I did was send an official complaint to the Barresh Council. I could have written it in keihu, but I chose Coldi because it had a far greater array of looking-down-your-nose pronouns. I could have made it informal, but I chose to use the official *gamra* channels so that the *gamra* stamps would show up on all future correspondence as well. The more I thought about it, the angrier I got, so when I finished that complaint, I wrote one to the new *gamra* Chief Delegate as well, expressing in the strongest possible terms that this wasn't going to be acceptable. Let him do something useful for a change.

Meanwhile, Nicha and Thayu had started wading through the morass of correspondence that cluttered my data storage system. A bit later, Veyada slipped into the room and sat next to Nicha to help him.

"Wow, there really is a lot of it," Thayu said. "I don't understand where it all came from. I see no relationships between the addresses. I don't even know where some of these places are." That was saying something. I would have rated Thayu's knowledge of inhabited worlds better than mine.

She flicked through a couple of messages. "They all want assurance that we're not going to give the Aghyrians significant control over the Exchange."

If I ever needed a reminder of how much the Exchange outage had spooked everyone, this was it.

"I don't even know why anyone would think that," Nicha said.

"Because people are stupid," Thayu said. "They weren't on that train with us. They didn't hear what the arsehole said. If they had, they'd know that we'd never give that idiot anything over our dead bodies."

Veyada was curious about what happened on the train and Nicha recounted Kando Luczon's words.

Veyada was one of the most patient, even-tempered and gentle Coldi I knew. He swore. "He said all that?"

"Pretty much in those words," Nicha said.

I nodded. There was nothing wrong with Nicha's ears.

Veyada blew out a breath and shook his head. "It's almost like he's here to deliberately cause as much conflict as possible."

"I said he's an arsehole." Thayu crossed her arms over her chest. "I'm impressed with Cory for still trying 'to make him see' what effect he's having on us. I'm pretty sure that it's all deliberate. Whatever we know about Aghyrian history is full of this sort of stuff. They were—are—manipulative people, whose aim it was to 'win' discussions, political shitfights or actual armed conflicts."

"Which makes it very hard to have any kind of meaningful negotiation with them," Veyada agreed.

I could see in Thayu's face that she didn't want a negotiation. Nicha was probably leaning that way, too. Veyada's expression was grim, as if he realised that likely there *wouldn't* be a meaningful negotiation, and Ezhya had probably asked me to intervene on the remote off-chance that I could stop a bad situation sliding into a war.

And damn, it, I hated letting Ezhya down, but it sure as hell wasn't looking good.

I sighed, leaned my head into my hands and sighed again.

I had to try. I had to keep my cool and keep plodding along. I had to keep a straight course. Take things one step at a time. Concentrate on the little things in the hope that they would add up to a big thing.

Change of subject. I gestured at the screen. "Veyada, legally, what am I allowed to do with all this correspondence?"

"What would you like to do with it?"

"Dump it in Delegate Namion's account so at least I can work again. I don't understand why all these people are asking me these questions—well, no, that's not true; of course I do know—but he's Chief Delegate, so if he wants to play he should play."

"I told you that you should stand for the position," Thayu said.

I snorted. She *had* to be kidding.

Veyada said, "Legally speaking, we're dealing with two conflicting issues. One: your correspondence is yours and you are responsible for it. On the other hand, *gamra* bylaws say that Delegates should not step outside the task assigned to them without consulting others."

Nicha snorted. "Have you ever done anything that's *inside* your assigned task?"

I said, "Veyada, does that mean 'Do as you wish'?"

"You got it."

"Hmm. Delegate Namion will be pissed with me if I send him the correspondence. He will also be pissed with me if I don't send it."

"So: send?" Thayu said.

"Yeah. Why not? At least he can't accuse me of keeping information from him." And I wouldn't have to worry about all those messages in the three seconds he would take to blow up and come blast my ear about it.

Come to think of it, I didn't even know him well enough to be certain that blasting ears was his style. "Let's do it. Give me the other stuff that needs to be dealt with."

Thayu sent me a much trimmed-down list of messages. In fact, once I had dealt with a decent number of messages by simply filing them, scheduling them or replying *Yes* or *No*, I started to see the last messages that had arrived in the account before I left, before the entire world was turned upside down.

The last one I had opened was a message from Marin Federza—

Crap. I should make some inquiries about him.

"Thay', have you seen or heard from Federza since coming back?"

"Thankfully, no."

"Me neither," Nicha said. "No great loss."

"I'm kind of serious. He was deposed as leader of the Aghyrians, sacked from his position as Trader Delegate, shot at when he was in my apartment, had the windows shot out of his apartment and his office trashed, and didn't come to the last assembly meeting before we left. He's not here and no one seems to be worried about it."

"He probably turned up and has simply gone back to his Trader life. He's got a house and an office in town. And since he's a Trader, he's probably travelling."

Nicha was probably right, but it didn't dispel my unease. Federza didn't seem the type of person who would just quietly disappear. "If I send him a message, that will get to him wherever he is, right?"

"The Trader Guild has their own satellites, so yeah. It will even bypass the regular public Exchange channels and, if he's off world, it will have no lag time or booking time." He still sounded as if he wondered why I bothered.

So I sent Federza a message, with apologies for my sudden absence and some other vague stuff. It was all strict business, and it was bullshit, but I would feel a lot better if he replied. I disliked the man deeply, but that didn't mean I wished him ill.

A bit higher up in the list was a message from Menor that I hadn't read. It said that he was going home to Hedron for a brief visit. In case we needed his services, he provided a list of dates that he'd be available. Very clinical and professional, avoiding the term "sperm donor".

Thayu stopped me staring at the screen and came to stand next to me.

"Oh," she said in a low voice. "Have you replied anything to him?"

"Wasn't that your decision?" I met her eyes. "We can call him now and you can be pregnant this week. The little Azimi brat can have a playmate."

"Hey!" Nicha protested. "You're talking about my son."

Thayu said, "What if we happen to be in the small percentage of people who do interbreed and I have a third child. I don't want to have to abort if it's yours." Tears glistened briefly in her eyes. "I don't want to forfeit my right to live on Asto. You will have to be careful, too."

"Does the two-child limit apply to me?"

"You're Domiri clan. I think it does."

"Veyada would know," I said.

"It doesn't," Veyada said, without looking up from his screen.

And as usual, Thayu was avoiding the final decision. I'd already had myself tested for compatibility on the off-chance and it was negative. The big Aghyrian population database showed absolutely no instances of crossbreeding between humans and Coldi. Earth humans did have Aghyrian roots, but they were buried very deep.

While this discussion had been going on, I'd kept an eye on the screen. There was no reply yet from Federza, not even an automated one.

Well, that was interesting. I was too busy and besides it was probably too late in the day by now, so I made a note to contact the Barresh Aghyrians tomorrow. Meanwhile I sent another message to his Barresh office. The Trader's office would often reroute messages through the Trader Guild's satellites. Probably something urgent had come up and he was off world.

But I still didn't like it.

I went to the admin office downstairs to check on the staff working there. They were looking after all my regular things: the household, bills, my accounts, *gamra* correspondence. I couldn't imagine how I'd once been lost for things to get these people to do. In the near future I would probably have to hire more staff.

When I came back from downstairs, Devlin was looking for me. "I have an urgent communication for you."

I went with him into the hub, where he pulled up *gamra*'s live video communication channel. He entered our code, and Delegate Namion's face appeared.

Well, that hadn't taken him long at all.

Devlin said, "The Delegate is here."

"Good. Let me talk to him."

"In private?"

"No."

Damarcian faces had a habit of always looking unfriendly and hawkish, but his face took on a super-annoyed expression when his eyes met mine through the screen.

After we had exchanged cool greetings, he started, "A couple of things I want to raise with you. I just received your message regarding the dig site. I'm afraid that this is a matter outside my authority. You will need to contact the Barresh Council to get access to the site."

"I already have."

"Then there is nothing more I can do for you."

"The captain has the whole history of the civilised world in his hands. He needs access to the site—"

"The council will decide who needs what."

"They will deal with it so much more urgently if there is a supporting message from you." I used the imperative-you, which was probably a fairly rude choice but I was tired and my patience was running out.

His nostrils flared. "Listen, Delegate. *We* did not ask for this man to come here. *You* insisted on bringing him—"

"I did so because his absence would neutralise the ship and would possibly give us information on these people and their aims."

"You did so of your own accord and without consultation."

"Tell me how I was meant to have consulted anyone from a secret place where the Exchange has no coverage!"

But there was no point in arguing and I would do best to shut up, because in typical fashion, I'd probably soon put my foot in it. And he was right: it had been my decision. A poor one, as it turned out to be. I still didn't see how I could have done anything better.

"Very well, I will deal with the captain's impatience my way. I can't guarantee you'll like it, and would really appreciate some support, but if there is going to be none . . . Is there anything else you wished to talk about?"

"Yes. Delegate, can you explain what this deluge of correspondence is doing in my inbox?"

"These are all questions I've received from the public about *gamra* in relation to the Aghyrian ship. I'm not qualified or authorised to answer them. I believed they were best suited to your office, but if you wish someone else to deal with it, tell me where to send them." Let's play innocent.

He harrumphed. I was sure he saw the choice where I was leading him: accept more work or admit that he didn't have a clue. His face remained blank, but I was sure he didn't like it.

He snorted again. "All right. Send everything to my office."

"Thank you. I will."

"In fact, Delegate, reroute everything from that address to my office."

That was not at all what I had in mind. "But it's my *gamra* correspondence address." What the hell?

"I will make sure that your correspondence gets returned to you. I doubt you have the staff to deal with this on top of everything else."

That was definitely true, but crap, I didn't want to send him all my correspondence for him to sift through. Imagine him reading the letters from Raanu.

I scrambled for something to say. I absolutely did not have the authority to refuse him. In fact, I had more authority to refuse Ezhya than I had to refuse the Chief Delegate. Never mind that Ezhya would never ask me anything half as invasive as that.

Because Ezhya trusts me.

That was the bottom line. Delegate Namion trusted me as much as I trusted him. And it *was* my *gamra* address, which technically, belonged to him.

Shit.

"Well, yes. I think . . . I can arrange that." I'd have to notify a few people not to send me anything until I got control of my account back.

But damn it, damn it.

He signed off and I went on a mad scramble to notify people to use my private account. Raanu, Asha, damn it, Margarethe Ollund. My father.

I was in the middle of scrolling through my incoming messages to see if any other private messages needed to be sent to my other account when Thayu came into the room.

"Are you coming for dinner?"

"Yes, just start without me. I'll be there soon."

"By myself?"

Now I looked at her properly. "No one else here?"

She shook her head.

Yeah, I couldn't let her eat by herself. I rose and took her hand, warm and dry in mine.

It had gone dark outside while I'd been in the hub, with just the faintest glimmer of orange remaining over the western horizon.

In the living room, Eirani was just coming to the table with a tray.

"Where is everyone?" I asked, while pulling back a chair.

"Veyada and Sheydu went out. They said not to wait." Eirani set the tray down. "They didn't say how long they were going to be."

"They booked a slot at the shooting range," Thayu said.

Eirani continued, "Deyu went with them. The young master Reida really wanted to come. Sheydu said that he was too impatient and told him to study. He's sulking in his room."

I thought that was a bit harsh. Reida had been studying a lot and had behaved very well recently. It seemed to have gotten through to him that being chosen to work here was a privilege and he'd do well not to waste this opportunity.

That said, Veyada was very strict on taking weapons seriously, not necessarily a bad thing. Guards should know how to use weapons but could not be trigger-happy. Reida had probably been a bit too keen.

Nicha was having dinner in his room with Xinanu, Eirani informed us.

So Thayu and I sat at the big table by ourselves. It was strange and empty and would have been romantic had I not been so annoyed at Delegate Namion's orders. I told Thayu about it.

"He wants you to send everything to him?" She seemed surprised.

"Yeah. Shows how much he trusts us."

"Is he even allowed to do that?"

"I'm sure he is. It's my *gamra* account. I shouldn't be keeping any secrets from anyone."

"That's ridiculous. He's using this to weaken your standing."

"Obviously. But tell me what I can do about it. There are avenues of appeal, but how attractive are they going to be in case I ever need his help?"

She snorted. Coldi did writs, not appeals. They did not tend to become dependent on people whose cause they fundamentally didn't support.

It was not as if I'd had any choice in the matter. I held up my hands. "All right, all right. Don't say it."

"Will you stand next time the position comes up?"

"Will there be a next time?" Chief Delegates were elected for life, until they died, resigned, were forced to step down or—in the odd case—were murdered.

"I'm sure there will be. Soon."

"I hope you're right."

How and when this would happen, I had no idea, but I knew I wouldn't stand, no matter how much Thayu wanted me to. If nothing else, I was far too involved with Asto to be an acceptable candidate.

I wondered when we had progressed from worrying about the accounts to plotting against the Chief Delegate.

"Why are you smiling?"

"I'm thinking about how we determine the fate of a lot of people in this room."

"That's the way it should be. The association is the strongest unit of society."

I didn't think she understood, but never mind.

Nicha scurried in from the hallway. He made a beeline for the table, emptied one of the breadbaskets into another, mixing two types of bread—just as well that Eirani didn't see this.

He then proceeded to stack bread, fruits and a bowl of salad into his empty basket.

"We're hungry," he said at my raised eyebrows, then picked up two cups, a jug of juice and his overflowing basket and carried the whole lot out the door.

Xinanu was going to have twins at this rate. I wondered what on Earth the two of them talked about by themselves in his room. More than anything, I felt sorry for Nicha.

"I hope that we won't have to suffer through this for very long anymore," I said to Thayu when Nicha was gone.

"No, we'll just have to deal with the Azimi clan."

"And with the council and why ever they blocked us at the site. I really can't believe that they didn't know who we were."

"How about you were blocked *because* of who you are. Or rather, because of who our dear captain is."

"They wouldn't be so petty, would they?"

"After he called all of the non-pure Aghyrians second-rate derivatives, and calling us the 'all-purpose colonising race' as if we're some sort of thing? After that stupid discussion on the train? The man is an arsehole."

"You *have* said this before."

"Maybe, but no one appears to be listening."

I was surprised at the anger in her voice. I'd been called much worse than any name-slinging by Kando Luczon. I guess I was used to the fact that most *gamra* people thought little about Earth and its inhabitants.

I said, "You know what I've been thinking? Some of this stuff that the council pulls is really, really childish. I can't believe that this petti-ness is the only motive for keeping Luczon from seeing the site. They can't just be in it to spite him, or spite us, or whatever. There has to be another reason."

"It's probably something stupid to do with local regulations."

"Probably, and I don't care how they classify someone as a local and what the rules are for historic sites. I don't care about their regu-lations. I need to understand if they ever plan on giving Luczon access to the site, because if he doesn't get it, he's going to get up to other mischief. Somehow, I prefer to stay in control of the mischief pulled by a four-hundred-year-old man from a civilisation that can travel outside the galaxy. I want him granted access. I want him involved in the dig. If nothing else, that's why he's here. Who knows what all those thousands of people aboard his ship think. I want him satisfied that he's contributing to something worthwhile."

"So, what? You've written to the council already. We've tried getting Delegate Namion to take up our cause. What else can you do?"

"I don't have time to wait in case the council might reply. For all I know, they're stalling on this issue and passing my message from department to department until I give up. Delegate Namion won't write a letter of support. Everyone is being stupid, so we'll play stupid back. I'll send Reida."

Thayu frowned at me. "Send him where?"

"To the dig."

"He won't get in either."

"Not to visit, to work."

Her expression cleared. "Ah." As spy. It would be perfectly clear to her now. She smiled. "I guess you could do that. This is where it gets interesting."

So when we had finished dinner and Eirani came in to clear the table, I went to Reida's room. At my knock on the door, a sullen voice inside said, "Come in."

As I opened the door, a waft of stale, warm air laced with the scent of Coldi sweat came out. Reida sat on his bed. He might be more focused on his study now that he was no longer attached to Delegate Ayanu, but right now he was, as Eirani had aptly called it, sulking.

However, when I came in, he jumped off the bed and snapped into a subservient greeting, which I reluctantly acknowledged. Reida needed it. He was quite insecure, having grown up in a neighbourhood where a good number of people didn't have the *sheya* instinct and would jeer at those who had it.

Urgh. Did he ever open the window in here? The room had an interconnecting door to Deyu's room next door, and the state of the unmade bed showed what the two of them got up to at night. I'd learned to see it as a good sign that finally that part of my association was working as it needed to be.

I began, "I have a job for you."

"A job?" He looked up, his expression hopeful.

I explained to him that I wanted him to get council guard uniforms, go to the dig site and find out what the deal was with not allowing anyone into the fenced-off site and what was going on there. He was to report to us every day on a number of different issues.

As I spoke, his morose expression cleared and made place for a smile.

"I know where to get those uniforms. And I can get a set of their equipment, too. I'll look just like the real thing."

"Just a reminder: I don't want to know where you got any of this stuff, because this is done without my authorisation." I was guessing he'd buy the uniform and equipment off the black market in Far Atok, because everything could be bought there.

"Yes, I understand, but thank you. You won't be disappointed with my job."

That of course remained to be seen, and I might yet receive a satisfactory reply from the council, but there was at least one happy person in my household today.

5

DELEGATE NAMION'S control over my message account came into being overnight. The volume of messages I received went from hundreds to precisely . . . zero.

"What the hell?" I complained to Devlin. "How am I supposed to work like this?"

I contacted the Delegate's office to ask if I could have my correspondence and was told by a sullen-voiced man that there wasn't any.

"That's impossible!" I said. "What about the agenda for the upcoming meeting? What about the captain? What about Marin Federza?"

"The agenda hasn't yet been released—"

"But the meeting is tomorrow morning."

"There was a last-moment amendment. You will get the new version after the Delegate comes in and determines the final items to be added. It's still very early, as you're sure aware."

How politely could one say *fuck off*? I wasn't going to give up so easily. "What about the rest?"

"I'm sorry. Neither of those people have sent you anything. We will send you the correspondence when it comes through."

I didn't believe him for one moment, but what else could I do?

Well, maybe the captain hadn't sent anything. He wasn't exactly communicative. And Federza was not my best pal either. He wouldn't feel the need to send me an immediate reply, especially since my message had been lame and nondescript.

I still had trouble believing it, but maybe there had indeed been nothing.

Maybe if I had a moment, I should go into town and check the Aghyrian compound to see if Federza was in there, not receiving my messages.

Maybe.

As outsider, it was pretty hard to imagine what went on inside that complex that took up an entire city block, ironically not far from where the ship was found.

Apparently there were people who never left this complex, and whose existence no one knew about.

Deep inside I sort of knew that I was just making excuses for not having to check out the situation. I mean—how easy would it be just to ask? No, I didn't want to see him, only to make sure that he was all right.

Then again, surely Federza had friends who would notify the right people if he had disappeared? Did that require action from me? For crying out loud, I disliked the man and he disliked me. I didn't, above all, want to give him the impression that I cared what happened to him.

Overnight, Xinanu's baby had decided to stay put. She came to breakfast briefly, with red-rimmed, swollen eyes. No matter how many times Thayu said *drama queen*, she did look extremely uncomfortable to me. Her stomach was so ridiculously swollen that she could barely sit, much less walk.

The assembly would sit tomorrow afternoon. Normally, I would be preparing for the meeting a few days in advance, but I had no idea what to prepare for. I guessed that after the previous debacle, no one had been too keen to invite Captain Luczon again, but the need to develop a unified plan to deal with the ship remained. I had asked for this to be put on the agenda. Didn't know if it was actually happening. I had a feeling Delegate Namion might leave it off, just to spite me.

On a personal level, I needed to find something to keep the captain occupied and happy to remain in Barresh. We didn't want him to return to the ship until we knew the ship's capabilities. Keeping him here and occupied with something that interested him was the best way of neutralising the ship.

But no one was giving me any assistance.

And the captain was downstairs, no doubt just as frustrated with the situation as I was, not understanding it. He had no loyalty to any *gamra* systems and he would be destructive if he was allowed to get angry, and I just did *not* know what to do about it.

I had no messaging account, because I didn't want to *send* any sensitive messages either, except to Delegate Namion, asking when control of the account could be returned to me.

You can use it. It works, was his secretary's chirpy reply.

That wasn't good enough, I told him.

He replied that he wasn't sure when they could transfer the account back to me. There appeared to be some sort of error, he said, because so much of that correspondence was coming in that should be going to his boss. He needed to investigate.

Bullshit. Those people were writing to me because they saw me as the person to answer their questions. No matter what position Delegate Namion held, they did not see *him* as capable of answering their questions.

I now wished I'd never decided to send him all those messages, but knew that would not have been anywhere near an adequate solution either.

It was about midmorning when Eirani came to notify me that a visitor had arrived and that he was waiting in the living room.

My first thought was *Federza*, because he had the tendency to turn up unannounced, but when I went into the living room, I found, to my surprise, Tayron Kathraczi seated on my couch. He scrambled to his feet when I came in and nodded a greeting. Each time I saw him, I wondered if, when all his fellows on the ship had been woken up, one would be able to see the difference between them and the Barresh Aghyrians. For one, none of the locals had his olive skin, which would have to be pigmented and not tanned, seeing as he spent his life inside a space ship. He wore his dark brown hair—with wavy curls—combed back from his forehead. It wasn't long enough for a ponytail and barely long enough to go behind his ears. His eyes were so black that you couldn't see where the irises stopped and the pupils started.

Whatever colour they were, Aghyrian eyes were always very intensely hued.

Without the presence of his captain, he looked less demure, and why oh why were all those Aghyrians so tall? He towered more than a head over me.

I gestured him to the couch, and we sat down. "How can I help you?"

"The captain wants to know if, since it is obviously not possible to see the excavation of the old ship, it would be possible to visit other sites. He wants to see Asto, even if we're told we can't land on the surface. He wants to see other artefacts that are preserved in this area. He understands that there are other items preserved in a place called Miran."

"I am aware of all the places you need to visit. I have to beg for your patience. None of those sites are easily accessible. Many have cultural significance and belong to local people. We need their permission to bring you there." For example, there were some incredible murals preserved from the time after the Aghyrians had landed in Barresh, but the site belonged to Pengali tribes, and held great significance for them. Many of those sites also were so well preserved because they weren't easy to reach; in one case going there involved a dunking in ink-black water inside a cave in order to duck under a wall. I needed Pengali permission to visit places like this. Visiting Miran was on another level of complexity altogether.

"My captain says you keep telling him the same story. He says he wants to hear a different story."

"I wish I could tell him something different, but unfortunately, I can't. It will take time to arrange the permissions."

"Is that necessary just for a visit?"

"It is, I'm afraid."

"My captain says he doesn't see the need for all these useless rules."

Was he even allowed to have his own opinion or did they all have to repeat what the captain said?

"I'm guessing there would be no need for permits on the ship." Especially not if the vast majority of the crew was in stasis. "But we're dealing with many different peoples and different nations. We can't just turn up, the same way that people wouldn't be able to visit your ship without getting your permission."

"Yet you turned up like that at our ship."

"I could not have entered the ship without your knowledge and permission." I still didn't think he understood the concept of borders or different people, or *culture* for that matter. "Look, I'll see what I can do, but I really do have to beg for your patience."

"We have travelled from outside the galaxy. Do not try to teach us about patience." He sounded miffed.

"I'm sorry. I just wanted to make sure you understood." This wasn't going well. One way or another, our conversations seemed to always butt up against a wall of wrong interpretations and misunderstandings. "I think we fail to understand your point of view. It's hard for us to comprehend the vastness of the universe when we have only travelled through such a small part of it. But feel free to explain. We are eager to learn."

"I don't know what there is to learn. There is a lot of empty space out there."

"Surely the ship jumped most of that?"

"Most, but not all."

"Did you . . . find anything that wasn't open space?" They'd been to the Andromeda galaxy, after all—what Coldi called the Renzha galaxy.

"We found interesting things, most of them of scientific nature."

"Any habitable worlds?"

"The Renzha galaxy is not a system as you would know it." Some small part in me still hoped that he didn't mean *you* to sound as condescending as it did.

"So—what then? Gas clouds and force fields?"

"Something like that. It is a *very* strange system."

"Surely the whole galaxy is not like that?"

"It's very hard to comprehend for someone who has not experienced it."

"Try me."

He gave me a penetrating, almost insulted, look. "You ask so many questions."

"Am I not allowed to ask questions?"

"Where do you get all these questions?"

"Where do I—what do you mean?"

"When the captain says that a thing is a certain way, then it is like that. There is no need for a question."

"We don't have a captain."

"What about . . . the man in the blue robe?"

I felt like laughing. Delegate Namion couldn't be further removed from a captain if he tried. "He is the leader of the assembly. Nothing else. He does not control this island. He does not control my life."

"Then who is your captain?"

"We don't have any captains."

He frowned.

I felt chilled.

"But let's go back to the question I asked. What did you see when you were in the other galaxy? I can't believe that there would not have been anything worth mentioning."

"You want to know this—why?"

"We know where you've been and we're curious. We want to know what the place looks like."

"We can report the differences in chemical composition and the differences in the nature of force fields. Is that what you want?"

"Just what it looks like would satisfy many people, but also things like maps to complement the ones we have."

"The captain will have to do that."

"Can you ask him?"

He returned a wide-eyed stare. Apparently, no one asked the captain anything.

We spoke for a bit longer, but I didn't get anything else useful out of him. Even when we spoke about Barresh, it was as if he completely missed my points. He twisted everything back to his ship and captain. He seemed to be incapable of discussing anything without mentioning his captain.

I blew out a deep breath when he was gone.

"I don't trust him," Thayu said, coming into the room. She had been working in the hub but of course had heard—and recorded—everything we said. "There is something he's not telling us."

"You say." I laughed. "Do you think there is something he *is* telling us? Because I don't know that he said anything useful."

"All those years cruising at high speed finding nothing, only to turn around and go back home with nothing more than a few chemical and mathematical data? It makes no sense at all."

"Well, we can't go and check. We have to take his word for it."

Thayu said, "How about we try to get that woman by herself and ask her some questions?"

"I don't know that we'll get a chance. Both of them seem to be glued to their captain."

I had randomly picked two of the captain's crew members so as not to give him the chance to bring accomplices, but I seemed to have picked the wrong people. I had never thought that the captain would be cooperative, but I had at least hoped that the two companions would be more informative, but they seemed incapable of thinking for themselves. Both of them were all *my captain says this, the captain says that* with no sign of their own thoughts or even a skerrick of personality. Brainwashed seemed to be the word for it.

I sighed. "I have to think about what we'll do with them. Right now, I think we might need to go into town. I should probably put in a regular application to see the Pengali sites to keep him busy, but it will take a while, not to speak of trying to visit Miran."

Thayu snorted. "What would you put down in the application as 'purpose of visit'? Study early Mirani settlement and change the course of history?"

We laughed. Those stupid Mirani forms. The nation of Miran surrounded the Barresh enclave, but most of those regions, like most of Miran, were sparsely-populated. They didn't want a flood of illegals coming over the border from Barresh and subjected visitors to ridiculous questionnaires.

Thayu said, "You know what? It would be far easier to apply for him to look at Asto. There are no rules for looking at a planet from orbit."

"Right. Your father does it all the time."

She grinned.

But she had a point. Although . . . "It would worry me to take him there. For all I know he'll try to do something stupid to force us down."

"He would be extensively searched before boarding any aircraft."

Except the things that worried me could probably not be found in a search. But Coldi, practical as they were, always dismissed the idea of mental powers: that a person could spin a web of small anpar threads like the Exchange. I'd even seen this done by that Aghyrian medico who had once visited me in my apartment. Little sparks flying from her fingertips.

We didn't know if the captain could do anything of the sort, but I wouldn't be surprised if he could.

All factors considered, looking at Asto from orbit was something we could organise quickly without much obfuscation from any authorities. It would just require the regular departure permits from the Exchange. I decided to go to the Exchange to get those permits in person, so at least I knew everything was approved.

While I was at it, I wanted to do a few other things in town.

We agreed that Thayu would come with me, but Nicha elected to stay at home. Was something finally happening? Hell, I hoped so, for all of us.

Nicha's second, Reida, was in town for the task I'd given him, and Deyu was there, too, running some errands for him, so Sheydu said she'd come while her son and *zhayma* Veyada sorted out some legal thing at home.

We were a strange and somewhat lopsided group going to the station, not balanced at all. Thayu picked up that I noticed that. She mentioned it to me when we sat in the train.

"Don't you mind that we're a strange group?" I asked.

"For routine jobs of lesser importance, no, it doesn't make a great deal of difference. We're all part of the same association."

With me on top, kind of bumbling through situations where, had I been Coldi, instinct would guide me.

Silver water flashed past outside the window. The train moved fast over the uninterrupted stretch of rails that ran low over the water between the artificial *gamra* island and the old city.

"You'd better hope that nothing of importance happens, then."

"You're nervous."

"That man makes me nervous. He talks but he doesn't answer any questions. He just states his points over and over again. He doesn't listen. He has absolute control over his companions. What they do, what they say, even what they think. There *is* no world for them outside the ship community. He says he wants to see these historical sites, and I understand why, but he's made me so suspicious that I'm thinking there may be something more behind it all. He doesn't seem to have any soft spots."

"He acts like the man who let thousands of spaces in his ship go unoccupied while the Aghyrian civilisation died."

"Yeah." I nodded. Just like he had been portrayed in Asto's historical texts. An arsehole.

6

———————

AT THE EXCHANGE, getting a permit to leave and come back ended up being really easy. In fact, the employee obviously wondered why we didn't do it through the auxiliary network. He didn't even want our names.

"I just wanted to come in to make sure that the permit was actually granted," I said. A small bit of certainty in this world which had become very uncertain.

"I will need a ship registration when you have it," the employee mentioned before we left.

Yeah, of course we needed someone to take us there. I had a feeling that someone would offer their services. I had a feeling that Asha Domiri was not far away. I supposed we could hire a craft if no one offered by the time we were ready to go.

On the way back out of the building, in the magnificent staircase, Thayu shook her head. "Sometimes I don't know why anyone believes any of the stuff you say. 'Make sure that the permit was actually granted.' That was the sole reason we went into town?"

Sheydu said, "Nup. The fun starts now. I'm guessing we're looking for Federza. Where are we going? Talk to the council or visit the Aghyrian compound?"

"Neither. We're going to Federza's office."

"I should have guessed that," Thayu said, her expression dark. She didn't like it when I did things she hadn't predicted.

Sheydu predicted it because . . . she was just being Sheydu, more than twice Thayu's age and three times the experience. One day I must ask her about all the places she had worked, but I suspected I wouldn't like some of the answers.

Thayu hadn't guessed because looking for Federza was not a thing a Coldi person would do, since Federza was not in their loyalty networks. He was supposed to have his own loyalty networks. Except he didn't. And I guessed in some sort of perverted way, he *was* in my loyalty network, if being a colleague could be called that.

Marin Federza's Trader office was in the old heritage four-storey building at the beginning of Market Street, a thick-walled, squat, cramped affair that you'd call ugly until you heard that the building was hundreds of years old and therefore, by Barresh standard, needed to be treated with reverence. Federza occupied one of the larger suites on the first floor. Because it was daytime, the metal gate at the bottom of the staircase was open and people walked in and out of the building.

Some of them greeted us when we came up the stairs.

The door to Federza's office was closed, and remained so after Thayu's knocking and jiggling of the handle.

Thayu harrumphed. "So, he's not home. Not that we'd thought any different. What's the plan?" I thought she sounded belligerent and didn't understand why. It was not like her to get upset about small things like failing to guess our destination. No doubt I'd find out what bugged her soon, but right now it wasn't very helpful.

"Reida broke into this office, remember? Last time I had to pick him up from the jail."

She shrugged. "I didn't get all the sordid details." There was definitely something bothering her.

I addressed Sheydu. "Reida said he broke in to replace the bugs in this building that we lost, but he was working for Delegate Ayanu Azimi stealing documentation that Federza had been intending to give up to *gamra*."

"Is there a point to this?" Count on Sheydu to lose patience quickly. Damn it, everyone was in a foul mood.

"Yes. While Reida was there, he placed new bugs."

Sheydu's eyes widened. "They're not ours. They're Delegate Ayanu's."

"I guess you want me to access them. I can't. I need codes," Thayu said.

"I have the codes."

She turned sharply to me. "What? Why didn't Reida give them to us?"

"Because of his loyalties, and because of the attack on Federza and he didn't want to be targeted as suspect. Because we went away soon after." And because Federza wasn't in anyone's loyalty network and there was no need for them to know about bugs in Federza's office. And also because it was Delegate Azimi's bug network. "Anyway, Reida only gave me the code yesterday. And tell me what's wrong, because everyone is snapping at me, and I'm just doing the best I can. This whole situation is fucked up, I know. This guy drives me crazy, and it's not even safe coming home anymore because Xinanu might bite off my head. I don't want any of you to start as well."

She sighed. "I'm sorry. We're all stressed." Nothing about what bothered her in particular. Too personal, I guessed, to be shared with Sheydu.

I pulled out my reader and passed Thayu the code that Reida had given me yesterday, and she went up to the door with her reader.

While Thayu did her thing, Sheydu and I stood a short distance back, pretending to wait for someone. We talked about the weather and the view from the balcony—into the back yards of the rich keihu families. Chatting with Sheydu was a hard job because she tended to give one-word replies, but fortunately I didn't have to make conversation for very long, because Thayu came our way. "I've got the security camera recordings. They're extremely short. Nothing happens."

"Nothing at all?" I couldn't believe that.

She shook her head. "But it's interesting to see where this whole bug network goes. It links up with bugs in the council chamber and the Exchange."

"Why? What does she have to do with the Barresh council?"

Thayu shrugged. Sheydu shrugged, too, but clearly the idea worried her. This was Delegate Ayanu Azimi, who had put her name forward for the position of Chief Delegate and had been voted down in what had had been, all things considered, a fairly tame election.

Interesting, if not what we were looking for. We considered going to the Aghyrian compound, although we would probably need a more solid reason to get a reply out of them.

"We should check the airport," Thayu said. I could hit myself in the head for not having thought to do that yet.

It was only a short walk down Market Street, across the main square where the stately, beautifully restored building of the Exchange looked out over a large public space dotted with trees and eateries. A good number of people were going in and out of the glass-fronted airport building, and I could see them going up and down the moving stairways inside.

We entered through the commercial foyer down the side into an airy hall where merchants and Traders were using check-in and goods declaration processes on the workstations scattered throughout the hall.

The far side of the foyer also consisted of a glass wall. It provided a view over the wide expanse of the tarmac. The public area was to the right, where I could just see a small piece of the modern terminal building, but all of the space directly ahead was taken up by private craft, most of them commercial.

I looked over the sea of varied aircraft, glittering in the bright sunlight. "Does anyone know which is Federza's?"

"The one over there." Sheydu pointed.

The craft in question was a solid, Asto-built model commonly used by private businesses. It stood at the far end of the private parking area.

When I held up my reader and magnified the view through the lens, I could make out the symbol of the Trader Guild on the side, together with the number I'd seen many times on the golden medallion that Federza wore: 8953.

Sheydu had gone to one of the workstations in the hall. I went to stand next to her. "What are you doing?"

"The craft is in location 743. I'm looking up how long it has been there." She pointed at the screen. "This one here."

The craft had arrived at the spot more than four weeks ago, before the day that Federza had been shot at. It hadn't moved since. Moreover, Federza also hadn't accessed his refuelling or cargo account.

I let out an exclamation. "Shit."

We exchanged worried glances.

"Does Federza have any friends?"

"One would think so," Sheydu said, although she sounded doubtful.

"None that have missed him or could have reported him missing?"

Thayu spread her hands. "I don't like him. You don't like him. I don't know that all that many people like him outside the Aghyrian compound, and if he's fallen out with them . . ."

"So what are we supposed to do about it? Do we ask the Aghyrians?"

Sheydu snorted. "They would be the first ones to know where he is. If they haven't been asking around for him, they probably know where he is, and I doubt they want to share it."

"True." But damn it, how could someone just vanish like that in a city as closely watched as Barresh? "What would happen if we went to the town guards and reported him missing?"

She spread her hands. "They're pretty incompetent but I don't know that it would do any harm as such."

"There might already be a record for the case. Otherwise we create one by reporting it. If the guards have a record, it will be someone's responsibility to do something about it."

"Don't hold your breath," Sheydu said.

Thayu, however, agreed with me. "I don't think they'll solve the problem, but once the record exists there is a case until he turns up. If nothing else, it provides proof that he's missing of the type that bureaucrats like."

We were not far from the guard station in Market Street.

It was in the same building as the jail, a place with which I was disturbingly familiar, but the main entrance was around the corner.

The waiting room was just as low-ceilinged as the jail office in the less upmarket part of the building around the corner. An officer in council black, with the silver five-pointed star on his chest, sat behind a counter that was wide enough to allow at least three people to work at the same time, but he was the only one serving people.

He was speaking to a keihu woman, who, from behind, displayed the typical keihu build: very broad in the hips and an enormous butt. She spoke with a broad local accent that would be considered uneducated. From the snatches of the conversation that I understood, I deduced that her house had been broken into and she was describing items that had been damaged or stolen. She was agitated, because she suspected the neighbour's son. The officer tried to calm her down. I had the feeling that there was some history involved.

A few people occupied the seats in the waiting area. They were all local keihu, giving us strange looks while we stood there just inside the door. A second officer appeared at the counter, probably alerted by the first. A woman gestured for me to go first, but I declined.

She went up to the counter. Meanwhile, the other woman had been palmed off to a junior guard who left the room with her.

The next in line, an old man, also gestured for me to go first. I also declined. He moved to the counter, but kept casting me nervous looks. Maybe he was afraid that I'd changed my mind?

That was typical keihu behaviour: they were highly aware of each individual's place in society. While Coldi had superiors and inferiors and their structure was rigid, if a group of Coldi was waiting for something and Ezhya walked in, none of them would give up their place in line for him. They knew their position, but they also knew their rights. Because position in society was determined through hormones, they did not crawl on the ground in order to appease a leader so that they might move up in the hierarchy. It had taken me a long time to understand that Coldi didn't work like that.

These types of differences in behaviour never ceased to fascinate me.

Eventually both the woman and the old man were done and it was our turn.

I moved to the counter and said, "I want to report a missing person."

His eyes widened when we gave him all the details, but he took everything down and promised to get back to me when they knew more. There was no prior record that Federza was missing, he said.

He seemed sincere enough that I believed him, but of course he was only an office worker. I couldn't believe that no one had any knowledge of Federza's disappearance.

I signed the report and he said that they'd contact me if there was any news. We left no wiser than we had come.

It was highly unsatisfactory and contributed to the seed of unrest inside me. A pan was going to boil over soon, and I was still looking for the kitchen.

It was only when we were outside that I realised where we should have gone to ask about Federza in the first place. I stopped walking and said, "The Trader Guild office." Damn, how could I have forgotten about that shadow society that all Traders considered their first home?

The building of the Trader Guild was a brand new affair right next to the airport terminal. The considerable funding advantage the Traders possessed over the Barresh guards was not evident just in the glass-fronted exterior. The air was cool and fresh. The floor was lined with soft rubbery material that dampened all sounds. There was a counter on the far side where just one man—dressed in the Trader Guild's distinctive carmine red—sat at a luxurious desk with new and modern equipment. No one waited at the couch in the corner which looked so comfortable that I would happily go to sleep there.

The man gestured for us to come over, and we crossed the soft floor, making little sound.

I explained, for the second time in a few minutes, what had happened.

When I finished speaking, the man rose and said, "Wait here. I'll get a supervisor."

He left through a door in the back of the room behind the counter and came back a moment later with another man in red. This man was Kedrasi, like the typical Trader Guild employees, small of stature, with flaming red hair and large pigment spots around his eyes.

He took us through the security door behind the counter. There was a corridor on the other side of this door, also with soft material on the floor, and newly painted walls. All along the walls hung heavy picture frames which contained manifestos, honour rolls and such things. The Barresh Chapter of the Trader Guild was very young in comparison with the Guild itself, but the building breathed a sense of stately history.

We entered a door about halfway down the hallway, into a small meeting room with a couple of armchairs around a low table. He bade us to sit down and did the same himself, facing us, holding a reader on his lap.

He nodded at me. "Delegate, it's an honour that you come to visit us."

It was amazing where the *gamra* uniform could get you in as honoured visitor, especially if you wore the all-blue. Even his pronouns were formal.

I explained the situation with Federza. How he had come to me, been shot at, how I hadn't seen him since.

He nodded all the way through. Clearly he knew what I was talking about. When I finished, he let a short silence lapse. Then he said, "It is a delicate situation. We are well aware that there is a problem, and that no one wants to talk about it. Most of it is taking place outside our authority." To an unfamiliar ear, Trader Coldi sounded like it had been stuck in the past for at least a hundred years, until you realised that they had a good number of native words and a highly simplified tense structure.

"What do you know?" I used professional pronouns. Even Coldi people rarely used those extremely formal ones that he used, and I wasn't about to change that.

He folded his hands on his knees. "Trader Federza has always been part of many groups and that makes him hard to trace. His membership in the Trader Guild should by rights have been his priority. He became *gamra* representative for the Trader Guild, but as the Aghyrians have no official entity, they never had more than casual representation. Trader Federza annexed that representation when occupying the position through the Trader Guild. The Trader Assembly was not happy about his divided loyalties."

"I heard that Delegate Namion has granted the Aghyrians the right to occupy a seat in the assembly." That was one of the decisions he had pushed through in my absence. Not that I would have voted against it. If the Trader Guild—dubbed a nation without land—could hold a position, then the Aghyrians—a nation whose homeworld was no longer habitable to them—should have one, too.

"They did. Feylin Herza was the first one to take the position."

"Then Marin Federza could have dedicated himself to representing the Trader Guild."

He nodded and pressed his lips together. "Don't make this widely known, but I have to be honest and say that the Traders in charge of the Barresh Chapter weren't highly impressed with Trader Federza's efforts as their representative. At times he seemed to be representing the Aghyrians over the Guild. Deposing a representative is not something the Guild does lightly, but they were considering it. I've heard stories that whenever they mentioned his lack of performance in the position to him, he made evasive replies. As we heard later, he was in trouble with the Aghyrians as well. He might have acted like their representative, but he was not their leader. He challenged the authority. He was aware that when the Aghyrians were talking to the ship, they should notify *gamra* and that the Aghyrians alone did not have the authority to negotiate with the ship on behalf of *gamra* as a whole. He objected to the state of affairs, but was shouted down within the group. He was going to raise it with you, but that was when he was shot at. The next day they replaced him as representative of the Barresh Aghyrians at your negotiations."

"That is what I suspected, but where did he go, and why did Tamerians shoot at him?"

"They were hired guns."

"Did the other Aghyrians hire them?"

He held up his hands. "No one knows."

He looked a bit too innocent for my liking. Not that I thought he knew an awful lot, but I did think he knew more than he told us. "Have you attempted to find him?"

"Not as much as we should, also being hampered by the fact that we don't have authority to make formal investigations."

"Neither do I, yet here I am. Sometimes informal investigations will do just as well as formal ones."

"It's different for you, because people accept that sometimes you need to step outside your authority to do something that you believe in."

Nice try, but sappiness wasn't going to work on me. "Any reasons you don't feel like this about Federza? After all, he's one of yours. The Trader Guild is said to be one of the strongest communities. Don't you all take the pledge of loyalty to the Guild above all others?" The precise wording of the pledge escaped me. If Trader Coldi still used a lot of formal expressions, the pledge was written in even more formal language. It was ancient.

"We're employees, Delegate. We don't take the pledge."

"But the other Traders in the Chapter did. There are at least—what?—seven other Traders here. None of them wondered where he was?"

"When that issue with the Aghyrian ship blew up, we assumed he was with his fellows. We understood the animosity between them only later. The issue didn't get as much attention as we should have given it."

"You forgot about him."

"If you want to put it that way."

I *did* want to put it that way, having spent far too much time with blunt Coldi people. I still felt he was holding back information, even if not about where Federza was.

He rose, signalling the end of the conversation.

I was about to do the same when I decided to be rude anyway, since that appeared to be my lot in life. "If you have nothing to tell us, then why did you call me in here?"

He gave me a startled look. "You're an esteemed Delegate. Should I have left you waiting at the counter?"

"The Barresh guards don't have a problem with seeing me at a counter."

His mouth twitched. "That's not how *we* do business."

"But you've not told me any business. I'm serious: If there is a problem, tell me, so that we can sort out where he is and why he disappeared. As you know, I can pull some strings if necessary." Like, Ezhya.

He hesitated. "What about . . . we don't want those strings?"

Now we were getting somewhere. "You don't have to use them." I glanced at Thayu and she made a hand signal to Sheydu, who rose and went to the door.

"Don't be mistaken that you can intimidate me with your fighting machines," he said, but he glanced at Sheydu's back nevertheless. Clearly nervous.

"There is no need to feel intimidated. I only want one thing: tell me what is going on. Federza was in my office when shots were fired. They were fired at me as much as at him. I have the right to take the perpetrators to court."

"Yes, but investigating that part is the task of the Barresh Council. Nothing we can do."

"I agree, but then tell us what was going on. Why Federza was shot at."

"I told you."

"Poorly doing a job does not justify shooting."

But whatever I did or said, he would not budge, even if he remained polite. At this point, Coldi would have found ways to issue a writ, or find out through networks what was going on, but I had no chance here. Federza appeared to have been without friends.

He led us back to the foyer. We met one of the Barresh Traders on the way. She was dressed in her turquoise and light blue outfit, carrying the cloak over her arm. She also carried a bag and a protective case that probably contained some kind of reader. She moved with the grace of a hunting cat, swaying her hip and tossing her hair carelessly over her shoulder. The hint of leopard-spotted skin protruded from under her uniform sleeves. She nodded a polite greeting to us and then used her tail to open the door.

"That was Yrrid Tiringga," Sheydu said as we walked across the square.

I'd heard that name before. Owner of one of the Pengali Trading licences, who came from a proud family that passed the licences from mother to daughter.

"What did you think of what he told us?" I asked.

"Mostly rubbish," Thayu said.

"Do you think he knows where Federza is?"

"Yes." She didn't even hesitate.

Sheydu was nodding.

"Then who is he protecting?" I asked

Sheydu pursed her lips. "With this vehemence? Delegate Namion."

"Nah," Thayu said. "Delegate Namion is too stupid to hush things up. My bet is on the Aghyrian leadership."

"You think so, huh?" Sheydu answered. "Traders are funny with who they'll pick to support. I think Delegate Namion, because the Aghyrians don't have any control over laws or rules that they might want changed."

"The Traders will support the people they think will win. When something blows up, Namion is the first one to go. He's weak, clueless. He's a stand-in for those who don't yet want to put themselves forward."

They argued over my head.

If I had to choose between who I thought was the most likely to have anything to do with Federza's whereabouts, I would pick the Aghyrians a hundred times over Namion.

But then. . . against this wealth of spying experience, what could I say? I was going to ask them how they were even certain that the Trader Guild was covering up for someone when Thayu said, "Stop."

We did. We were on the far side of the main square where there was a good deal of building activity. I pretended to be looking into a yard. Thayu was talking to Devlin on her comm. "Can you get a fix on them?"

I couldn't hear Devlin's response.

Thayu pulled my arm and yanked me to the side of the street. I knew better than to shout out or resist, even if I almost tripped. We went into a little side alley that ran between two garden walls. She ordered me, "Get down."

There was a door in the wall to the right, with two steps leading up to it. It was probably a servants' or delivery entrance. Leaves had piled up on the steps, especially in the corner in front of the door. I sat down on the steps. There was a collection of food wrappers and empty drink containers, as well as dead leaves and other rubbish.

Between the wall and a bush, I could just see a small section of the street. People walked past in a leisurely pace. They were mostly locals, either merchants or servants of the rich families.

But then a different group came past.

They were all quite stocky and dressed in a variety of clothing that looked as untidy as the local dress, but wasn't local.

They were olive-skinned with brown hair. They walked past slowly, looking to both sides. One of the men was looking at a screen. He briefly turned in our direction. Thayu and Sheydu raised their guns, but the men continued on their way.

We waited a while before coming out of our hiding place.

Sheydu said, "I'm finding this continued presence of Tamerians in Barresh disturbing. Everyone is quick to yell out 'hired guns' when they are mentioned, but I think there is more to it, and I think we should investigate where they come from. Maybe that will tell us a bit more about who is hiring them."

I said, "Or why."

She shook her head. "We know why. Kando Luczon is in possession of some of the most advanced technology anyone has ever seen. No one can stand the thought of any of their enemies getting their hands on it."

7

———

ON THE WAY BACK in the train, we discussed our unease about the various things that were happening around us.

Sheydu didn't like the Tamerians. To be honest, I don't think anyone liked their presence, but I liked even less that no one could explain why they were in Barresh.

I mostly felt uneasy about Federza having gone missing after trying to alert the *gamra* assembly that the Aghyrians were talking to Kando Luczon long before the ship got involved in the stand-off with Asto's military.

"I just don't like that captain, nor his robotic helpers," Thayu said. "If they knew enough about us to specially seek out the Barresh Aghyrians, they would have known that they *should* have sent their correspondence to *gamra*. My guess is that they've been spying on us for years. I don't trust anything that man says. He's not interested in a peaceful reunion. He wants us divided and he is doing all he can to maintain disagreement."

I had a disturbing thought. Everyone had heard the rumours that the Tamerians were an artificial race, but— "If that ship was communicating with the Aghyrians, they might have been talking to others, too. Do you think anyone made the Tamerians according to specifications the Aghyrian ship sent them?" After all, these were the people who had *made* the Coldi people—and were convinced there were flaws in the Coldi genes that they needed to fix. The Tamerians might well be their start-over, second try attempt.

Thayu and Sheydu gave each other a disturbed look. I would probably never know what Asto's military had found out about Tamerians, but my question might have hit close to the mark.

"Well," Thayu said, leaning forward with her elbows on her knees. And then again, "Well . . ." Her face had a disturbed expression as if she was trying, but not succeeding, to find reasons why the truth would not be as I suggested. "I'll . . . see what my father has to say about this."

Clearly something going on there.

The sunlight had turned golden by the time we came back to the apartment. Because I was out, no one was required to be at the door. Evi and Telaris must have gone out for errands, or maybe they were in bed.

The hall in the apartment was deserted, eerily quiet. A couple of lights blinked in the hub, but I didn't think Devlin was in there.

Thayu announced that she had some work to do and made straight for the hub. I suspected she intended to talk to her father.

I said that I was going to get changed out of my formal clothes for dinner and set out for the bedroom—and one moment I was walking across the hall and the next moment my left foot slid out from under me. My left leg shot forward and I landed awkwardly on the left hand side of my butt with my right leg folded under me.

Ouch. What the. . . ?

"Cory!" Thayu stood at the door of the hub, looking into the hall. "What happened?"

"I fell." I pushed myself to my knees and ran my hands over the tiles. "It's wet here. Slippery."

Eirani came in, carrying a bucket. She clamped her hand over her mouth. "Oh, Muri, I just went to get this bucket to put over the wet tiles. You didn't hurt yourself, did you?"

I hadn't and was about to tell her, but at that moment a sound came from deeper inside the apartment: the crying of a baby.

I stared at Thayu, and then met Eirani's eyes. "Has Xinanu had the child?"

"Yes, Muri, and she's gone."

"What do you mean, gone?"

"She had the child and left."

"Isn't she supposed to stay until the child is feeding properly?"

"Muri, tell me, has that woman ever done anything properly?"

Well, maybe not, but . . . "Where is Nicha?"

"He should be in his room, but dinner will be ready soon."

I ran to Nicha's room. The sound got louder when I opened the door.

Nicha sat on the chair by the window, holding a little squirming bundle in a blanket. I went to stand next to him. The baby's face was all scrunched up from crying, the skin red, flaky and blotchy. His mouth was open, with only a ridge of gum, and no teeth. A tiny hand had wormed itself out of the blanket and opened and closed into a fist with each cry.

"He's so small." I wasn't terribly familiar with newborns, whether on Earth or here. I'd only heard that Coldi babies tended to be small.

"He makes a lot of noise," Nicha said.

"Is he drinking yet?" Eirani asked.

Nicha shook his head. "He doesn't want the thing in his mouth."

A baby bottle with a soft teat sat on a table next to him, filled with the yellowish, rich milk that had sat in our cooling cell downstairs for the past week or so.

The room was an absolute mess. The bedding lay on the floor, as well as a good number of Nicha's books and clothes. A cupboard door stood half open. The contents all lay on the ground.

"What happened here?" I asked over the crying of the baby.

"Oh, don't ask," Eirani said. "She didn't like something and she started throwing things around."

"She wasn't feeling very well," Nicha said, still defending Xinanu.

"That is no reason to make a mess of the room," Eirani said. "When we aren't feeling well, most of us crawl into bed. We don't make a huge scene."

Nicha picked up the bottle and pushed the teat in the open mouth. The boy turned his head to the side and continued screaming.

"She should have stayed," Thayu said. "It's in all contracts. Feed the child until it takes a bottle."

"There are many things she should have done, if you ask me,"

Eirani said. "Making that scene in the hall definitely wasn't one of them."

I glanced at Nicha, and he looked away. It was that embarrassing, right?

He nodded. "We had a fight."

I wavered between saying "Another one?" or "That was long overdue." It had irritated me a lot that Nicha had accepted and sometimes even defended the way she treated him.

"She started packing her things. Screaming at me. It made no sense what she said. Anyway, here I was trying to calm her down and she started throwing things around. Then she ran into the hall. A lot of the staff had gathered there out of curiosity, so she started screaming at everyone there. I mean, she was really abusive and rude. Even Eirani was not taking it any longer. She and Devlin were trying to drag her back into the room, and then she pulled away, fell to her knees and gave birth."

"In the hall? Just like that?"

"Yes, Muri, it was outrageous. With everyone watching." Eirani stuck her chin in the air. "I know you look down your nose at my people, but at least we don't make a spectacle like that. There are many things that are meant to stay in private, to be shared only with loved ones and best friends."

I remembered the wet patch in the hall, and tried to imagine what would have happened in that spot, and failed utterly.

While we spoke, the little boy had quietened down a bit. He appeared to have noticed my voice and turned his head so that he could see me. His eyes were very dark, still lacking the golden flecking of the irises. But apparently, unlike human babies, Coldi babies were quite aware of their surroundings.

Nicha picked up the bottle and held the teat to the boy's mouth. He turned his head away sharply and nosed Nicha's shirt. His little hands clawed the fabric while he started screaming again and turning his head further and further away from the bottle. It was a frustrating thing to watch.

Thayu said quietly, "Give him to me."

Nicha did. Thayu held him, squirming and all, in the crook of her arm while she sat on the bed and opened up the top of her uniform with her other. She held the boy to her breast. He latched on. She winced. "Ouch."

It was quiet.

"Is that going to work?" I thought milk tended to dry up.

"Not really, but it will keep him happy for a little bit. If I did this every day, I would have more, but for now, he might calm down. When he's not so frustrated, he might take the bottle."

I'd noticed how over the past two years her breasts had become smaller. She said that they would eventually shrink back to nothing if she didn't have another child. This had happened to Sheydu, which was why I had never suspected that Veyada was her son.

There was already a sign that the baby wasn't happy with the offerings. He was starting to squirm again.

Thayu held out her hand. "Give me the bottle now."

Nicha did, and Thayu inserted the teat in the corner of the little mouth. He latched on. His eyes widened as if in surprise. He drank in long, noisy gulps.

Nicha watched, fascinated, and Thayu's eyes glittered while she looked down at the little helpless creature who was yet unaware of all the controversy that would break out over him.

"Have you named him yet?" she asked.

"Ayshada."

I sat down on the corner of the bed. "Well then, Ayshada Azimi, welcome to my household." I stroked the top of his head, warm and soft with almost no hair.

The first of the next generation. Things in our house would never be the same. And yes, we should get on with providing a playmate for him, or he was going to annoy Eirani.

When he had drunk his fill of milk, his eyelids started drooping. The little hand fell slack. Thayu rose from the bed and lowered him into the bassinet.

Nicha nodded at her. "I clearly have a lot to learn."

He carried the bassinet with us to dinner and while we ate, I spotted him looking down at his sleeping son with a tender expression.

His mother, with whom he had grown up, was very sick. She had connections with the Azimi clan and even if Xinanu hadn't been Nicha's partner of choice, this child was probably part of a contractual obligation between the two clans that I couldn't even begin to understand.

But despite the manner in which fatherhood had come upon him, he seemed to be enjoying it. He *had* been looking to have a child, and his agreed woman had broken her contract. Maybe he hadn't walked into this quite as innocently as the stories let us believe.

8

––––––––––

THAT NIGHT, I discovered that babies don't like sleeping when adults do. Twice, Nicha came into our room with the screaming baby for Thayu to calm down. Thayu, being Thayu, went back to sleep immediately, but I lay awake, worrying about things that might be happening where I couldn't see them, things that would happen if I didn't achieve certain other things, and things that had already happened, but I didn't know about.

I worried about control of my *gamra* message account and messages Delegate Namion's assistant said weren't there, and potential ones that *would* be there and I didn't want him to read.

The second time Nicha entered the room, I got out of bed intending to go to the kitchen to find something to eat, but when I let the door to our bedroom rattle shut behind me, I sensed movement in the hall. Someone was just shutting the door with a soft snick.

"Devlin?" The figure was too short to be either Evi or Telaris. They would be outside, and they would have let this person in, wouldn't they?

"What is everyone still doing up?" a Coldi voice said. Young, male.

It was Reida. He found it necessary to make a subservient greeting. I touched him on the shoulder. Both he and Deyu had trouble dropping that behaviour, no matter how many times I told them. Maybe I should just ignore it and get used to it.

I said, "The baby has been keeping us awake. He needs feeding all the time and Thayu is helping Nicha with it."

"Isn't it in the contract that she should stay for a while?" I had sort-of expected him to make a surprised remark about the birth, but of course, being Nicha's second, he would already know.

"That's another story for another day. Why are you here? Is it safe for you to visit?"

"I have to be a bit careful. I told them at the dig site that I was from the northeastern barracks, except I'm not, and sleeping on the street makes you dirty, so I had to go somewhere to wash. I'll be gone before daylight."

"Did you find out anything interesting?"

"That's what I was hoping I could tell you."

"Come." I pulled him into the living room where I turned on a small light. Ouch— that hurt my eyes. Reida was still wearing black council gear. He wore his hair loose, kept out of his face by the clip that held his earpiece in place. Very much like the local young men wore it. But he was right. He did look a bit scruffy and smelled of marsh mud.

We sat down on the couches in the living room facing one another. His belt bristled with guard equipment.

"You've actually done a really good job of looking like a council guard," I said.

He snorted. "This?" He indicated his belt. "Most of this doesn't work. It just looks good."

"Yes, it does." Although I assumed that the equipment was probably dated and a real guard would be able to see the difference straight away. "What have you found out?"

"There is some really strange shit going on."

"Tell me something new."

"Well, it was actually quite easy to station myself at the dig site. All I did was claim to have been sent there from the northeastern guard division. I expected checks—yes, I have a pass—but the guards are clueless. No one ever asked me for identification. They just told me to stand on the footbridge to the station and stop anyone wanting to access the site. The fellow in charge of the dig is someone named Adaron Namitu. He's an academic and seems to know what he's doing, but he's very slow. People keep putting pressure on him to work faster.

I don't understand why they don't get people in from the Outer Circle. At Asto, people have been digging up this stuff for hundreds of years."

"That's the question, isn't it?"

"At night we all have to leave. There were rumours that the Council was getting Tamerians to do the night shift, and we all have to leave before they arrive. I was curious, so I hid in the reeds—which is why I look like this."

The dried mud on his uniform made grey patches on his knees and lower legs. There were also splatters on his shirt.

"Tamerians did arrive all right. There were two. They pulled down all the side flaps and stood outside. That was pretty boring. I had to crawl all the way to the beach and it was really muddy."

I restrained the urge to laugh. "Do you know who hired them?"

"They're saying the Council. It's not because of the Tamerians or the night shift that I'm here."

I raised my eyebrows.

"I actually managed to wander into the tent yesterday and I had a look at what they're doing. They've sealed off the site by driving plates into the ground and pumping the area dry, but there is nothing much to see except stinking mud and roots and rotting weeds. They're taking the mud up in buckets and rinsing out the dirt until only sand is left. Then they dry it under all these lamps that you can see lighting up the tent at night, and pick all the little fragments out. It takes forever and most of the things they're finding are tiny metal fragments. They pick them all up with tweezers and then they go into a little jar. One per grab sample. They record exactly where each sample came from. It's all very slow."

Yes, that was how it was done.

"Then yesterday, they started uncovering this rock-looking thing."

"Thing?"

"Yes, it's in the middle of the site. It looks like a rock with stuff growing all over it."

"What sort of stuff?"

"Oh, I don't know, the rubbish that grows on rocks that lie in the water. Slimy plants and all that."

"Water life?"

"Something like that. They all seemed very excited about this rock. It's right in the middle of the site."

"In the middle of where the ship used to be?"

"Yep."

That was odd. I had not heard of any meteorite strike that would either have brought the ship down or would have hit it afterwards. "What were they saying about this rock?"

"That's the thing: it's not a rock. It's got all sorts of . . . stuff inside."

"Stuff?"

"Yeah, machinery. Electronics. I couldn't see it very well."

"What do you mean?"

"Well, a couple of the academics had a deep scanning machine and the image was coming up on the screen. I was sort of standing to the side, pretending not to be there. I couldn't come too close, because I didn't want to show them that I was interested."

No. That was true.

"But I got a copy of the scan."

That was Reida: he would get to the important part in a roundabout way, but when he did get to it, the wait would have been more than worthwhile.

He pulled out his comm and an eyepiece projector—which I didn't even know he had—and scrolled through the menus on the apparatus. Then he passed the eyepiece to me. "Just move with your eyes where you want it to go," he said.

I *had* worked with eyepieces before, but admittedly that was a while back. The projection that seemed to hang in the air before me was blurry. The two little buggy antennae hung so close in front of my sleep-affected eyes that I blinked, which sent the projection flying through the menus.

Crap.

"Sorry. I'm not awake yet. That kid has been keeping us up."

I relocated the image and redisplayed it. It was a white and blue monochrome . . . something. A blobby indistinct shape that resembled a cloud, or maybe a giant peanut, if the scale down the bottom was anything to go by.

"Is this it?" That was a disappointment. How could anyone tell what they were looking at, let alone draw conclusions from it?

"Blink."

I did. The image changed. It was still blue-white and blobby but the blobs were in different places.

"What's the idea of this?"

"Blink again. They're cross-sections, like you were cutting the thing into thin slices, but without actually damaging it."

I blinked, and now a square shape materialised out of the indistinct blobs. Another blink and it became thicker.

"It's an encasing."

He nodded.

I blinked again, and now some of the inner content of the "rock" became clear: a section of straight lines with interconnecting wires, a couple of slabs that looked like boards with plugs, some cross-sections of cylinders of some description.

I scrolled through the whole thing, and then reversed the order. The shape of the—clearly artificial—contents came out clearly. I didn't have enough technical knowledge to even begin thinking about what all this was for.

"Can I make a copy of this?" I'd show it to Thayu in the morning.

"You can have it."

I pulled the eyepiece off. "The whole thing?"

"It's all yours."

I wondered where he had gotten the eyepiece. Those things were not cheap. Surely someone would miss it?

Reida announced that he needed to wash and go back, so he went to the bathroom and I went back into my bedroom where Nicha had gone.

Thayu stirred when I came into the bed.

"Hmm, what's going on?"

"Reida came back."

"What did he have to say?"

I told her in a few sentences what Reida had told me. She sat up, a silhouette in the dark against the faint glow that came in from starlight and lamps outside. I gave her the eyepiece and she blinked through the images as I had. The glow from the tiny projector lit her face. I could only see light spots, no details of the image.

"I have no idea what this thing is. I'll get some people to run functional analyses on it." If she said "some people" she almost certainly meant high-level Asto intelligence officers.

"We could simply ask our captain."

Thayu snorted. "What is the chance that he'd tell us the truth? Or that he'd let us analyse these images? He could make such a stink about this data that everyone knows who's got it, who's supposed to have it and who doesn't. He'll probably find out about this anyway, and we'd best send it off before he starts complaining about information being in enemy hands. I'd think the assembly would argue against him and in favour of us, but with this idiot in charge, I don't know anymore."

"Exactly where do you want to send it? First Circle intelligence?"

"Nah. There is a group in the historical wing of the Inner Circle that does models of similar scans. If someone discovers an object at their building site, they notify these people and they turn a scan into a three-dimensional shape that you can test to see what the function of the object is and how important it is that it be preserved."

"Send it."

"I will." She grinned. "Of course they work for the fleet as well."

Of course.

She shifted to the edge of the bed and swung her feet over the side —and froze. "Wait. What's Joyelin Akhtari's name doing on this document?"

"Is it?" I didn't recall seeing that. To be honest, I didn't recall seeing text at all.

Thayu pulled the eyepiece off and gave it to me. She had the projection paused at the very last slide, which just contained the last fuzzy section of the layer that contained the marine growths. "Where is it?"

"In the top corner."

There were a number of lines of blue text in that corner, all of them in Aghyrian—which I hadn't mastered very well. The text was in Aghyrian script, too, not in Coldi notation, and I was even shakier on that subject. But yes, now that Thayu told me, I saw it, too. "What else does it say?"

"Not much. Just something about where it's meant to be sent, I think. We need to have this translated." Again, to be done by the army.

Thayu left the bedroom in her nightshirt. I followed her across to the hub where we sat by the dim glow of a couple of lights. If I found it hard to see anything, I could only imagine what Thayu would see. She couldn't switch the main hub on, because Delegate Namion still had control of the account, and he would be unimpressed if we passed this information to the Asto military.

I used the special line I had with Ezhya, which I couldn't use too often because someone would pick it up. It was the middle of the day in Athyl and we received an immediate acknowledgement of receipt. Ezhya sent these messages without even thinking. I had no doubt that he would process the material later.

For us, it was time to go back to bed.

When we were about to climb into bed, the baby started crying in the next room. We heard Nicha get up and mess about with the bottles.

"I should go and help him," Thayu said.

"He'll call us if he needs help." I slid my hand under her thin nightshirt. Her skin glowed with heat. I ran my hands over the soft mounds of her breasts. Was I crazy or had they become fuller?

"This is another thing you should do," Thayu said in the dark.

I rested my hand on her stomach.

"You should write to the Azimi clan and complain about her departure from Barresh before her contract was even completed."

"Oh, I don't want to—"

"Yes, you do. Breach of contract is a serious clan matter. Nicha is deeply offended. *I* am offended by her behaviour. Ask my father. He will tell you what to do."

I was afraid he would, very much so.

I even sort of agreed with them. Xinanu had been rude and didn't leave us with much choice, but on the other hand, I was getting annoyed.

All this stuff—the Council's refusal to let us visit the site, Federza missing, Xinanu's behaviour—was keeping me away from dealing with the actual problem at hand: what to do about Kando Luczon and his companions and thousands of crew on the ship.

9

——————

BECAUSE *GAMRA* operated on its own time of twenty-three and a half hour days and Barresh operated on Ceren time of twenty-eight hour days, the *gamra* assembly meeting was on before dawn.

I didn't think I'd slept much when Eirani woke me and I sat up with a shock, feeling all sweaty and shivery. It was still dark outside and the air that came in through the open window carried a definite bite. Urgh.

I let myself roll out of the bed, poking Thayu in the side. She went, "Hmmm?" and lay back down while I went into the bathroom.

The light, when I flicked it on, hurt my eyes, and lit a red welt on my chin where an ingrown hair was starting to make its displeasure known. For crying out loud. That always happened when I was stressed. At some point I was going to have to go back to Auckland for another treatment of my skin. Most of my facial hair was gone, but every now and then, a nasty sucker like this sprang up.

Thayu came in, her hair mussed up and the impression of folds in the sheets in her cheek. She held out her reader. "He's finally sent the agenda for the meeting."

That was none too early. "Any items about the ship or the captain?"

"No, it's all internal matters."

As I had thought. This did not improve my mood.

I didn't always go to these meetings, nor did I need to. Attendance was only mandatory if there was an issue to be voted on. Out of consideration for some of the assembly's elderly delegates, those voting meetings were usually scheduled in the afternoon.

I read through the agenda while Eirani did my hair and while I held my reader with one hand and a slice of bread in the other, getting angrier with every line. Budget this, report that.

"Seriously, what the fuck? Not even a single mention of either the captain or the dig site?"

"They've passed responsibility to the council," Thayu said from inside the cupboard where she was getting changed.

"That's ridiculous. Whose idea is this?"

Eirani complained, "Do sit still, Muri, because I don't want to have to redo this plait again or you will be late."

Finally we were ready to go. I caught Thayu throwing a sharp look at the door to Nicha's room. Of course now that we had to get up, the little monster was fast asleep.

Even at that early hour, Telaris stood at the door. He raised his eyebrows as we came out. No, he didn't need to come, I told him when he asked, and also, please go to bed because there might be work to do when I got back.

He nodded, but remained at the door.

Well, whatever. He was a big boy and could look after his own well-being.

Neither of us said anything on our way to the assembly hall. All around us, other candidates were coming out of their apartments, many of them looking equally unimpressed with the time of day. It was not so much that meetings were held at this time, but that the time in relation to Barresh time kept shifting so much. Yes, I understood why they did it, and yes most worlds had shorter days, but right now the massive four-hour difference was not welcome.

The meeting turned out to be very boring indeed. As always, it was quite dark in the hall with exception of the floor surrounding the speaker's dais and the brightness of the spotlights made my eyes feel even grittier than they already were.

We sat through discussions about funding and operational details that were comprehensible only to those people with intimate knowledge of the Exchange. A lot of the delegates' boxes around us were empty.

I had trouble staying awake.

But then the time for questions arrived. Thayu had to poke me in the side or I would have missed it. I scrambled for my prepared statement, couldn't find it, so I had to write a hasty replacement from memory and sent it off not a second before applications closed.

The secretary read out the submissions, of which there were only three.

When my name came up, Delegate Namion looked suspiciously in my direction. Maybe he always looked suspicious. I was starting to see ghosts everywhere.

I stood up in my box and asked him, without much preamble, why Kando Luczon had been refused entry to the dig site, and stated that he should be one of the people allowed access to the site.

Delegate Namion gave me an annoyed look. "I remember telling the Delegate that it is a matter for the Barresh Council."

"No, it is not. The Barresh Council is free to instate their own rules, but *gamra* can override their decisions if this is deemed to be in the interest of all member entities." I had looked that up.

"I cannot see a reason we should take such action. While excavation is in progress, it is only fair that the party conducting the work gets the say over who is allowed on-site."

"The captain and his companions can help with the excavation. They have important knowledge about what we might find. Their entire ship is built using the same technology."

"If we give them access to the site, there will be a lot of other people who will want access, too. There simply isn't the room in this small excavation area."

That had to be the lamest argument I'd yet heard. "We have this man here and he or his companions will become extremely impatient if they're not allowed to do anything."

"Is this of importance to us? Who brought this man here in the first place?"

"The reason I brought him was to preserve the peace and break the standoff."

"Whose fault was the standoff? *Gamra* did not provoke them. *Gamra* did not follow them or push them into corners where their only option was to use violence. It could well be that your employer wants these things to happen, but I cannot see why we should be beholden to these people's wishes. The captain is a most rude and unforgiving man. I don't wish for him to think that in our world that sort of behaviour gets rewarded. He can wait. He can sit at the table when we resume the talks about the Aghyrian claim that's still outstanding."

"Certainly, that claim should be killed as soon as possible." In fact I was surprised that it hadn't been declared void already.

"Not if the claimants let it stand."

Letting the claim stand, of course, suited any conservative person well enough. That's what he seemed to be saying: bury the process in bureaucracy and eventually people will forget about it.

There were just too many places where I could see openings for manipulation.

I asked him, "So what would you suggest that I let these people do? They want to access the historic sites. They are going to get impatient if I have to deny all their requests."

He held up his hands as if he wanted to say, *That is not my problem*.

But it was my problem, and yes I knew that it had been a gamble, but I couldn't possibly send Kando Luczon back to his ship without having seen anything, because he would wake up all his crew and come back to get that information by force, as well as everything else he wanted.

Delegate Namion gestured at another delegate.

"Hang on, I wasn't finished."

"We are finished with the current subject." The tone in his voice was cold.

"This is about a different subject."

"I only noticed one submission from you."

"One submission that contains two questions."

He glanced at his screen. His scrunched up in an expression of distaste as he saw that I was right. He said nothing.

In the hostile silence, I went on. "Yesterday I filed a missing person report for Trader Marin Federza. I want this to go on the

record as having been said in this room. I've looked through recordings of the past meetings, but cannot see any places where people
have discussed the fact that Federza hasn't been seen since his apartment was shot at." It had gone very quiet in the hall.

"Why does this need to be mentioned here? Trader Delegate
Federza has been replaced."

Yes, I noticed the Kedrasi Trader Delegate in the box—her hair
stood out like flaming fire in the glow from the spotlights. Still very
keen to attend all meetings, I guessed, because Federza would never
have come to this early morning sitting.

I returned her nod. "I know that he has been replaced. I am
concerned for his safety."

"He's a trader. He's travelling."

"He is not answering my correspondence. Unless my correspondence is being held up somewhere." I glared at him.

He glared back. "We're still in the process of setting up filters to
direct the appropriate messages to my account."

"Was there anything from Trader Federza?"

"I'm not a message boy."

"I would appreciate if control to my account could be returned to
me, along with *all* the messages that have arrived in the last two days."

He didn't say anything, didn't move. I gathered that there hadn't
been a message from Federza.

I said to the assembly, "If anyone here has any information about
Trader Federza's whereabouts, you know where my office is."

I sat down to an increasing murmur of voices. The Trader delegate
gave me a strange look. Disturbed, almost. She might be living locally,
I don't think she'd been here long. I had no idea what the people in
the Barresh Chapter of the Trader Guild had told her.

By the time the meeting finished and I left the hall, it was light
outside. Both suns were above the horizon, bathing the island in a rich
golden glow.

Neither Evi nor Telaris was at the door to my apartment, and the
hall lay equally deserted. I went into the bedroom to get changed. Out
of curiosity, I opened the door to Nicha's room, and found that it was
dark inside.

Nicha lay in the double bed, on his back with his head on the pillow, his eyes closed and mouth slightly open. The infant lay curled up on his stomach, his little head on Nicha's chest.

I shut the door as quietly as I could.

"Is he still asleep?" Thayu had been grumpy because she had to get up early and she sounded even grumpier now.

We had breakfast at the dining table. Neither of us said much. We were both tired. We weren't getting anywhere. Kando Luczon was going to be extremely unimpressed and some people, possibly including Delegate Namion, were actively obstructing us. I mean—how long could it take to redirect messages relating to a particular subject?

"What can we do?" I asked myself as much as Thayu. "Everything we do is turning into a mess. I don't even know why it's our task to try to find Federza. We don't have time for it."

"Then don't. He's not our responsibility."

No, he wasn't. But I couldn't forget how he'd been genuinely scared when he came to my apartment, before he was shot at.

I let out a deep breath. There *was* no time.

"I'm going to get Veyada to dig out every single law he can find that says that *gamra* has to make a decision about the captain and the ship. The only thing they do is bullshit around the margins. Meanwhile, we have the captain getting into the security accounts."

"Security reported that they fixed that."

"Not for long, I bet."

"Until they find out what else he's been getting into."

It disturbed me deeply. I knew that on Earth a lot of modern technology contained chips that had little preprogrammed routines that Coldi had planted there, and that the Exchange could access, if necessary.

What if the Aghyrian technology—the very one Coldi had used as blueprint for their development—had similar hidden routines?

"I promised him that he could visit the historical sites. He *needs* to see some of these sites. How long is it going to be for the Pengali or Miran to grant me a permit?" Which, fuck it, I couldn't receive if Delegate Namion was going to hang onto control of my message account.

"I think we should take him to look at Asto."

"That might be the most logical solution, but I'm afraid that he will either do something stupid to himself or to us."

"He hasn't come here all this way to do stupid things. He won't be in control of the craft in any way. You have the permit already. We should arrange it to keep him occupied."

"All right then, let's do it."

10

———

WITH THE EXCHANGE in operation, a trip to Asto wouldn't be anywhere near as long and uncomfortable as my previous one. Not long after he became fascinated with me, when I was very new to this job, Ezhya had taken me to look at Asto from orbit a few times. Looking at stars or some other celestial phenomenon was his euphemism for a private talk, or some other private activity. In a way it galled me that I had to do this with a very unpleasant person. I had *good* memories of floating in orbit and seeing the planet's surface pass under me while sipping some kind of liquor.

I spent much of the morning trying to organise a pilot, without a great deal of success. They were busy. They wanted exorbitant amounts, or they didn't take tourists. I was left with two I didn't particularly like but which I would use if there was no other option. Thayu remained conspicuously quiet in this matter, so I half-suspected that she was working on something else. My guess: her father.

After lunch I went downstairs to tell Kando Luczon about the trip. No need to notify Delegate Namion by sending the message through the account that he was spying on. Lilona opened the door this time. I told her about the trip and that we would contact her when it was organised.

She acknowledged my efforts with her usual empty smile.

When I came upstairs, Devlin notified me that some correspondence had come through in my account. I guessed Delegate Namion had figured that he couldn't hold onto *everything* that arrived in the account without being asked to explain. Most of it was boring stuff, but one was a message from my father, presumably sent before he received my message not to send anything to that account anymore.

In any case, the message contained nothing important.

My father had bought a new boat. It was a classic catamaran with a kitchen and three double cabins. He lived with Erith—my Damarcian stepmother—and an ever-expanding herd of animals, to which he had recently added a camel—yes, seriously—so who was going to occupy all that space on the boat? Oh yes, I got the hint, Dad.

While I was reading, transported to salty sea breezes and dolphins gambolling at the bow—and that surfboard that sat in the storage room downstairs and that I'd promised Raanu I'd use to teach her to surf—someone came into the office.

Devlin. "I'm sorry to disturb you, but you have a visitor."

Again, I thought *Marin Federza* and while following Devlin to the living room, formulated a response that would be neither unfriendly nor give any indication that I'd been waiting for him.

However, when I entered the living room, I found Asha Domiri standing at the balcony door overlooking the marshlands beyond. It was now late afternoon, and the room filled with golden sunlight.

"It's a nice sunset," I said, and it was, with a flock of little sheep-like clouds, pink-edged and bright in contrast to the dark purple sky directly above.

"For this place, yes, it's a nice effort." He nodded. He was aware that I didn't like to do subordinate greetings and today didn't seem to have a problem with that.

"Have you seen your grandson yet?"

"Not yet."

I had been going to ask why he'd come to see me, but put the pieces together: Thayu had spoken to him yesterday and he was going to offer transport for us, Kando Luczon and his companions to look at Asto from orbit. He trusted Kando Luczon as little as I did.

"We'll go and find Nicha." After breakfast, I had seen him potter about the apartment with the baby.

He was just coming up the stairs, carrying his son in a sling that hung over one shoulder. The baby was awake, looking around with a slight frown on his little face. His skin was no longer wrinkled, but full and soft. His hair was a soft fuzz on top of his head, slightly blue-purple metallic-looking already, but still light in colour.

Asha nodded at his son. "Well done. What's his name?"

"Ayshada."

The name seemed to please Asha.

Nicha held the baby up to his father. Asha stroked the little boy's head with a hand that looked massive in comparison with the baby's head. He was so tiny, and looking around so peacefully, that it was hard to believe that he had kept everyone awake last night.

"He'll be a handful of trouble," Asha said in a rare personal comment. "Take good care of him." Then he nodded, signalling that the time for chat was over. He met my eyes. "I need to talk to you."

"That would be a good idea. I think Eirani is about to serve dinner. Why don't you stay and we can have our discussion afterwards?"

"It's . . . sensitive. I'd like to go somewhere else. Just the two of us."

That was interesting. "I guess we could go to one of the eating houses." Eirani would not be impressed, but it wouldn't be the first time that I didn't attend dinner at short notice.

"I'd like to go to a place where we can disappear in a crowd, not be recognised and pointed at."

"We could go into town." He would definitely be recognised on the island.

"All right." This was getting ever more curious.

I had to make some preparations. One simply did not catch the train into town with a guest of this calibre. I asked if I should bring guards, but Asha said his guards were shadowing us all the way. They were bringing Evi and Telaris along, and anyone else would be notified if we weren't returning at the agreed time.

Devlin called a water taxi, which we caught from the jetty at the back entrance to the building. It was one of those flat-bottomed marsh boats with a jet engine at the back. It had three benches for passengers. In past trips I had learned that the back row was where you wanted to be if you didn't intend to get wet. Asha and I sat down next to each other on this bench. The driver, a young Pengali man, asked if we were ready, and when I said we were, gunned the engine.

As we pulled away from the quay, I couldn't see any guards, but they would be there, even if I had no idea where they hid.

The trip was fast, windy and noisy and left no opportunity for talking. As the outline of the *gamra* island receded in the distance, I had a strange feeling that Asha might be trying to get me alone on some kind of journey. The resemblance with the manner we'd been whisked away to go to the Aghyrian ship was eerie. Maybe there was trouble at the siege area, where a fleet of Asto's military ships surrounded the sleeping giant that was the Aghyrian ship. I might not come back here tonight.

But in that case . . . wouldn't Asha have insisted that Thayu and Nicha or Veyada and Sheydu come as well? And last time he had told me to pack a bag.

Asha's face looked no different from the way it usually did: stern but otherwise unemotional, while the warm wind and occasional spray of water battered our faces and strands of hair blew in our eyes.

I had asked the driver to drop us at the airport jetty which was next to the station.

From there, it was a short walk up a slight incline, past the fence where you could see the craft on the tarmac. Asha's familiar unmarked craft sat at the far end. A plainly dressed guard stood next to it. I didn't miss the bulges of guns in the sleeves of the jacket. I didn't miss the broad shape of the shoulders and judged the soldier to be female. Did Natanu have a sister?

A train had stopped at the station soon after our arrival and we walked up the hill, mingling in the crowd. We chatted about innocent things. The weather, the building activities in town, whether or not I was going to get that pilot's licence that I'd promised Ezhya to get. Every time the subject changed, I expected him to mention any of the serious issues we faced, but he did not. Maybe it was because it was quite busy on this path, maybe because of something else. I didn't know. I wished those Inner Circle people would stop doing this. Maybe he only wanted to talk about his family and the Azimi problem, but if so, why did he need to make me so nervous over going out to a private dinner?

It was almost dark by the time we came out onto the main square. The place was busy with people milling about and choosing which place to eat at, people sitting at eateries, people lining up at the popular places. The air was full of chatter and cooking smells. Of course one could not make a fire in Barresh, but electrically-fired oil burners were a way that stall-holders had found around that, and deep-frying just about anything was very much in fashion. Much of the food smelled heavenly and contributed a lot towards expanding waistlines. Mine, too, I was afraid.

We walked past all that activity and chose a small Pengali-run eating-house in the quiet end of Market Street. It seemed a casual decision, but I had no doubt that Asha had planned to go here and already had his guards stationed at strategic positions where they would have been scouting out the surroundings for most of the afternoon.

We sat at a little table under the giant trees that lined this part of the street. He commented on the trees, and I told him how the entire street used to be lined with these trees down to the square, but that the ones closer to the airport had been blown over in a terrible storm.

A tiny little light in a jar of pink glass stood on the table. Not glass, of course, but real Pengali-cut diamond. There were whole cliffs of this stuff at the escarpment, waterfalls running over cliff faces made of pure diamond. Most windows in Barresh were made of it, as were drinking glasses and bowls. There was the regular clear variety, there was pink, there was yellow and amber and a kind of purple-blue that was the most expensive variety. The Pengali had developed ancient, time-consuming processes to cut it.

This eating-house was a Pengali place, proudly run by an all-Pengali staff with uniforms that allowed for their tails, singlets that showed off the patterned skin on their shoulders and a variety of exquisite artwork on the walls. Whenever I came here, I resolved to learn more about these ancient people, and somehow, that wish got lost in the bureaucracy and other "more important" things that crept on my to-do list.

All around, people were talking to each other in keihu or Pengali. Locals mostly, some of whom gave us curious glances. At one point, I spotted Telaris in a corner, in the company of a Coldi woman in dark clothing. Just letting me know he was there, I thought.

A waiter came to bring our orders in clear bowls with little metal tongs. It was Pengali fare: fish, noodles, mushrooms, all grown and harvested locally. Asha thanked the waiter in a gesture unusually friendly for him. Then he fixed me with a serious gaze, and I knew that we had arrived at the important part of what had so far been a strangely relaxing outing.

"We must discuss the Azimi case. That woman has to be one of the most terrible drama queens I have ever had the displeasure of coming across. I gather she complained a lot when she was in your household?"

"She was not very nice to the staff even if they tried their best to please her."

"She has also been complaining since she got home. The clan elders have told her that she's wrong."

"Delegate Ayanu is still in Barresh." Even if she lost much of Ezhya's favour and the race to become Chief Delegate. "She hasn't spoken to me about it." In fact, she hadn't spoken to me since we had rescued Reida from being locked up in her office. "Is she still the clan leader?"

"She is. I don't know how much she agrees with Xinanu, but there *will* be a complaint."

"What is there to complain for *them*? Xinanu is the one who didn't stick to the contract."

"She says she had reasons not to. Frankly, I think it's best not to wait for their complaint and lodge one of your own. That's what I'd like you to do."

"Do I have to? To be honest, I'm glad that she's gone. I don't want her to come back to fulfil the rest of the contract. We can manage between the three of us."

"I understand that, but the point is, she offended us when she broke her contract. You must ask for compensation on behalf of the Domiri clan. This is important because the Azimi clan must not think that they can get away with this. They know it's coming and they are already formulating their response."

I sighed. Veyada had told me as much. It seemed the matter was unavoidable. "What if the Azimi clan has a valid counter-claim?"

His eyebrows rose. "Do they?"

"I took Reida from them. He was captured in Delegate Ayanu's office because of a claim they had against him. I intervened and freed him. More recently, I used their network bugs."

He shook his head. "Disputes of property are not clan matters.

They won't try to offset your relationship contract claim against theirs. They can't. Different parts of the law."

"Can this wait a while? No one seems to be in any great discomfort, and there are a lot of other things going on that require my attention."

"Preferably not. With clan situations, the longer you let a thing fester, the worse it gets." He went on to tell me how to compose and lay out a claim document. He had me type it up on the awkward keyboard projector of my reader, which projected the keys over the surface of the table, my glass and part of my bowl. The table just wasn't big enough.

To my human mind, making the claim was an extraordinarily petty thing to do in the light of the situation. Xinanu was home, we were happy, we didn't want her back and there was so much more important stuff to do.

But he insisted.

I had to redo the whole thing three times before he was satisfied with it. "Send it."

"Now?" It seemed a strange thing to do while at a relaxed dinner.

"Why not?"

So I did. While watching the message disappear off my screen with a kind of trepidation, I asked, "What do I do with the response when one comes in?"

"It should be pretty straightforward. Veyada should be able to help you with most of it, although he is better versed in *gamra* law than clan law. If you run into trouble, ask me."

I registered that he had not asked me why I had used my personal account instead of my *gamra* one.

We were silent for a bit, watching the other diners. Then he insisted on paying for the meal.

In all, I thought the evening had been quite amicable and for once, I was happy with the way I had remained in control of events. I needed help with this clan claim, and he had given it. I could handle it now. That certainly had to be a step forward from being dragged out of my house on some goose chase where I was only informed at the last minute what it was all about. I was sure that he knew many things that would be of benefit for me to know; but for once, he didn't appear to want to talk to me in order to use me as vehicle for his aims.

Maybe I was getting the hang of this father-in-law thing after all.

We left the eating-house and walked back in the direction of the airport, but we hadn't gone far when he stopped in the shade of one of the big trees.

I stopped too. "Is anything wrong?"

For a while, nothing moved except his eyes, studying the street where, as far as I could see, nothing out of the ordinary was happening. Just the usual evening crowd going about their leisurely business.

"Not yet," he said. "But I might have to ask you for a fairly large favour. I'm hesitant about this and haven't mentioned it yet tonight, because I think I finally understand what you're about, and what I'd be asking would be contrary to your philosophy. I'm hesitant because I respect you."

"Well," I said, and my voice sounded high. Did I say anything about the evening having gone well? "If you don't ask I can't say yes or no. So why don't we have a drink and you tell me about it?"

"A drink is good. But understand: there is no saying no."

I looked into his eyes and knew that the entire night had been a smokescreen, even the bit about the Azimi claim.

When dealing with Asto's military, you were never, ever, on safe ground.

I hesitated.

At some point in my life, I was going to turn a corner where I knew so many secrets that I would become a representative of Asto. Maybe that point had already been reached. I'd been let into military secrets that no one knew. But so far, knowing those secrets had helped establish peace for *gamra* as a whole. I suspected that he was now asking me to assist in an act of war, which *would* turn a corner for me.

On the other hand, a strong Asto presence preserved the peace. I'd hate to think what would happen if Asto's hold on *gamra* diminished. We'd have Barresh Aghyrians, *zeyshi* Aghyrians, Damarcians all fighting for control and a largely ineffective bureaucracy that never decided anything in time.

If he—and through him, Ezhya—thought it was important that they get me on side with this slightly less peaceful thing—whatever it was—then perhaps I should trust them that it was for the better.

I took a deep breath. No saying no, huh? "All right. Let's go."

11

———————

I **LED HIM TO** one of my favourite bars: located in a secluded, tree-covered courtyard surrounded by commercial buildings that were closed and dark at this time of the day. As was almost mandatory for Barresh, there was a fountain in the courtyard, with little tables surrounding it. I half-expected him to say that the venue was not secure enough with all the balconies overlooking the court-yard, but his guards must have judged security adequate because he said nothing about it, although he did appear distracted for a little while, probably listening to a report via his feeder.

I ordered my usual: a local liquor made from flowers. As I suspected, Asha wanted zixas, and this was indeed one of the places that had a permit for serving it.

We chose a table near the fountain's edge, where a little waterfall fell over the edge into a drain, and disappeared into the ground. Most of these fountains were part of Barresh's elaborate drain system that kept the islands dry and habitable.

We sat down, facing each other.

His expression was a lot more serious now than it had been earlier in the evening.

"You are positive you want to hear about this?" he asked. "Knowing that when I tell you what I'd like to do, you don't have the option of backing out?"

My heart was hammering. "I am assuming that you would never ask me if you didn't think there would be a benefit to the peace."

"A benefit to the *established* situation." Which was not entirely the same as "peace". According to some, Asto had entirely too much power. I'd spent the last few years making sure that I wasn't seen, not in public at least, to be favouring one side or the other.

Ezhya had placed me in charge of negotiations about the Aghyrian claim, because I was seen as neutral. Had I turned the corner when I'd gone to Athyl to secure Ezhya's position? Maybe not, because any of the people who would have taken over would have been detrimental to the peace in the region. I'd definitely been let into some deep military secrets when I went to break the standoff between the Aghyrian ship and the military, but that, again, had been because people saw me as neutral. Oh, Asto exploited every bit of that neutrality. They had *bought* me a seat in the expert panel section of the assembly, I was well aware of that. And I was *not* entirely neutral, because I happened to believe that a strong Asto was vital for peace in *gamra,* and I also happened to count Asto's Chief Coordinator as my friend.

But deliberately stepping out of that neutrality? That was mine-riddled ground.

I licked my lips. "Do you think that the situation is serious enough that I should risk my position?"

"I don't ask any of this lightly. When you agree, you may be seen by some as betraying *gamra.* I think we can both agree that the current leadership is rotten to the core. In their quest to counter what many see as evil Coldi dominance, some principles have been bent or forgotten. As Coldi, we can't do anything about it without appearing to further our own position, which of course backfires and pushes possible doubters in the other direction. None of this would matter much—in fact it *hasn't* mattered one bit for many years—if we didn't have the Aghyrian situation. And we've found a couple of factors that converge disturbingly."

I realised I didn't really have the option now to back out anymore. He seemed to have started on his story already. Had probably been bursting to do so all night.

A Pengali waitress came to our table to deliver a tray with two small glasses. One contained a cloudy greenish-yellow drink that I recognised as mine, the other a clear blue oily fluid. That glass had a little lid that fitted it perfectly.

Asha rotated the tray so that the glass with the green liquor faced me. It was cooled and condensation coated the outside of the glass.

I lifted the glass and took a sip. I quite liked this stuff. Not too strong and very mellow.

He lifted the other glass off the tray and took off the lid. A thin trail of vapour rose from the blue fluid. It was zixas, one of the most red-coded, utterly poisonous drinks invented by the Coldi. It wasn't legal for bars to serve it to the general public, so you had to know where to get it and I'd guessed right that he wanted it.

He lifted the glass to me and drank a good gulp. The breeze carried the faintest waft of vapour to me. It made my eyes water and my face tingle. It wasn't unpleasant, but holy crap.

He set the glass back down and put the lid back on. "So, the Trader Delegate disappeared, but no one seems to care a lot."

"Um . . ." Out of all the things I had expected him to talk about, Marin Federza's disappearance was probably the least likely.

"Let me summarise some things. Somebody—and this is somebody who is in league with those who control, or know how to get help from, Tamerians—is keen for certain things to stay a secret. These are things to do with the Aghyrian ship, its whereabouts, its occupants, its trajectory, its history. Delegate Ayanu—Azimi, the same clan we've had some trouble with recently—had the information briefly before your rascal spy took it off her and you presented it to the assembly. As, I add, was entirely appropriate. I know that you get annoyed with the boy, but my son chose his seconds wisely. Hang on to that boy. He'll pay you back any investment in him many times over."

I really did wonder how he knew all this.

"Question: that information about the ship that the rascal stole from Ayanu's office, that's been picked over and analysed many times, would that have been all that's available about the ship?"

Damn. Of course not. I opened my mouth—

"No, don't answer that. There is a lot more, of course. Whether it was all covered in easily understood conversations with the Barresh Aghyrians, I very much doubt it, but all communications from that ship, including the considerable anpar wake it created when coming in, will have produced information. Where is all that information?"

"I . . . I don't know. I assume that the Exchange collected it and passed it onto appropriate authorities and that they're working on it, or looked at it and informed us of any information they could glean."

"What have they told us? At the very beginning, they told us that they deduced from the anpar wake that Kando Luczon was aboard the ship."

I remembered that. It was just after I'd returned from Asto. We'd all been so shocked that we hadn't even asked what else there was.

"They've told us nothing since. Do you believe that none of the Exchange data could have added additional information?"

"When you say it like that, not really."

"Now who controls the Exchange?"

"*Gamra*."

"In theory. In practice, who controls it?"

And that's where my insides went cold. The *gamra* Barresh node of the Exchange was the only privately-owned Exchange in all of the settled worlds. Who owned it? The Damaru family, but ultimately, the round-waisted men of the Barresh council.

Who had teamed up with Delegate Namion to stop me or Kando Luczon getting access to the dig site? Even using Tamerians to do this. Tamerians that *might* have been developed by the Aghyrians to "replace" the "faulty" Coldi.

Which, by itself, was an aim that suited the Aghyrians and anyone not Coldi in the *gamra* assembly.

Oh shit.

Asha took the lid off his glass and lifted it to his lips for another sip.

I asked, "That thing that's buried under the ground in the lost ship that Thayu sent you that scan of—"

"She sent it to the History Division in the Inner Circle."

"Yes, sure." I met his eyes, unsmiling. I felt like he was joking, but his showed none of it. "It's some kind of communication device, isn't it?"

"Too right."

"And you're still fearing that there might be other relays orbiting Asto in the space junk clouds."

"Not fearing. We know that these things are present there. We've noticed that some appear to have moved recently."

"Moved?"

"Judging by maps, some of them older than me."

"Have they moved by themselves?"

"That's the question. There is no way to find out unless we send drones out there to bring in every single piece of space junk and analyse it. But we know some of the junk clouds have reconfigured, more often than we would have expected them to do as a result of collisions. Some satellites have moved. We just don't know which ones or how. Doing a complete sweep is impractical within the time frame we have."

"Time frame?"

"The main ship appears to be waking up."

"I thought you couldn't communicate with it."

"We can't, but there is increased activity and increased radiation and heat output. You saw that huge hall with all the stasis pods along the side? I think those people are being woken up. Maybe the process was set in motion by something we've done, maybe it was set in motion a long time ago, but they're definitely waking up."

I remembered the vastness of that hall with all those pods around the walls. Thousands of people. No, thousands of Kando Luczons. "What will they do?"

He spread his hands. "I'm guessing they're not here for the annual occultation festival." This was a big celebration in Barresh's calendar, when one of the suns went behind the other.

"If all this is true, I really need to get on with talks with Kando Luczon."

"I understand he's an unpleasant character?"

I sighed. "Someone asked him in the assembly if he was the arsehole who could have transported thousands of people off Asto when the meteorite impact was imminent, but didn't, and I would have loved to have risen and cheered with the rest of the delegates."

"I guess hanging around long-term in the isolation of space can make one an 'arsehole'." He met my eyes.

I couldn't work out if he was joking or offended. *He* spent a lot of time in space.

Delegate Wilson, you suffer from a serious case of Foot-In-Mouth disease.

I took a sip from my drink. My ears were glowing, and I hated it when they did that.

He continued. "Can you give an honest answer to a question?"

I looked up at him. *Even more honest than that?*

"Do you think you're making any inroads with this arsehole character?"

I shrugged. He seemed to have latched onto the word "arsehole" and adopted it as his new favourite. How embarrassing. "It hasn't been easy. Sometimes I feel that we're speaking to each other in two different languages. Their understanding of society is entirely different. The trouble is we have no reference points to tailor our approach or responses. If only the historic texts or surviving information from the time of the Aghyrians contained data about how their society was structured—but they don't. Surviving information is all about technology. It seems the reference to society is lost."

Asha laughed. He clapped me on the shoulder. "I like you. You're a very good diplomat."

Oh? I frowned at him.

"Using eighty-seven words where just one would have done: No."

Geez, thanks. "Well, I guess you're right. But it's early days."

"We don't have early days. Or I should say: early days are all we have. There will be no late days. We need this solved now. We need an agreement or understanding from them about what they'll agree to do with that ship, where they'll stay and where they won't go, and where they won't interfere. Failing that, we need to defend ourselves."

"Defend ourselves" was not a term one wanted to hear from the mouth of the leader of the largest army in the settled worlds. Hell, what information did he have that I didn't? "So, what would you do in my position?"

"Ask for assistance."

I frowned at him.

He continued, "I heard you're planning to take the captain on a little excursion to watch his beloved home planet from orbit. If I were you, I would allow the military to tack onto this expedition to run certain . . . reconnaissance programs."

"But that's—"

"Outside your mandate. I know. That's why I suggested that once you know about this, there is no going back."

"Nice trick." I took a sip from my drink. The liquor didn't taste half as sweet and mellow as it should. He had me by the throat, and he knew it. Yet again, the only inroads we'd made with the captain were that we now knew that the rumours about his self-absorbed character were not rumours. "What would these reconnaissance projects be?"

His lips twitched.

"You're asking me to take a major risk. It's only fair that I know what you're going to do with my commitment, if I give it."

He snorted. "I suspect that once he's up there, our captain will have some way of contacting the relays in orbit. Once he does, we can identify them."

"And destroy them?"

He nodded, once.

"What if they're . . . unimpressed?"

"There is no 'What if?' They *will* be unimpressed, but unless they let us know all the missing pieces in their story, we're going to make every damn attempt possible to stop them coming into the Ratanga cluster. I'm guessing that they came back for a reason to do with us. In other words: they may need us, so they can't destroy us. But they're going to do something. The increased energy output of the ship probably means that they're gearing up for whatever it is."

"I thought you had them cornered?"

He snorted. "I have no illusions that we control them. They're probably happy to sit where they are now. I very much doubt that we could stop this ship, or even destroy it, if we wanted. We've run analyses on it and I'm worried about what the engineers tell us. These people travelled between galaxies. We don't know what sort of forces operate in that void. We don't know what they found at that other galaxy. Because I'm sure that they found things that could change our world, but they're not telling us. I don't trust them."

I didn't trust them, either. We were on the same page on that issue. "I had hoped that by taking the two companions, we might be able to extract some information from them, but they've acted like mindless, faceless robots."

"That's probably because they *are* mindless, faceless robots. They were probably creations of the original Aghyrians, like us. Except they lost control over us when the meteorite struck and we survived on Asto free of their control. Could you imagine what our life would have been like if they had still been here? We were meant to be an 'all-purpose colonising race'. What if they would have used us simply to do hard work on new colonies, only to kill us off when the work was done?"

Damn. "So now they have created the Tamerians for the purpose of getting rid of us?—I mean, the Coldi."

He laughed. "All right. I know where you stand in this matter. It's just that you haven't yet admitted it to yourself."

My ears were glowing again. Yet he was probably right. If I could turn myself Coldi, I would, even if just to give Thayu the child she wanted.

"It's my guess that the captain's two companions are probably also artificial. Slaves or minions. It wouldn't have mattered which of those people in the ship you'd have chosen as companions. They would all have been like this. When we were in the ship, did any of them except the captain ever say anything useful to you?"

They hadn't. Hell, he was probably right and he had spent a lot more time on board the Aghyrian ship than any of us. "But the Coldi became independently thinking people. If these Aghyrian companions are not machines, they can be tempted to think for themselves as well."

"After four hundred years of living like minions? I don't like your chances."

"Allow me to try." Although what I would do to get the companions to talk, I had no idea. But I had to do it, because if I let him have his way, we'd be guaranteed to head for armed conflict that, by his own admission, Asha wasn't sure the Asto military could win.

And he knew it.

He pursed his lips. "All right. I will prepare for the sightseeing trip. If you can do your thing and get them to talk, that's where it will stay. We take the trip, let them look at Asto from orbit, take them back. If you haven't made any significant progress by then, we'll proceed with some more intensive questioning during that trip." He picked up his glass and upended the rest of it in his mouth. "Another one?"

"Sure." I gulped the rest of my drink while he hailed a waiter.

He hadn't put the lid back onto the empty glass, and the few oily remains of zixas were trailing wisps of vapour into the air. The sharp, acid-laced smell was starting to make me feel dizzy. I was trying to come up with a way that I was going to isolate the two timid Aghyrians from their master, but failing. One of the most important ultimatums of my life, and I had no idea how to go about it.

Asha put another full glass into my field of view. He lifted his glass to me.

I asked him, "So, is there anything you'd be willing to share on the subject of the information held back by the Exchange about the ship?"

He began a long and technical reply about anpar wakes and how the military's equipment had picked up snatches of information, most of it incoherent. He said those snatches presented a worrying picture that suggested that the ship had been sending information for a long time. They were unsure who received the info, because of the relays used in the system.

"We've been out to destroy those. They're easy to detect once they're active. Not so much where the information went. The Exchange holds the full anpar readings, and we cannot request access to them except by assembly approval. The whole *gamra* system is already set up to limit Coldi influence as much as possible. We don't even need the Aghyrians to hold us down. The rest of *gamra* is succeeding magnificently already."

To sum up, there was not a great amount of information known, but the more I thought of it, the more likely it seemed that the Barresh Aghyrians weren't the only group that the ship had been communicating with. How long had this been going on? If they had indeed been sending information about how to produce Tamerians, then it must have been at least twenty years. The thought made me dizzy.

More drinks arrived at the table. I didn't even remember who ordered them.

Asha seemed happy. He got into *gamra* politics, and women— concerned, apparently—that I hadn't tried out enough of them.

There was a block of time, in between stumbling out of the courtyard, and arriving at the *gamra* island, that was erased from my memories.

I had no idea how we got back. I vaguely remembered stumbling into the bedroom where Thayu was already asleep. I vaguely remembered lying in bed feeling like I was on a ship on a rough ocean.

12

———

I WOKE UP with a shock, with bright daylight streaming into the room. The curtains were open, the side of the bed empty and the room tidied.

Well, what the. . . ?

I sat up, looking around, confused.

Ouch, my head.

Ouch, my eyes.

I stumbled from the bed into the bathroom. A look in the mirror confirmed that my eyes were red, a by-product of the zixas fumes I had breathed last night.

My feeder must have signalled activity to Thayu, because she came into the room, wearing her *gamra* uniform.

She smiled at me. "Big night out?"

I groaned.

"I can smell zixas."

"Seriously, I didn't touch the stuff. That stuff is pure poison. It would kill me." I must be the first person to get a hangover from breathing the fumes of someone else's drink. Damn it, I felt terrible.

"I'll let you recover." She headed back to the door.

"No, Thay' don't go."

She stopped, raising her eyebrows.

"It's . . . not good. I need to talk to you. Call Nicha. Veyada, too. Sheydu as well. I need ideas."

She frowned at me. "Call them in here? Like this?"

I looked down at my pale chest, where the laser had missed some hair follicles and a few dark blond hairs stuck out of my pale skin. I would have to go back to the clinic in New Zealand to get regrowth on my face and chest removed. At some point, a diet would probably also be a good idea. "Tell them to come to my office. Let me get changed first."

"Reida is still out. Should Deyu be there?"

"Yeah. All right." I'd not yet discovered much use for her. She seemed timid, but since she was in my association, she should probably be there, too. "Oh, and I want Evi and Telaris, and Devlin. But give me time for some breakfast."

Thayu left and I scrambled for clothes and to make myself presentable. I tried eye drops from the medicine cupboard, but they stung like hell—I said a few interesting words—and made my vision blurry. Great. Go to save the world while having the universe's biggest hangover. Wasn't I just a model picture of the patheticness of humanity?

Apparently, Eirani was running some errands in town, so I had to do my own hair. Eirani would do this plait from the back that captured all the stray hairs, but I could never manage more than a loose ponytail. I went down to the kitchen myself. The cook was just lifting a tin of fresh megon nut bread out of the cooking bath. The tin sat, still steaming, on the bench. He used gloves to undo the clamps, releasing the heavenly smell into the kitchen. He cut a big piece for me, which I sprinkled with herb oil. I sat at the big, flour-dusted table in the kitchen to eat it, being careful not to burn my fingers. It was heavenly.

He made me *manazhu* as well, without complaining that it was not a local drink or that it stank or any of the things Eirani would say about it.

I took the steaming hot cup back upstairs. It was time to dump on my faithful association the seemingly insurmountable task I'd agreed to last night: get Kando Luczon or his companions involved in a productive negotiation or face having them forcefully interrogated by Asha's soldiers.

In the light of the morning this task seemed even more ambitious than it had last night.

My office was the first room to the left at the top of the stairs.

The sound of voices came from inside and I found Thayu, Veyada and Deyu already in the room. The latter sat in the big chair that faced the desk. Thayu and Veyada stood next to the chair. I'd told Deyu several times to stop making subservient greetings to me, but she was always awkward with that order. The instinct was very strong in her. There had to be a reason for the odd pairing of her—Omi clan, from very modest business background in Eighth Circle—to Reida— one of the very few remaining Ezmis at Asto, strongly affiliated with the *zeyshi*—but I hadn't found the reason yet.

Devlin came in after me, as well as Evi and Telaris and Sheydu.

Nicha entered last, carrying his son in the sling. He shut the door and the rattling of slats as the traditional Barresh door, unrolling, made the baby squirm. Nicha patted the lump in the sling until he settled.

I looked around the circle of serious faces. They were my trusted team, and I hated dropping on them what I was about to tell them.

I started telling them about the things that Asha had told me last night. Several times there were sharp intakes of breaths. I spotted Thayu shaking her head in a most worrying fashion.

I ended with, "The short story is that we absolutely need to get agreements out of these Aghyrians and we need to start talking with them. If Kando Luczon is not going to cooperate, and it doesn't look like he will, we must get it from his two companions. First, we must find reasons to separate the two from their captain, and to get them to talk. We know nothing about these people, their wishes or fears, and I'm afraid there isn't the time to be either nice or subtle about this. I want your thoughts on how we should go about this in a manner that we get the cooperation we need, and that is least likely to start the first-ever one-hundred-year intergalactic war. I'm asking you because my mind is blank. I'm a diplomat and I talk—far too much some say—but talking is my thing. Talking has failed us so far."

To my surprise, Deyu was the first to speak. "Reida would know."

I nodded. Yes, he might, and it was a pity that he was still in town, but the work he was doing there was also important to me.

Sheydu said, "I can do bombs, if you need them."

Deciding whether or where I needed them was, apparently, my job. Fair enough.

Thayu looked like she was thinking, Nicha stroked his son, also in thought, but it was Veyada I was watching, because out of all of the team, I counted him as significantly more intelligent than the rest of us.

But it was Devlin who spoke. "The two companions are guards of some description, right?"

I shrugged. "I might have pushed them in that position. I don't think they were originally. I'm not really sure that aboard a ship like that one needs guards."

Thayu said, "When we were at the ship, I saw the woman working at that stasis facility. She's more likely to be a medical worker of some sort."

That would make sense, that with the majority of crew in stasis, personnel awake included a medical team to perform maintenance operations on their human cargo.

"Hmmm," Devlin said. "I thought we might interest them in a security problem, but if they're not security workers then that's not going to work."

"Shouldn't we then present them with an interesting medical question?" Deyu said. Her voice sounded quite young. In Earth years she would probably have been only eighteen or nineteen. Coldi started mentoring at thirteen and people became legally adult at seventeen.

Everyone looked at her. I was glad to see that I wasn't the only person in this house whose ears betrayed them.

She continued in a slightly nervous voice. "My father started his business running a workshop that makes and repairs furniture. He said his early years were hard. He didn't get enough customers and he spent a lot of time touting his business, his skills and craftsmanship. He never did very well until he realised that all those people in the area where he lived just weren't interested in his nice furniture. He says, 'You can't sell furniture to people who don't have a house,' and that's true. The area in Eighth Circle where he lived was very poor, and many people lived in such cramped conditions that there wasn't room for furniture. My father grew up there, so that's why he had stayed in that area. After he realised that, he went to another area where people have bigger houses. Another tactic for my father would have been to start selling something else, but he chose to move because he likes furniture-making. He's doing all right now."

Her cheeks went red. It was the most I'd ever heard her talk. From memory, Deyu's father had gone on to become involved in the Sector Council, and was regarded as an influential honest man in his small part of the mega-city of Athyl.

Deyu went on, "That's what we should do: move somewhere else, even if only in speech. These Aghyrians aren't interested in talk and negotiations, so we don't try to sell them negotiations. Are they even interested in ever settling on a planet again? We don't know. But they are interested in genetics. So we talk genetics. They know as little about us as we know about them."

Sheydu said, her voice dark, "The reason that no one has said anything important to them is because we're afraid what they would do with the information."

Deyu's ears went even redder. She looked down at her lap. "Well, it was an idea."

"It was not a bad idea," I said. "I happen to think that offering them something that might interest them could be a good tactic."

Sheydu sniffed.

"We've already taken them through the regular questions, like where they came from, what they want, what they know, and haven't gotten anywhere, so it's worth a try. But we must find a question small enough that it only interests the woman and not the captain. Not something that affects entire races. Something personal." And as I said that, I got an idea. I looked at Thayu. No, I couldn't possibly do that. On the other hand . . . "Thay'." I gestured to her. She rose and came with me to the corridor.

I spoke softly to her. "I've got an idea I want to run past you to make sure you're all right with it. We've got to interest this woman with genetics and it has to be something personal, so I thought I could tell them that we wish we could have children, and is there any chance she might know about a way that we could?"

Thayu stared at me.

My heart was hammering. Next thing, she was going to get angry with me and accuse me of using our personal suffering for a public aim to embarrass her, or something like that. To be honest, the move felt a bit tacky to me as well.

Thayu enfolded me in a hug so strong that I had trouble breathing. I managed to say, "I'm sorry, I'm sorry. I won't do it if you don't like it."

She let out a tiny squeak. "But I do want you to do it." Her eyes glittered. "They know so much more than we do."

"Oh Thay', you know there is very little chance that they can change anything in our situation, and you do understand that this is not the aim of the exercise?"

"I do." She wiped her eyes. "But if there is any question left to ask about our chances, I want it asked."

The Coldi mind continued to find ways to surprise me. Somehow, I seemed never to have understood that the only emotion the Coldi truly lacked was that of embarrassment.

13

WE MADE A PLAN.

Thayu and I would go to the apartment together. We would wear no uniforms and take no guards, although they would stay in close proximity, of course. We would ask for advice on a personal issue in an informal, almost secretive way.

Our past experience indicated that Kando Luczon was thoroughly uninterested in people's private struggles, so we guessed that he would listen for a bit and then withdraw himself from the conversation.

Hopefully the woman Lilona would continue.

If it looked like we were having success in drawing her away from the captain, we would try to make her leave the apartment. She might want blood samples taken or need to use certain equipment. We would offer to do that at the hospital. We would pounce and ask her some forceful questions about the ship and their intentions once we had her out of the apartment. *After* we asked the questions about fertility, Thayu insisted.

Sheydu and Veyada took the speculation a lot further than I liked, talking about making direct threats to her, and to the captain, and about taking her as a hostage.

I so very much wanted to tell them that this sort of thing was not on, but I couldn't.

All the planning brought us to lunchtime, and while lunch wasn't much of a feature in our house, certainly not on the scale it was in town, I didn't want anyone fainting on the job, so I asked Eirani to supply us with a good meal. We sat at the table in the living room, a big varied and noisy team.

Ayshada had decided that he'd behaved well enough for today, and demanded noisily that he be fed. This was done by Nicha, and when he had to eat, by Sheydu. Ayshada remained very much awake after he finished his milk, and Sheydu proceeded to tickle him, to which he responded by making gurgling noises. It was the oddest sight ever, a fierce killing machine cooing at a two-day-old baby. But she had given birth at least once, and obviously cared enough about Veyada to pair up with him. The fact that he lived with her also meant that it had been *her* contract and her decision to have him.

It occurred to me that Xinanu's departure was the best thing that had happened this week—no, make that this year—and that I would be utterly happy to withdraw my claim against the Azimi clan so that I never had to deal with them again. I wasn't going to ask Devlin if they had responded yet. It would be great if that issue could stay out of my hair until after the Aghyrian crisis was settled.

When lunch was done, we went to the bedroom to change. We would wear informal clothes. We would not carry weapons in visible places. I didn't want to take any at all, but knew that was a battle I'd never win.

"Light armour," Thayu said, tossing the rigid body-hugging vest onto the bed.

I picked it up. It was heavy and hot. "Is that necessary? These people have thousands of ways to kill us that don't involve shooting a projectile or charge at high speed."

She just glared at me. Like the gun, I knew this was a losing battle as well. Her plain tunic and loose trousers hid her armour well. The pockets and folds of the garments probably also held all manner of guns.

I got dressed and we met up with the others in the hall.

While we went to talk, Evi and Telaris would casually hang around the fountain in the atrium a few steps from the door of Kando Luczon's apartment. They often relaxed there, but this time they would be ready to take action if necessary.

I felt sweaty and shivery when walking up to the apartment's door. Probably an aftereffect of last night; but with every step we took, I became less sure that it was such a good idea to exploit our painful personal situation to get what we wanted. Thayu might say she had no trouble with it, but I had a hard time believing that.

Thayu knocked on the door.

It took a while before it was opened by the young man Tayron. He raised his eyebrows, looking from me to Thayu. "You didn't let us know that a visit was planned."

It was hard to discern any kind of emotion from his voice. He could be annoyed, or happy or surprised.

"We're not on official business. We have a deeply personal issue we'd like your advice on."

He looked over his shoulder where Kando Luczon came into the hallway and eyed us with his usual hawkish suspicious look. He wore the loose robe that he had also worn on the ship, complete with the broad armbands that seemed to have some sort of electronic function, but probably wouldn't work here. Not for the first time, I wondered what the three of them did when they were by themselves in the apartment.

I nodded to him. "Excuse us for disturbing you without notice. As I told your companion, we're here for personal reasons. We have a question that I hope you or your staff can help us with." Thayu had been happy to let me do the talking. She said that she would likely be too rude.

I could see hostility warring with curiosity on his face. No, I hadn't messaged him as I usually did. I didn't want to advertise my actions to Delegate Namion.

Then he glanced at Tayron, who stepped back, opening the door further. "Come in and ask your question."

We followed him to the living room on the far side of the apartment. I went first and Thayu behind me. The broad hallway bisected the apartment, with all the rooms to either side. The ones on the left backed onto my downstairs storeroom and staff office. The apartment's main living room was at the end of the corridor. The windows, overlooking a neatly maintained garden, were on the western side, which made it quite hot, like my own living room and our bedroom. Yet he seemed to have all the vents that brought cool air from the atrium closed and the window and garden doors were closed as well.

They had moved the furniture around: the dining table now stood at the far end of the room, the couch and one of the armchairs against the wall. A second armchair stood in the middle of the room, like a captain's chair on a ship. This was where Kando Luczon took his place, leaving us to find seats at the table. The woman Lilona already sat at the table. She met my eyes, but said nothing. She didn't greet us. She didn't get up to offer us drinks.

Not that I really wanted any, just having had lunch, but in any other house, a visitor would be offered refreshments.

It seemed that along with the sense of living in the open air, these people had lost their sense of civility. Was that what happened when you lived cooped up in a ship with the same people for generations?

When I just started training, I'd often been baffled by Coldi customs, but I didn't recall ever having felt like I was floundering as much as this. They looked like people, they moved like people, but in their behaviour they might as well have been lions.

In the awkward and unfriendly silence, I started out explaining why we had come. That we were lovers, that we were, obviously, from different races, and that we would love to hear if there was any chance at all that we could have a child.

Kando Luczon's face showed intense dislike. "She is from the all-purpose colonising race. I do not know why they were ever allowed to keep their fertility. I certainly didn't agree with it. It was that idiot Waller Herza whose idea this was. And look at this place today! I was right." He spread his hands.

I had no idea what was wrong with Barresh and its varied population, and after getting a taste of his opinions on it, couldn't say I was highly interested in finding out.

In the further tense silence, I then outlined some of the known genetic connections. That the Coldi and Mirani Endri sometimes interbred. That a famous research project by a scientist on Earth called Richard Morton had proven that humans from Earth had Aghyrian roots.

While I was speaking, Lilona's expression had pricked up. She asked me some questions in a timid voice. She knew what Thayu was —and that earned her some disapproving looks from Thayu—but didn't know about me. Earth was not a place they were overly familiar with, but after some cross-referencing, expressions cleared.

"We seeded a population there, a long time ago," Kando Luczon said.

He eyed me up and down, as if seeing me in a different light. He said something to Lilona, who took one of their screens and pulled up a diagram. I could see her screen, but didn't read Aghyrian very well and this variety was even less familiar to me. Tayron came to sit next to her. They spoke quietly, pointing at various places in the diagram.

Kando Luczon sat in his chair and supported his chin in his hand. He stared at Thayu, already looking bored with the discussion.

Thayu stared back. If the daggers in her eyes were real, he would have been dead a hundred times over.

"We need to know certain things," Lilona said eventually.

"You need blood samples?' I asked.

"We do. We don't have any equipment to take them."

"The hospital does," I offered without trying to sound too keen.

"We also need equipment to analyse."

"They might have that as well. I'm sorry, I know nothing about medical things, but I can take you to the hospital and you can see what they have and you can ask the lab staff. Many of them are Aghyrian." My heart was hammering in my chest. It did sound like an innocent enough proposition, didn't it?

She said something to the captain, but he said nothing and didn't react. Then she spoke to Tayron. He replied, his tone flat.

Lilona got up from the table and disappeared into the hallway. I frowned at Thayu. What was going on?

The feeder told me that she wasn't sure either. *They really don't show any emotions.* Coming from a Coldi person—who were often accused of not showing emotions—this was a major statement. It confirmed the unease I had felt about these Aghyrians.

The captain sat staring into the distance, and Tayron looked out the window.

With any other person, I might have chatted about the weather, but all previous attempts to chat had fallen into a black hole. Not only were they unfamiliar with the concept of weather, they were uninterested in it, or, for that matter, in other harmless subjects, like the scenery or clothing.

You couldn't chat with them, because they didn't know how to chat.

These people were not super-humans. Well, they might possess the genetic base from which all humans were descended, but as a society, they seemed incredibly broken.

Lilona came back to the door. She had put on the shirt with the blue piping that we had supplied for the *gamra* meeting they attended a few days ago. This wasn't the right shirt for a trip into town, but I let it rest. They didn't understand "appropriate" either.

The captain and Tayron seemed happy to let her go—and I felt guilty because they possessed a healthy dose of suspicion in some areas and seemed naïve and trusting in others, and we were going to betray what little trust they had.

We left the apartment. It was now the middle of the afternoon, and, being the dry season, sunlight was at its hottest. I was pleased to see that thunderclouds were building up over the top of the escarpment in the east, although it would probably take a few weeks until they were big enough to roll over the city every afternoon. The sky directly above was cloudless, if a bit hazy, but still clear enough to show double-edged shadows, although the suns were very close together and would go fully behind each other later this week for the occultation festival and the crazy parades that accompanied it.

I explained all this to Lilona on our way to the station, and it met with the usual reaction: indifference and silence.

Thayu rolled her eyes at me several times.

Through her feeder, she asked me why I kept trying. I truly didn't know. I guessed our different brands of humanity couldn't stand continued silence when in the company of others. That was the point of company: that some form of communication took place. Otherwise you might as well live alone in the jungle.

We're communicating Thayu said through the feeder. *We're not making any sound.*

That was true. Did the Aghyrians have a similar type of communication? There were rumours that some were telepathic, but if they were, their processes didn't work on us.

The train arrived and we got in.

I could see Evi and Telaris at the end of the wagon, pretending to be travelling by themselves. I looked around for others, most importantly Coldi in unmarked non-uniform clothing, but none were obvious to me.

I sat opposite Lilona. If she was really in her sixties, she looked remarkably young. We had wondered if they used some type of rejuvenation treatment or if her younger looks were a function of conditions in the ship.

I had asked about this before, but as with most things, had received at best an inconclusive reply. I guessed it was hard for people who travelled across galaxies to understand the concept of age and time—both planet-bound concepts—but their inability to relate to anything that mattered to us was profoundly disturbing.

She was, however, more forthcoming when I asked her about her work on the ship, which was to prepare the pods and their occupants for long jumps. Normally the stasis pods would contain gas, but for jumps they would be filled with gel that would slowly be frozen over what I guessed was a period of days before the jump. Once the jump was completed, the reverse process would take twice as long.

"So when you jump, you freeze the entire crew?"

"Everyone who isn't needed for the operation of the ship." And apparently they could run that behemoth ship with a crew of about twenty.

"What do *you* do for the jump?"

She frowned at me.

"It sounds like jumping these kinds of distances is dangerous enough that you protect most people by freezing them. What about you and the other crew?"

"We're selected to perform this task."

It sounded like it was an honour. "But isn't it dangerous?"

"The survival of the main population is the most important aim of the mission. Some need to be awake to ensure that the ship is healthy."

"But do you do anything special to protect yourself during these jumps?"

"We monitor the health of the crew. It's very important." Her voice acquired a slightly angry edge.

Was she deliberately not answering my question? "All right then. What happens when you go into a jump?"

"They take a long time. All the while, we adjust the pods."

"Isn't there a way to do this automatically?"

She gave me a startled look. "All the internals of the ship are completely powered down during a jump." She sounded indignant. How stupid of me not to know this.

At the same time, I sensed something inherently horrible about these jumps. Having travelled through space myself, I had tasted the acute discomfort that comes with being locked in a tin can with no gravity. The forms of space travel I had tried had been controlled and relatively easy, but extensive safety briefings brought home the fact that when the system became stressed because something went wrong, crew might need to take desperate measures to stay alive. The emergency supplies contained items such as adult nappies for when confined to one's room unable to go to the bathroom, and scrapers to take ice off the walls in case of heating failure and other items whose purpose I was happy not to know.

If the ship's internals were powered off during a jump and a jump lasted days, the crew might be confined to a small compartment, where air, temperature and heating would slowly deteriorate. They might need to wear hard vacuum suits, and live, eat and shit in these suits. Shields would be off, so radiation might penetrate the ship.

Hell, maybe even half the non-frozen crew would not survive a jump, and they weren't allowed to complain because it was an honour to serve the ship.

I shuddered, once more reminded how much we put our lives in the hands of technology even when travelling through the Exchange.

"I'm bound to the ship," she said, and her voice sounded proud.

That declaration chilled me even more.

I had asked her before what that meant, and had received an incomprehensible reply about biometrics and some micro-technology to do with blood. It seemed a biological thing, like our feeders. I suspected that a lot of the terms she used were wrongly translated, but Coldi just didn't offer a correct translation.

I imagined that if a modern human met a Neanderthal, the level of communication would be similar. True transfer of information was impossible.

As the train slowed down at the approach to the airport station, my overwhelming thought was that we were the Neanderthals, and they could pull out a magical weapon the likes of which we hadn't begun to consider, and they would kill us all.

On the other hand, if a modern human and a Neanderthal faced each other in a stone axe fight, the Neanderthal would win.

Axe fights it was.

Welcome to the Stone Age.

On further consideration, if a modern human faced a Neanderthal in a modern home, the Neanderthal would strangle the human with a power cord.

As long as the Neanderthal could pick the time and place of the fight, he would win if no magical weapons were present.

All this assumed that they didn't develop some form of mutually understood communication where the modern man could make it understood that there was no need for a fight and they could be sharing a beer instead. Did Neanderthals like beer?

All right, so we were the Neanderthals. I had tried very hard, but so far failed miserably, to see the hand holding out the beer. In fact, we seemed to be facing an entirely different situation. If three modern men walked into a Neanderthal village of two hundred with the intention to take the village, they'd bring guns and make short work of the whole tribe. That seemed closer to the situation we were facing. The guns were on that ship that was waking up and that, by his own admission, Asha might be unable to stop.

The comparison made my head hurt.

14

———————

WE GOT OFF the train at the airport station with a big group of other people, most of whom looked like they were going to the markets. They were, for the most part, domestic staff dressed in grey with little splashes of blue or sometimes colours of whatever house they worked in. It was a happy, careless, chatting ensemble. We followed this group up the sloping road past the fence around the airport. This part of the path was exposed to the weather and right now facing the western sun. Lilona had to stop, wiping sweat from her forehead.

"Not used to the heat?" I asked, mentally chalking up the climate as a distinct advantage to the Neanderthals.

"It makes you wet." That was clearly a great source of annoyance.

"Don't you do exercise on board of your ship?"

Lilona gave me a blank look.

"Didn't you see the pods for muscle stimulation?" Thayu asked.

"No, I didn't."

"They were in one of the labs to the side. You could see in through the open door. People were asleep while machines moved their arms and legs."

"Sleep walking." The ultimate solution for people who hated exercise. That would have been weird to see.

Lilona was looking at the aircraft on display at the airport. From here, we could see the private area, including Asha's craft.

"Do they look anything like yours?" I asked her. *Keep trying, Delegate Wilson.* The more questions I asked, the more likely I would get an answer that gave away more than she intended to share.

"They're flyers for use in the atmosphere. How can they look much different? They need an aerodynamic shape. They need a carrying area."

"Tell me then what yours look like." I had already seen some of their smaller ships, in the big hall where we had entered the ship. That whole docking hall had been dark and powered down, consistent with the fact that most of the crew was in stasis.

She was still squinting at the aircraft. "The wing area is bigger."

Thinner atmosphere? Thayu said through the feeder.

Or thicker, less need for engines, more friction, more gliding action. I pictured the images I'd always seen as a child, of designs of colonies humans had planned but that had never been built in the cloud tops at Venus.

"They're made from hardened resin."

Thayu filled me in. *Some type of plastic, produced on board the ship.*

Lilona eyed us, as if sensing the conversation that went on through our feeders.

I started moving again, uncomfortable that the shuttle that was the subject of her scrutiny happened to be one that belonged to Asto's military.

"What is the most important thing that you notice about being on a planet?" I tried a different, more comfortable angle.

"Everything stinks." A surprisingly frank reply. It was as if, being away from the captain, she was coming out of her shell.

Like the Coldi, Aghyrians had a keen sense of smell. "It stinks like what?"

"The recycling plants."

"Are you familiar with them? Did you work there?"

"Everyone has to work there, especially the crew who are bound to the ship."

"Is working there a form of punishment?"

She gave me her usual blank look. It was impossible to figure out what went on behind those blue eyes. Sure she would understand *punishment?*

"We do shifts," she said, her voice soft. "It is very hot there and it stinks. Some of the equipment can malfunction and cause harm."

It was the first time that any of them had said anything that could be remotely classified as emotional. "You don't like working there?" I prompted.

She gave me a blank look. "It's part of our tasks."

"Does it scare you, working there?"

Another blank look.

I tried again, "Does it scare you, being out of your ship, with so much open air that stinks like a place you hate and where there are no safe places to hide?"

"We have the captain."

Which, again, was not an answer.

It went on like this for a while. I asked innocent questions and Lilona replied in short sentences.

Thayu was meant to keep an interested expression and not act like security personnel, but she appeared to have given up trying a long time ago. I suspected that had he been here, even Veyada would have started fidgeting by now. Along with embarrassment, patience was another state of mind that Coldi seemed to be incapable of feeling.

Even though the conversation consisted of starts and stops punctuated with long silences, I was starting to see a pattern. Sometimes she replied in answer to my question, sometimes not. If she got to the point where she stopped replying, she always said something about the captain or the ship, as if that was a fallback answer when she was unsure of what to say.

I found out that most of the people that she looked after in stasis were women. She didn't ever appear to have been in stasis herself. Maybe it was a long-term thing that you could do only once?

To my questions about jumps—how many they did, how far, how long they took—she answered that the captain knew about those, and my question about what they ate on board met with the same reply: the captain knows.

Both she and her male companion had beautiful teeth, so I asked if the food caused any problems, but that was also a matter for the captain.

As we walked onto the main square, past all the eating-houses towards the tramline, I confirmed my opinion that theirs was a closed society where one person had a lot to say and the others more or less blindly followed him. This didn't make much sense for a people of the Aghyrian intellectual calibre, but at least I was getting answers, as long as my questions remained innocent, because I ran into a wall as soon as I slipped in a question about why they were doing certain things.

"What" or "How" questions were apparently all right, but "Why" questions were not.

Yes, of course I was recording all of this, although with the rumbling of the train, the city and aircraft noises and later the tram, I wasn't sure how much I'd be able to decipher on the playback.

The hospital was on the northern side of the island at the end of the tramline from the main square. It stood on a little rise—and Barresh was extremely flat, so a little rise meant a knee-high hillock—surrounded by a new housing development built entirely on stilts over the water. Most of the stilts supported slabs of concrete that made up the ground and streets, but spaces had been left in between, where it looked as if water ran through canals. Right now, the development looked bare in the blazing western sunlight, but the slabs included large, wire-bottomed boxes filled with sand and mud where native trees had been planted in beds of rotting leaves and anchored with rope. Within a year the trees would send roots from the concrete to the muddy bottom, providing a natural anchor for the artificial structure.

We were met in the hospital foyer by a worker in the research division whom I had contacted before leaving the *gamra* island. Of course the Aghyrian compound had its own genetic research division—where we were not allowed to go—but they also funded a department in the hospital that collected genetic information from locals and anyone else who came in. Most importantly, they had access to the Aghyrians' giant database of genetic material.

I had met Jacina Emiru before, when I had taken my compatibility tests and she had put me on the giant map of Aghyrian descendants that continued to be the research centre's magnum opus.

She took us on a tour of the lab, a bright and airy facility which combined technology from Asto, from Asto's *zeyshi* faction, from Damarq, Hedron and smatterings of techniques from other worlds. She explained to Lilona all the facilities they had and the type of research they did. Lilona asked to see the map. Jacina took us to the conference room, where she brought it up on the large three-dimensional projector.

It was an awesome sight, this giant tree with a multitude of branches that each held a multitude of little dots representing data points. One of those represented me; another was Thayu. Jacina herself probably had a dot, as did the tailed Pengali assistant who had been working in the lab and whose dot could probably be found on one of the tree's lowest branches.

Lilona sat on the bench next to me. Her face didn't show emotion, but I liked to think that she was at least mildly impressed. This graphic represented over a hundred years of work. Originally started by the Barresh Aghyrians under the initiative of Daya Ezmi, they had opened it up to the public when the value of this treasure became clear. Many people from all over *gamra* came to Barresh just to see and study this tree, and sometimes add to it. I considered it the pinnacle of human research, not for the level of difficulty or newness of technique, but for the fact that if everyone contributed, we could make something truly awesome.

Lilona finally unfolded her screen and brought it to life with a touch of her hand.

She asked Jacina if she could import one genome file, and when that was done, another, for reference. Then, with a few quick strokes, she translated the data to her notation, and then imported more files, including mine and Thayu's. I felt a bit apprehensive about letting her have a copy of my genetic material, but in order to get her to answer a question, we needed to provide her with data. This entire tree relied on sharing data and openness. But that data defining my little chromosomes would go back on that big ship with her. Did I trust the ship Aghyrians not to do anything untoward with it?

Well, actually . . .

I hid my unease by offering to go and buy dinner because it looked like Lilona was going to be a while and it was that time of day.

I left the hospital in the dusk, walking over the bridge that connected the hospital to the surrounding new development, where I'd been assured I could buy dinner. A few stars already blinked in the purple sky above. The bright pink dot that was Asto hung low over the horizon, a tiny little crescent glowing in the light of the suns already below our horizon.

Asha might be staying in the guest quarters on the ground floor of my apartment, but his home ship probably sat in orbit, watching us, waiting for me to obtain the information they needed, to sign agreements of nonviolence with the Aghyrians and disclose whatever knowledge they had obtained in that other galaxy.

And I doubted I'd be successful. Yes, there had been some progress made today, but it was a slow, two-steps-forward-and-one-step-back process.

When I stepped off the walkway, Telaris detached from the shadow of a wall and joined me soundlessly.

"Just buying dinner," I said.

He nodded, but continued to walk next to me.

"Everything all right?" I asked him.

"We've been talking to Reida," he said. "He says he has important news and is on his way back to the apartment."

Dang it, and I wasn't going to be there. "Can you tell Devlin to ask Nicha to deal with it on my behalf?"

Telaris said he would. Then he said, "Any luck yet?"

"We agreed not to commence the forceful questioning until we left the hospital."

He nodded, again in silence. I didn't like it. I didn't know what he expected me to do. Push Lilona with her back against the wall, point a gun at her face and start asking questions? Not my style. I doubted I'd even get the answers I wanted from that tactic. She'd probably just flip out and start blathering about her captain. For all I knew, she might even self-destruct.

"Asha's guards are here," Telaris said a bit later. "They'll be waiting on the town side of the bridge. How long do you expect to need?"

"Not sure." And then, "I don't like the idea of putting pressure on her, Telaris. Who is to say that she doesn't have some kind of system built in that warns the captain and all sorts of other people when she is threatened?"

"We'll have to risk it."

"I don't know that she will answer our questions."

"We can only try. I think Asha has given us enough reason to do so."

In other words: leave it to security, dumb delegate, and stop meddling.

Did Ezhya ever feel sorry about the pain and pressure his guards applied to people who disobeyed his rules or possessed information that he needed?

I was about to ask where Evi was when the very man came walking down the street carrying a couple of parcels.

Dinner.

Evi gave them to me. The food he bought was green-coded—because that was what keihu people ate, and there were not many foreigners in this part of town. It had been intended for himself and Telaris, but he assured me that he could easily go and buy new food. I took the parcels and went back inside.

While I had been away, Lilona had produced her own tree based on the files from Jacina.

"The very tips of the branches represent all the people alive today." She pointed to one solitary branch on the left of the tree. "This is you." She looked at me. Next, she pointed to a line that went straight from the trunk into the air. "This is me." Then she pointed to another branch to the right of the straight line. It lay close to a couple of branches that represented a relationship cluster that would contain the Mirani Endri and keihu. "This is her." she nodded at Thayu.

I stared at the distance between the lines. The further apart in the tree, the less relationship. My courage sank. Every bit of anecdotal experience said that we would never have children, but seeing it like this cemented the facts. I really wished I'd pushed harder for Thayu to agree to using Menor.

Thayu was looking at it as well, blinking. It seemed that the truth had finally sunk in. I could see it on her face. And she did want another child, and did not want to use a surrogate.

Damn, what would this mean for us?

15

LILONA WAS FINALLY in her element. She went on at length about each of the different races both past and present, oblivious to Thayu's silence and morose expression.

It seemed she had already forgotten the question I'd asked her and was getting carried away with all this data. I had no doubt that geneticists would find this extremely interesting, so I let her talk as much as she wanted. Also, because I felt extremely hesitant about what would happen the moment she stepped outside this building.

Apparently, the Coldi had been created by stripping the unused, "junk" parts of the Aghyrian DNA, replacing it with altered code and turning it on. Underneath the added altered genetic code, Coldi and Aghyrians were identical, because all the original Aghyrian genes were still there.

Which was why Aghyrian throwbacks happened.

"They happened because there was contamination," Lilona said. "Waller Herza thought that it was fun to contaminate the new people with his own code. He was always a selfish man with an interest in self-aggrandisement."

"I think it went differently," Thayu said, and she sounded snippy. "Our origin stories tell us that there were thirty-five couples. There were meant to be thirty-six, but a stasis pod failed and one of the men died. The woman who was meant to be his partner was woken up before the meteorite strike and had a baby the natural way. She survived in the chamber when the meteorite hit and after the dust had cleared, years later, went on to open the cubicles so that your 'all-purpose colonising race' could actually get out of their boxes, because if she hadn't done that, they'd all have died from eventual power failure."

Thayu was not a person of a lot of words, and for her to say this would have taken a good dose of anger. The significance of her outburst went straight past Lilona, who had magnified an area of the tree on the screen and sat squinting at the data. "This group is very varied."

Thayu spread her hands and rolled her eyes, but Lilona didn't see or didn't understand the gesture.

I checked the names in the group she was studying. They included Marin Federza, Feylin Herza and Sadet Arwan. "Those are the Barresh Aghyrians. The genome was pieced together from your throwbacks, surviving Aghyrian strains and a single direct survivor."

Now she gave me a startled look. "Survivors?"

"There were two kinds of survivors. The Mirani Endri are virtually pureblood Aghyrians descended from a ship that landed on the Mirani highlands. They never interbred with any other races other than Coldi. There was also a single direct survivor, a woman called Anmi, found in a stasis chamber as baby. You will find her genes in the Herza and Federza families." I didn't know why I felt so fierce about defending them. After all, no one particularly liked the Aghyrians, but they were part of Barresh and most of them were half-decent, even if they were often rich, entitled arseholes.

"There were survivors from the meteorite strike?" Her voice was soft.

"None that are still alive today, although their grandchildren are."

"How did that happen?" She sounded shocked.

I told her what I knew about the babies that had survived in buried chambers, that most of them had been found during building activities in Athyl about three hundred years ago, and that the last one found was Anmi, the mother of the Aghyrian compound in Barresh. Lilona asked what section those babies belonged to and I had no idea what she was talking about.

Then she wanted to know what Anmi looked like.

"Like many Aghyrians, pale-skinned with deep black hair and eyes. They're all very tall."

"Pakshar," Lilona said, and by her tone, I gathered that was not a good thing.

She went on to explain that there had been two rival nations on Asto, those of Aghyr and Pakshar. Both had built magnificent capitals that lay across the river from each other. "You could see from the top of Aghyr into Pakshar. Aghyr had buildings of knowledge and study. Pakshar had temples where people with outspoken personalities were worshipped."

We knew that Athyl was built on the ruins of Aghyr, and that the desert valley that ran across it was likely to have contained a river. Pakshar was likely to have included the flat country that today took up some of Athyl's outer circles. The *zeyshi*-controlled desert was probably all that remained of the Pakshari plains.

Lilona said that the people in Aghyr were "rational", the people in Pakshar were not. They were—and here she used a strange word that I deduced from her next description to mean something like "spiritual". She kept pointing at her head. Maybe she thought they were mad.

"Our scientists were rational, but Waller Herza, he was half-Pakshar, and he betrayed us. Through him, all of the science in Aghyr became contaminated."

What with, I couldn't understand but I didn't think it was a contamination of the biological kind. With religion? With opposing thoughts?

"The contamination happened through him, with help from his scientist friend Perling Dinzo."

Something clicked. "Dinzo, that was Anmi's clan name. The survivor woman who started the Barresh Aghyrian settlement."

"Perling Dinzo's daughter survived?" She seemed horrified.

"I don't know who she was, except that the local Aghyrians regard her as their mother. Did you also meet her father?"

"Oh no, the captain taught us all this."

And here we had the captain again, a fallback answer in case of doubt.

I was starting to feel distinctly uneasy about this transfer of information. These people had memories longer than an elephant's, and held more massive grudges than the Sicilian mafia. Whatever these

"contaminated" or "irrational" scientists were supposed to have done,
apart from the very sensible thing to save as many people as they
could, apparently it was ground for a very strong reaction from the
"rational" crowd, whatever they thought was rational about coming
across a vast swathe of space to trade grudges with a culture that died
fifty thousand years ago. What had they come back here to find? An
empty planet waiting for them? Were they here to get rid of the Coldi,
the local Aghyrians or both of them?

Thayu met my eyes. I didn't need the feeder to know that she
shared my apprehension.

Time to put an end to it, she said.

Yes, time to go home. Time to get ourselves "accidentally"
ambushed by "strangers" in the form of Evi and Telaris and Asha's
guards, time for the interrogation, whatever that might bring.

It had gone completely dark outside and the rest of the research
lab was quiet.

I rose, feeling sweaty. "I think this lab is about to close. Maybe we
should go home and come back later."

Lilona said, "You can come to our apartment to discuss further. I
have what I need."

"All right then." I nodded to Jacina, who appeared slightly bewil-
dered by the events.

"I do have one more question," Thayu said as she got up. "You still
haven't told us whether there is any chance at all that we might have a
child."

I cringed. *Thay', please.* I thought she would have understood, but
science was never her thing.

Lilona pursed her lips and looked at the screen. She sniffed. "Not
without a lot of effort."

"But not impossible?"

"Well. No. But there would be some very heavy treatment
involved, and I would be hesitant about giving that to adults—"

"I'll do it," Thayu said.

"No. It wouldn't work for you. You already have two sets of genes.
We can't strip genes in adults, we can only add. It would have to be for
him. But we would need a lot of work to find out if it's even possible. I
couldn't do that by myself. I need the team and the lab at the home
ship."

Thayu looked at me, and I looked back at her. She smiled. My heart was hammering. That was just not what I'd expected to hear, at all.

Holy fuck.

"You said 'a lot of work'?" I asked, hesitant.

"Many, many tests to see if we could get the extra genes to stick, or if we could turn them on. It is probably still impossible."

"Could you try?" Thayu asked. Her eyes shone.

"Not now. I need the lab on the ship."

"But later?"

"Later, maybe."

That was assuming that she would return to the big ship. Which, at this point in time, we were trying to avoid.

I couldn't bear to meet Thayu's eyes.

We made our way out of the building through corridors shrouded in semidarkness. I felt sick and sweaty at the same time. Altogether not happy about what I'd found out.

So. They could change my genetic makeup by adding an extra gene set to my junk DNA. But they'd been to worlds outside the galaxy and had discovered nothing new there? Did I have to believe that?

The more I learned of these people, the less I liked them.

As we left the hospital's entrance, I thought I spotted movement on the artificial island. That would be Evi and Telaris, and Asha's people would be nearby. I couldn't see them. I was afraid to look in case I gave them away, knowing that they were closing in on us as we crossed the bridge from the hospital to the artificial island.

Thayu, in front of us, reached the end of the bridge and turned left in the direction of the tram station.

Lilona and I stepped off the bridge. I braced myself for the attack, but it didn't happen. We turned left, following Thayu.

I held my breath, waiting for someone to pounce from behind.

It didn't happen.

Surely Asha's people would be waiting at that dark section of the street ahead? My heart was thudding, sweat running over my back underneath the armour. Thayu was still in front of us, and I couldn't see her face.

We made it past the dark section of street unhindered.

Thay'? What's going on? Where are they?

I don't know. I didn't miss the disturbed feeling that came with the statement.

Can you contact Devlin?

We kept walking, now almost at the station. It was clear to me that the attack wasn't going to happen, because there would be people on the platform and other passengers in the tram.

Except the platform was deserted, and the tram, when it arrived, empty.

I glanced at Thayu while the tram slowed down, unsure what to do. Evi and Telaris were meant to be with us at this point, and they were yet to arrive.

Get on, she said. *Above all, we can't let her know that this was meant to be a trap.*

True, but something must have happened.

Could be anything. It's unfortunate, but they're my father's guards. They will have used their judgement and will intercept us somewhere else.

All right then. I couldn't say that I liked it, but I saw no alternative. I would make sure that they were notified of my displeasure.

The tram groaned to a halt. The doors opened—

—and someone charged out of the doors and ran into me at full speed. Thayu shouted. I fell backwards and crashed onto the platform on my backside.

Ouch.

The other person had fallen after tripping over my legs, sprawled on his belly. He was now getting up, brushing dust off his clothes. He was young, dressed in black and—

"Reida! Whatever are you doing?"

"Don't get on the tram. There's Tamerians. Run!"

He didn't say where the Tamerians were, and as I scrambled to my feet, I didn't see any, but despite his tall tales, I'd never known Reida to lie.

"Come!" I turned around and headed off the platform with Reida. Thayu and Lilona were behind me.

"Where are the Tamerians?" I asked him.

"I managed to give them the slip at the next station. They're waiting for us there. They'll probably find out that we didn't get on the tram soon. They'll be running this way."

"I'll get a water taxi," Thayu said.

"I think we're better off walking through town," Reida said. "I have some news and you may want to act on it."

"Do you know where Evi and Telaris are?"

"They're at the previous station trying to keep the Tamerians in check."

Damn, I hoped they were safe. I hoped Asha's guards were there as well.

"Cory, wait!" That was Thayu.

I stopped. While we had been going at a decent jogging tempo, Thayu and Lilona had fallen behind. Thayu was standing with her hands at her sides, the pose she took when she was annoyed. Lilona stood doubled over, panting, supporting herself with one hand on a wall.

No exercise aboard that ship, huh?

Thayu spread her hands, clearly annoyed. "We can't protect her going through town when she can't run when we need her to."

True. "Maybe we should get that water taxi after all." And here I was thinking that I was unfit and weak.

"No," Reida said. "There are more Tamerians on the outside of town than inside. Once we're on the water, they'll only need to pick us off. There is no shelter out there. They have excellent night vision." In contrast to one of the "mistakes" supposedly made with the Coldi people.

I said, "We need a vehicle. It's a good run from here to the airport and we should take her back before we do anything else."

"She won't survive a run across the island," Thayu said, her voice dark.

Lilona still stood at the wall, now vomiting up her dinner.

"Better check if she is all right." Thayu walked back, leaving myself and Reida in indecision.

His eyes glittered in the dark as he scanned the surrounding rooftops. "We can't stay here for long."

No, we couldn't, but Lilona was in no state to run.

"What is the news that you found?" I asked him. "Is it why the Tamerians have taken an interest in you?"

"Yeah." He pushed a strand of hair behind his ears. "I know where Trader Federza is."

"You do? How did you find out? Where is he?"

He lowered his voice. "It's a long story, but he's in the jail."

I gaped at him. Surely he was kidding. "I went there and notified the guards that he was missing. Why did they say nothing?"

"Apparently, he went there for his protection and no front desk staff was allowed to say anything about it. Someone tried to contact me instead, but that gave me away as working undercover at the dig site so I had to bail and run because . . . those Tamerians are fast."

"What does he need protection from?"

"His own folk, against the Tamerians. I think he knows stuff, and he's been trying to tell someone."

Shit. And then I thought of all the things Asha had said about the Exchange and the anpar wake and all the missing information about the Aghyrian ship.

I felt cold. "We have to go and get Federza. He's likely to have information about that ship."

Thayu nodded, her face grim.

Lilona had straightened. Her face glistened with sweat in the light of a street lamp. Whatever Captain Luczon said, I wondered how healthy the Aghyrians truly were.

"We need to go," I said to her. "I don't know how or which route we'll take. We'll use a vehicle if we can find one."

Lilona gaped from me to Thayu and back. "My captain." Her eyes were wide, her face pale. To be honest, she looked like she might faint at any time.

Thayu said, "The captain's fine. We're not at the island yet. Nothing is happening there."

Reida called, "Oy!"

He pointed at the other side of the road, where another tram had turned up. He ran. We followed much more slowly, Thayu supporting Lilona as she often did with me when her running speed was more than I could manage. Except I could outrun Lilona by a long margin. We were slow. Reida was going up the steps to the platform.

The tram doors opened—

—And someone rose on the roof of the vehicle, firing a wide spray of charges into the dark.

Thayu pushed Lilona into a garden bed where she fell unceremoniously into the bushes. With her other hand, she extracted her gun and returned fire.

"Take cover!" she yelled at me.

I scrambled into an alcove in the wall surrounding a yard and pressed myself into its dark shade. Ew. Why did these things always have to contain rubbish bins? I felt under my clothing for the light-duty gun Thayu had insisted I carry.

Found the gun. Turned it on, seeing the green light flicker into life with a sense of relief. I'd had enough training to know that I *could* protect myself, if needed. The gun wasn't going to be much good at this distance, and I knew better than to fire it. It would only anger Thayu.

Another man had come out of the tram, gun raised.

No one fired for a very tense silence. I could see some of the tram's passengers sheltering behind a maintenance shed.

"Where is Reida?" I whispered.

Thayu pointed, but I didn't see him.

The two Tamerians inched towards the edge of the platform. The first one jumped off—to be taken care of by Reida who had hidden in the shade of the overhanging platform.

The second one took a hit square in the back.

Thayu laughed. "On the roof!"

It was Evi. Telaris was there, too.

Good. Now I felt a lot better.

Lilona, however, didn't, if the sounds from the bushes were anything to go by.

16

———————

WE GOT ON the tram with much rejoicing.

While we had been in the hospital, Evi and Telaris had been called to Reida's aid. He had run into trouble at the previous station. Apparently the Tamerians, too, knew where Federza was and didn't want us to know it.

The mess from that struggle was still evident when our tram passed. There were a lot of guards on the platform, the tram drivers' station had its door smashed in and there appeared to be a body on the platform, but it was hard to see because of all the spectators.

Reida, Evi and Telaris sank to the floor of the tram and relied on us to report on what was going on. Fortunately, no one checked the tram as it stopped at the station—Sheydu would have had something to say about that—and we continued on.

A few passengers had gotten on and they gave us strange looks, particularly when Evi was unstrapping his spare gun to give it to Reida, as well as a few bits of electronics. Telaris was speaking to someone, probably Devlin, probably to send over reinforcements. We could use Sheydu, in particular if there were explosives involved.

We got off the tram one block away from the guard station. The trams didn't go through Market Street and this was the closest stop. Some of the new trams had no drivers, and a disembodied voice took the place of the driver yelling destinations into the cabin from the front seat. When we were getting off, such a voice stated that the northern line was closed and all services would terminate for the night because of an emergency.

"Oops." Thayu looked at me and waggled her eyebrows. Very pretty eyebrows they were, too.

Reida found it funny.

Lilona was barely following us off the platform, pale-faced. I wished we had time to take her home, but we should act while we'd managed to sidetrack the Tamerians on the subject of our location.

We took a shortcut behind the main council hall, a tree-lined alley shrouded in darkness. The council buildings were all empty for the night.

It was not the sort of place one would want to be on a night like this, with Tamerians lurking about. Evi and Telaris were our eyes, because Indrahui night vision was excellent. In one spot, we disturbed a pair of Pengali lovebirds. They scurried off, tails still intertwined. Sheesh, were those kids even old enough?

Evi laughed.

Thayu touched my hand.

We stopped at the entrance to the alley and could see the dingy entrance to the guard station jail across Market Street, past the trunks of the still young trees that were nevertheless already a decent size. Something moved in the shadows a few steps to the right. I took in a sharp breath, but everyone else remained relaxed. It turned out to be only Veyada. Sheydu was with him. She had climbed the wall of the council complex and now sat atop, holding her gun and watching the street. Her backpack stood next to her on the wall. I guessed it contained her gadgets to make explosives.

She would be in view of security cameras where she sat, and I guessed that was probably the point of sitting there. Why, I didn't know.

The jail office across the street was lit but unmanned. The light was of the local light pearl style, a sickly greenish glow that washed out all colour, reminiscent of the really old fluorescent lights that some of the Earth ships still used.

"We'd be pretty visible if we cross the street like this," Thayu said.

"They're probably all over the area watching us," Reida said.

"Then there is no way to get there other than with violence."

I said, "I think there is. Why don't I just walk in oblivious to all that's going on? They're not going to take shots at me in the middle of town."

"No, you can't do that," Thayu said. She'd been watching me a lot since we had left the hospital, as if she had latched onto the idea that somehow my genes could be changed so that I could father her child.

"I'll be fine. You made me wear armour."

"That doesn't mean I want your arms or legs shot off."

"They're not going to shoot me in the middle of town."

"They shot at Federza."

"What? When he came in here?"

"No, when he was in your office."

"That's different. They were in the reeds and could easily clear out quickly. Here, the only places where they can hide are easily identifiable. The tree up there. The window and balcony. There are enough of us to keep an eye on those places."

Thayu sniffed. "I knew this would involve you putting yourself in the line of fire. I'm coming."

Telaris was undoing his belt. He slid off one of his devices and handed it to me before doing up his belt again. It was a military-style receiver, much sturdier than the one I had in my pocket. "At least take that."

Thayu rolled her eyes. "I should have known that. You're all in cahoots with him putting his life on the line. We're supposed to protect him."

Telaris grinned.

I said, "Sometimes a situation requires a person with a gun, sometimes it requires a person with a big mouth."

She sniffed. "Sometimes I think your mouth is bigger than the rest of you. I'll come."

"All right then." I nodded. "We should also take Lilona." I didn't want to have her on the visit, but I didn't think she'd handle being shot at very well and inside the building was probably the least likely place for that to happen.

Reida would accompany us across the street, and Evi and Telaris would stand guard in front of the door once we had gone in, while Sheydu and Veyada would remain where we stood to spot approaching danger and distract it.

We stared off across the street, through the open space that would, many years in the future when the trees had grown, again be in the shade. My heart was hammering, but nothing happened and we reached the door safely.

A chime rang in the office when I opened the door. The sounds from the street dimmed when the door shut again. Thayu leaned on the counter, looking sideways at the screen on the desk. Reida remained next to me, and Lilona sat on the seats next to the door. She really didn't look her best.

From elsewhere in the building came the sound of footsteps and a moment later a guard appeared from behind the counter. This man I knew, too, from the times I'd picked up Reida here.

His eyes widened when he saw me. "Delegate, you must be mistaken. I didn't notify you about the young man—" He noticed Reida, who grinned.

"I understand that you have someone else in here who normally lives on the *gamra* island."

"No, why should I? We have no say over anyone from *gamra*. We don't hold those people here."

"Can I check?"

"What?"

"I'd like to check downstairs, because the man we've lost may be hiding here."

"Whatever are you talking about?"

"I have it from reliable information that you hold Marin Federza here."

"What? Of course I don't. He's a respected citizen."

"Then if you don't, can you take me downstairs to check?"

He huffed. "I can't allow just anyone off the street to walk in wanting tours of the jail."

"I'm not anyone from the street and I don't want a tour of the jail. If you don't want to come, why don't you give me the key and I'll go by myself." I held up my hand. "Just in case you feel in any way stressed about this person's presence in your establishment, I'm offering to take him off your hands."

He hesitated. "Do you know what you're dealing with?"

"I know enough. Our security is strong enough to withstand any kind of pressure from our Tamerian friends."

They only tended to shoot from a distance anyway. Whatever

Tamerians were, smart didn't appear to be one of those things. And so every artificial race had its problems. Fancy that.

He put the key in my palm, hesitant. I walked past him to the door—

—and it opened from the inside, almost hitting me in the face.

An armed man ran out. I jumped aside. He shouted and pointed the gun at me. Lowered it again.

He blew out a heavy breath.

It was only a Barresh guard. "What were you doing?' he yelled at his colleague in keihu. "I'd almost shot him. I thought this was one of those . . ." Then he looked at me, as if realising that I understood him. "What are they doing here?" Then he frowned at Reida. "He's the one normally behind bars."

The first guard said something to him in a low voice. The second guard nodded, again glancing at me. "He said they'd take him?"

The first guard gave his colleague a warning look.

I said, "You do have Marin Federza here. I want to see him."

The first guard wiped sweat off his upper lip. Unless I was mistaken, they appeared nervous and very much on edge.

"Come." The second guard jerked his head and disappeared through the heavy door behind the counter. I handed the key back to the first guard and followed him. Thayu was close behind me. Reida and Lilona followed him.

We plunged into the darkness down the circular staircase that reminded me strongly of a medieval dungeon. The steps were made of limestone blocks that had become slippery with the constant seeping moisture.

"That smell," Reida said. His voice sounded disturbed.

The smell was typical for many of the old cellars of Barresh. These were not cellars for dry storage. They were for drainage and cooling, as most of them were below the ground water level and water seeped through the stone and evaporated. These structures always smelled of algae, wet stone and must.

The guard waited at the bottom of the stairs until all of us were down and the door had shut behind us. He was a tall fellow, broad in the shoulders rather than round-waisted. He possessed several tattoos on both sides of his neck, visible because, unlike most keihu men, he wore his hair short.

"I don't know how keen he'll be to go outside with you," he said. "To be honest, he's paranoid. He says there are people with military-grade weapons waiting to pick him off outside. We've tried to get him to leave several times already, but he's flatly refused."

"How long has he been here?"

"A week or two." He scratched his head. "Seems longer than that."

"Is there another way out?"

He laughed, spreading his hands. "What do you think? This is a jail."

"Was a jail. This is no longer the main jail."

"No, but we hold miscreants here to cool their heels after a brawl or rowdy night out."

Didn't I know about that.

"The other building is newer and may smell better, but it's much worse for the inmates."

True. That jail had a "termination room". Local judges favoured the death penalty over long prison terms.

The winding staircase was on one end of the passage and from where we stood, we could see all the way to the other end. The doors to the cells consisted of metal grates and all of them were dark, some closed, some stood open.

A glow of light came from an open door at the end of the passage.

"I guess he's down there."

"Yup. I hope he's not going to blow up when he sees you." Clearly, the prospect terrified him.

We set off down the corridor.

Reida muttered some words as we walked past the cells. Occasionally, when he was stressed, he reverted to *zeyshi* dialect, and this was one of those occasions. I now wondered how he had found out that Federza was here, and was unsure I wanted to know. Asha had said that Reida was gold, but that didn't stop me feeling deeply disturbed by certain parts of the young man's life, such as the times when I'd come here to rescue him from one of the cells.

The rooms at the end of the passage were not cells. They looked to have been a guard's station. This seemed a stupid place for a guard station—I would have put it next to the stairs—but then I realised that the wall at the end of the passage dated from a much more recent period than the jail itself, and from memory, it was not the new jail on the other side of the wall. That institution was at the back of the corner block.

After the darkness of the corridor, the light in the guard station seemed impossibly bright. The room contained a pair of scruffy couches and a low table, the surface stained with moisture spots.

Federza sat in the far corner at a dining table that had been turned into a desk. When I came in, he rose.

I couldn't work out whether the expression on his face was happiness or annoyance or all of the above. I remembered him the last time I had seen him, when he came into my apartment scared. Was there anything I had missed then? He'd obviously been more scared than he'd let on.

"Delegate Wilson." He shook my hand, Earth-style. He had travelled there. His grandfather was the legendary Daya Ezmi, the founder of the Barresh Aghyrians.

He gestured at the couch and I sat down. The cushion released a waft of musty air. He sat on the other couch. Thayu and Reida remained near the door while Lilona sat on one of the chairs at the table.

Federza frowned at her. "Is that . . . ?"

"She's from the ship, yes."

He stared at her, and she looked back at him, pale as she was. From his looks, Federza did not belong to the dark-haired, Pakshari, group of Aghyrians, even though his family heritage said otherwise. His hair was bronze and his eyes the colour of beach sand: beige, almost yellow.

He rose again and bowed to her. "I cannot offer you much in the way of refreshments, but I have clean water."

"It's all right," she said. "I haven't been feeling very well."

"Do have it checked out." He sat down again, still looking at her.

Something intense about the exchange went beyond words.

Thayu frowned at me. We were under the ground so the feeder didn't work. I would have loved to know what she made of this.

"Tell me what happened and what led you to coming here," I asked Federza.

He blew out a breath and leaned his elbows on his bony knees. "It goes back a long time."

"Something like twenty years when your people first started talking to the ship?"

"I don't know. I wasn't involved. I didn't become aware of it until a few years ago. At first I thought it was just too silly for words, but then I saw the proof and wondered why no one had told *gamra* about the ship. But our leaders said the information and the ship was ours and no one else had a right to speak to it."

"Except they did speak to others, didn't they?"

Federza glanced at Lilona. She shrugged. "I work in the lab. That's what I do. The captain makes decisions about which information to give out."

Proof that she knew at least something, and felt uncomfortable discussing it.

I asked her, "Did you, at any time, know who he was communicating with?"

"No. Just the new inhabitants of our home planet, he said."

And he'd lied, unless he had been talking to the *zeyshi* group, too. That was a distinct possibility.

"I don't know how much of a setup it was," Federza went on. "I still don't know. I don't know what their aims are, but when I started questioning, people became defensive."

" 'People' meaning the Aghyrian leadership?"

He nodded.

"I became more and more convinced that the approaching ship should be mentioned to the *gamra* assembly, but they continued to overrule me. In the end, I copied the information and took it out of the compound, but they found out. That's when they sent the Tamerians after me. When you disappeared to the ship, I had nowhere to go. I came to the island but it was full of Tamerians. I couldn't leave a message for you because they would have intercepted it. They have bugs everywhere. Except here."

"You went to the guards for protection, and they put you in jail." Which, all things considered, was a pretty smart thing to do. "But you can't get out."

"They will kill me." He sighed. "Since our last meeting, I've learned more disturbing material." He passed his reader to me. I tilted it so that the image faced the right way up. It was a block of unfamiliar code.

"Look at the date," Federza said.

I did. It was twenty years ago. I would still have been in high school at Taurus, before I went to Mars, before I lived in Athens with Nicha. "What is it?"

"Genetic code and instructions."

"Where did this come from?"

"The Exchange picked it up but never released it, because they looked and couldn't find the origin, and because nothing else ever came from that direction, they filed it and forgot about it. But someone received this data and worked on it for years. That man you killed in my office, I had his genetics analysed. It matches with this." He gestured at the screen in front of me. "This is Tamerian. No one knew where it came from, no one knew where it went. No one recognised it for what it was. No one worried about it."

No one had known about the ship.

"They were communicating with people back then."

I looked at Lilona. She sat staring into the distance. With her limited understanding of societies, what was the chance that she had no idea what we were talking about?

"They were. It all went to Tamer, although the Exchange doesn't have any proof for that. They used old satellites that had been floating around amongst other space debris."

I nodded. "The Asto military destroyed them as soon as they sprang to life." Asha hadn't told me how long they'd been doing that for and how long each satellite had been transmitting when they destroyed it. Hell, information like this could be transmitted in a few minutes.

Federza said, "I'm not sure there would have been that much point in destroying them after the fact. They have so many of these potential relays that we can't keep track of them. Even if each communicates only once before it is destroyed, they still get a lot of material through before all of them are gone."

"But I don't quite understand why they're after you." I would have said he was just paranoid, if there hadn't been that attack on him while he was in my apartment, and if his apartment hadn't been ransacked.

"No. Most of this was known already, even if no one did anything about it." He met my eyes squarely.

The sandy colour always made me feel strange. The ship Aghyrians didn't have such interesting eye colours. Theirs were more human: brown or blue.

"They were after me because I know who made the Tamerians. I'm not the only one who knows, but because I was going to take the communication with the ship to the assembly, they judged me a risk."

"This is about the Barresh Aghyrians, isn't it?"

"Yes and no. It's a cartel, not a single person, and mostly they're investors, they don't do any of the work. That's why they're doing it at Tamer. Because if they did it on a *gamra* world, it would be traceable."

Tamer was a dreadful, dangerous world that colonists had left mostly alone. It was inhabited by impenetrable thickets of live forests, trees that were half animal, half plant; and by fierce predators. There was a research base somewhere on a tall mountaintop, but that was the only settlement I had ever heard of. Tamer was about as Wild West as they came. "So these investors are mostly Barresh Aghyrians?"

"Again, not all. Some names I'm certain of, others I can only guess."

A series of loud pops sounded above our heads. Thayu and Reida looked at the ceiling. Reida formed his hand in the shape of a gun.

Gunfire? Up there?

"Any chance of sharing names before we go out and get ourselves killed? The more people know, the less chance the secret dies."

"They're very secretive." He sighed. He had aged a lot in the past few weeks. Yes, he still cared too much about his appearance, but damn it, I hadn't given the man enough credit. *That's what happens when you behave like an arrogant dick. People take a long time to warm to your good deeds.*

I appeared to have misjudged him badly.

He said, staring at his hands. "The one I'm completely certain about is Joyelin Akhtari."

I blew out a breath. She would still have been Chief Delegate if she hadn't been pressured to resign. Then again, maybe the pressure had provided her with a perfect excuse. And I should have seen it. I'd even suspected her, but never had any proof. Never had any reason to look for it, and probably wouldn't have found any had I tried.

"She has provided a lot of money for the project."

"Tell me honestly. Do you know if she was ever involved in Amoro Renkati who killed President Sirkonen?"

"No."

"But she never took active steps to discourage them either."

He shook his head. "No, she didn't. I was quite friendly with her at the time, and she knew they'd eventually implode, so she left them alone and pretended she never heard of the organisation."

"You're not friendly with her anymore?"

He laughed, not in a happy way. "Would I be here otherwise?"

"Well, I don't know. There seems to be an entire shadow society that's dedicated mostly to ending the Coldi domination in *gamra*."

"Pretty much."

"That's why the ship Aghyrians helped them by making Tamerians."

He completed the train of thought. "Except the shadow society didn't realise that these ship people aren't interested in helping them end the Coldi domination at all. The ship people hate everything about what our society has become. Because it's not ordered, and we're dirty, and we—heaven forbid—interbreed. That man is a fucked up nutjob. He probably always was, even in his day when he neglected to save the thousands he could have saved."

At his point, looking into his sandy eyes, I finally realised—much too late—that Marin Federza and I had always been on the same page, and that I'd just been too blinded by some of his behaviour that annoyed me to see it.

Lilona was watching this exchange with wide eyes.

I cringed. I could just about hear her say, "My captain." Except she didn't. She was staring at Federza. Was she shocked by all this? Did she even understand it? It was impossible to tell.

I asked him, "So, tell me this: back when we had the trouble with Amoro Renkati, you gave me their contact because someone supposedly had a job for me. You didn't send me in there because you wanted to convert me to their cause?"

"Hell, no. I sent you in there because I knew you didn't take bullshit, and I wasn't in a position to do or say anything about it myself."

He'd been distant and aloof to me because he'd been afraid to be seen as an enemy by powerful people in the Aghyrian group. I remembered how *he* had sought me out in the clothing store downstairs.

How I'd thought that he was trying to talk me into joining his cause, while he was actually trying to warn me and inform me. Which he had done quite successfully. And it had taken me this long to see it. Damn, I'd been an arse.

My ears did their thing again, but fortunately it was dark so no one could see it. "So, what can we do now?"

"You can come and join me in this prison."

"Not likely."

"I was afraid you'd say that."

Another misjudgement on my part that had come to the fore in the last few weeks. Traders were allowed to carry heavy arms and were said to be a backup if a conflict erupted and no guards were present. They were said to be happy to use their weapons. Not Federza: he was afraid of armed conflict.

"Well," I said, scratching my head, reordering a couple of major pieces of the story in my head. "We could go back to the island and set up a secure zone there. Ideally, all of this should go before the assembly as soon as possible, but since there is no session planned and many delegates won't be at the island, we should probably alert Delegate Namion as soon as possible."

"Are you kidding? He's one of the people whose investment in the Tamerian project I haven't yet been able to prove."

I stared at him. "Delegate Namion? You're serious?"

He nodded, slowly. "He and a good proportion of the Damarcian upper-class delegates are involved. I've got evidence of payments made by Delegate Vitani, who is Delegate Namion's brother-in-law. The Damarcians never got over the fact that the *gamra* headquarters were permanently moved from Damarq to Barresh. According to them, Damarq was ideal, neutral ground."

"Well, yes, but back then, the headquarters moved to the home of the elected Chief Delegate, didn't they?"

"Yes." It was also why *gamra* could never be on Asto. When Isandra Andrahar won and she lived in Barresh, and Barresh at the time was dilapidated, the council purpose-built the island, and the railways, and they did such a good job that the assembly voted to make it permanent.

Federza snorted. "The Damarcians say that Barresh is a stand-in for Asto. Too close. So they and a number of other investors acted on this mysterious data that had been sent to them to produce this super-human race that was going to challenge the Coldi and with them, the entire established order."

"But if Delegate Namion is involved then that would . . ." *make all of the island unsafe. Would make all of the city unsafe.*

He nodded in response to my unvoiced fear.

Shit. Reorder all the pieces in my mind again.

"I still think we should set up a safe zone on the island. I *still* think being at the *gamra* island will offer us protection. Once *gamra* shows clear bias in the direction of the Tamerians . . ." *Asto would be here in a heartbeat, and they wouldn't be coming for tea.* That thought shook me deeply.

I continued, although I must sound incoherent by now. "Well, I think we have a much better chance at staying safe at my apartment." I was clutching at straws of sanity. In one hit, it looked as if the entire world had gone nuts.

Which dumb, ignorant, utterly stupid young diplomat had said that *gamra*'s excessive formality prevented violence?

Shit. Shit, shit, shit.

Thayu had been listening with a darkening expression on her face. She now looked at her reader. "Evi says Asha's guards have a van waiting outside. Backup has arrived and we should be able to get to the island safely. He says they flushed out some snipers and other undesirables." Presumably related to the noise we'd heard upstairs. "Now is probably our best chance, while the Tamerians regroup." She put the thing back in her belt. "I hate not knowing what I'm fighting."

"We'll do a good deal of research when we get home."

She snorted. "And I'm not dressed for this either."

That was my fault, of course. I still managed to underestimate how quickly a situation could blow up.

"What do you think?' I asked Federza. "Are you taking my offer for a ride out of here?"

He pursed his lips and thought for a bit, staring into the distance. "Yeah. All right. Either way, my days are probably numbered. Might as well die trying to save the world as we know it."

He rose and collected a number of things into a bag.

Then he offered Lilona his arm and led her into the corridor, saying something about food supplements that he could provide her with that were certain to make her feel better.

My head was reeling.

I wondered how much she had understood of the conversation. In any case, it must be painfully clear to her that unless Kando Luczon backed off and came clear, there would probably be an armed conflict of some kind—that Asha wasn't sure the Asto military could win. Especially not if the ship could count on the assistance of goodness knew how many Tamerians. Although I wondered how long that collaboration would last, because I was sure that Kando Luczon had no loyalty to anyone who would help them. If Coldi were an "all-purpose colonising race" meant for front-line work, and not meant to be fertile, I could only imagine what the ship folk thought of the Tamerians.

Damn.

Evi and Telaris waited at the bottom of the stairs, each carrying a military grade weapon that I was sure didn't belong to them. The keihu prison guard was also there.

We were halfway up the stairs when Federza stopped. "Wait."

He squeezed past us and went back down. He ran down the corridor and came back a moment later with a set of noodle tongs. "These are mine. My grandfather gave them to me." He stuck them in the inner pocket of his jacket and continued up the stairs.

That was when the explosion struck.

17

THE GROUND TREMBLED.

Evi, who was at the front of the group, tumbled a few steps down. He was followed by a couple of bricks that we managed to duck but that bounced down the stairs until they landed in the puddle at the bottom.

Then the light went out and we were plunged in total darkness.

"Great," the guard said.

"Everyone all right?" Telaris asked.

Several people said that they were. There were a couple of big thuds upstairs. People running. A crash. Shouting.

"What now?" the keihu guard said.

"There's an emergency light in my room." This was Federza's voice.

"If we can find it," Thayu said. Being Coldi, she saw even less in the dark than I did, and it was so pitch black that I wasn't sure if that was possible.

We managed to get down the stairs, while the noise from the guard station above us intensified. Shouts, alarms, rumbling. People running.

"Are those shots?" Telaris said.

"Likely," said Federza. "Likely Tamerians have been in hiding in the surrounding buildings ever since I came here."

It seemed like every curtain you shook around the place had

Tamerians falling out of it. *That* thought was frightening. Just how many of these emotionally blank fighting machines were there?

We listened. I didn't hear any shots, but Indrahui ears were better than any of the rest of ours, and mine especially were still ringing from the explosion.

We shuffled along the walls, running our hands over the rough, algae-covered stone. Evi at the front would shout if something came up, like "door" or "pillar" or some such.

We finally reached Federza's room, where he shuffled about finding a light. A pale glow filled the room. It came from a glowing orb that sat atop a wire coil. This was the oldest and most basic form of light in Barresh, cheap and efficient. The pearls were charged at the solar plant. They glowed when two pieces of metal came in contact with the surface. I kept some of these things in a cupboard in my apartment, too. They were great for power outages, even if the greenish light looked like something out of a zombie movie.

"Now what do we do," I asked, looking around the circle of pale faces.

"Wait until it calms down upstairs?" Thayu said.

"They'll probably come down here before that time," Reida said.

"We could dig in and defend ourselves," the guard said.

Thayu protested, "What with? We have two decent guns, a couple of single-shot jobs, no explosives, and most of us here have no training."

There were some nods at this.

She looked at the ceiling, searching for a vent of some such. "There has to be another way out."

The guard shook his head. "We can't escape. It's a jail."

Federza said, "Ha, ha, ha."

But Thayu said, "You want to bet?"

The guard gave her a suspicious look.

"It's an *old* jail," Federza said. "As far as I know, no one has done anything to actively upgrade security in the last hundred years."

Reida was frowning. "Isn't there a drain behind the cells on the other side of the corridor?"

The guard frowned at him.

"When it rains, you can hear the ringgit calling inside the drain. It echoes and it's really noisy, and it's annoying because you can't sleep, but it means there is a drain pipe somewhere, doesn't it?"

Oh, for the advantage of having a team member with a propensity to get himself arrested for petty offences, like climbing into rich council daughters' bedroom windows.

Thayu took out her equipment and started doing a scan of the corridor and the cells opposite the guard station. I let her do her thing, and wandered to the stairs by the feeble light emitted by my reader. A wall at the top of the staircase had collapsed and an avalanche of bricks blocked the way. It probably wouldn't be impossible to get out that way, if it weren't for the fact that we'd probably be watched by whomever was firing guns up there; and I didn't want to take chances guessing which side they were on. There was still a lot of noise upstairs: people running around and shouting, things falling down, doors being slammed.

I only hoped that Sheydu and Veyada were all right, and that Nicha had been smart enough to stay at home. His son needed him.

I went back to the end of the corridor where Thayu had completed her scan.

She reported on her findings at the table that had been Federza's desk. "It shouldn't be too hard to get out."

The guard made a disbelieving noise.

"No, it isn't—and of course there is a big difference between trying to escape from a cell without anyone noticing, and trying to get out of the jail with the blessing of the guards."

He said nothing.

"Right. So, Barresh is a lot like Athyl. Going places in secret usually involves walking through tunnels, even if in Barresh, they're tunnels for drainage, not the remains of an old civilisation." She glanced at Lilona, who sat with her hands jammed between her knees. Not feeling well, I thought.

Thayu flicked to another screen on her reader which displayed a three-dimensional schematic produced from her scan. "Our little jail-bird here is right. A fairly large drainpipe runs behind the cells on the other side of the corridor. We're unlucky that it's a fairly recent pipe, not one of the old system, which have walls of soft stone; but we're lucky that it's a recent pipe because it contains a one-way valve, which is in the storeroom opposite this room. It's not wet season yet, so the drain is fairly empty. If we push out the valve, we can get out that way."

"Only one problem. The door to the storeroom is locked. The key is upstairs," the guard said. "If you can get it, you might as well leave the station that way."

"We don't need the key."

The guard raised his eyebrows. "You can't force the door open."

"Our colleague Sheydu, who is not here, regularly has serious things to say about security, both on the island and in town. All of your security infrastructure is based on the capabilities of people like yourself, and maybe Pengali capabilities. This is a serious mistake. We'll give you a demonstration." She jerked her head. "Reida. Open the door."

Reida got up from the table, grinning as if he'd been waiting for this moment. He went into the corridor and retreated a few steps until he stood with his back to the opposite wall. Then he ran to the door and kicked. The door shot open, clanging into the wall. The lock fell out and bounced over the floor, shedding rivets and other little parts along the way.

"That open enough?"

The guard gaped at Reida. "Those times we locked you up in here, you could have just escaped like that?"

"Yup."

I rarely ever saw the full force of Coldi strength and it was a beauty to behold. No doubt Thayu would have had even less trouble with the door.

The guard scratched his head. Reida smiled at me. He said in a low voice, "Those cell doors are bolted with a huge piece of metal. I couldn't break that. Believe me, I tried."

Thayu kicked the broken lock aside and went into the room, shining the light from her comm over the walls. The storeroom contained piles of crates and boxes, most of them with Mirani script that I couldn't read well enough to guess the contents.

She directed the light to the upper right corner of the back wall. "There."

The valve was a box the size of a good suitcase set into the wall near the floor. Inside the recess were two metal slabs with a rubber rim. In case the jail flooded, water could escape through here, but because the flaps opened only in one direction, water couldn't come in if the drain was full.

Reida pushed open one of the flaps and stuck his head out.

"Urgh." He came back inside. "Something dead in there."

"How far down is it?"

"Quite a way. If we get the tallest people to go out first, they can help the others." That was a nice way of saying that they thought I needed help to get down.

Marin Federza had already taken off his pretty shirt and put the bundle into his bag. He wore a plain undershirt of khaki fabric that looked locally produced: felt made from fibres of a seagrasslike plant.

He put his arms through the handles of his bag so that it sat on his back, while Reida knocked out the metal division between the two valves. Federza's shoes were sturdy but quite pretty. They wouldn't be so pretty after all this.

He stuck his head out through the valve. "Someone hold up this piece of metal, or it will slam onto my fingers." Not a word about smell or dirt. A few weeks ago, I would have expected him to complain about getting dirty, but I didn't know about Federza anymore

Reida pushed the flap up and Federza stuck one of his legs in, shimmied his body through and pulled through his other leg. He made me think of a giant grasshopper when he did this, all thin limbs and elbows and knees. Then he let himself down while still holding onto the edge. Reida held the valve open so that it wouldn't slam on his fingers. A waft of humid air came into the storeroom. It smelled like mould and decomposing leaves that had been in water too long.

"All right, here I go." His voice sounded hollow out there in that drain. His head and hands disappeared. There was a scraping sound and a splash, and a voice said, "Shit."

"You're all right?" Reida asked through the hole.

"Yeah. It's just really slippery down here. All right. I'm ready for the next person."

Lilona was the next tallest. I gestured to her. "Come on, in you go."

She took a few steps forward and stopped. She looked at the hole, her eyes wide.

Reida held a hand out to her.

I wondered how strong she was. Not very, judging by the thinness of her limbs. Reida let the valve fall into its original position and grabbed her hand which she held out reluctantly. She dropped to her knees.

Reida pushed the valve back open. Lilona peered into the dark gap. "It's dark and dirty in there." Her legs were trembling.

"Unfortunately, dark and dirty is all we have," Reida said.

"But I can't . . . My captain says . . ."

This wasn't going to work. I said, "Thay' you go first. Then you can help her."

Thayu dropped to her knees, wriggled backwards through the hole and jumped down on the other side.

Scrape, splash.

"Oh, shit. It really is slippery down here."

"No one ever believes what I say," came Federza's voice.

The guard went through next. He was a fair bit wider than either Federza or Thayu. His hands were visible in the opening while he hung onto the edge. We heard him ask, "How far down is it?"

Thayu replied, and then he was gone too, accompanied by a couple of swear words in keihu. Next, Evi and Telaris, and then it was my turn. I stuck my foot in the dark hole, wriggled through sideways. Thayu waited at the bottom of the drain with a small light. She was right, it was quite a way, and the drain was a concrete tube with curved sides and nothing to hold onto on the way down.

I let go, slid down the side and ended up in the smelly, stagnant puddle at the bottom. "Oh, fuck."

They all laughed.

"Shh," Reida said. "Hurry up, because someone upstairs is trying to get in. Come on, down you go." The latter to Lilona.

She climbed onto the ledge, awkwardly, trembling. Reida had to help her get her second leg out. Then she froze.

"Come on, let go." I tried to walk up as far as I could, but could only reach the bottom of her legs. And even doing that almost made me slip.

"No," she said. "I can't." She sounded terrified.

I tried to imagine what it would be like growing up in a sterile, neat ship and then being asked to shimmy into a disgusting hole and slide into a disgusting drain, and could not. "Just pretend you're a kid and this is a slide." Did the Aghyrians even have kids? If they did, did they have childhoods anything like ours?

She just hung there, helpless. I couldn't reach her properly because of the curve of the tube and because the concrete where I would like to put my feet was covered in algae and as slippery as fuck.

"Come on!" I called to her. "Let go. You're just going to slide down the side and end up in the water. You won't hurt yourself." *You might teach us some Aghyrian swear words.*

"No."

"I'm coming out," Reida said, now sounding urgent. He managed to get out while Lilona was still hanging onto the edge. "I think they're inside. Come on." The latter to Lilona.

"No!"

"Freaking let go. You're the least likely to hurt yourself. You're the tallest of us!"

But she was paralysed with fear.

Reida grabbed her hands and forced them off the ledge. She managed to grab onto his legs to stop herself sliding down.

"No!" she screamed. "No!"

Reida let go, and the two of them slid unceremoniously down the side of the tube into the water. Reida quickly scrambled to his feet, cursing and wiping his hands on his trousers, but Lilona sat in the water, crying.

"Come on, get up." Thayu was trying to drag her to her feet, but almost slipped herself. She cursed. "Come on. We don't have all day!"

"My captain, my captain," Lilona was crying.

"I don't give a fuck about your captain," Thayu yelled. "Get the fuck up and stop being stupid." In our relationship, I was the one who did all the swearing, and if she started, that was a fair indication she had enough, in this case of Lilona's behaviour.

"Wait, Thay'." I pushed past her, almost slipping in the sludge.

Reida called out. "What are you doing? We have to get out of here before they discover us."

Yes, but I had just realised that something monumental had happened. Emotions had broken through Lilona's mask.

I crouched in the sludge and took her shoulders. Pushed her chin up until she looked me in the eye. There was something inherently Coldi about the gesture, and even that fitted the situation.

"Calm down. It's all right."

Her face was dirt and tear-streaked, a far cry from the emotionless mask she had worn for the past days. Her bottom lip shivered. She whispered, "No. No."

"Tell me what bothers you. But be quiet because we don't want to advertise where we are. And get out of the water. It will make you sick."

She carefully climbed to her feet. Her legs and right side were covered in dripping, slimy mud. She trembled so much that she almost slipped again. I leant her my shoulder to steady herself. Her hands were so cold that I could feel it through my shirt and armour.

"Come now."

We shuffled forward. It was slow going and Lilona wasn't getting any steadier on her feet. She kept quiet, but continued sobbing quietly. I asked her if she was scared but she didn't answer that. Then I asked her if she was cold, seeing as that might be an easier-to-understand emotion. She said she wasn't. Her hands felt like ice.

She didn't mention the captain once.

We went a short distance until we came to an intersection. Here the recent concrete drainage tube joined a much older, square tunnel. A stone grate above let through a smattering of light—from a street light probably—and a whiff of fresh air. The soft stone walls were covered with moss and ferns and various types of fungi. A trickle of water flowed through the bed of the tunnel, and there was a narrow walkway along the side, wide enough for one person. We walked in single file, slowly because the stones were slippery and Lilona wasn't steady on her feet.

A chorus of ringgit echoed through the drain from elsewhere. Thankfully they were quiet in our section of drain—the noise could damage your hearing.

Every now and then, the council sent men with smoke bombs into the drains to smoke the creatures out, for all the two weeks' worth of relief that brought.

A bit further down, the drain opened into a channel. At the end, I could see an arch-shaped patch of light where a streetlight stood at a jetty where the channel boat would moor. A tree next to the drain entrance obscured the street and houses above. I suspected that we were somewhere in the block between Market Street and Fountain Street.

The ledge along the side of the drain widened out. This was part of the very old drainage system. There was a little platform at the edge of the water where in the old days servants would come to draw water for their households. There was also a semicircular bench, called a lovers' seat, where people would sit in the relative coolness of evaporating water in the extremely hot and humid days before the start of the monsoon. It was quite pleasant here where the cool moist air mingled with the freshness above. The walls were made from limestone and covered in ferns and moss. The occasional ripple in the water indicated water life below.

"Wait here," Thayu said. Her voice echoed in the hollow space. She had stopped at the lovers' seat bench and unstrapped her belt. She laid out her weapons and equipment and rearranged them. For what purpose, I didn't know.

I helped Lilona down to the stone bench where she sat, shivering. I said to Thayu in a low voice, "I'm worried about her."

She didn't react to the fact that we were talking about her.

Evi crouched and looked into her face, holding both sides of her head. "She's hypothermic." He pulled down her eyelids with his thumb. "Look at how narrow her pupils are. It's some kind of shock."

"I guess running to the station from here is out of the question?"

"We should take her to the hospital."

"I'm not going back there." The island had a small medical post. That would have to do, when, or even if, we got there. "How bad is it?"

"I don't know. I'm not familiar with this. I don't know what prompted it."

"Unfamiliarity. She must have gotten too scared." I crouched next to Evi. He was right. Her hands were really cold, and she had freaked out badly when Reida dropped her into the tunnel. "Come. We'll take you back." Although I wasn't sure how we were going to manage that. "Back to your captain." I cringed at the thought of explaining to him what had happened, although on second thoughts, he might not even care about her.

She was shivering. Telaris took off his jacket and wrapped it around her, but it didn't seem to make a difference.

"What are we going to do?" I asked.

"Reida and I will fetch us some transport," Thayu said. She had strapped all her gear back on. Everything now sat on the outside of her clothes, clearly displayed. It never ceased to amaze me how much stuff she could hide under regular clothing. She glanced at Reida and hooked her thumb at the tunnel's entrance. "Come."

The Barresh guard cleared his throat. "Well, if you're done with me, I would like to go back to the Guard Station and report that I'm still alive."

"Don't tell anyone that we were with you, at least not yet," I said.

"I was going to do the opposite. Warn them so that they can provide backup security for you."

Thayu pulled a face behind his back.

"We have evidence that at least certain sections of the Barresh guards are compromised."

"You don't trust us?"

"Not unless we're sure that your unit isn't one of the compromised ones."

The guard gave a *how dare you?* huff. "Well, that's just . . . quite a heavy accusation."

"Again, this is a trustworthy source, and it may not apply to your unit."

"I would think not."

"But do us a favour and keep the news back a bit. Even if your unit is perfectly fine, and the whole office where you work is perfectly trustworthy, there still *are* sections in the guards that are not fine and that contain Tamerians, maybe under false names."

"Well . . ." He scratched his head, clearly disturbed and no longer denying my statement. "Well, if you wish . . ."

"Yes, thank you, I do wish to keep it quiet. Go back and report on the collapse of the jail. Tell them how you got out if necessary."

"What am I supposed to say about you? They know you went down. It becomes a lot more complicated if a delegate of *gamra* is involved."

"For the time being, you're going to tell them that we're buried under a pile of rock."

"Well . . . they're probably in the jail already, and it wasn't that big a pile of rocks that came down the stairs. They're going to discover you're not there if they haven't already."

"I know. That's why we must hurry."

Thayu and Reida were off, and the guard left, too, after having agreed not to volunteer information about our location.

Evi and Telaris said that they'd guard the entry to the tunnel, leaving me with Lilona and Marin Federza on the lover's seat.

It was very quiet here. Somewhere in the darkness, water trickled into a deeper pool. The familiar sound of meili squabbling in a tree drifted in from the entrance.

I sat on the stone bench next to Lilona. She was staring at her knees, while holding her arms clamped around herself. "You really have to make an effort to walk. It won't be far." And when she didn't react, I added, "I'll take you back to your captain."

No reaction, but her eyes widened briefly. Fear? Happiness? It was hard to tell.

Federza walked around the bench and sat on the other side of her.

I continued, "Aren't you happy about that?"

She looked at the tunnel entrance. Avoiding me?

There was nothing to do but to continue talking. I was probably annoying her, but time for finding out what Asha wanted to know was running out. I couldn't see myself putting pressure on her—she'd probably go into a deeper shock—but I had to keep trying. "I don't know what sort of society you have on that ship out there, but you are safe here. In this place, no one can hear what you say. You don't even have to go back on the ship. You can stay here, with our Aghyrians. They will look after you"

She looked at me, and then at Federza, who nodded, once.

"Whatever anyone aboard the ship is making you do or say doesn't apply here. We have our own laws, and they will protect you, if necessary."

Again, a glance at Federza, whose corner of his mouth moved up. The scramble through the tunnel had left him with smudges in his face and his normally sleek hair looked dishevelled with wisps having come loose from his ponytail.

"You can say to us what you want, because your captain can't hear it."

She spoke in the merest whisper. "He knows."

"He knows what?" I sensed a very small victory.

"Everything you say or do. Or think."

"When you're on the ship, maybe, but not here."

She looked at me, puzzled, as if she truly didn't understand that the micro-cosmos that she was used to didn't extend beyond the walls of the ship.

Her expression sent a chill through me. Ages ago, as part of my degree at Mars University, I'd done a project on how truly frightening dictators control their people, like the sect leaders whose followers were so dedicated that they would kill themselves for their master. I remembered reading through reports of how the victims were scarred for life, and had often been vulnerable people to begin with. When pushed, they would at first deny any wrongdoing by the leader.

"It's the truth. We don't have the same system. If we did, he wouldn't have access to it. Besides, there is no coverage in this tunnel."

She turned to Federza. Again, he nodded. He pulled out his reader and showed her the blank screen. "See? I can access anything that's stored on here but if I want to talk to someone, I can't."

She turned back to me.

"Speak out if there is anything that we can do for you or the other crew of the ship."

"Oh, no, you can't. Their schedule is set from within the ship. We set it before we left."

"They're waking up?"

"Soon they will be ready. They will do as the captain says. It's his journey."

"But not yours?"

She stared at me. Blinked. That question probably cut too close and she wasn't ready.

I tried a different angle. "Do you have any family on board the ship?"

"No. Dashtari is my world." Her eyes glittered.

"This is where you came from?"

"It's my home. It has soft green oceans and floating islands that follow the ocean streams to where the fish and the floating gardens are."

So they *did* settle worlds out there. "So the captain lies when he told us there was nothing out there."

"The captain would never lie. There *is* nothing. For him."

"What do you mean?"

"He wants to own a place and the people in it. He says that humanity owes it to him that anyone is still alive. He said that Asto was his, that it was back to the state he left it in."

"But he lied and it was occupied by the Coldi and still too hot for you." Although that would change over the next fifty to a hundred years.

"The captain . . . does not want to talk to any of you. He doesn't want to collaborate. He wants no agreements. He wants to destroy you."

I nodded. That didn't surprise me either.

The sound of an engine came from the mouth of the tunnel. It appeared Thayu and Reida had annexed a channel boat, which they now brought upstream. I hoped the water was deep enough here.

Lilona continued, "The captain wants to start again, as he says. But we're tired. He's had two opportunities at making a new world—"

"Two worlds you settled there?"

"No, there are more. But he could have come to this world and started here, but he didn't like that there would be Pakshari refugees aboard his ship, so he refused to save anyone. He could have set up a settlement on this planet, but he left instead. That was the first opportunity he didn't take. It was very hard on the crew. They were at minimum supply levels and they had little breeding stock. When people challenged, he put the whole crew in stasis and made the jumps himself. They found Dashtari and built a settlement there. People were happy, but he refused to work with them. Because they were doing it all wrong. So he left them."

Thayu steered the boat to the water drawing point in front of the bench where we sat. It drifted sideways and hit the stone. She jumped out.

I looked at Lilona. "Wait. Are you saying that there are people left on that planet?"

"Many. Or, there were many people there when we left. Don't know about now. We will never see it like that again. So much time is lost when the ship jumps." Her eyes glittered. "When we left, they were facing problems with adaptability and disease and wanted to use indigenous material to overcome the problem. But the captain didn't agree. It was 'not pure' he said. But the world had changed and people didn't listen to him anymore. They were going to use the native material anyway. He got angry. Any of the families who still owed debt to him had to send him crew. He was going back and reclaim Aghyr."

"So that is how you came to be on board?"

She nodded.

"What about the other crew?"

She kept nodding. A tear leaked over her cheek.

"This guy really is a first class arsehole, isn't he?"

"A . . . arse . . . hole?" Lilona looked confused.

"Eeeyup," Thayu said, standing with her hands at her sides. "It's the part of you that your shit comes out, unless shitting is beyond you."

"Thay—"

She faced me, muddy, wet, with filthy hair, but her eyes were blazing. "Don't make any excuses for them. They're all arseholes! They've been keeping the most important information from us."

"She was controlled by this guy."

"Oh, that's just an excuse. I don't believe any of them anymore."

"I have a feeling that he controlled her with something like our feeders."

"He doesn't. We took all the scans and there is nothing unnatural in them."

"Because our equipment doesn't pick it up, it doesn't mean it's not there." I could think of technology that didn't show up on scans. Even Coldi technology included wetware—biological tech, for example the bacterial screens.

Thayu snorted. "I don't believe any of it. They're laughing at us. Oh, we're so happy to be back. Playing the *old man wanting to see his home one more time* card. No, we're not going to tell you that we were hounded out of our new colonies by our intergalactic peers and oh did you realise that we've got a whole ship full of arseholes about to jump containment lines coming to your doorstep. That's what they're like! Sorry if I don't roll out the welcome mat."

Thayu, that's really not helpful right now.

But there was still no reception here so she couldn't hear me.

"We can talk here all day, but we need to go," she said. "Don't know what's brewing out there, but something is brewing. I picked up a lot of surveillance activity on the scans when we were out there."

"Tell me quickly, what is the captain's plan?" I asked Lilona.

"He is the captain. He does not share his plans."

"Then what was he looking for?"

"The relays. The one in the ship, in the place where we can't go, is powerful, but there are others."

"Other ships?"

"No, they float about in space. You probably never noticed them."

But we had, and Ezhya had committed to cleaning up the space junk in an effort to find all those old things that were still operational.

"What are they for?" They were satellites, weren't they?

"You know how in your jump system, you use nodes which create a jump line?"

"Yes, but they have to be activated from both sides. Your ship would have a sling of some sort."

"It does, and that's the problem. Because this . . . sling is not very precise. It generates a funnel on both sides of the line, and especially the exit funnel is a problem. Its diameter depends on the size of the ship. It's often more than a hundred times wider than the length of the ship. That's a nuisance for a small ship, but with a very large one, it's a real problem, because with a funnel that size, there is a real chance that something gets caught in the mouth and the ship hits it when it exits. There are quite a few asteroids in the system."

Yes, we knew about those.

"When the ship left, the captain seeded relays along the way to generate the field that allows the ship to jump home in the same way your system works. We can't jump yet because the relays in this area are disturbed. A number aren't working. We need to reconfigure them in order to generate the jump line."

Shit. All those satellites we'd thought forgotten, abandoned and drifting and now moving into position? It was a fucking Exchange array.

I raised my hand to my mouth. I had to talk to Asha, urgently, before the ship jumped, before Captain Luczon's army of human war drones was going to be unleashed on two planets I loved deeply.

Lilona said, "We must bring the ship here. There are three thousand of my people on board, and supplies are running critical."

But bringing the ship here is just what the captain wants, so that he can defeat us with a bunch of crew who are slaved to him.

Thayu met my eyes. I didn't need the feeder to know that she understood the seriousness of the situation.

She said, impatiently, "Is anyone going to get into this boat?"

18

———

W**E SCRAMBLED** into the boat. It was one of the channel ferries. It had a flat bottom and wobbled a lot even when we got in one by one, with Reida holding the vessel steady. Lilona found it scary, and Federza told her to sit on the row of seats closest to the engine. It was noisy, he said, but less wet and bumpy. He insisted on sitting at the front. He had a gun, he said, so he could help protect us. He sat at the front bench, looking very dapper.

I struggled not to laugh. Did he realise that she was off the dating market courtesy of her captain?

"All in?" Thayu flipped a lever that reversed the airflow through the engine. It blew a waft of hot and humid air over our heads that made our hair fly. The boat reversed out of the tunnel at a good speed.

She cut the engine again to slow down to pick up Evi and Telaris at the entrance. Telaris was dripping wet.

"How was the water?" I asked him.

He grinned.

Thayu gunned the engine and turned the boat around.

"Hang on carefully," I said to Lilona. If this was going to be like racing through the aquifers at Asto, we'd better hang on very hard.

And yes, it seemed it was. The channels were narrow. Walls and trees and jetties and other boats flashed past. Fortunately, it was night and not busy. Unfortunately, Thayu was Coldi and had extremely poor night vision although from the way she was driving that boat you would never tell.

We raced at a crazy speed through the canal, turned left—

Reida yelled, "No, you need to go right there!"

"Just who is driving this thing—Shit." We had come to a dead end.

"I told you so. This goes to the markets. The channels don't cut across there." Reida pointed.

She turned around, and Evi swore. "Tamerians!"

In one movement, I pulled Lilona off the bench and pushed her between the seats. On the row in front of us, Federza had done the same. He lay on his back with his gun clutched to his chest.

Thayu was steering the boat. That left Reida, Evi and Telaris to defend us. Thayu hit the reverse thrust, and a few shots hit the water in front of us. Evi returned fire, but the sniper was on top of a roof, and he couldn't get a clear shot.

Then Thayu hit the thrust so hard that Telaris in the front almost fell over.

We raced through the narrow canals. In places, there were signs up with maximum speeds for boats. I didn't need to see the controls to know that we were going much faster than that.

I realised to my horror that they had no interest in keeping Federza alive. They wanted him dead. They probably wanted us dead as well. Tamerians moved in the shadows, and they could get away without trouble, especially if Joyelin Akhtari had anything to do with it. After sixty or more years in the Chief Delegate position, she would know exactly how and where to get the documentation to easily clear all the security checks.

It was our luck that this was a highly populated part of town. There were houses on the sides of the canals. There was the occasional surprised citizen who got a fright when we came past. It was our misfortune that there were no direct canals from here to the airport. The main square was the highest point of the island and the airport and train station were on the other side. We would have to backtrack through the eastern part of the island and go around—and the canal between the two islands was notorious for bogs on the northern side. Or we could take the longer route around the south. And Thayu wasn't that familiar with these canals. And they were windy, and narrow, with many dead ends.

There was just no end to them. We went left, right, left, right, with Thayu often having to make the decision in a split second. I had no idea where we were going. I don't know that she had an idea either. We had to turn around twice.

Eventually, I could see the canal opening up into the water ahead where moonlight glittered on the water, but there was a lock at the end, and it was closed, because it was night time and the tide was out, and because it was the dry season.

Damn it.

Thayu killed the engine and jumped out. The water was only thigh-deep, which the instruments would have told her. "Come on, lift it over."

We all jumped into the water, including Lilona. She was neither strong nor skilled in physical work, but she helped, her face screwed up with the effort. It was as if something had shaken loose in her brain.

The lock wall was only low. At the moment, it served to keep water in the canals.

We lifted the boat onto the lock wall, slid it over and plunged it into the reed bed on the other side. Because it was the dry season, the ground was only muddy, not under water. The boat slid over the mud easily enough, but walking was another matter. With each step, I sank in ankle-deep soft mud, and each step was a fight with the mud about who was going to keep my shoes.

By the time we had traversed the reed bed, both moons were high in the sky, visibly tracking across the starscape. They moved so fast that they would set and come around for a second lap before the night was over. Right now, they provided the only light, a silver glimmer over the water.

We had ended up on the southern side of the island and would now have to go all the way around the point and back up northwest to the airport.

Thayu jumped in. "I'll go a bit further out there where it's deep enough for you to get in."

We were supposed to follow on foot, I gathered.

Federza and I went first, with Lilona. Reida, Evi and Telaris kept a close look on the houses and the edge of the island.

The reeds were thick, and wherever I put my feet, a bunch of ringgit would skitter away, thrashing in the water and occasionally taking flight, although they didn't usually fly at night. I'd heard the creatures described as mudskippers with wings, but they had legs as well, and looked more crustaceanlike with the armour plates on their backs, which they used to make the terrible mating call racket.

It was muddy and slippery, and too dark to see where I put my feet.

I reached the boat first. Federza climbed in after me and we were just helping Lilona when there was a shout. Reida pointed at the island where some sort of flying drone had taken to the air. He and Evi and Telaris raced for the boat. The engine roared into life. We took off across the open water.

The drone followed us.

The boat was built for sedate ferry services in the canals. It had low sides so that people could easily get in and out. It had a flat bottom so that it could operate in knee-deep water. At speed, with whatever small waves the wind whipped up, the flat bottom slapped on the surface, throwing up a spray of water each time it hit. Without a decent keel, it was as wobbly and unstable as hell.

At one side, Federza was yelling, "Faster, faster," and Evi was yelling at Thayu to keep the boat steady so he could aim.

Whatever was that thing?

We were losing ground on it. At this rate, it would overtake us even before we got to the next point, and solid ground where we had a chance to shoot it.

Even Thayu was looking over her shoulder.

Then we rounded the point, and the wind got stronger. There were more waves here. Each time the bottom of the boat slapped onto the water, a huge spray washed over us. Thayu slowed down briefly so that we could move closer to the front to weight to boat down. She tried to stay as close to the reeds as possible, but there were snags like washed up tree trunks that we couldn't afford to hit and that she wouldn't be able to see.

Evi and Telaris were now shooting at the drone, hitting it, too, but it had a shield and the hits glanced off. Very soon it was going to reach us.

The thing carried a laser burner, Evi informed us. Farmers used these things to clear fields of vegetation, minus the shielding. It would need to come straight over the top of us before it could fire.

Thayu zigzagged over the water—

And we hit a choppy wave, just as the bow of the boat slammed into the water. The wave broke over the side. Flooded the boat. Water washed over my shoes and the lower half of my legs. The boat slowed so abruptly that Telaris toppled over the bow, face first, into the water. I watched him fly out as if in slow motion, throwing an object in the general direction of the boat. Evi reached out to catch it, but it was too far to the right—Evi almost made the boat tip over—and it fell in the water. It had been his gun, I realised.

The boat barely still floated in its swamped condition, so I jumped over the side, sinking in a mixture of mud and rotting leaves that released a smell of farts. We were a good distance from the sandy southernmost point of the island. There was no way we get there before the drone reached us.

Evi had jumped after his partner's weapon. Telaris had scrambled to his feet and was wading to where it had fallen. Thayu still stood at the back of the boat, yelling, "Get down everyone, get down now!"

Reida, who had Telaris' second gun, took up position and aimed at the drone that was rapidly approaching.

Even Federza had produced his weapon, which I had never seen. He yelled, "Take cover."

I pulled Lilona's arm hard enough to make her topple over the side of the boat. I pushed her down behind the rim of the half-sunken boat and let myself sink in the water. The rim was too low to offer any protection, so I took a deep breath and dived below the surface. It was dark and extremely muddy down here and I could see nothing, just feel the movement of Lilona's legs, whatever she was doing.

A sharp snap echoed through the water. Someone jumped into the water next to me. A much bigger big splash followed, further away.

I couldn't hold my breath any longer. When I surfaced, it was quiet and the sky was empty.

Thayu, Evi and Reida stood watching the wreckage of the drone that lay in the water, producing thick clouds of steam and smoke. Telaris sat on his knees in the water on the other side of the boat. Federza and Lilona stood behind me.

Thayu said, "Uh-oh. Time to get out of here." She was staring at the shore.

At first I saw nothing, but then I noticed some pinpricks of light moving through the reed beds.

Could even hear their footsteps, when the wind carried sound our way, and the wind was unusually squally tonight.

Evi and Telaris tilted the boat so that the water sloshed out. The bag that contained Federza's pretty shirt drifted out with the water. The owner went after it.

"Come on, hurry up," Thayu said.

We climbed back in. Telaris was cursing, draining water from the plasma chamber of his gun. Thayu attempted to start the engine. It sputtered and went out. It was drenched. We were drenched.

Thayu tried again. "Come on."

Another sputter.

"Come on, we don't have all day." She slammed her hand against the side of the jet inlet tube. It made a loud clang.

The engine started with a whoosh and a spray of water.

I had expected her to keep going parallel to the shoreline in the direction of the station, but she turned sharply to the left, away from the island.

I protested. "Where are you going? You're not going all the way to the *gamra* island in this thing?"

But clearly she was doing just that. I knew that she had been taking commando-style training directed specifically at situations in Barresh, but the day that I'd punted across this stretch of water with her in the boat petrified with fear didn't seem that long ago.

It was a hair-raising, uncomfortable and cold ride, but we encountered no more drones or Tamerians.

We moored at the jetty in front of our building. *Gamra* security came to check, but Evi and Telaris managed to palm them off. If they saw we had Federza, they might tell someone who shouldn't know. We could no longer trust anyone.

I was by now so cold that my legs were stiff and Thayu had to help me up onto the jetty.

"Aren't you cold?" I asked her.

"I didn't go for a swim."

True, but—the difference in her confidence between our first trip and now was astonishing. Sheydu loved saying, *Every difficulty can be overcome with training*. It was one of the Coldi proverbs. I had never realised how true it was and how Asto's security and defence training pushed people up against the things that terrified them, and helped them overcome their fear.

We tied the boat on the jetty, where the ferry with its timetable displayed on the back looked very much out of place.

How they'd get a canal ferry back to the main island would be someone else's problem.

We were safe, for the time being. We needed to establish a secure zone. Evi and Telaris were already working on it, even though Telaris still seemed sour about dropping his gun in the water.

19

———————

THERE WERE GUARDS in front of the door to my apartment. Unfamiliar ones, in silver temperature retaining suits wearing red sashes. And there were additional security people whom I recognised as Asha's guards, wearing silver suits, black or grey non-uniform clothing and no red sashes.

I glanced at Thayu and she showed me the screen to her reader, which contained a message from Devlin.

It seemed that in our absence, Ezhya had arrived and that he had been entertained in my absence by Asha and Nicha.

We went inside and found more guards in the hall. They knew who I was and waved Thayu through—she disappeared into the hub— but were not familiar with Federza and Lilona. We looked like bandits, all dirty and wet, and the guards wanted to see their ID. They inspected Federza's gun—a solid, civilian-style Trader weapon—and he showed them his Trader medallion. They were fine with him after they saw that. Lilona was another matter. We'd supplied them with a temporary ID, but the card had no personal history, no *nothing* associated with it.

"She comes from the ship," I told them, and then wasn't sure if it had been a good thing to say this, because they insisted that she be taken to a room elsewhere in the apartment and they were going to guard the door.

Eirani came scurrying into the hall.

"Oh, Muri, I'm so glad that you're back." Her eyes widened. "Whatever have you done to yourself? You're all dirty and wet."

"I'll tell you when I get a chance."

"You must come and put on some dry clothes."

I switched to keihu, which I only spoke to her when there was a security reason, so I hoped she got the message. "No time right now. Can you look after my guests, especially Lilona? Make sure that she gets dry clothes and a safe room on this floor. They will want to guard her room."

Her eyes widened briefly. "The room next to the office? The view is nice there."

"No, on the other side." That view was exactly the problem. "What about him?" She glanced at Federza.

"He'll stay here, too."

"Can he stay in the room next to the office?"

"Definitely not."

"But we're running out of rooms, Muri."

Asha and his entourage had taken up residence in my usual guest quarters downstairs.

"I don't mind staying in the same room," Federza said, in perfect keihu. "She needs help, anyway."

Eirani's gave him a scandalised look. She very much disapproved of people sharing a room who were unmarried. "But, Muri, there is only a double bed in that room."

"I'm sure we have a spare bed somewhere that can be taken up. Arrange it."

"Yes, but why not the room next to the office? It's much nicer."

"Someone will shoot at the window. This is an extreme security situation. No one is allowed to set foot in that room except these two people. No one is allowed to look into the room from outside. No one will be entering this apartment while they are here."

Eirani's mouth formed into an O. "Well, then, I better get going. Come."

She scurried off, and Lilona and Federza followed her. Thank goodness for Eirani. I upset her with my requests sometimes, but she always came around and did as I asked.

The sound of Coldi voices came from the living room, where I was greeted by the most unusual sight ever: three grown men, two of whom were extremely powerful, sat on their knees on the carpet tick-ling a baby.

And by the look of things, Ayshada was loving all this attention. Nicha had told me that he could grab things and squeeze but couldn't yet coordinate his eyes with what he ended up grabbing. In this case, that was Asha's finger in one of his little hands and Ezhya's nose in the other. He had his thumb up one of Ezhya's nostrils and the rest of the hand balled into a fist as if trying to grab, but not comprehending what he was grabbing. Ezhya made cooing noises as he probably was used to making to his own baby daughter. It was a strangely relaxing and reassuring sight.

I said from the doorway, "I can see that *someone* has the world in his hands."

They turned around, with Ezhya gently extracting his nose from the baby's grip.

He started laughing.

I guess I was a bit of a sight: muddy, dripping wet—in fact Jonisa, one of my newer members of domestic staff, was mopping up the water in the hall right now and complaining to Reida about the state of his clothing, because he was the only one she dared complain to. Evi and Telaris were shedding their equipment and lots of mud and sticks in the hall, but she didn't dare complain to them. They were much taller than she was, much broader, and very, very black.

Reida was saying, "We save everyone's butts, and I come home and what do I get? Complaints that I make the floor dirty!"

Nicha stifled a snort of laughter. I went to shut the door.

Asha and Ezhya rose. Nicha picked up his son. Faces turned serious.

On my way back to the sitting area, I grabbed a dishtowel from the cupboard, spread it over the carpet and sat down. "Better not make the couch dirty."

Ezhya nodded.

Asha nodded.

"You brought a couple of other people into the apartment," Ezhya said. It was not a question, but it carried the sense of: *Is this going to be a security issue?*

"Federza is with us," I said.

Ezhya's eyebrows flicked up. No doubt he remembered the last interaction between the two of them, where he had pulled Federza up by the front of the shirt and spoken some choice words to him. That had been over the Aghyrian claim, an issue that had been thoroughly forgotten and pushed aside by the current situation.

"He's one of Akhtari's cronies." Amazing how, now that Joyelin Akhtari was off the scene, people came out with harsh opinions of what they really thought about her. What if everyone had voiced those opinions earlier? Maybe something could have been done.

"At one stage he might have been with her, but he's not, anymore."

Both men gave me sharp looks. Changing one's loyalty was not something Coldi did easily or often, and usually it was accompanied by big changes in the person's living circumstances. Often, also, it was just a rearranging of loyalty lines within the same camp. Like Veyada and Sheydu had come to me, but were still well within Ezhya's camp, and would always remain so.

Simply changing one's political allegiance without far-reaching, and often violent, outward changes was unheard of in Coldi society.

"We'll see," Ezhya said. No, they wouldn't fully trust Federza's change of mind. Ever. Except Federza had largely acted in his position all along. Acting was also something that was considered a dubious activity in Coldi society.

"How much do you know?" I asked both men.

"My daughter briefed me," Asha said. It was, too, the first time I had heard him publicly refer to her as such. "That's why we're both here."

"So you know that the ship has communicated with groups other than the Barresh Aghyrians, and that this communication has been going on for many years. You know that Joyelin Akhtari is one of the main financial backers of the Tamerian project, and that Delegate Namion might be involved, too?"

"We know."

"There is more," I said. "More and worse." I went on to recount what Lilona had told me after Thayu had left. That Kando Luczon had left behind an Aghyrian community that had settled on worlds they had found in the Renzha galaxy. That he had fallen out with them because they wanted to supplement their limited genetic material with local genetics. That he had forced people to provide crewmembers, and that those crewmembers were slaved to him or the ship.

That he had no interest in peaceful discussions, not with us or with the group who had financed the Tamerians. "You do know about the relays, right?"

They did. I guessed those were the main urgency right now.

"I have people working on that," Asha said. "These things are a bugger because they're not big and in their inactive state they're absolutely impossible to see. We're talking here about an active component that's the size of a fist. The Astronomy branch is dealing with that headache." The *military* astronomy branch, that would be, somewhere in that giant station that orbited Asto, that could, at Ezhya's command, disgorge a burst of fire power the likes of which the galaxy had never seen, and that Asha *still* didn't judge adequate to destroy this ship.

Ezhya blew out a breath. Asha shook his head.

Nicha stared at me, an expression of horror on his face while he held his son to his chest. A little hand clawed at his shirt. I didn't know that Nicha had known *any* of this, or had realised the seriousness of it.

Everyone was silent for a while. Sounds drifted in from the hall: Eirani talking, soft conversations from the hub, where Devlin and Thayu would be busy. Maybe the others, too. I suspected Thayu was conducting a second meeting to bring the rest of my association and staff up to speed with the situation.

Then I asked, "What am I supposed to do next?"

"I think the time for you alone to do anything that's going to impact this situation is over," Ezhya said. He spoke slowly, deliberately with a sense of dread to his words. I knew the gist of what was coming. He pushed his reader over the carpet to me. "This is why I'm here. This is why we're both here."

I wiped my hands before picking it up. There were drops of water running down my arm.

The screen displayed a document.

In bold characters at the top, it said,

To the occupants of the ship reported to have come from the Renzha galaxy: Intention to take defensive action, Beniz-Yaza system, Ratanga cluster.

To local authorities: this is a notification only, from Asto's Chief Coordinator. Not for debate or voting.

Underneath, it said,

The Beniz-Yaza system in the Ratanga cluster contains the home worlds of the Coldi, keihu, Mirani and Pengali people. We have lived on these worlds in their present state for many thousands of years. We will view any invasion of this system by non-declared ships as hostile. Any foreign vessel not known to the Exchange approaching the system will be eliminated. Any piece of foreign equipment in orbit in the system will be destroyed. If you want to speak to us, speak to our representatives directly. We urge that you do this as soon as possible.

The document contained, damn it, *miyu* pronouns which I knew existed but had never seen anyone use before.

The most famous use of them was in the declaration that had almost led to an invasion of Hedron by Asto—and both were Coldi worlds.

Miyu pronouns were for declarations of large-scale war.

I looked from Ezhya to Asha and back again. "Something else has happened, right?"

"The ship has turned on power and fired what we think are auxiliary engines, possibly to kick up the main reactor, which is still dormant. There has been no change in their lack of response to us. We will be sending this declaration to them."

I doubted the Aghyrians would understand Coldi writs and the deadly seriousness that lay underneath the fairly matter-of-fact language of the text.

"I want you to present it to the *gamra* assembly as soon as possible. Call an emergency sitting if there is none planned. Those willing to join us in the defence of our system will be welcomed. If it comes to an armed conflict, we will allocate privileges in accordance to their involvement."

I'd been afraid that he'd wanted me to do this, but what else could I say? It was yet another way in which people would say that I was a mouthpiece for Asto. "I will. There will be fireworks. The assembly will be hostile to this."

"There will be not nearly enough fireworks. We have to get rid of that idiot they voted in."

I nodded. I agreed. *Gamra* could never function with Delegate Namion at its head. "He's only been in the job for a very short period of time."

"Long enough," Ezhya said.

"Too long," was Asha's judgement. "Depose him. Immediately."

"I can't. I'm not . . ." *an influential figure.* Although I should probably acknowledge that I was becoming influential, in my own way. "I can't just . . ." *When the process has broken down measures must be taken to prevent further damage.* That was a quote from the *gamra* manual itself. If we could prove Delegate Namion's involvement with the Tamerians, then he was as good as gone, but one didn't make it to the top by being stupid and his tracks would be well covered.

I spread my hands. Let them sink again. If they thought I was going to stand for the position and challenge, they were wrong. I would never stand up to *gamra*'s constant scrutiny. I was not impartial. I was not made of endless patience. I had not covered any of my tracks.

In amongst all the conflicting feelings and thought that ran through me, I found some sanity.

"I know the *gamra* assembly well enough to know that they get easily distracted by details. Not that I call the attempted deposing of a Chief Delegate a minor detail, but compared to the approaching ship emergency, it is. Let's not try to distract them with internal politics. We can always depose him later. I dare say we don't even need to get our hands dirty in that process."

Ezhya nodded. He rubbed his upper lip, and then he nodded again. It was at times like this that he scared me most. I couldn't believe that I'd said something that he hadn't considered, yet he acted like I had, and as if he was arranging the pieces in his head.

"All right," he said. "Don't waste any time with the assembly. I have better things for you to do. I'll just send it to them, if I can use your equipment."

"Sure." At the same time it occurred to me that my *gamra* account was still routed through Delegate Namion's. That would be an interesting message for him to intercept.

Ezhya continued, "As for any matériel support, is there any group in the assembly you judge capable of giving us useful support?"

"Kedras is also in the Ratanga cluster. They're small, but they have the Trader Guild. Their new *gamra* representative is Kedrasi."

"Hmmm." A look passed between the two men.

Asha said, "The Trader Guild is not a military organisation."

"No. It's not. But they have a lot of ships."

"They do. Hmmm, not sure if I can do anything with that, but leave it with me."

Ezhya gave him one of those mysterious hand signals. Asha seemed happy.

"What about the captain?" I asked.

"We have him under strict observation. He will receive this document as well."

"He'll likely misinterpret it."

Ezhya snorted. "Misinterpret? How much clearer can we be about: do not come here or we'll blow you to pieces?"

"He hasn't shown any understanding about any of the things we've attempted to talk to him about."

"That's why it worries me that you have one of his crew here."

"She's been very helpful today. I would not have known all the things I just told you if it weren't for her."

"Nevertheless, I would be much happier if she were with the others under the guard of my people and not with that . . . fop."

"Look, I will take responsibility for them. They will stay here, guarded by my staff. They will not jeopardise our actions."

"The only way that man won't jeopardise anything is if he's dead."

If nothing else, that remark showed me absolutely how important loyalty was in Coldi society. Federza was perceived as wavering, untrustworthy. He had a lot of damage to repair, if it could be repaired at all.

"Please. I trust him. Leave both of them here."

"We'll see." That was by no means an encouraging reply, but the best I could hope for.

"Whatever we do must not preclude giving assistance to the ship crew who want to escape. The crew are not there of their volition and their supplies are low. They are weak and sickly. The mission to retake Asto is driven by the captain only. Let's not act in a similar manner to his actions when refusing to save people, if we can."

"If we can," Ezhya said. It was painfully clear that he thought we couldn't. "If the ship backs off when we issue threats. If he's willing to agree to restrictions on where the ship can travel."

Asha snorted. "What's the chance you'll get that sort of agreement out of a man who's stayed the same course for four hundred years?"

We let the answer hang between us.

Nicha looked decidedly disturbed.

Ezhya said, "We *will* fire if that ship turns up here and if the ship is unresponsive to our demands."

"I do wish that you'd consider a diplomatic solution, if I can broker it."

"Haven't you tried that already?" His voice was disturbingly serious.

"Yes. I may have gone about it the wrong way. The captain, I think, is a dead loss. I do not, in any way, endorse the assassination of anyone, and the captain is a major historic identity, but I guess I wouldn't be disturbed or surprised if somehow during skirmishes he didn't . . . survive."

Ezhya laughed a loud. It was a rare enough sound that it was both uplifting and threatening.

I went on, even though my ears were starting to betray me. Those damn ears. "I think there may be a reasonable chance that we can separate the crew from the captain, as long as there are no hostilities, as I understand from the crew member we had with us today that most of the crew will have left family behind."

"All the more reason that a second mission of theirs will eventually follow the first one."

"Which may not be a bad thing if, but only if, we can see the present mission to a peaceful end. From what I understand, the settlers of those new worlds have no love for the captain, and this appears to be one of the primary driving forces of his decision to make the return jump."

"He can't rule the people over there, so he wants to rule people over here."

"Pretty much."

"Whichever way, he wants to rule something."

"Yes."

"He's downstairs under guard. At the slightest order from me, any of these people here can go there and assassinate him. We can do that, if it solves anything in their internal hierarchy."

That was as close as Ezhya got to asking advice. "It's not entirely that simple. He *is* their absolute leader, but they use the term *bound to she ship*. This appears to relate to some kind of physiological connection. I don't know how this works, but the ship's systems appear to have a need to ensure the safety of those with this distinction. The woman we have in here is also bound. The ship might have been set to follow them regardless of what the outcome of their visit here was."

"How likely do you judge the chance that the crew will obey the captain?"

"Very high."

"If we take out the captain?"

"Even higher."

Asha made a hissing sound. "So, we have a ship unlikely to respond to a writ, already on its way here in response to the captain's distress or command. We have a dedicated crew who we can't access before they get here, who are unlikely to suddenly change allegiance anyway, and who are slaved to the captain and will carry out his commands, whether or not he's on board the ship."

I nodded. "Pretty much."

"And out in the Renzha galaxy, there is at least one, but possibly more, inhabited worlds of these people, possibly infused with truly alien genetic material, who might come after this ship?"

"I am not convinced *those* people would have any interest in coming here, or if they did, that they'd be hostile; but yes, that's what I understand."

Ezhya folded his hands and leaned forward on his knees. His expression was dead serious now. He looked at Asha in a way that made me feel small and insignificant. "Our first and foremost priority has to be to destroy their relay network so that they can't jump. It's a monumental task, and one that may be impossible."

"This is where I can see the Trader Guild being useful," Asha said.

Ezhya nodded. "Yes. I can see that."

Asha said, "Once they jump, destroying the ship may not be easy. If I had command on that ship, I would jump as close as possible to either planet as I dared, because any weapon that's going to destroy a ship that size can't safely be fired close to a planet's atmosphere."

"Anything that size can't jump close to a planet."

"Possibly. We have to run calculations on that."

"They can't. I want you to run calculations on any possible config-uration of the array of Exchange nodes that they have remaining out there. I want to know which are the most likely locations the ship will appear when it jumps with the array's current configuration, or if we can even speak of a configuration yet. I want to know which nodes we need to destroy to keep the jump from happening, if indeed that's possible."

"The larger ones," Asha said. "We've already been destroying as many as we can. Some are quite small, others much larger. We don't have the time to check what each node does, but it's safe to assume that the larger ones fulfil more important roles."

"What is your assessment of the structural integrity of that ship? What do we need to breach the hull?"

"They're well shielded. Their shield processes capture energy and feed it back into the engine, possibly also into weapons systems."

"As it would, with a deep space vessel. Can we overheat it?"

"Not with regular weapons. With the sling, maybe."

Ezhya nodded. "How fast can you bring it over?"

"It needs to go through six jumps."

"Time loss?"

"Without checking, my guess is about a day."

"Do it. Now."

Asha went quiet and his expression blank. I guessed the order went out to his fleet right this very moment and somewhere deep in space, people would be frantically packing and stowing and cleaning up a ship that was normally used for exploration and research purposes, now to be used as a prime weapon.

Ezhya was chillingly serious now. For thousands of years, Asto's society had deliberately selected the most physically able and mentally capable people in their top tiers of society. Children were born without Circle membership. Testing started at age five and for the top tiers, finished at seventeen. These two men were the smartest and toughest in all of Coldi society. I would argue in the entire galaxy. They calculated every step of their actions with consequences far down the track.

Their decision was to go to war.

Then Ezhya got up. "I guess that's it."

"What can I do?" I asked, and my voice sounded insecure. I hadn't realised how my jaw was trembling and I was sweating from the tension.

Ezhya faced me. For a moment I was wondering if he was going to question what I was doing there, because the preparation for war was sucking his attention to all three of his feeders at once. I felt very small, and insignificant, and utterly clueless on how to behave. These two men were so much more powerful than I was and I didn't understand why I had ever thought that I could call either of them a "friend".

There was turmoil in those gold-flecked eyes, and I could no longer meet them. I looked down, felt myself take up a subservient position even though I'd sworn that I would never do this unless I judged it wise, and only under pressure at that. That had been my human side speaking, my stubborn conviction that all people are equal and that I could match this man. I was stupid. I could not.

He didn't touch my shoulder, but a firm, thick-fingered hand moved into my field of vision and pushed my chin up. "I thought you wouldn't do that anymore except when protocol dictates."

I met the gold-flecked eyes. "I'm on very shaky ground. I can't say I've ever participated in a war council before."

He laughed out loud. "Neither have we."

"Tell me what I can do to help, with the understanding that I would be very much in favour of avoiding the firing of weapons. There are thousands of innocent civilians aboard that ship who never chose to come here and given the choice, would rather go back home."

"We do not favour that option either. If the sling can get here in time, it might not be strong enough to work. I'd prefer not to have to try. As for what you can do: I understand that there is a relay buried in an excavation site on the outskirts of town."

"There is."

"It appears important in terms of communication with the ship. It's bigger than the ones we've found in space, although we don't yet know why or how, mainly because that stupid council is keeping people away from the site. That scan you sent was helpful, but we haven't yet had the time to fully analyse it."

I nodded.

"At this stage, there is only one sensible thing that we should be doing with it: destroy it."

"Yes." Absolutely, I could do that.

"Then go. *Iyamichu ata*."

"*Iyamichu ata*." Into a real battle this time.

20

———————

THERE WAS NO TIME to lose.

Ezhya and Asha left to arrange their respective business. I understood that Ezhya would take full command of Asto's entire fleet, and would gather as many ships as could possibly make it back to Asto. If the sling could be back in time and if it was fired, he would do it.

After Asha had left the room, Ezhya said to me, "I don't envy your task. It's easy to go hunting and shooting things in the depth of space. They're often things that shouldn't have been there in the first place, and no one complains, even if it was a ship with troublesome occupants."

There had been suggestions that Asto's fleet had been hunting Tamerians, and this was as close as an admission that this had indeed been the case.

"All these things become massively more complicated when there are settlements and authorities involved. I would caution you to stay clear of the Barresh Council and the various powerful interest groups involved in this site. I would advise you to obtain the proper permits and have this relay, wherever it is, dismantled and taken apart to the level where the individual pieces just become parts and no longer fulfil the function they've been designed to fulfil. But we have no time for all of that. Therefore, go out there tonight. Take your association, make sure they are absolutely loyal to you, take arms and blast the thing to pieces. I have on my *gamra* account a prepared statement that I will send out the moment you get into trouble. It will be a notification that you've been relieved of your position so that you can be tried in the Barresh court and don't need to face the *gamra* court. It will arrive backdated two days ago. You can send that on as evidence that you were acting of your own accord. If you run into trouble."

"Delegate Namion still filters all my mail anyway."

He snorted. "When all this is over, I'll have a thing or two to say about that." He lowered his voice. "When this is done, I will call a council of supporters to make sure we get rid of this idiot. If by any chance you get an opportunity to do it earlier than that, by all means, go ahead. You have my full, utter, undivided support. This extends to taking you into protection and offering you unlimited residence in Athyl."

I met his eyes, my heart hammering. Shit, this was serious. Was he telling me that he would condone any of us assassinating Delegate Namion? I didn't even dare ask. Didn't want to go there. He *trusted* me, and that was so much appreciated.

There was a slightly awkward moment. He had to go, I had my work laid out for me. We might never see each other again.

We'd been through all the formalities, war declarations and protocol. A simple "goodbye" would never do. I held out my hand, and he clasped it in a bone-crushing grip—never shake hands with a Coldi person, Nicha used to joke, and by hell, how true that was. He put his other hand on my shoulder and held me briefly in a very human, very earthly hug.

Then he was gone, crossing the hall in fast strides, drawing his red-sashed guards from the hub room and the door. I would have thought the hug had been a dream, but I could still feel the warmth of his touch.

Right, then. To work.

I called, "Thay', Nich'!"

They had both been in the hub, and came to the door. "Everyone, in the living room."

They weren't used to me issuing orders, but they nodded, absolutely loyal. They knew that something very serious was up.

I asked Eirani to bring some refreshments up; and cakes, nibbles and tea arrived at the same time that people started turning up.

Nicha without his son, Thayu, Veyada and Sheydu who had been downstairs and Deyu and Reida who had been in the bath and came in wearing bathrobes and with wet hair.

Also Evi and Telaris.

We settled around the dining table. Eirani poured tea.

I began, "We have a nasty job to do tonight." And I continued with a summary of what Ezhya had told me and what we had to do.

"Shouldn't be too difficult," Reida said. "Usually there are only foreign guards at night. Usually Tamerians. They don't question or ask for more pay."

I asked him, "Do any of these Tamerians ever introduce themselves? Do they have names? Do they talk or mingle with others?" *Can they be talked around into cooperating because I hate killing people?*

He raised his eyebrows. "Very little. They give one-syllable names. Pok, Mil, Sang, names like that. I don't think they're real names. I don't think they're capable of holding a conversation or relating normally to people."

Sheydu nodded. "That concurs with my assessment. They're not superpeople. They might be strong and good at physical combat, but they have no skills in negotiation."

"They're made to blindly obey," Veyada said. "Like the Aghyrian crew themselves."

"They're not that good at fighting either," Reida said. "I haven't even done that much training but I bet I could could wrestle them to the ground."

"Now don't you go and take unnecessary risks, young man," Sheydu said. "The plan is we go in quick, do the job and out quick, before anyone sees us or before we run into trouble. No wrestling matches."

Reida nodded, leaning forward on the table. Absolutely loyal.

So the plan was deceptively simple. Go to the dig site, overwhelm the guards, preferably without killing them, and destroy the relay which Reida had shown was inside the ruins of the former ship.

Deyu then wanted to know why I was so obsessed with not killing the guards. "I mean, they're Tamerians, not really people at all."

I was going to reply, but Sheydu cut in. "Young lady, that is how the Aghyrians think about us, and once you start down that road, there really is no end to it."

Deyu had the grace to look ashamed, and I met Sheydu's eyes. Had I just been mistaken about them all along and did they understand me better than I thought?

"Killing people is a last resort," she said. "But when it needs to be done, it needs to be done."

There were nods around the table. It was just that the parameters for getting killed in Coldi society were so much more sensitive than on Earth or even in *gamra* society. Shooting first, ignoring a writ, or being deemed troublesome by a higher authority were all likely to get you killed, and of course once the *sheya* instinct came into play, laws no longer applied and all bets were off.

I handed the meeting to Sheydu, who spoke in brief sentences about weapons we would take—full armour and two guns for everyone, including me—and explosives she would carry. Her backup was Deyu, who nodded bravely, but looked terrified.

Thayu reported that the military astronomers had already started calculations to find the most likely spots where the ship would jump. They were compiling lists of relays that needed to be destroyed with urgency that would be drip-fed to the ships that needed them. The expectation was that this process would need to run half a day at least for calculating time, for crosschecks, for matching of items in the giant database of space junk.

She added, "But I expect the checking to go out the window when they get pressed for time. It's more important that they try to stop the ship than that they avoid taking out operational satellites."

Then Veyada reported on legal implications of conducting an attack on the island.

He reported, "Being on the island proper, and none of us being citizens of Barresh, we're all far outside our mandate. If the council wants to prosecute us for a hostile act, they can. If *gamra* hears of it, they will drag us to court."

I told them that Ezhya would send a backdated message to temporarily take us out of *gamra* duty if something went wrong. I presumed that if something went wrong in space as well, he had people on the ground to send it.

Veyada said, "All right, that takes us off the hook with *gamra*, but the Barresh Council will have classified the site as heritage property and there are conservation laws dealing with this listing. Barresh takes their history very seriously. They have arduous application processes if you simply want to see the site. Never mind blow a hole in it. We could apply to have the offending object removed, but that would probably take the best part of a year to clear the Heritage Committee, the Public Safety Committee and the Committee for Protection of Agricultural Habitat." He counted off on his fingers.

I stared at him. "Fuck all that. Let's go throw some bombs."

Nods. Coldi were people of action. They disliked endless talk. For all that the two people were on related branches in the tree of humanity, their personalities were vastly different.

I said, "We're going to be facing Tamerians."

Reida rubbed his hands. "I'm looking forward to that. Those guards were useless pricks."

Again, there were nods all around. If the Coldi absolutely had to acknowledge that someone else had created them, they wanted to push home the fact that they were more adaptable and stronger than other people

"Later, we might need to deal with people who financially support Tamerians." Like councillors, like Delegate Akhtari. We should get off our backside and move these Tamerians out of town.

"I will shoot them personally," Sheydu said. "They have no idea what they're playing with."

Her bravado was uplifting, but ultimately false. The people who supported the Tamerians were powerful *gamra* identities and would be unlikely to put themselves in a situation where they could be shot.

It was an occasion for full battle gear, with the rare added condition that none of us needed to hide the fact that we were armed.

I went with Thayu into the bedroom to get changed. I shed my wet clothes in the little bathroom that was attached to our bedroom, wondering if I'd ever wear them again.

You've wondered that so often in the last few years. Thayu came in. She was in her underwear, a short body-hugging singlet and a pair of loose shorts, both brown. Her metallic hair hung loose over her shoulders. "Need to get a hair tie."

I reached for her as she passed me. Her skin was warm and made me shiver.

"Hey, you look out of sorts." She sounded cheerful but I didn't miss the serious undertone.

"I don't think I've ever done anything more dangerous."

"Going into your president's office and searching through his records wasn't dangerous? Going to Asto wasn't dangerous? Defending the hub wasn't dangerous? Going into the ship?"

"You know what I mean. Those things were dangerous, but rarely affected a lot of other people if something went wrong."

She nodded. She did know.

I hugged her and the hug turned into a passionate kiss.

Then she said, "We will survive because we have the best people. If it comes to a conflict, Kando Luczon won't win, because his people only support him out of fear. When we take the fear away, there won't be any support left."

"I hope so." I couldn't face telling her what Ezhya had told me, especially about being given clearance to live in Athyl, which would be a very special kind of clearance indeed. I didn't want to alarm her.

I hoped that this was going to be over soon. My body didn't handle sleepless nights as well as it once had and just looking at that bed made me feel tired and gritty-eyed.

We went into the hall where a silent group was gathering. Everyone wore full battle gear. Telaris had even procured a military style gun. I wasn't sure the weapon was legal, but I didn't care. They were here to protect me, and we were going to destroy the relay, no matter what.

We discussed how to get there. The train was not a good idea because we'd be too visible. The ferry was gone, Sheydu informed me. If it had been day, it would have been picked up by some hapless council worker, but at this time of day, I assumed Ezhya and Asha had taken it to the sand bar where military ships landed on the water without knowledge of the Exchange.

Then Thayu came into the hall. "It's all organised."

She didn't say what, so I assumed some other type of boat.

We left the building, a tight group of heavily armed people. Thayu walked next to me, Nicha on my other side. Deyu and Reida were in front of us, and Sheydu and Veyada behind us. Evi was at the very front and Telaris at the back. It was a perfect unit, even in Coldi eyes. Sleek, symmetrical, a full association with two extra guards, a configuration Ezhya would use often.

We definitely weren't going towards the station. We weren't going to the water taxis either. I asked Thayu about that.

"Too risky," she said. "You never know how reliable the drivers are. Any who come to the *gamra* island might well be paid for information about who they picked up, where, and where they were taken. We're doing something different today."

I was wondering what that "something different" could be because it sounded ominous and not entirely without risk.

We crossed the main thoroughfare that ran across the island from the station to the assembly hall. We didn't talk much, but with all of us walking at a good pace, just our footsteps made enough noise to bring people to their windows to look. They were silhouettes against the light. I was sure many more watched in darkness.

About halfway down the passage, Thayu turned to the *gamra* domestic staff and maintenance quarters. I still had no idea where she was taking us.

Think agriculture, she said through the feeder.

Agriculture. There was plenty of agriculture around Barresh. Most of it involved some type of water farming, often using enclosed field like paddies. Most local crops grew or floated in the water. The people of Barresh had farmed this area for thousands of years. They used low, keelless punts to ferry their harvest to town, but recently some larger commercial farms had started up, and they used—

Damn it.

You know?

Yes. Solar planes.

Not much later, we arrived at the place where they stood, black and silver lightweight structures such as flew over lily crops spraying fertilisers. These particular vehicles, though, did not belong to farmers but bore the logo of the island's security.

"I didn't even know security had these things," I said.

"You wouldn't, because ironically, they fly them at night. On battery."

Obviously.

"They are ideal for night surveillance. They make very little noise and are slow enough to allow for crew to take observations on the ground."

Telaris groaned. "Why do these things remind me of some place I prefer not to remember?"

Yes, one day that seemed much longer ago than it was, we had flown around a hot and horrible part of eastern Africa in one of these things, although that particular plane had been of Indrahui make. We'd crashed it in the desert, we'd attempted to fix it, we'd been caught by some very unsavoury characters. We'd been brought to the place in the desert that was a mansion, a bunker, a factory and a prison all in one. We'd . . . killed a few people.

My stomach *still* churned at the thought. Do you know what happens when you repeatedly fire a charge gun at a person and their insides evaporate into steam?

Trust me, it's better not to know.

Damn it, I really didn't want to think of this right now.

But I did wonder what had become of Henri, the cocky Canadian-Ethiopian pilot.

A group our size required two planes. Thayu was going to fly one, Sheydu the other. I had learned that all of Ezhya's guards had to learn to fly, so we had a backup pilot in Veyada.

I went with Thayu, Nicha, Deyu and Reida. Thayu didn't like having both Evi and Telaris in the other plane, but they were both big and heavy and we had one more passenger, so we needed to have the lightest people.

Thayu had clearly flown one of these things before. I knew she went out for nebulous "training" activities, but hadn't been able to picture just what she did until now.

We all climbed in by a tiny little light from Nicha's comm. He was handing out night vision goggles at the door. Thayu, Reida and Deyu each got one, but he didn't have enough for me. Deyu offered me hers, but I told her to keep it. Coldi night vision was notoriously poor, and they were the ones who would have to do the shooting if there was any shooting to be done.

The seats were cramped, with a narrow space down the middle that didn't deserve the name *aisle*. The plane wobbled ominously when Nicha shut the door and wriggled into the seat next to Thayu.

We took off after the other plane and glided low over the water. Nicha instructed us to have weapons accessible.

"We land around the point and approach from an angle that's out of view from the dig site."

The latter meant flying all the way around the island past the airport—low under the approach path I assumed—and around the northern side of the island, maybe even around Far Atok because we couldn't fly through the channel between the two islands and we weren't allowed to fly over the city.

It was an eerily pretty route even in the dark. The giant trees wouldn't come into flower until the very start of the wet season, and they were now virtually leafless waiting for that to happen. They stood like skeletons against the streetlights. Occasional houses displayed lights on the porch or in upstairs windows. Sometimes a person walked on the street. It was past midnight and even the eateries had long since closed and sent their staff home.

It was warm in the cabin, and I grew very sleepy.

Next thing I knew we were skimming low over the surface of the marsh and moonlit water rushed past just below the cabin.

Damn, I'd fallen asleep.

The bottom of the plane must have already bounced off the water once, which is what had woken me up. I pushed myself straight in my seat.

I felt hot and sweaty and guilty, because Thayu hadn't seemed able to sleep, and I felt I shouldn't sleep then, either.

The plane hit the water again and slowed so much that it floated to a stop. Thayu gunned the engine to push the plane as far into the reeds as it would go. She got up and opened the door. Cool dry air came in.

"Guess what? We'll be getting wet."

I was happy that I had listened to the advice to put on my temperature-retaining suit and my waterproof boots. They were hot right now, but it would get cooler very soon, especially if we ended up getting wet again.

The little nap had refreshed me somewhat and I felt clear-headed when I jumped after Thayu and Nicha. When Reida and Deyu were out as well, we could drag the plane even further into the reeds.

"That won't be going anywhere soon," Thayu said.

I wanted to ask what would happen if we needed to get out in a hurry, but Thayu said the planes would be picked up by island security regardless of what we did. We would not be using them to get back. It looked like everything was under control.

The other plane had already landed, but it was too dark to see where the others were and I had to keep my attention on following Thayu as she pushed through the reeds.

The ground was soft and wet, and walking over a thick and springy carpet of decaying leaves was a slippery affair. We didn't want to use comm lights so the feeble light of one of Ceren's little moons was all we had. Wearing the infrared goggles, Thayu could possibly see more than I did. She would see where the others were, and indeed when we stepped out of the reeds onto a small beach, there they were, seated on the sand, a couple of dark silhouettes barely visible to me.

"Did you check it out?" Thayu asked.

"I did." This disembodied voice was Sheydu's. "There is a lot of activity at the site."

"What? At this time of the day?" I asked.

"Look here." She held up her IR scan screen, which showed the point of the island seen from the air. The water came up as black in the projection. The beach was grey, because it still radiated heat from the evening. A bunch of lighter grey blotches represented the houses that backed onto the beach. The tent showed up as a bright and clearly demarcated grey square, surrounded by a good number of light grey dots. Some were even people-shaped.

"Seventeen of them," she said. "More than what Reida told us."

Another question: had they possibly seen us?

"What do they all guard this place *from?*"

"Isn't that the question everyone wants to know?" Thayu said.

"And why is that light in the tent still on?"

No one knew the answer to that.

Reida said, "When I was here, no one ever spoke about a night shift at all. You just would see the Tamerians arrive. Usually not more than two or three."

"They were not appointed by the council, were they?"

"Most people assumed that they were. The rumour went that they were sick of keihu men not wanting to work at all and not doing the job properly if they did."

The cliché that keihu were lazy really needed to go and die in a hole. It was utter rubbish.

"But?" I prompted him.

"It does seem strange, looking back. Presumably, the council would have to pay the Tamerians more than the locals. Why would they do that?"

The unspoken truth hung between us: because someone in power knew that there was something valuable at the site.

"It puts us in a difficult situation," Sheydu said. "We were counting on two or three Tamerians. There are seventeen. They have excellent night vision. They have an elevated position. The distance between us and them is exposed marshland where we can't run or hide."

Reida said, "Everyone keeps banging on about this night vision—"

Sheydu spread her hands. "Because compared to them, we can't see a fucking thing at night, even with these dreadful goggles—"

"I know, right? But we get others in with ever better night vision."

Sheydu let her hands drop. "Others?"

"Leave it to me. They're on their way."

"They're what? You have a bunch of Pengali turning up? Why would they help us?"

"Because this is *their* town, too, and they've been excluded from any decision-making."

And Pengali, I remembered reading somewhere, were great at rallying behind causes. Once they believed in something, they were the best rent-a-crowd, bar none. It was getting them to that stage that was the hard bit. Whatever did Reida used to do during his nocturnal trips to town, in which he frequently ended up being arrested by the Barresh guards?

He was very closely related to the *zeyshi* I reminded myself, and *they* had developed into a powerhouse in the hugely populous Outer Circle.

Sheydu was drawing something on her reader and showed it to us. It was a map.

"Unless you can tell us exactly when and where these Pengali are going to show up, we'll have to do this alone. We don't have much time until daylight and it's got to be done before the first crack of dawn."

"They will be here before then."

"If you say so. But meanwhile we'll plan as if they won't, or won't be much use. All of us will go in armed and ready. There will be no wussing about sparing lives." I believe she directed that at me. "There will be dead bodies. Ideally, there will be seventeen of them, and none of them will be any of us."

Damn, I was starting to feel sick. Ezhya had spoken of how the political fallout and aftermath of this worried him, but I preferred that to a shooting match.

We divided in smaller groups, each with a clearly defined task. I was with Thayu and Telaris and we were supposed to make our way to the site in as straight a line as possible. Good. We could manage that.

We were not meant to fire unless in absolute self-defence, at least not before they knew of our location.

Once on the site, it would be my task to distract the guards with talk, while Sheydu organised the explosives.

What should I talk about? I asked.

That was up to me. Whatever I could think of as reason why the three of us would be clambering out of a marsh in the middle of the night.

Yup. Because that's what silly *gamra* delegates do. They take nightly trips and get themselves stranded in places where no one has any reason to be at pretty much any time of the day.

We went fishing or something, Thayu said.

Except I didn't fish.

Now you do. And you got hungry and there was no fish in the house.

That's just lame.

The purpose is to keep them talking and distract them, not to provide a credible excuse.

True. But could one even talk to Tamerians?

So much potential for things to go horribly wrong.

Several groups split off straight away. Nicha went with Evi, and Reida and Deyu went off together—into town by the look of things. Veyada and Sheydu stayed with us. Sheydu carried her pack with many pockets that bristled with gear. She made an effort to walk lightly, but I guessed the pack was really heavy.

Our group walked along the beach until we reached a small sandy outcrop where a couple of megon trees grew.

The megon tree had been found to be an extremely distant relative of the paperbark trees on Earth which in turn had its roots in now-extinct tree species that used to grow on the edges of rivers in

Athyl—the Aghyrian first wave colony-seeders never *just* sent people. They sent entire colonisation packages which included seeds of crops. In its natural state, the tree usually consisted of one or multiple straight trunks with weeping branches, like a wilted, sad-looking pipe-cleaner brush. It also had peeling bark which locals used for making cardboard. But unless cleaned, harvested and pruned, it was a scruffy kind of tree, and the few specimens on the point were every bit typical representatives.

Because it was the end of the dry season, they were also in flower, and the heavy scent hung over the water. The oil that exuded this scent was sold as a fire retardant all over the settled worlds.

It also meant that we could not use the trees as cover, because the oil would mess with the firing reliability of our weapons.

So we stuck to the edge of the sandy beach, where it was very open and exposed and the reeds were low and there was a muddy exposed tidal area where a couple of ringgit did their noisy mating call.

We rounded the point and were met by the sight of the brightly-lit tent. There were people hanging around outside it, people silhouetted by the bright lights inside, people patrolling the walkway and the bridge from the shore to the train station. The train platform was brightly lit, even though there was no train in sight.

A shout rang out somewhere at the site.

And that's when all hell broke loose.

21

—————

SEVERAL PEOPLE in different parts of the site opened fire in our direction.

Thayu pushed me down faster than I could drop myself. I landed on my belly in a patch of sand.

Oof.

At least it wasn't mud.

Charges flew over our heads, bright trails in the darkness that petered out somewhere behind us. One stream hit a branch of a tree a short distance from us. It exploded in a shower of sparks, but they went out long before they hit the ground.

"Shit," Thayu said. "They're doing that on purpose because that's going to release a lot of oil into the air. I hope Veyada and Sheydu can get their weapons covered in time."

Thayu peered in the direction of the trees. She was wearing a pair of infrared goggles without which she would be virtually blind. Of course Tamerians had excellent night vision. We had not yet discovered what their weakness was.

Evi and Telaris were our night-vision specialists. Evi had gone with Nicha—I had no idea where they were—and Telaris lay on his belly behind a log a few steps in front of us. His gun rested on the log. The safety was off, which I knew because the tiny light on the back of the grip was orange. Telaris concentrated on the headgear that he wore that would be projecting an image that only he could see. He moved the gun accordingly. Apparently someone walked from left to right, but I didn't see them.

Someone to the right of us fired at the dig site.

And again.

Both charges hit the timber structure that surrounded the white tent. There were no people on this part of the walkway. I guessed the shots had been fired by Sheydu with the heavy gun, in order to take out one of the escape routes from the tent.

A guard at the walkway returned two shots, but they hit the reed beds harmlessly. At least I hoped. I didn't know where Evi and Nicha were.

A couple of people came out of the tent to look. The sound of voices drifted on the night air. I wondered what language they spoke. I wondered what they said. I hadn't, to date, heard a Tamerian say anything at all.

They spread out over the walkway, moving slowly, alert, watching and listening.

Thayu started crawling forward. I was afraid that I'd lose track of her, so I followed close behind. We passed Telaris, who looked like he was going to provide cover for us.

My heart was thudding like crazy. This sort of stuff was definitely not my thing, although I found myself doing it with disturbing frequency. Each time, when it happened, I had the same thoughts: I should get some training. I should get a heavier gun. The weapon in the bracket on my arm wasn't even mine. It belonged to the team. I didn't own any guns, because, you know, *guns!* but I was rapidly losing count of how many times guns had saved my ignorant, self-righteous butt, and I really, like *really*, should do something about getting a dedicated, fitted and weighted weapon for myself.

Next week.

If, at that time, I was still alive.

And if I was, I would probably forget about it.

Until next time.

I looked over my shoulder, but it was too dark to see any of the others: Telaris and his gun and Veyada and Sheydu.

I hoped they had everything under control. I was only in contact with Thayu, who told me through the feeder to stop worrying and keep crawling.

But it was so exposed and they were going to see us.

We've got it all going as planned.

Glad to know it. Better if I knew how they were going to stop those Tamerians shooting our sorry butts.

Stop worrying.

But I had to worry. I was a diplomat, not a commando fighter. Yeah, yeah, I should learn a bit more of this stuff.

Dog, meet tail.

A fairly long period followed when we crawled through the reeds. Thayu was going too fast for me to attempt to be silent. I slipped. I got wet—again.

Two guards stood on the walkway between us and the tent. We could see them clearly because the tent stood out like a bright yellow rectangle with the glow of light inside. Both men were peering into the darkness, clearly expecting trouble. Sometimes one of them stopped and used binoculars or a scanner and transferred the image to a reader. I could see the blue-green glow of the screen. He would look at it and then he would walk a few paces and repeat the process.

Maybe they were waiting for reinforcements.

A moment later that reinforcement arrived. Footsteps echoed in the stillness, and another guard came down the walkway that led to the station. Where had he come from? I hadn't seen a train arrive. In fact I was positive there hadn't been a train.

The new guard passed a few others, greeting them as he continued on, and rounded the corner to the side of the tent that faced us directly, where the two other guards were still peering into the darkness.

The newcomer said something.

The two guards turned to him—

And the new guard fired a gun, twice, in close succession. Both guards fell.

People shouted all over the site. Heavy footsteps thudded on the wooden walkway. Men came from around the corner.

Someone else in dark clothing climbed onto the walkway from the reed beds below. This figure moved in a lithe and cat-like manner. Coldi, likely female. I would have thought it was Thayu, but she was still with me. In quick succession, she despatched three of the men, while a fourth was shot by her partner. The Coldi woman was Deyu, and the first fake guard was Reida, of course.

A flap opened and a guard came from inside the tent.

He was hit in the chest by a beam from somewhere to our left, towards the water. I hadn't realised that anyone from our party was out there. In fact, someone fired from our right-hand side and I was almost certain that this was either Nicha or Evi. I couldn't see Veyada and Sheydu anymore, but they could never have travelled that distance in the short time since they had been with us under the megon trees. They were Coldi. They would never choose to go into the water of their own volition. That shot had come all the way from where the railway tracks were.

A couple more Tamerians ran to that side of the tent. I saw a weapon being fired somewhere over the water. I saw the streak of light fly over the water. It struck the side of the tent, the walkway and the guards all at once. The walkway collapsed. A man screamed. Something heavy hit the water.

A guard fled the scene, but a second streak of light hit him. That part of the walkway collapsed, too. Someone was splashing around in the water, calling out, but his voice stopped when a third streak hit him.

Holy crap, that was some sharp shooter there.

It seems Reida's local backup has arrived, Thayu said. *Stay close to me.* I could feel that she was very cautious about this support.

I didn't need to be told twice. Telaris had now also joined us.

Do you know who these people are? I asked Thayu.

Pengali is all I can guess. He's got a lot of friends in places in town where you or I would never get a foot on the ground.

I figured as much.

She added, *It's why they're here that worries me.*

I got that.

We kept going forward. We hit a patch of reeds where the water was thigh-deep and we had to wade holding our guns above our heads. Just as I was looking forward not to getting wet anymore.

A tense silence hung over the marshland in which our sopping footsteps sounded incredibly loud. Just as well there weren't any Tamerian guards left in a position to fight because we were in the open, terribly exposed, with nowhere to go.

Thayu whistled. Reida or Deyu whistled back. A tiny light went on. Someone whispered, "Quick!"

Deyu.

Thayu splashed through the remaining muddy ground to the walkway. She climbed up, helped by an outstretched hand from Deyu.

"Come up here now." Thayu stuck a hand over the edge and, when I grabbed it, hauled me up to the level of the railing with one arm. I climbed over the railing. The wooden boards felt dry and solid under my feet after ploughing through that mud. By the muted light that filtered through the tent's fabric, I could see the muddy state of my boots. For crying out loud, that was two pairs ruined today.

"Anything going on inside?" I asked.

There were some thumps from Telaris making his way onto the walkway.

"It's been quiet," Deyu said. "We haven't been inside yet. These guys were kind of defending the tent." Not very well, she clearly thought.

"Where are the others?"

"Nicha and Evi are on the other side. Sheydu and Veyada are just coming up now." I followed where she looked with her night vision goggles. She was right. Veyada was just helping Sheydu up.

"Who was shooting over there?" I gestured at the blackness of the night away from the island where a faint glimmer of moonlight reflected off the water.

"Just some of our friends."

"Pengali?"

"Anything wrong with that?"

"Are they in a boat?"

"No, they're on the rails."

Of the train that went out there. Holy crap. "What if a train comes?"

"There aren't many this time of day."

True.

"Pengali are smart and they can climb really well."

I formed a mental picture of a bunch of Pengali in tribal outfit perched on the struts that supported the track bed. That would work, if they had a means of getting up there. Except the tribal outfit. They would probably be wearing something sensible and dark. Or, being

Pengali and in possession of beautifully-patterned skin, very little at all.

Thayu walked over to the tent flap, but the body of a Tamerian guard lay in front. "Move him out of the way," she said to Deyu, who went about doing it, dragging the man by his feet to the far side of the walkway. She was going to push him in the water, but he wouldn't fit between the boards and the lowest beam on the fence, so she left him there.

Truly, no one cared about Tamerians. There would be no family—he probably had none—and his body, and that of the others, would most likely be pushed out into the marshes on a joint burial float with no gifts and no flowers.

I didn't know why I thought about this. I guessed it disturbed me that so many Tamerian deaths had gone unreported and bodies had been left unclaimed. I couldn't get my head around the fact that no one seemed to care.

Thayu pushed up her night-vision goggles and peeked through the gap between two pieces of heavy fabric. "There are people inside."

Shit. "Are there? What are they doing there?"

"Right now? Hiding under the tables."

"How many?"

"Sixteen or so. Have a look."

She moved aside so that I could get to the flap. I carefully lifted the fabric.

Around the perimeter of the tent was a second walkway that surrounded a rectangular hole which I presumed to be the dig site. Along much of this walkway stood long tables with light suspended above them. Bathing in the glow were hundreds of flat trays, each containing a thin layer of soil. The lights produced warmth that dried the mud, I guessed.

At the far end of the tent, opposite from where I stood, a number of people had been picking little fragments out of these trays of dirt, if the vials and tweezers on the table were anything to go by.

Chairs were strewn over the walkway and the people, wearing coats, facemasks and gloves, cowered under the tables, casting fearful looks to our side of the tent. They were ordinary people, research assistants. Keihu, Pengali, Kedrasi. Just doing their jobs.

Shit. Getting innocent civilians caught in this project wasn't part of the plan. That was why we were here at night. I dropped the tent flap into place.

"What are they doing here at this time of the day?"

"Don't ask me," Thayu said.

"What are we going to do about them?" Reida had assured me that there were only Tamerians guarding the site at night. Those we could shoot. We had not planned on having to deal with innocent civilians.

"Move them out before we blow the thing up," Sheydu said.

Count on her to make a blunt remark. Never mind that she was right, and never mind how we were going to get them far enough away that they wouldn't see the explosion and wouldn't have questions that might get certain people—like the Barresh Council—to interfere with what we were trying to do. We really couldn't use *witnesses*.

But did we have an option? "All right. Who's going to do the moving? I don't want any of us to be recognised." Evi and Telaris, especially, were well-known in town as my guards. Everyone knew Thayu and Nicha, too.

"Reida will do it," Thayu said, having been privy to my thoughts through our feeders and agreeing with them.

She gestured Reida over. He was quite a sight. Muddy, wet and covered in sticks as we were, carrying a military-style weapon that I was sure wasn't his and belonged to no one in our household. He was bleeding from a cut to his cheekbone, and his attempt at wiping the blood had only distributed it all over his face.

Thayu spoke briefly to him in a low voice. I made no attempt to listen in. Most of it would be in spy code. Reida understood. His face looked solemn. He might be keen to measure himself with a Tamerian —and his muscled arms looked so impressive that I would hate to be that Tamerian—but he definitely didn't see fighting as enjoyable or frivolous. Asha was right. That young man had come a long way, both as a fighter and a provider of mysterious Pengali backup.

He turned around and held up two fingers.

Thayu whirled around, aiming her gun at the darkness. With barely any sound, a small figure climbed onto the walkway, followed by a second one. Both female, near-naked, Pengali and carrying fearsome guns.

They were much smaller than any of us and they regarded us with their huge, roving brown eyes. Both dipped their head in greeting to me. One of them waved her tail over her shoulder in the way Pengali greeted each other.

I said, "I'm honoured to have your help." I didn't speak their language beyond a few words relating to food—another thing on my long *if I have some time* list.

Both followed Reida into the tent.

The people under the table huddled closer together. A keihu man at the front of the group shouted. "Don't come any closer!" He held a piece of wood.

"The boss says you have to leave," Reida said.

"We're not going anywhere," the man said.

"You don't understand. You are *going* to leave. I'm not asking. I'm ordering."

"I have my orders, too. This site is ancient and precious. It belongs to the people of Barresh and not to you filthy . . ." He was getting agitated. His eyes were wide. I wondered if he'd taken something or what possessed him.

"Get. Out! Or I'll use this." Reida held up the gun. He strode in big steps towards the table.

A woman squeaked and crawled out from underneath the table. She ran for the exit in the far corner. A young man followed her, and so did a middle-aged Kedrasi woman, who was still wearing her face-mask. The man with the piece of wood was shouting at them not to abandon their principles and let a dirty foreigner dictate what happened to a precious historical site.

"Get out, get out!" Reida shouted at the remaining people.

One by one, they all chose safety over historical treasures, until the only one left was the man with the piece of wood. He drew himself up, waving the wood in front of him. He was taller than Reida, but faced with a Coldi young fighter holding a gun, the gesture was ridiculous. His entire behaviour was ridiculous.

"Come on, man, go," Reida said, annoyed, gesturing with the gun.

"You can't make me." His face was set in a stubborn expression.

Reida pointed the gun at him. "You want to feel the end of this?"

The man said nothing. He stood perfectly still for a little while, staring, wide-eyed, at the business end of the gun. Definitely not in his right mind.

Something must have clicked in his brain, because he lowered the piece of wood.

He retreated a step, and then another.

Reida followed him, still pointing the gun.

"Yeah, yeah, I'm going." The man dropped the wood on the walk-way. He retreated faster in the direction of the exit.

I gestured at Sheydu to come over with her gear. She hefted the pack onto her shoulder, ready to go in.

The man had reached the exit, but when he was about to go through, he almost crashed into someone who came in from outside. Someone with a gun. Not one of our group. A guard. *Not* Tamerian. Damn.

He called out, "What's the meaning of this?"

All of a sudden, there was a lot of action. The crazy researcher ran outside. Other people ran in. Guards, dressed in grey with the *gamra* blue band around both arms.

In amongst them, a tall man in a flowing blue robe entered the tent.

Oh, shit. What the hell was Delegate Namion doing here?

22

———————

EVERYONE FROZE. Delegate Namion and his guards on one side, Reida and his two Pengali assistants on the other.

Delegate Namion looked pointedly at Reida's gun, still levelled at chest height, where a moment ago the nervous research worker had been backing away, and where it now pointed at the Chief Delegate.

Reida lowered his gun, mumbling an apology. My heart was thudding. Reida had a lot still to learn about *gamra* protocol. I was pretty sure that *he* wouldn't easily be forced into doing silly things with that weapon, but I wasn't so sure about the Delegate's nervous guards.

Reida and his two friends retreated slowly to our side of the tent. Faced with a couple of heavily armed *gamra* guards, there was nothing they could do.

There was nothing any of my association could do. Only I could handle this situation. I pushed the tent flap aside and entered the brightly lit space.

The Delegate's guards turned to me, raising their weapons, but lowered them again. One of them nodded a greeting. "Delegate."

Delegate Namion raised his eyebrows, and the greenish glow from the lights above the abandoned tables made his tigerlike irises—yellow with a black rim—even more yellow. Even without the harsh light, he looked like a scarecrow.

"Well, this is quite an interesting occasion, meeting you here," he said. The tone in his voice betrayed his surprise, and it didn't sound like it was a pleasant surprise.

I bowed. Not strictly necessary, but giving me time to think. Seriously, what the *fuck* was he doing here? "That sentiment is mutual. I was told only council workers could come here."

"Clearly," he said. "And that's why you're here at this odd time? Snooping into the site where you've been told not to come? Really, does that justify the dead bodies outside?"

"We'll talk about them if we can find any who are not illegal Tamerians."

"They're appointed by the council. They have nothing to do with me." It was a very curt reply.

Liar. "By the council? Aren't there enough local young men out of work? Does the job require thugs of this calibre? Just what are they protecting the site from?"

"Tell me, Delegate Wilson, what *you* are doing here, completely outside your authority, I should add."

Out of all the things I could have told him, I decided to tell the truth. "I'm here to destroy this thing."

He took in a sharp breath. Stared at me. Whatever he had expected, *that* was clearly not it. "Surely you are kidding?" His voice was soft. Genuine surprise this time.

"I wish I were."

"But I don't understand. This site contains historical artefacts thousands of years old."

"Yes. One item has to be destroyed, urgently."

He huffed. *"Has* to? Who says that?"

I made an attempt to explain about the array, and that the ship was going to use it to jump. I was forced to leave out huge chunks of information that involved things that I didn't want to tell him, things that he knew, but I couldn't let him know that we knew them, too, and things that were related to his activities that might lead to defamation claims from his side until such time that we could prove them.

Without these things, my story was incomplete and didn't make much sense. His expression showed it. This was a disaster. We couldn't possibly have run into a worse person here.

He spread his hands in a theatrical gesture, as he did when he spoke to the assembly. "And that is why you want to destroy this ancient artefact? So that the captain can't get his hands on it? So that a ship that's powerful enough to jump outside the *galaxy* can't return here? They can jump here any time they want. They don't need whatever it is that's small enough to have been carried here in this ship."

"They can't. They're too big and it would be too risky that they hit something. They need this array."

He huffed again. "But then to destroy this thing . . . I would have thought you to possess more sense than that. Especially to come here in the middle of the night to do it. Illegally. You know what the inside of the Barresh jail looks like?"

I did, but wasn't going to enlighten him. "Ultimately, it is necessary because the captain has not come here in peace."

"No, of course not. He wants his planet back—"

"Which is a ridiculous claim—"

"Which is a valid claim."

"Have you asked him what he plans to do with the Coldi people? *Fix their genes*, because apparently, they are faulty. Haven't you listened to what he thinks of anyone else, including you or I? Don't allow him to fool the assembly into thinking that if he doesn't think much of the Coldi, he's part of your team by default. Because he's not. There is only one team he's on: his own. And I'm not even sure it's a team. The two people with him are slaves. This man does not come in peace."

"And that is a reason to destroy this significant historical site?"

"It would be a pity about the site. It's equal to the one in Miran—"

"Ha! Miran." He obviously didn't think much of *them* either.

"And there are a number of very similar sites on Asto. Much is known about the original design of the ship that can't be gleaned from this site and the state it's in. It's really *not* well-preserved, and the only thing that is preserved at this site is dangerous."

"How do you know all that? You're not a historian. Why don't we take a real expert's view on that? Oh, but you've just chased them all away with your armed thugs."

"Please. We don't have time. The array is reconfiguring. The ship will jump as soon as it's done—"

"But this is a major historical site!"

"The future is always more important than the past." A Coldi proverb.

He snorted. "I know what team *you're* on. You're rubbish. Your reasons are rubbish. You're not impartial. Everything you say is rubbish, and you know it. Have a look at this."

He walked a few paces to one of the long tables and flicked a lever up. A couple of bright spotlights came on near the ceiling in the middle of the tent.

They lit a rectangular area cordoned off by metal plates driven into the soft marshy ground, the gaps between them sealed by bright blue building putty. A pump hummed while keeping the water level down.

A wooden staircase went from the perimeter walkway into the site, where it ended at a platform that hung over the muddy ground. A couple of smaller platforms hung suspended over the ground from beams that spanned the area from one side of the perimeter walkway to the other, so that people could access the site without stepping on anything.

Most of the ground inside the excavation was muddy, with little fragments of rusty metal and other bits visible as little specks from where I stood. Someone had put out pegs with flags on top, presumably to outline the shape of what had once been a ship.

The remains were so fragile that if someone had dug through it by accident, they would barely have noticed.

With the exception of the dirt-encrusted object in the middle of the site.

If I hadn't known any better, I would have judged the dark lump to be a barnacle-encrusted rock, half out of the ground. Except there were no rocks in Barresh.

The thing was dark and slimy-looking, covered in so much marine growth and encrustation that it obscured the shape. Someone had put little posts around it.

That had to be the thing that Kando Luczon had been looking for. Perhaps the thing that the Tamerians had been looking for. The relay that had responded to the signal from the ship.

"That is the thing we need to destroy. If you step aside and we get some time, we could dig it out and—"

"Dig it out? Never!"

Oh, crap, it was so easy to annoy this man. Everything about him seemed to be designed to rub people the wrong way. Maybe he'd been voted in because people figured he'd annoy everyone so much that he wouldn't last long, buying various groups a bit of time to mount a proper election campaign. Maybe he knew that, too, and had resolved to be as annoying as he could possibly be within the short space of time that he was in the job.

I should *not* let him rile me so much.

"Inside that lump of growths is the thing that sent the burst that almost fried the Exchange and that made a wall collapse."

He snorted. "That? I'm sorry, but if there is any piece of equipment in that rock, it has long since stopped working. I'm sure you have seen the state of the rest of the ship."

"I'm sure you have seen the scan of the site. The captain has confirmed to me that this thing is here. The ship communicated with it. There are satellites up there in orbit around us and around Asto, and there are ones trailing us and Asto at the LaGrange points. Most of those look like pieces of space junk no bigger than a fist. We've managed to learn from the captain's companions that those pieces are manoeuvring into position to form an array of Exchange nodes which will allow the big ship to jump. This here in the ground is a vitally important node because of where it is and because of its size."

He again eyed the lump in the sand as if rearranging his thoughts. I saw it as a hopeful sign. He *had* to be reasonably smart to have made it this far.

I continued, "Right now, a lot of people are working very hard to destroy as many relays as possible. I'm sure you read the statement Ezhya Palayi sent from my account to the *gamra* assembly."

He snorted. "I *highly* disagree with this kind of unilateral action."

"They do have the right to defend their own world."

"But why the hostility? That will only provoke the aggression that Asto so dearly wishes to see. Why go to such lengths to stop them? They will come anyway. We have no technology to stop them. I can only imagine that you want to stop the ship jumping because the Aghyrians will want to displace the Coldi."

"These Aghyrians want to displace *all* of us. These people do not come here in peace. They come here to wage war."

He snorted. "Well. That's news to me. Why haven't you raised that with the assembly? We could have instated a negotiating team."

What do you think I've been doing? "The most damning evidence against the Aghyrians has only come to light overnight. We heard from Marin Federza."

"Marin . . . Federza?" *That* seemed to shake him. "He's . . . not here, is he? He's gone . . . to Guild headquarters at Kedras, hasn't he?"

"Yes," I lied.

I would have laughed at the utterly confused face he pulled had the situation not been so serious. I would love to have known what he'd been told about Federza. Something that was obviously a lie, because he seemed genuinely surprised.

"Federza had some very interesting data that I will be presenting at the next assembly, but first, I have to make sure that we will still *have* an assembly. We have to stop that ship coming into the system. Step aside, and let us destroy the relay."

"Never." He crossed his arms over his chest.

"But I explained to you—"

"A lot of tall tales and false accusations, that's what you told us. Nothing substantial."

"Oh, there will be plenty of substantial evidence." *Including evidence against you.* "I would go to the assembly if there were time. I would even call for an emergency meeting, but we don't have that time. We have to destroy this thing as soon as possible. Before the array can form and the ship jumps. Tonight. So please stand aside and let us—"

"No." He placed himself at the top of the stairs that went down to the dig site. "If you do that, you'll have to destroy me, too."

"Don't be stupid."

"You dare call me stupid? Do you even know what you are saying? Do you know that I have the power to sack you and send you home to your miserable little planet, or better still I'll send you to Asto since you seem to love them so much."

A strange wailing sound echoed over the water outside. The walkway thudded with the sound of people running.

"What was that?" Delegate Namion said, turning his head to listen.

A high-pitched squealing noise echoed over the water.

People yelled in the distance.

23

———————

I **HAD NO IDEA** what was going on. The sounds and voices were unfamiliar, not close enough to be anywhere near the tent.

One of Delegate Namion's guards went to have a look—and came back a moment later, pushing a Pengali youth in front of him, holding him by the hair. The young man kicked and tried to yank his hair free. His tail lashed up and around the guard's arms. The guard grabbed the tail and pulled it until the young man's feet almost left the ground.

You did *not* hold a Pengali by the tail. A woman, also Pengali, ran into the tent letting out an angry shriek, attempting to stab the guard with a fearfully sharp diamond knife. The guard tried to fend her off with his free arm. He wore armour, clearly.

Delegate Namion retreated while this fight was going on.

In the chaos, I gestured to Sheydu, who was looking in through the tent flap on the other side. I gestured, *Quick*.

She ran across the walkway and jumped over the side railing onto the platform below, landing with a heavy thud that made the planks under my feet shudder. Coldi strength never ceased to amaze me. If I'd have tried that, I would have broken both my legs.

She slid the pack from her shoulder.

Two more Pengali had entered the tent, as well as another guard in response to calls for help from the first. They had restrained the woman with the knife, but the youth had managed to free himself.

Delegate Namion had retreated behind the tables where the researchers had been working. He was shouting at all of them to go outside and continue their fight there, while the guards struggled to get the situation under control. They were *gamra* guards, both Damarcian. I didn't know that Damarcians made decent guards. Damarcians were thinking people who valued knowledge highly. They were thin and often moved awkwardly, and these were no exception.

Sheydu often rolled her eyes at the *gamra* guards' competence, and I had come to see how she was right in many instances.

She couldn't complain about these particular clumsy ones, because she used the chaos to unpack things from her bag in quick and efficient fashion. She laid out one glob-shaped wad of explosive, and another. Then a bag that went around the explosive that had a highly adhesive surface. Then two tiny buttonlike devices that she pushed into the soft material before closing the bags and tying them tightly at the top. She tapped her reader against the parcel where lumps indicated the position of the devices. They each emitted a tiny flash of light.

She flicked through a few screens on her reader. I recognised the "Device Activation" screen. Working. Contact.

She gave me the *all systems go* sign.

I needed to get all these people out.

But the struggle between the Pengali and the guards attempting to arrest them had spread. More Pengali had come into the tent. If these were all Reida's supporters, Reida should call them off.

I checked the time.

Asha's craft would be up there, destroying as many relays as possible. Ezhya would be doing the same, maybe talking to the sling, too, while it made its way back. I must make sure that that terrible weapon was not used.

I gave Sheydu the sign. She jumped from the fixed platform to one of the suspended ones. It swung back and forth with her weight. Carefully, she lowered one of the bags onto the encrusted surface of the relay. And then the other one. Tapped on her reader. Jumped back onto the fixed platform. The two explosive bags lay on the muddy surface like someone's discarded garbage. The bags were white, so stood out clearly. A little light blinked at the top of each.

Sheydu ran up the stairs. "Get out, get out!"

The skirmishes stopped. People looked at her, and some noticed the white bags on top of the "rock".

An expression of horror came to Delegate Namion's face. He lunged for the gun on a nearby guard's belt.

"Get out, get out!" Sheydu ran over the boards, out of the tent. She jumped over the side into the darkness of the marsh.

I followed her outside and climbed on the railing, hesitating, looking at the dark gaping void where there would be a wet landing in the mud some metre and a half below.

"Jump!" Sheydu called from the darkness below. I couldn't see her.

"Come on!" Thayu yelled. She jumped.

Splash.

I jumped.

There was a flash behind us. And another one.

I landed in the mud and fell to my knees. Water splashed in my face.

"What the hell was that?" Nicha.

"I think Delegate Namion must have fired at those bags," I said. I was the only one to have seen this.

Thayu cursed. "Oh, he fucking didn't—"

An explosion bloomed out from the tent. The sides blew out. The roof blew off. The walkway shattered, sending support poles crashing sideways.

Thayu pushed me down on my belly. In the water, of course. Various pieces rained down around me, some of them quite large. I covered my head with my arms.

"The stupid fucking idiot shot at the explosive!" Sheydu yelled somewhere close by.

Now that the light from the tent was gone, it had become seriously dark. I couldn't see a thing. I didn't imagine that Thayu and Sheydu saw any more.

People splashed around us. I had no idea who they were. I couldn't hear them because my ears were ringing. I could barely figure out where Thayu was, and if everyone would just stop yelling I might just be able to hear what any of them said.

Someone pulled me up onto my feet. A deep voice said, "Come." It was Evi.

He more or less dragged me along, not in the direction of the point behind which we had left the planes.

I protested, "We have to go that way."

"No, our transport is right here."

There was a hoverboat in the reeds that I hadn't seen because it carried no light at all, and both little moons had long since vanished below the horizon.

Evi pushed me in and I sat down on the first bench I encountered. Damn, I was shivering. The driver was small, likely Pengali. The dark, heavy person who sat next to me turned out to be Veyada. I sensed Thayu on the bench behind me. The boat reversed out of the reeds. Where the others were I didn't know. The night was black and chaotic and hopefully my team would have a better idea of what was going on than I did.

But . . .

"We're going in the wrong direction." I could see some pinpricks of light *behind* us.

"Nah," Veyada said.

The driver turned the boat in a half-circle, steering it towards . . . one of the pylons that held up the railway tracks. A ladder led from the water to the track bed. There were people up there. There was also a train, with all its lights off. What the hell?

The side of the boat thunked into the concrete of the pylon. A Pengali on the ladder caught the rope that the driver threw at her and tied it to one of the rungs, chatting with the driver. After years in Barresh, the Pengali language, consonant-filled, with harsh and guttural tones, still sounded utterly foreign to me.

Someone called, "Cory!"

Nicha was up there.

I rose and crossed the few wobbly steps to the ladder, stepped from the boat and climbed up. A thick layer of moss and algae covered the rungs of the ladder. It felt disgusting, slippery. I climbed slowly, making sure that my grip or step was secure before hauling myself up. Nicha held out a hand and pulled me up onto the track bed, behind the train. The cabin had a little door at the very back, which stood open. A few pinpricks of light pierced the darkness of the cabin. Something moved, showing up only as a shadow against the light. Too tall to be Pengali.

A Coldi voice said, "Delegate? Get in."

Holy crap, it was Deyu.

"Since when is hijacking trains our business?"

"Since Deyu used to be a train driver in Athyl," Thayu said next to me.

"Did she?" Here came the important bits about why Deyu was with us.

More people were climbing onto the tracks behind us. I recognised the solid form of Telaris. Sheydu was there, too.

"Are we missing anyone?"

"All here." Reida said.

"Even if some of us are a bit bruised," Sheydu said. She sounded exhausted.

"Did anyone see Delegate Namion?"

No one replied. A chill went through me.

"He shot at the explosives," Thayu said, her voice dark.

"Stupid." My mind filled with dark thoughts. What would happen if, by chance, Delegate Namion had not survived that stupidity? "Do you think that the relay is fully destroyed?"

"We'll have to check in the morning," Sheydu said. "Not much good hanging around now and getting caught."

"Yes, we must get out of here soon."

"We'll check with my father," Thayu said. "No need to come back to this mess."

And it was a mess that we would definitely hear more about. Tamerians had been getting killed all over town without much publicity, because they were only Tamerians and no one knew them or cared about them, except perhaps other Tamerians—not that I'd ever seen evidence of that. But if any of the *gamra* guards, the council workers or, heaven forbid, Delegate Namion, had been injured, then the proverbial shit would hit the fan at lightspeed. And then I might well need that protection Ezhya offered.

"Get in," Deyu called from inside the train.

We walked over the track, careful not to slip. Evi, at the front of the group, reached the door first. He climbed up the little ladder and disappeared into the cabin. Then Thayu. Then it was my turn. I put my hand on the ladder—

"Shit," Nicha said behind me. "Look over there."

We looked.

A faint glow emanated from the water where the excavation had been, a bright spot under the water that lit the sad remains of the tent and the walkways with a ghostly blue-green light.

"Does your explosives cause that?" Telaris asked Sheydu next to him.

"No. They shouldn't." Her voice sounded uncertain.

The water *moved*. It bubbled and churned as if it was boiling. In fact, it *was* boiling because steam billowed from the water in the same way it did at the volcanic vents. The light became brighter and brighter. That thing that looked like a rock had detached itself from the muddy bottom and was rising. Sharp beams lanced from cracks in the encrusted casing, making the steam glow.

As the thing broke the surface, big chunks of the casing fell away.

The object underneath was so bright that I couldn't even make out the shape of it. It emanated a low pulsing hum, that was painfully familiar. This was the sound that had disturbed the Exchange operation at times. The sound that had destroyed the back wall of the house at the edge of the island.

Telaris raised his gun and aimed. He squeezed the release. A bright beam crossed the night sky, hit the light source—

The beam glanced off.

"The bombs didn't work." Sheydu stared, her face lit with a ghostly green glow. "What the fuck . . . Those two babies were big enough to destroy a military cruiser. Each." She was covered in mud. The sleeve in her suit had ripped and blood had soaked into the fabric.

We probably shouldn't have been surprised that the explosives weren't strong enough to destroy an object that had lain dormant but operational in the mud for fifty thousand years. Or maybe Delegate Namion's actions had prevented the explosives from working properly.

Nicha said, "Listen."

He held up his comm and turned up the sound: the same pulsing deep tone that we'd heard several times before.

Whatever the reason, the explosion had awakened the relay. It was live. It was calling the ship to come home.

Despite both Sheydu and Telaris firing at it, the thing rose and rose in the air, quickly fading to no more than a bright speck of light.

We stared after it, standing on the train tracks, a sense of despair coming over us.

Shit. I was far too tired to go after it and save the universe. I didn't even know how. I'd go home and hide in bed when Asha and Ezhya learned of our failure.

Then Thayu said in a low voice, "My father says that the Aghyrian ship has turned on all its outside lights."

No, this wasn't the summit of our failure. It was the beginning.

WE CLIMBED INTO the single carriage and sat, wet, dirty and dejected, on the floor between the benches. Few words were said.

The floor of the carriage had started humming, and outside lights came on. I felt terrible for leaving like this. I should stay and make sure that the injured were taken care of and that no one died because they'd fallen unconscious in the water and there was no one to pull them out.

But my decisions were not my own. Ezhya had placed absolute trust in me. He had asked for me to complete this task. He would not be impressed that we'd failed and he would probably issue further orders. I could do nothing but wait for them and his inevitable disappointment in me.

I could hear myself making excuses to him. *Look, most of the time I did hare-brained things they ended up going my way.*

It didn't matter. The one time it was important, I failed.

The door to the control room was open, and Deyu stood inside, with the schematics of the railway tracks on front of her.

"I can take us straight to the island," she called.

That was good. I felt mortally tired. I stank. I was hungry. That probably applied to all of us. All we could do now was go back and prepare for war. Hopefully most of it would be fought in space. Hopefully it would consist mainly of bluff and a bit of fireworks as satellites were destroyed so that the ship could not jump. Hopefully both Asha and Ezhya would survive.

Evi and Telaris sat sideways in the aisle, leaning against the seats. Evi leaned the back of his head on an armrest and Telaris leaned forward on his pulled-up knees. Thayu had crashed face down on the floor and was already asleep, but Nicha was doing something on his reader that appeared to be holding his interest.

After a while, he got up and went to the cabin. He spoke to Deyu. She pointed at the tracks on the screen. Something about turning sideways. She nodded.

Nicha came back into the cabin. "Change of plan. We've got to go after that thing and destroy it with heavier firepower. My father has sent us a ship and crew. He and Ezhya are tied up sweeping up as many relays as they can around Asto. A shuttle will be on its way down to pick us up."

Shit. Go into war? Like this?

"And something else. Ezhya tells us to bring the hostages."

"All of them? Even Lilona?"

"Yes, he says all of them. He wants to use them as bargaining chips."

"He's expecting the ship to jump?"

"He wants to be prepared for all eventualities."

Shit. Shit, shit, shit.

I didn't want to do this. I believed I could fully crack Lilona given more time. She was deeply unhappy, missed her family and was beginning to see that there was life outside the ship and away from her all-knowing captain.

But I'd sworn loyalty to Ezhya. There were times that I could stubbornly argue about his way of doing things. This was not one of those times.

We turned onto the train line that went from the *gamra* island to the main island, and Deyu had to go slowly over the switch to the southwestern track. The squeaking and clanging of brakes and couplings under the floor of the carriage woke Thayu. She pushed herself up, wincing, looking unimpressed and annoyed. "What's happening?"

"We're going home to get the Aghyrians and then to the airport." I told her what Nicha had said.

"Oh, fuck." She rubbed her face with her hands. There was a large red blotch on her cheek where it had been pressed against the hard floor of the cabin. She leaned against the side of a bench and rested her forehead on her knees.

No one said much while the train rushed low over the water. This was now the second night without much sleep, and all of us would need to rest soon. I could schedule rests for everyone in turn, maybe. Before the shuttle turned up. After we'd secured the captain and Tayron in my apartment. I'd probably have to keep Lilona separate. They might consider her a traitor.

My mind was jumping all over the place.

I hoped I wasn't forgetting vital things. I hoped Veyada and Thayu and Nicha were in a state to pick up my mistakes.

At the *gamra* station, we were met on the platform by a puzzled railway worker. She had, evidently, turned up to work early so that she could do some maintenance before the first commuter trains arrived.

She watched all of us, dirty and bedraggled, stepping out of the carriage.

"This is not a scheduled service?"

"Nope," Deyu said, handing her the engine's master control comm.

"Where did you get this? It's an offence to steal train controls."

I decided to step in. "The carriage is undamaged. None of us sat on the seats and we didn't make anything dirty or wet. There's going to be some major shocking items hitting the news today. I don't think a harmless joyride in a train is going to register high on the list."

Her eyes widened. "Delegate?" I didn't think she had recognised me up until then. I guessed looking in the mirror was going to be a shock to me.

"We might need the carriage later to take us to the airport. It's a very important mission. Is there a chance that it can stay here until that time?"

"Well that . . . depends on where you got it. Most of our vehicles are in use in the morning commute."

"If we need it before then?"

She shrugged. "Maybe. I might be able to move it further into the tunnel so that it doesn't disrupt the early services."

I thanked her and we continued up the stairs.

"It never ceases to amaze me how you talk your way out of trouble," Thayu said. "She was all about calling the guards on Deyu before you started speaking. How do you even do that?"

"That's because I have a reputation of doing silly things and people are curious so they give me the benefit of the doubt."

"No," Veyada said. "That's because you don't make melodramatic claims that later turn out to be nothing but hot air. When you say that something is serious, it actually is. That's called judgement. Up here." He tapped his head. "That's why all of us are here with you."

I met his eyes and damn it, near lost it. I was pathetically bad at accepting compliments. I only ever expected to get blowback because that's the only thing I usually got.

But damn. *Damn it, Veyada.*

It's true.

But I just failed the entire team.

No, technology failed us. Delegate Namion was an idiot. Many things went wrong. It was not your fault. Maybe the relay could never be destroyed that way in the first place.

He was probably right about all those things.

We emerged from the stairs onto the wide boulevard that crossed the island.

I sent Telaris, Veyada, Reida and Deyu to collect the captain and Tayron, while allowing the others to go home for a change of clothes and a snatch of sleep.

Everything was quiet in the apartment, and even all of us coming in at the same time did not bring Eirani upstairs. It would probably be at least an hour before she started stirring, and complaining about the dirt we'd traipsed into the hall.

"Go get cleaned up and to bed quickly, before the staff wakes up."

Nicha made a beeline for his room and his son, and Thayu declared that she would have a bath first. Her voice carried an edge that betrayed her utter fatigue.

Reida agreed to leave Eirani a note that we possibly wanted an early breakfast.

I hesitated in the hall, seeing the blinking lights in the hub, knowing that there would be messages for me, even ones that had *not* been filtered through Delegate Namion's office. Possibly *important* messages.

But a voice in my head that sounded like Thayu's said, *Go to bed.*

I guessed that if it was urgent, like *really* urgent, they would know how to reach me.

I looked at the door to the guest bedroom in despair. I'd notify Lilona immediately before we'd leave. No need to do that now. She might freak out. Hell, in her situation, *I* would freak out.

I walked into the bathroom to find Thayu in front of the mirror, digging with a pair of tweezers in a wound in her side. Her face was white, her lips set and her hand trembled.

Damn. I hadn't even known that she was injured.

I ran to her side. "Wait. Let me do that."

She made a weak protest. I guided her to the bench, easing her down on her side with the wound facing up. Whatever it was had gone straight through her suit.

"It went between the front and back plates of the armour. Bad luck, I guess. It's not deep. It hurts like fuck."

"We need to glue this. You might have to stay here."

"No way. We live together, we die together."

"Thay' please." I extracted the first aid kit out of the cupboard along the back. I was feeling sick, too tired to deal with this.

Evi came in and similarly recoiled at the door. "Oh, fuck. What happened?"

Thayu said, "I don't know. I fell on something. A branch I think."

Evi nodded. "Megon tree wood. The splinters give off a sap that hurts like blazes. This will probably get infected."

"Never mind that. I'll go to the hospital when we're done with this emergency. Just stick a bandage over it."

Evi helped me pick fragments of wood out of the wound, clean it, glue it and bandage it up. I scooped a bowl of water from the pool and washed Thayu while she lay on her side. She had fallen asleep.

I left her to rest, briefly dived under the water, came back and lay face down on the bed in our bedroom.

The next moment, someone was at the door.

"Cory, get up. The military is here."

Shit. I rolled from the bed, feeling terrible. My face felt bumpy with the creases from the sheets. Eirani came in, complaining about fuss and all these people in the apartment without her knowledge.

Thayu snapped at her, "You don't have to feed them. Just let them wait."

She fussed with my clothing while one of the other staff brought breakfast. It was indeed getting light outside. Eirani very much disapproved of eating breakfast on the run, but it happened regularly, especially when the *gamra* assembly sat at awkward times.

She also disapproved of my battle gear. "That is protection worn by guards," she said of my armour, and she purposely avoided the guns on the table.

Thayu was ready and came briefly into the room, stole a slice of bread off my plate and went back out.

"The captain is ready," she said.

"What about Lilona?"

"Not yet. You said you'd wait until we were about to go. Do you want me to go to the room and call her?"

"No, I'll do it." I set the empty plate on the dressing table and rose.

In the hall, I was met by two Coldi in dark clothing. Their faces were blank, their words few, their weapons clearly displayed. Asto military. Women both, I thought, but couldn't be sure about that.

They stood on either side of the antique bench that was only used for ornamental purposes, but where today Captain Kando Luczon sat with his companion. They had not bounds his hands, but both wore leg braces that would not allow them to run.

The soldiers greeted me briefly, the captain and Tayron ignored me, as usual. The captain's face was blank, but I couldn't help suspect that he knew something was going on. We couldn't discover how their readers connected with their ship, but they had to communicate with the ship in some way. I thought. I hoped. Because if the captain saw the size of Asto's fleet, he might realise he could never win, even if he destroyed all of them today. There would always be more ships.

I went down the corridor and knocked on the door to the guest room.

Eirani hadn't told me anything in particular about Federza and Lilona, and I presumed they had been asleep while we crawled through the mud.

Why didn't he open the door?

There was no time to wait, so I rolled the door aside and went, Coldi-style, into the room.

It was dark and stuffy inside, with the blinds over the window.

These blinds were the ones that came with the apartment and I had removed them in our bedroom because I liked to wake up when daylight came.

I knew that the large bed stood close to the window even if it was too dark for me to see it, but the staff had put a smaller bed against the wall near the door—and it had not been touched.

My heart jumped briefly but then my eyes had adjusted, and the low light that filtered through the curtains revealed Marin Federza and Lilona Shrakar both in the large bed, sleeping, as Thayu and I sometimes did, spooned against each other. Federza's arm, pale-skinned with the Trader Guild emblem tattooed on the shoulder, lay over Lilona's side.

He stirred briefly but relaxed again.

Whatever I had expected to find, this wasn't it. Yet in a heart-breaking way, it made sense. Here was a man whose world had been destroyed by the very people he had grown up with, people he had trusted. Here was a woman who was scared, escaping a situation akin to slavery, also having lost all that was dear to her.

And I had come to destroy their fragile happiness—

Lilona opened her eyes and squeaked. Federza rolled over and reached for his gun—which fell off the bedside cabinet.

"Calm down, calm down!"

He sat up and regarded me with blurry eyes. "Man, you gave me a fright."

"I'm sorry. Things are happening. I need her to come."

"Where to?" His voice sounded suspicious.

I explained briefly to him what had happened. His eyes widened and as I spoke, he got up from the bed and faced me. His eyes blazed with anger. "So you want to return her to this dreadful man and hold her as hostage with them?"

"I don't really want to, but I see no other op—"

In a huge step, he crossed the room. He grabbed hold of the front of my shirt and pushed me back into the tiny bathroom. I tripped over the rug. My backside collided painfully with the washbasin. "Hey!"

The door rattled open and Thayu ran in, followed by Evi. I gestured that all was fine. They remained outside the room, but didn't shut the door.

"You can't do that!" Federza hissed in my face. "Just now that she has been saved. She will think that we betrayed her."

"It's not my choice either. Ezhya wants all three of them there. I can see his point."

"It is your choice. You've had plenty of times of speaking out against him. Of all the times you've spoken up against him, you choose this one occasion . . ."

"Not today. I can't speak up. This issue is much bigger than us. Look . . ." I was thinking on my feet. "I'm still hopeful that I might be able to negotiate a peaceful solution even if the ship turns up here. If she gets left behind, the captain will use her as bargaining chip against us."

"It's all right, I have to go back anyway," said a soft voice from behind us.

Lilona had come out of bed and slipped on one of the loose bathrobes that Eirani kept for guests. Her hair hung loose over her shoulders. She resembled some elflike creature.

Federza turned to her. He let go of my shirt. "I'm not having you go back to that monster."

"I have no choice. I'm bound to the ship." She held out her arm, where little globs of light pulsed under the soft skin on the underside of her forearm. "It's calling me."

Federza's face hardened. He crossed his arms and stepped between me and Lilona. "Then you will have to take me, too."

25

———————

MARIN FEDERZA was not to be dissuaded, even though Lilona said that he should stay here. He said that if she had to go with the ship, he would come, but I suspected it wasn't that easy. I had no idea what to do about it. I didn't think Ezhya would be happy about this. But I was already arguing against him in my mind. If nothing else, some stupid, trivial part in my brain argued, we could use someone who spoke Aghyrian.

As we went into the hall, even Lilona was trying to dissuade him.

But Federza was adamant. "I've got nothing to live for. They took all my jobs, my safety, ransacked my business and ruined my reputation. I understand that we may die or that this tyrant—" He glanced at the captain. "—controls your life and will control mine as well, but I refuse to let you go alone."

I resisted the urge to groan. We really could not use this type of delay.

And then I saw them lying there, against each other. I'd sometimes joked that I'd never seen Federza with a partner and all sorts of speculation circulated at the island about that.

And I remembered that deep and dark place I'd traversed when I was convinced that Thayu had a contract with Nicha and was off-limits to me, and the light that entered my life when he told me she was his sister.

Would I deny a man that happiness?

And I was so fucking tired, and didn't want to deal with it—couldn't deal with it without bursting into tears because amongst all the hostilities and talk of war, love bloomed where it couldn't, like it always had, since the start of humanity.

Since the time that a scientist called Waller Herza had noticed trouble in the pods of one of the colonising race's couples, had failed to save the man and had fallen in love with the woman. Marin Federza and the Barresh Aghyrians were descended from their daughter, born a few days before the disaster. Those stories of love had been scratched into the walls of the aquifers where she had survived for years with her daughter, and then woken her fellows when the air cleared.

I waved my hand. "All right, come with us then."

There was no way the Asto military would have Federza on their flight, so he'd be stopped at the airport. They'd do my job for me and separate the lovebirds. I was a fucking coward.

We assembled in the hall, most of us still looking tired.

"I don't think it's necessary for all of us to go," I said. "There is probably not enough room for all of us on the shuttle either."

The silent military men in dark clothing nodded. One held up three fingers. This could mean two things: three levels of association, seven people, or two to the power of three, eight people.

I glanced at Thayu, but she didn't know. *It depends on whether that's part of military or civilian sign language.* We could ask, but that would look silly so they probably wouldn't even reply.

I was going to be bold and guess eight people.

Myself, Thayu. Nicha wanted to come, but I didn't want him to.

"You need to look after your son," I said.

"He's in good hands with the girls." He'd taken two keihu nannies who each did half of the day.

"But imagine if something were to happen to you, would you want him to grow up with his mother?"

He pulled a face. That argument settled it for him. He sent Deyu to represent him. Reida wanted to come, but Nicha said, "You're going to be poked, prodded and provoked the moment you walk on board that ship and they see your clan. You'll be learning how to handle it, but I don't think you're there yet, and don't think it's a healthy learning environment."

Reida nodded. Not a month ago he would have scowled, but he simply nodded.

"I'll take you to the firing range if we get a bit of time," Nicha said, and Reida was, at least outwardly, happy with that.

Veyada and Sheydu would come, since they were well-known in the military, having been part of Ezhya's guard.

The other numbers would be made up by the captain and his two companions. The eighth person who might or might not be refused would be Marin Federza. That way we wouldn't be unpleasantly surprised if he wasn't allowed to come down with a member of our team.

It was time to go. Sheydu already had the hostages up standing near the door. Thayu stood next to me, a warm, heavily armed presence. I hoped her wound was better, although it would certainly have to be looked at later. I'd heard terrible stories about megon wood splinters.

It was time for goodbyes.

"Well, um . . ." I faced Nicha awkwardly. Just what did one say in a situation like this?

Thayu glanced at me. *You know what to say. Say it.* Her expression was penetrating. *Sometimes I think you're doing this deliberately.*

Do what deliberately?

Being obtuse. You understand Coldi society as well as any of us, but occasionally you'll feign ignorance because you don't like a particular custom.

True. Surely they didn't want me to—I was not a major leader.

You're the head of our association.

All right then. No option, really.

I said, "Iyamichu ata."

Nicha looked down in the subservient position. He replied, "Iyamichu ata."

I touched his shoulder, very formal and appropriate. I had always thought I would hate it, but there was something apt about the situation.

Soldiers going to war, coming back either victorious or dying for the cause.

He said, "Cory, be careful, please."

Then I hugged him. It was a human gesture, viewed by both soldiers with looks of deep suspicion, but then again, we had both grown up on Earth and hugging was a thing one did there, especially if one was going to war.

It was time to leave. I followed Thayu, tired like my footsteps were dragging, like I desperately didn't want to go—which I didn't—fighting thoughts that I might never come back, and I didn't want to go down that rabbit hole, because I would lose it, and that would definitely be viewed as inappropriate by these career soldiers.

The door thudded shut. We walked along the gallery. The last I saw of my apartment, just before going down the stairs, was a piece of Telaris' dark-skinned arm.

Back to the station, where the train still waited in the little space of rails beyond the platform, presumably built as a safety margin in case a train overshot the platform.

The station guard had provided a proper driver—because one needed a licence to be a train driver in Barresh—and Deyu sat with us. On a bench this time, like normal passengers.

She looked a little pale but oh so serious.

Very little was said on the trip to the airport station. I sat next to Thayu, missing Nicha already. Federza and Lilona sat opposite us. They would occasionally meet each other's eyes and their gazes would linger longer than necessary. Or he would touch her hand in a way ever so slightly longer and more intense than if the touch was accidental.

Sheydu and Veyada were guarding our other hostages. None of them said anything during the entire trip. I suspected Sheydu and Veyada were communicating through their feeders.

The train stopped at the far end of the platform of the airport station.

The two soldiers led us away from the station, not via the regular path along the airport fence, but to the left, past the section of shoreline where the landing area joined the water, and up a little path on the other side. There was a gate where two more soldiers waited, as nondescript and genderless as the other two. They didn't even greet each other, although the new soldiers greeted me, accompanied by a quick glance at my Domiri earrings.

They nodded briefly at Sheydu and Veyada—both Palayi—and did a barely noticeable double take at Deyu, who was Omi, not at all a clan that populated the ranks of security officers or administrative assistants. They let the captain and Tayron through with steel faces.

As if their height and lankiness were not enough to distinguish them, they both wore leg ropes and manacles.

When Federza wanted to step through the gate, the guns went up. "Halt. What are you doing here?"

Federza opened his jacket and showed them his Trader medallion.

"What is he doing here?" one of the soldiers asked me.

"He insists on coming here with the third member of the Aghyrian crew."

The soldier looked both Federza and Lilona up and down. He—or maybe she, whatever—did not show any emotion. Not a smile, not a single sign that Federza's efforts to protect Lilona were worthy of hope or a smile.

"We don't take any external passengers on board unless under strict instructions."

"External" was a euphemism for non-Coldi. I guessed I fell under the "instructions" part. "He is a Trader."

Behind me, Thayu said, "Come on, can we just go through? We have work to do."

The second looked at me. His eyes had been distant when his colleague was speaking to me, but now they came back into focus. "Asha says you determine the team."

That meant that I would be responsible for mistakes, too. If there was trouble. If this developed into a full-scale war.

I didn't miss how Federza touched her from behind, a subtle and fleeting touch to the back. I tried to approach it from a logical perspective. She was the only ship Aghyrian that we'd had any type of useful conversation with. He was the only person to whom they were likely to listen.

I closed my eyes. "He comes." I would probably regret this. It would be a story I'd tell Ayshada when he was a teenager. *Did you hear about the time I forced a military deep space ship to carry a non-Asto Trader representative?*

"They will be restrained aboard the main ship," the soldier said.

"I don't care." Federza put his chin in the air. "Myself and the lady are not criminals, but see it as you wish."

Damn the man. I was *proud* of him. I didn't think that would have been possible.

The craft on the other side of the fence was a lot smaller than the shuttle that Asha normally used. Just a simple shuttle with the bare essentials. Only four crew. Room for ten passengers.

We climbed the gangplank which retracted the moment we were inside.

The cabin had no luxuries whatsoever. The crew seats were behind a pressure door, half-shut, and the rest of the cabin resembled a cargo hold. Bare metal plates made up the floor, the walls and the ceiling. Bundles of leads were strung over support struts overhead and in corners.

It looked like this ship was normally used for cargo. Two rows of antigrav couches had been moved in. They were big and bulky things, which was why there could only be ten in the ship.

Federza and the three Aghyrians went in the back row and the rest of us in the row behind the pressure door.

I sat directly behind the navigator, looking onto the pilot's instruments. Once we'd taken off, the door would close and I would of course no longer be able to see that.

I was given a mask, which, when I put it over my face, released a burst of hot air. I followed instructions. Lie down in the reclining chair. The soldier closed a lid over me. It had a little window through which I could see a small section of the control panel, the back of one of the pilots' heads and a bit of window.

Thayu was in as well.

The craft shuddered with thumps of things being shut and secured. I sensed movement in the bench when someone took the couch next to me. Air hissed as the mask was turned on and there was a snap from the lid closing.

My fingers on the armrest found a few buttons. One operated a light inside the pod. There was a lever to open it from the inside with dire warnings that it was not a good idea to do this in the event of a hull breach. Thanks for reminding me.

A tinny voice came through a loudspeaker in my little capsule. "Crew, prepare for liftoff."

I turned off the light inside my pod and lay back in the couch. Through the little screen inside the helmet I could see the sky, which was starting to turn blue on the eastern horizon. Would this be the last sunrise I'd ever see?

The floor was humming now, and the tinny voice in my helmet was rattling off technical details, the meaning of which went completely over my head.

Sweat ran over my chest. It tickled but I couldn't wriggle my hand up far enough to wipe the drops. It was so hot in this damn thing.

The humming increased, and all of a sudden burst into an explosive roar. The pressure on my chest increased. Some machine pumped air into my pod with a loud hiss that gave me a fright. Through the little screen I could see only sky.

Thay?

There was no reply. I guess I couldn't count on the feeders working inside a military ship. I tried to turn my head but the downward force was too great. I didn't know that I could have seen her in the pod anyway. The little screen inside the pod went dark. What was going on? Panic closed like a vice on my chest. I knew, somewhere in the back of my mind, that everything was under control, that I shouldn't worry, but right now the situation was reminding me, with the bluntness of a freight train at full speed, that I *didn't* like space travel.

I thought I passed out for a few seconds.

Then, slowly, the pressure eased to make way for another feeling that was far too familiar: weightlessness. And I hadn't brought any sickness medication.

Great. The universe was going to send me to war throwing up. Here comes Spewy the Hero.

I closed my eyes because anything else would just make it worse. It got quiet. The engines must have stopped or were only running at low speed. A blue glow filtered through my eyelids when the screen came back on, showing the curve of the planet backlit by sunlight. Numbers scrolled over the side of the screen, but I had no idea what they meant.

I might have drifted off for a bit and was jolted wide awake by some heavy thumps and sideways shifts that made the ship shudder.

I guessed this meant that we had docked at the larger ship in orbit, but the jolting was much rougher than I had felt on previous flights.

After a while, there were clanks and clicks, and then someone opened the pod from the outside. The lid folded up and a muscled figure floated in the space before me. Thayu. She pulled out a bag that she carried tucked in her belt, and handed it to me in case of embarrassing emergencies. That made me feel better.

She touched me gently on the cheek. "Hey, you look terrified."

"I *am* terrified."

"It's a military ship. Not built for utmost comfort of passengers."

"I noticed."

"The pilots are already tracking the relay, and we'll come within range soon. Once we've dealt with it, we'll join the rest of the fleet."

I pushed myself out of the pod. "All right then. Let's go and hunt some satellites."

26

WE WERE STILL weightless even though we were in the main ship. On the previous trip I'd learned that a rotating habitat, and artificial gravity, was a heavy drain on the ship's systems and interfered with weapons operation. A large ship might have a rotating habitat when travelling or observing, but the moment they entered any level of alertness, all rotation stopped.

Of course, Coldi did not get motion sickness.

Sheydu was helping Veyada out of his pod. It seemed that he had used his enforced imprisonment to catch up on some sleep. Smart Veyada. If anything that flight had made me feel more tired.

The crew had lowered the pressure door and were moving about. One operated the mechanism next to the door, and it opened, letting in a waft of ship air: clean but perpetually too hot.

Damn, I'd almost forgotten about that.

This crewmember said, "You are cleared to proceed to the command room." I *still* had no idea of the gender of any of these four soldiers and this bugged me far more than it should.

"The four hostages will remain on board this shuttle under our guard."

I nodded, unsure where I stood with them in terms of ranking. I should have expected something like that. Asha and captain of the main ship would never let non-Coldi into any area of significance.

At the door, I turned around. The four crew were just now freeing the hostages from their pods. I met Federza's eyes in between two dark-clad backs. His expression was . . . determined, observing. I didn't *think* he looked angry, but Traders were notoriously good at hiding their emotions. He seemed to have accepted his fate, whatever it would be.

Thayu preceded me out of the cabin through a narrow tube that led into a busy docking area of a much larger ship. It resembled the setup I had seen in that giant space station that orbited Asto: a fairly narrow space with high walls from which protruded brackets that each held a ship. The ground, irrelevant as it was, hid out of view in the darkness below. Our was the only non-fighter ship that I could see.

We floated into the open space.

"Stay here," Thayu said, yanking the tether on my belt. It attached to the outside of the ship with a sticky pad.

There seemed to be a traffic highway past our ship, "down" into the darkness and "up" to a rectangle from which yellow light radiated: crew hurried past, pulling themselves along a railing on the wall.

My tether had a metal loop, too, and Thayu showed me how to attach it. Then we followed the other crew to the square entrance. It was a corridor, with entrances on all sides.

This was a deep space ship, built for long-term travel in weightlessness. The sides of the corridor could each function as walls or floor. Most of the time, they ticked the "none of the above" box. Two tether railings went through the middle: one for traffic in each direction. Thayu pulled herself along at a decent clip.

Veyada and Sheydu followed me, with Deyu, who looked at everything with wide eyes: at the doors, the control panels, the crew in desert pink uniforms, which she would never have seen, since Asto military didn't go uniformed when mingling with the public. Some crew greeted us, some even with subservient greetings.

From the corridor we went up through a manhole into another corridor and then straight ahead to the ship's control room, where the narrow corridor widened out to a huge, funnel-shaped space.

Deyu whispered, "Wow."

And it was quite impressive. All around the walls, people were busy at workstations. From the design, I guessed this room could rotate, but right now it didn't and all the workers were attached to their part of the perimeter with their tether clipped to a "seat". There were easily over a hundred people in the room, stuck to the inside of the funnel-shaped walls like bats in a cave. The far end of the room—the "mouth" of the funnel—was taken up by a huge window in a couple of segments. A bank of screens and another workstation hung in the centre, suspended from the window frame. A serious-looking officer in uniform sat there. I guessed this was the ship's commander.

When this officer noticed us, he—I thought it was a he anyway—unclipped himself from the seat and floated towards us with deadly precision.

A brief flash of panic flared up in me. He met me as the leader of our respective associations, and I was expected to *feel* whether I was higher or lower in rank than he was. As recently as last year I would always have erred on the side of *lower* because I thought that would please people, but Veyada assured me that this wasn't true at all. Just getting it *wrong* was a source of annoyance. Getting it *wrong* could mean the difference between having a successful cooperation with the other association and trying to break a stone wall with water bombs.

What was it? I didn't know. I lacked the instinct.

And he already threw his tether pad to the wall and reeled himself in. He decided I was . . . *higher*. He looked down, holding his arms by his side, palms facing backwards.

What the fuck?

I touched his shoulder, sweating, feeling ready to faint or vomit, or both.

"Don't be so nervous," Thayu said softly in keihu because no one else was likely to understand it.

That was easier said than done. I wasn't ready for this. Oh hell, I wasn't.

The captain introduced himself. His name was Ledaya—male indeed—and his clan Domiri as evidenced by the blood red stones in his earrings. My clan.

In fact, all of this ship was likely to be run by people from the Domiri clan.

I guessed I should have known that. I just hadn't been thinking clearly. Too tired, too stressed out and too busy keeping the contents of my stomach where they belonged.

He told us to join him at the command module in the middle of the hall.

Of course he was much more adept at navigating the open space to get there. I misdirected my push off the wall and Thayu had to come after me to stop me drifting into some highly bemused workers.

Great. Making an idiot of myself already.

When we arrived at the command platform, me with my pride slightly dented, he gave a hand signal. The light dimmed and a giant projection sprang up in the void, consisting of many glimmering dots. Most of them were white, but some, clustered in groups, were blue. Two red circles intersected the projection, one inside the other. Those, I made a guess, were the orbital paths of Asto and Ceren. A little orange blip indicated the current position of each planet.

Each planet possessed a cloud of dots. "At some point, the array will form a network of anpar lines. We have a number of different models for when we think this might happen. The trouble for them is that over the years so many of the relays have drifted off-course. They have come to life to change their orbit. As soon as they fire an engine, we can detect them and destroy them. We have calculated a number of different configurations that they are likely to take up before the ship can jump." He enlarged the area around Asto until the planet became a neat yellowish sphere. "It's likely that they'll be using this cloud here around Asto. The relays have drifted and are bunched up at the LaGrange points. They will likely need to spread out further to get any kind of resonance happening between them. Some have started to move. Estimates for them to form a decent array at their current speeds is between a few days and a week."

"Are all those dots relays?" The sheer size of the cloud was astonishing.

"They are. The known ones, at least."

"What about the blue ones?"

"Those are the ones we've destroyed."

There were many more white ones.

The monumental task only became clear to me then. "All those need to be destroyed?"

"Ideally, yes, but some might not have any function. Some could be more vital than others. There are a lot of unanswered questions.

There may also be some relays that we don't yet know about. That's likely."

Damn. Finding them all and destroying them was a huge task. "Forgive me for saying this, but it seems futile to chase just our one little dot here at Ceren."

"It's not *just* a little dot. It's bigger and more powerful than most of the others and fulfils a special function in the communication with the ship. We don't know what that function is."

He zoomed out again and now enlarged the area around Ceren, which was devoid of dots, apart from a single one in low orbit.

"This is the one. We are on an intersecting orbit and will come into range shortly. You're welcome to stay here and watch."

A little floating platform appeared from below. It looked like an upside-down mushroom with a thick stalk.

Crew in pink uniforms attached the floor to the command platform and pulled seats out of the central stalk, insofar as one could talk about seats in zero-g. They looked a bit like giant spoons, where one sat in the spoon's bowl, held in place by a belt.

All around us, below and above and to the sides, people were working on their individual tasks. The navigator section was on my left-hand side, if the giant screens with diagrams and lines were indeed maps. I thought weapons were directly above. There were a lot of people with very serious faces in that part. Below my feet I thought were the ship operations and maintenance divisions.

The entire command centre was a hive of busy but controlled activity.

The land underneath us was starting to change. Low golden sunlight stroked the pristine, forest-covered hills of the southern slopes of the Mirani continent, way beyond where the nation of Miran petered out in uninhabited swathes of dense forest. This land was deserted, dangerous and cold. In places I thought I could see patches of snow.

Ceren was an overwhelmingly cold world, with huge ice caps and an ocean filled with icebergs that drifted to quite low latitudes. I could see some of the icebergs now, breaking off glaciers, pushed into a corner of a fjord by currents and the wind. The water was azure blue, the forested hills dark green with patches of snow.

It was really harsh, infertile country down there.

We continued into the eastern sunlight. The suns were so close that they almost touched. We rounded the southern tip of the continent, a rock-strewn, barren, icy place, where it was hard to see where the sea ice started and the land stopped. There were thousands of islands here, a giant archipelago that extended along the length of the western coast to just south of the Barresh delta.

Even when it wasn't dark, one rarely saw this much of the world on a commercial flight. Ceren was an agricultural world, underpopulated because of its cold climate even if ironically, Barresh was decidedly tropical.

"There," said one of the navigators.

A flurry of activity followed between the navigators and the weapons crew. Snatches of jargon flew to and fro. The navigators at the projection communicated with at least two groups, one of which was in the control room, the other elsewhere. Ledaya watched the activity with sharp eyes from his command chair.

After a short period of frenzied activity, he said, "Permission to fire."

Navigators peered at their controls, faces tense with concentration.

A shudder went through the ship. I peered out the window, but didn't notice anything until a faint glint of light bloomed and flickered out.

One of the navigators said, "Positive."

I guessed that was it? I didn't dare ask. Everyone seemed busy. Thayu watched the goings-on with sharp eyes. Did she understand what they were doing? With the many jobs Thayu had done, I didn't *think* she'd ever done a stint in the military, but it wouldn't surprise me if she had.

This stealth warfare thing was not half as exciting as I thought. I attempted to lean back against the central stalk of our platform, as far as one could speak of leaning back in weightlessness, and go to sleep. But as I closed my eyes, the light from the projection and the thousands of white and blue dots turned into streaks when filtered through my eyelashes. Ledaya had again zoomed out so that all locations near both planets showed up. The dots formed an almost half-circle which, when I squinted, all looked like they were connected to each other through streaks of light.

I opened my eyes, and I lost it again, but the streaks reappeared when I squinted. It was an effect of light reflecting off my eyelashes or something, but the resulting image made me think.

A bit over a year had passed since we first heard from the Aghyrians. Back then, I remembered Ezhya talking about the alignment of the planets. This happened only once every five years. Ceren's years were long. We were now almost at the quarter point and Asto was about a quarter of an orbit ahead of us. The relays were mostly in orbit around Asto. A good number of them had drifted to the Trojan LaGrange points, which were in the same orbit, but ahead or trailing the planet by a sixth of the orbit.

There were also a handful in the Trojan LaGrange points of Ceren. The only relay at Ceren itself had just turned blue.

Supposing the ship was not going to use an area with a high concentration of relays, but an extreme spread of them? It now had relays in positions that spanned a third of a circle around the two suns. Supposing the ship needed as many of these relays to connect with each other as possible, and assuming that they would focus on the jump point, which, if I was the captain, I'd choose to be the L_1 LaGrange point on the inside of Asto's orbit—well, I didn't know that, but let's assume it.

All those relays would then need to focus at that point. Their means of communication was probably not terribly fond of the disturbance caused by stars. Which meant that if Asto and Ceren were on opposite sides of the suns, the array was huge, but communication poor. If both planets were at the same point, the array was small but the communication excellent. Which meant that now Asto was racing ahead, we were going into a long period of poor communication and they would probably jump sooner rather than later.

I explained this to Thayu, and she said, "Shit. I don't know that that option has been included in the calculations."

She undid her belt and floated over to the command module where she spoke with Ledaya.

"They produced three possible models," Veyada said.

"We assumed that a certain concentration of relays would be necessary to produce a strong enough signal," Ledaya said, joining us on our mushroom platform.

"What if the larger ones are resonators or boosters?"

He frowned deeply, staring at the projection. "We just got rid of the only relay at Ceren. Ceren's trailing cloud would be about to go out of range. That would explain some things . . ." He fingered his upper lip. "I've been getting messages that the ship's engines are ramping up, and we haven't been able to understand why, since our calculations didn't have any of the arrays in a useful formation for a number of days. Engineers suggested that it might be for tests, but to me, it looks like they will jump soon. Which means . . ."

He pushed himself to the command module and spoke urgently into his earpiece. All around us, people stopped working and listened to commands we couldn't hear. There was a sense of urgency in the air.

"Are we going to jump?"

"It seems so," Sheydu said.

"Our work here is done," Thayu said. "I've just been connected to the ship loop. He says we're going to join the fleet to destroy some relays around Asto. Oh, and my father has just received word from the Trader Guild that they're ordering all their ships to go up as well."

"They're not armed, aren't they?"

"No, but they can haul in relays in the hold and destroy them manually."

"That sounds like a slow process."

"It is, if you have only a few ships. There are over ten thousand Trader ships. Not all will be able to come in time, but the majority will."

Shit. This was happening. This was a race against time.

The crew was full on preparing for a jump. Unnecessary processes were shut down, anchor belts and tethers properly attached, workbenches stowed and uniform buttons done up. I didn't know why the buttons were important, but enough of the crew were doing up their buttons for it to be noticeable.

A warning started blaring to secure loose items and use belts. A countdown number flashed in the middle of the window behind Ledaya's command chair.

I knew what to expect and still felt cold with nerves.

The countdown reached zero. For a moment it seemed like nothing happened and my heart filled with panic that the Aghyrian ship had yet again disabled the Exchange.

Then everything went white, and slowly reassembled itself in rainbow colours.

The scene outside the window had changed. Immediately below was a decent-sized disk displaying the eroded pink surface of Asto, crisscrossed by channels. The projection in the middle of the command room had adjusted to reflect our new locality. I could see many little specks that I presumed to be other ships. The space station, too.

"Are those all military ships?" I asked Thayu in a low voice. "Or are they Trader ships?"

"No, the Traders are at the LaGrange points."

Damn it, I hadn't realised how big Asto's fleet was. I could likely see only a small part, too.

"Where is the sling?"

"It's still on its way."

Ledaya made another announcement to the crew, and the frantic activity resumed.

"He's ordering everyone to stay in their seats in case the ship needs to move quickly. We'll be doing an orbital sweep and will be firing at any bit of debris we find."

The crew was certainly very busy. Other ships were busy, too. One by one, the white lights turned blue. Someone was making good progress at Asto's leading LaGrange point. The white dots at Ceren's leading LaGrange point were almost extinguished, too—wait. There was a *white* light that didn't belong in the projection. A white dot at Ceren.

I said, "Look there."

But people had already seen it. The captain, too. He was talking to someone—Ezhya or Asha—making wild gestures. Yes, he had destroyed the relay. Yes, he had checked. Yes, he had fired twice just to make sure.

And yet there it was: a white node, not just live, but *communicating* with the few relays at Ceren's leading cloud.

Shit.

Alarms started blaring. Lights were flashing. Crewmembers were talking in their earpieces. Compared to what you might expect a scene of panic to look like, it was still calm and ordered, but the pronouns were all imperative. *You do this. You do that. You hurry up.*

A couple of white lights in Ceren's cloud went blue.

But something else was happening in the cloud around Asto: a couple of the dots were growing filaments, like fungus. The threads connected with other dots.

Ledaya was shouting orders now. Some lights turned blue, but more and more of them sprang into being, connecting to the growing network of nodes, linked up with blue-white filaments of light.

The network grew. It connected to the nodes in Asto's orbit—and some winked out again because they were still being destroyed. But it grew outwards inexorably, and grew, and grew—

Until the whole thing resembled the web-like projection of the Exchange network that you could see when you stood at the observation window at the Exchange: a web of strands of light that were constantly moving and jiggling.

And pulsing, like the beating of a heart.

For two flashes the entire network pulsed in unison.

Then the flight deck went dark, and the windows went dark. Of course. They only *looked* like windows but were viewscreens. The screens went dark. The instruments stopped blinking and transmitting. In that deep silence, a wave of . . . something made the ship hum and shudder.

"We've lost contact with command," someone said into the darkness, which might have been the understatement of the century. I thought the voice was Ledaya's but I couldn't be sure.

And then, a moment later, "Yes . . . yes. We're working on it." It was Ledaya indeed. He lit a small light on his workbench that cast his face in an eerie glow from underneath.

Then he said, "Fleet Command reports that the Aghyrian ship has jumped."

27

THE CREW worked frantically to re-establish power to the command room. First the light came back on in the cabin and then the viewscreens flickered back into life.

The scene out there was surreal. Ceren was just big enough to form a little half circle. Asto was a brighter and much larger half-disk. Both were side-lit by Beniz and Yaza, which, from our position, were much further apart than they were when seen from Barresh.

Against the backdrop of ink-dark sky glittered thousands and thousands of bright specks, which moved in the same direction we were moving. The closer ships resolved into distinct shapes. They were, as far as I could see, mostly Asto military, the square and clunky vessels that few people ever saw and that mostly hung around in the dark depths of space.

The crew also managed to bring the projector back to life. It showed a vibrant white-green dot that trailed filaments of light.

That was the Aghyrian ship. I guessed those wisps were the anpar wake, even if I'd never seen this. The operator enlarged the area and then enlarged the view at the giant viewscreens.

The dark, giant behemoth that was the Aghyrian ship floated between Asto and the suns.

It was massive, many times bigger than the largest ship in Asto's fleet. Fifty thousand years ago the generation ship had left, having refused help to the beautiful, green, dying planet. Today it was back, looking on its homeworld's scarred surface.

Most of the crew in the control room would not have seen it before. People sat silent behind their workstations, staring at it. Coldi military would be strongly discouraged to show emotions, but their utter silence and pale, quiet faces were scarier than shouts and panic would have been.

They would have heard Asha's statement that normal weapons couldn't destroy this ship. There was no doubt in their eyes. It was plainly obvious. They had no weapons to destroy it, except perhaps the sling, but it wasn't due to arrive for the best part of a day.

The navigators had managed to re-establish contact with the fleet and were talking to other ships in low voices. I could see the details flicker over the screen.

"Our leader speaks," Ledaya said, amplified through the command centre.

There were some clicks and hisses of static and then a voice resonated through the area. A voice that had spoken sternly to me and had offered me protection before I left, protection that might be futile depending on what that ship did.

Ezhya said, "People of Asto and all who have loyalty to me. Today we stand before a challenge that is bigger than any we have faced in the history of our civilisation. I may ask things of you that I have never asked before and that, hopefully, I will never have to ask again."

He used *miyu* pronouns all the way. All people in the command room listened. Not a single glance went to the instruments or screens. Ezhya had their undivided attention.

"While I am with our fleet, I look upon this intruder and know that our impressive arsenal of weapons may not be enough to deal with this ship. We do not know what they want but we know that they have not come in peace. I am calling on all my people to help defend our beautiful world against the menace. I have given orders to appropriate people to take action. If you find you are subject to an order that appears to be outside your normal routine, this is why. The orders may seem extreme, but I'm hoping that they will be no more than precautions."

"He's ordered all the citizens to seek shelter in the aquifers," Thayu whispered to me.

Shit.

"We have a number of advantages. We are many, and our numbers continue to increase. We have recalled as much of our fleet as feasible. We have full cooperation and assistance of the entire Trader Guild. The Exchange is operational. The Kedras military is on its way. Hedron has sent ships, due to arrive soon. And we have the captain of the ship as hostage. We will be using all these advantages to their fullest extent."

Ledaya glanced at me from where he sat.

"Meanwhile, I expect your full loyalty. As people, we have been through difficult times together, and we will get through this together. We are one. Iyamichu ata."

The whole command centre exploded with the reply as more than a hundred voices shouted, "Iyamichu ata!"

I merely repeated the words, but Thayu shouted, and Sheydu and Veyada, and Deyu, her eyes glittering.

The shout made the air vibrate as if the very metal of the hull rang with the sound of many voices. A number of people raised fists.

Ledaya called out, "Iyamichu ata!"

And again the crew replied as one. Serious faces. Raised fists.

It gave me goosebumps.

Asto was going to war.

As the crew sank into frenzied activities, Ledaya gestured me over to the command module. I undid my seat belt and floated over to him.

Ezhya's face was still displayed on the screen in front of the captain. Ezhya, too, sat in some kind of ship. Not a very large one, I thought. Possibly his own.

Ledaya moved aside so that I could face the screen.

Ezhya nodded when I came into view.

He said, "You have the captain there with you." It was not a question.

"We do indeed."

"Tell him to put that ship into a stable orbit. Tell him that he will have one last chance to speak to us. Tell him that any move towards the planet will be seen as hostile and will draw fire."

I wasn't going to mention the fact that we had nothing to destroy the ship with. He knew that. I saw it in his eyes. This was going to be classic Coldi bluff.

"Can the captain and his companions be brought here?" I asked Ledaya.

"They can." And he ordered, "Bring the hostages. Blindfolded." A cabin lackey hurried off to do it. Or maybe he wasn't a lackey. The disturbing part about the Asto military was that they rarely displayed ranking on their uniforms. Coldi *knew* who was ranked high and low. It was in their instinct.

I said, "Is the ship speaking to anyone?"

"No," Ezhya said. And then: "Their engines are running at low speed. They will want to execute a series of short burns to insert themselves into a stable orbit. We'll allow them to do that as long as they don't come any closer. After that, I rely on you to keep him talking. They've made it clear they're not interested in any form of communication with us. Keep him occupied."

"Until the sling turns up?"

"Until they come within range of the station. The sling can't be here before that time."

Shit. No one came close to the station. Not even the commercial flights did, and everyone aboard those were Asto's citizens.

"Is the station . . . armed?"

"There is a plan." All right so he was not going to answer that. "All I want you to do is make the captain believe that we're still interested in negotiating."

"Yes." I believed with all my heart that we should still try to negotiate. "As far as I can tell, the ship is slaved to the captain and one other crew member we have here. I am unsure what their tasks are. They haven't been very helpful."

"Talk to them. Keep them busy. I don't care what you say to them. I don't care what the result is. Just keep them busy."

"What if I can broker an agreement?"

His face hardened. "The time for agreements is past. If they were going to agree to anything we offered, they already would have done so. If there was anything they wanted that we could give them, they would have asked." The *miyu* pronouns unsettled me deeply, but oh, I understood. It was just that I would have considered him a friend, and now he was deciding over matters of war that would affect the lives of many. It was disturbing.

I signed off, and saw his face disappear from the screen, wondering if, when and where I would see him again and how much the world would have changed by then.

A couple of soldiers floated in through the square entrance in the base of the funnel shape of the command room. They pulled with them a platform with a plain flat base, unlike the mushroom-shaped one where we had been given seats. This particular one was probably used for moving freight through the ship. There were no seats, no stalk, only hooks on the "floor" to tie down the cargo so that it didn't go drifting into space. Four people "sat" on this floor, secured around the waist, wrists and ankles by brightly-coloured cargo straps: Kando Luczon, Tayron Kathraczi, Lilona Shrakar and Marin Federza. Their eyes had been covered by blindfolds.

"Do they really need to be blindfolded?" I asked Thayu in a low voice.

"You know the rule: *no one* sees the room of the upper command in Asto's military, unless you're upper military."

Kind of silly, but pointless to discuss. This was not my territory and not my terms.

I felt chilled that Ezhya's use of pronouns of war triggered my association to do the same.

I detached myself from the seat and floated through the control room. To one side—it was pointless to speak of left or right anymore —navigation crew were monitoring the progress of the ship, in particular in the giant formation of military ships that floated with us. Thayu had once explained the intricate systems of controlling where everyone jumped and how fast they moved when large sections of the fleet were in motion.

I grabbed the edge of the platform that held the hostages and swung myself up. I attached my tether to the hook I recognised to be destined for that purpose and reeled in the wire so that I didn't go floating into space.

One day I was going to be an expert on this.

To be honest I was astonished that I'd so far been able to hang onto my breakfast. Running ragged on high adrenalin apparently suppressed motion sickness.

"I've been given one last chance to come to an agreement with you about our future interactions," I started. "Ezhya Palayi of Asto has given you his position. Your ship is allowed to stay in orbit at its current distance from Asto for the duration of the negotiations, but—"

"What negotiations?" Kando Luczon turned his head towards me. His eyes were covered but his mouth was set in a stubborn line.

My mind flooded with a sudden revulsion and a feeling of deep hatred. This man had been given the most amazing life, a dream that people had died for: to make a jump in time and see what the future brought. He could have used it to help people, to warn people or simply to tell interesting tales. But no, all this man had ever done with the astonishing gift he'd been given life was be an utter dick. Frankly I was out of patience with him. "You're right. The time for negotiations is over. My allies keep telling me that, but I guess I was too stubborn to see it. I understand it now. Once I would have wanted to help you and your crew. I would have given you a place to live in safety—"

"We are not interested in anything you can offer us."

Frustration boiled over. "Then why did you come here? To disrupt our peaceful lives and to manipulate some of us into fighting against each other? How long has this been going on? Twenty, thirty years? Why? Do me a pleasure and tell us that."

"We made mistakes." His voice sounded prim.

"And you come here to make them worse? What do you care anyway? It's not your life anymore. None of us here are your problem or remotely your property. I was moved by your plea of an old man wanting to see his home once more, but I can see it for the lie it is. I don't believe anything you say anymore. The best thing you could do is leave us alone because if you stay here, things will end badly."

"Those people out there, they have nothing that can damage our ship."

"I would not want to put that to the test. Have you seen the size of the fleet out there? Do you know how many people are watching you? Do you know that they will try and try again until they can find a little hole, and they will rip it and make it bigger until it's so big that no one can plug it." That was how Coldi society worked: they kept trying, they waited until someone made a mistake. Above all, they worked together, as one.

"You still have nothing that could damage our ship. We refuse to let ourselves be dictated. We will go exactly where we want."

This was predictably not going well. Lilona was vigorously shaking her head. It didn't matter. Keep him talking, Ezhya had said, so that's what I did.

Marin Federza sat next to Lilona, holding her hand. He said, "It could be that the captain might consider retreating in exchange for permission to live on one world." What he said was nonsense. We already knew that he wasn't interested, but damn it, Federza appeared to understand what I was trying to do. I had never considered that possible.

I added to his words, "My colleague here is right. We could provide a community for all of the crew to live in, give them care and clothing and food—"

"We don't need worlds to live on. We don't need anyone's permission. The ship has been self-sufficient for generations."

"But it isn't!" Lilona cried out. "We're sick, and we're made to believe, every time things get worse and we become weaker and more sickly, that this is normal. Yes, we can live to very old ages, but we are too weak to enjoy it. I can't walk as fast as everyone. I feel sick all the time. I'm one of the healthier people, but compared to everyone here, I'm so weak. We get told that we're all healthy, but we can't even reproduce naturally anymore."

Tayron snapped at her in Aghyrian. She replied in an equally angry tone.

"I am trying to assist a peaceful solution." Federza sounded weary. I could only imagine what he had been going through since I'd come here and he had been left behind in the shuttle with the three Aghyrians.

Kando Luczon said, "The solution is that if everyone leaves us alone, there will be no problems and no weapons fired."

"You can't go wherever you like. This is not your world anymore."

"According to your own laws, it is. According to those laws, there is a group of people still waiting for a response to their legal claim against the occupiers."

Wait. The Aghyrian claim, had the captain been behind it? Had he contacted the *zeyshi* Aghyrians with promises of riches or land or power? Was that why, despite a few vocal voices, the claim had been largely forgotten since news of the ship had broken?

Holy shit.

I gestured for Veyada to come over. I absolutely needed to have a better witness than just the recording of this conversation, but at that very moment, an officer in the communication division yelled, "Action!"

In various parts of the command centre, people sprang into frenzied activity.

What the hell did that mean?

Ledaya took the projection off the schematic map and showed a live image. The quality was poor, shown at higher magnification than the image was intended for. I had no idea what the bright spots meant. Except they appeared to be moving. A spot in the middle flared with white and four other spots ejected a trail of bright sparks. Damn, the ship's engines had increased burn.

I whirled at Kando Luczon. "What are you doing?"

"We are resuming our planned course."

Damned if I understood this man, damned if anyone could get through to him. "There are hundreds of ships here that will fire at you if you come any closer."

He did not respond to that in his usual non-communicative mood. Did he even understand the concept of war?

"Call the ship to resume its earlier orbit, now," I yelled at him. "We have one chance to stop a fight."

Damn it, damn it. The vector already showed that the ship was dropping in orbit, on a direct route to the station. There was no way that anyone could tell me that the Aghyrians didn't know about the station. This was deliberate and provocative. Someone was going to fire. A lot of people were going to die. . . .

He said, in a dry tone, "Processes have been set into motion. It's inevitable."

"Stop those processes! If you're bound to the ship you have means of communicating with it."

They might even be aiming for the station. The ship might not have weapons of the calibre to make any impression on Asto's fleet. But they could use the ship itself, built to safely traverse intergalactic debris clouds at speeds we could not comprehend. They would have no trouble with a space station. Did the military even have enough time and docking space to take their giant workforce off the station? Surely they had some means of changing the path of the station? If they did, would it be agile enough?

This started to sound like Asto all over again.

Fuck, fuck, fuck.

I pressed the button on my tether and reeled myself in until my knees were firmly jammed against the cargo platform facing the captain. My mind overflowed with the things I wanted to do to him: shoot him, pull him up by that stupid robe of his and punch the teeth out of his mouth, or at least slap him in the face.

But I couldn't do any of that.

Because I was a negotiator and I never lost my temper. Because, if I would attempt to do those things, I wouldn't be very good at it. Because it was not my style.

So I just sat there, like a hunting cat ready to spring. I was trembling all over. One day, when Kando Luczon was no longer important to the peace, I was going to go up to his front door, and when he opened, I'd shoot the fucking bastard. Just like that. Until then, I was a coward.

"Cory," Thayu said, her voice soft. She was floating towards me.

I turned around, and almost lost it at the look of concern on her face. Even though our feeders didn't work, she acted like she knew what was going on. I loved her so much. I didn't care what she wanted me to do. I'd do it.

She put her hand on my arm. The warmth of her palm radiated through the fabric of my sleeve.

"Leave them for the time being. The ship will probably move soon, and we have to be secured."

She accompanied me back to our upside-down mushroom with seats.

The weapons command below my feet was in a state of frantic activity. Ledaya enlarged the view of the Aghyrian ship and surrounding space. A few ships were already lining up, small specks against the behemoth.

"What can they do against anything that size?"

Veyada said, "I suspect they'll try to create a diversion so that a small crew can break into the ship from the outside and disable the shield."

I remembered how we had entered the ship, and how the pilot of our shuttle had no control over where we went. How could anyone try to breach the shield? What did they know that we, having visited the ship, hadn't seen? That ship knew exactly what was going on around it.

A couple of smaller craft flew in formation quite close to the Aghyrian ship.

I thought I spotted a burst of fire from one of them. I presumed it was firing at the big ship, but I couldn't see whether or not it hit its target. All I could see was the futility of it.

A flash bloomed out from the big ship. That definitely hit the target as the small ship disintegrated. And another one and another one. The small ships had disintegrated into a cloud of debris.

"That seems like a stupid move," I said, feeling sick.

Thayu said, "Those were drones. There were no crew aboard those ships."

"Who told you that?"

"Standard engagement manoeuvre. I'm surprised they're falling for it. Watch what they're doing down there."

In the command centre, weapons crew were frantically analysing and calculating. Clearly I had misunderstood the point of the drones. They had been deliberately sacrificed to collect valuable data on the nature of the ship's weapons. Screens displayed ranges and possible weapon types.

Kando Luczon sat quietly, his back straight, his legs folded and his hands on his knees. Next to him, Tayron sat in exactly the same position. Lilona had slumped over. Her shoulders were shaking and her cheeks glittered with tears. One of her hands lay in her lap, but Federza held the other. Under the soft skin of the underside of her arm, a row of angry red lights flashed. She tried to pull her arm free, but Federza held it firmly.

"Kill me. Just kill me. He's using my connection to communicate with the crew. I don't know how long I can hold out. Kill me, now, before he orders them to attack."

Tayron hit out at her, lightning fast. But he wore a blindfold and missed. He leaned over and grabbed Lilona's free hand, twisting her arm.

She screamed at him in Aghyrian.

Federza snapped something at Tayron, and Tayron spat at Federza.

I called out, "Hey, that's not how you treat a crew member." I pushed off my seat and floated back to the platform.

Thayu was with me. She took her gun out of its bracket, and pushed the end against Tayron's head. "Do you feel that? Do you know what this is?"

He lifted his chin. "Killing me will have no effect. I'm not bound and my position on the ship is of no importance whatsoever. Kill her, if you need. She has fulfilled her purpose."

"Is that how you talk about the people who have given you a life-time's worth of service?" Thayu poked harder. "The Delegate is very nice and even tempered. If he weren't here, if it was up to us, you'd be dead many times over. I guess you haven't come here to be shot by us, so you might like to—"

"Action!" someone shouted.

I turned around so that I could see the projection. Thayu turned around. Crew all throughout the command centre went quiet.

The navigator zoomed out. He overlaid the projection of the thousands of little dots, each representing a ship, with an image of light filaments interweaving, all connecting to the same point in space.

The array of nodes blinked and pulsed again. In the split-second before the lights went off and the command room went dark, I saw a bright shape: a second ship had jumped.

We hadn't even known about a second Aghyrian ship in the system. This was not a visit to their place of origin. It was an invasion. These Aghyrians had lied to us about everything.

Alarms started blaring, voices were more agitated than before. In amongst all the military's urgent voices, I heard Ledaya's shouting orders. We had lost contact with Fleet Command, but the weapons people could fire at will.

Why I had had no idea.

We had no defence against these people at all.

28

FIRST THE INTERNAL lights and screens came back on.
The weapons team started up their systems immediately. The crew were tense, with hands on the controls. Waiting for orders, waiting for the outside feed to come back online.

First the viewscreens flickered into life. Without the scope feed, Ledaya couldn't enlarge the live view, and the unenlarged version was not very informative. Ships were no more than little dots against the starscape, if we could see them at all.

Then the three-dimensional projection in the middle of the command room came back up. Several people took in sharp breaths, but I didn't understand why.

"What is that thing?" Deyu whispered

I stared at the projection, confused by the mess of trailing jump wake lines that resembled old spider webs strung over bare tree branches. Ledaya enlarged an area further.

A long, stylus-like shape resolved in the projection, visible only because it trailed anpar filaments as if it had just flown through a dense concentration of spider webs.

That shape was familiar.

It looked like—No, it *was* the military sling.

"How the hell did they end up here?" I asked.

"They must have figured out how to use the array," Thayu said.

"And the Aghyrians, not expecting them to be able to do this, had not closed the line or dampened their wake."

Sheydu shook her head. "That is a major miscalculation."

Seated in the command chair, Ledaya balled his fist.

A few of the crew did the same, smiles on faces, and with shining eyes.

There might have been the odd, very uncharacteristic, cheer.

Everyone went back to work. Data scrolled over screens, commands rang around the room.

The sling ship kept a good distance. It was still smaller than the Aghyrian ship but not that much shorter. It went through a series of engine burns that kept it directly behind the Aghyrian ship and that positioned it so that the focus point of the output beam was focused on the ship. It was hard to see that from our position, even in the projection, but Thayu explained it to me.

Space warfare, people had told me on many different occasions, involved long periods of manoeuvring with very short periods of intense action. It also involved extraordinary amounts of physics.

"I don't understand why the Aghyrian ship doesn't move away," I said. "They have to realise that this thing is a weapon."

Thayu said, "I would stay, too, if I had as much confidence in the integrity of my shields as they seem to have. They would be running calculations to determine where and how they can move through a series of configurations where the sling will always be pointing at one of our ships as well as theirs. Well—I don't know that they're doing that, but I would."

"Maybe you should run a pirate fleet or something."

She smiled, nervously. We were both nervous. Everyone was nervous. I didn't like all this waiting. I kept looking at the clock ticking down to the moment the ship would come into range of the station. I trusted that Ezhya was not going to let that happen.

Ledaya held his hand up to get my attention. "Tell the hostages how the new situation stands. One last chance."

I was still floating next to the platform where the Aghyrians sat. The tether line hung slack. I reeled it in, pulling myself onto the platform.

I faced the captain, who still sat with his back straight.

"A ship has just jumped that will give the Coldi military a big advantage if it were to come to a fight. I plead you to change your ship's course, or the Chief Coordinator will order to have this weapon fired. I don't want that to happen. You have a crew of thousands. We have no desire to kill these people."

"You have a very high opinion of the strength of your weapons."

"You have a high opinion of the strength of your shield."

"Yes. I'm not worried. You, on the other hand, are all afraid. You're afraid that we are going to hit that precious base of yours, and we will. And there is nothing anyone can do about it."

"You cannot murder all these people yet again!" Lilona yelled at him and continued in Aghyrian.

He replied. I didn't understand what he said, but the disdain dripped from his voice.

"Why does she allow him to talk to her like that?" Deyu whispered.

Ezhya's voice came through the loudspeaker. "We have the sling aimed at your ship. Change course, or there will be a warning shot."

We waited.

Kando Luczon's face was impassive. Was there any communication between him and the ship going on?

And waited.

No one spoke; barely anyone dared move. All those crewmembers in the command room watched the three-dimensional projection. The Aghyrian ship's engines remained off. The clock counted down.

Kando Luczon said nothing. Lilona sat silently crying, pulled as far from him as her bonds allowed. She held Federza's hand.

In the heavy silence, Ezhya's voice sounded loud. "I do not see a change. I'm out of patience. Fire."

No one moved; no one spoke. Not even the faintest whisper or beep of a machine broke the silence.

Kando Luczon sat with his chin in the air, as if he were meditating. We had tested all three of them for equipment, and found nothing. Yet I still didn't believe that nothing was there.

We waited. And stared at the projection. My heart was thudding like crazy.

Too long.

Damn, it didn't work. The sling was damaged or jammed, or the ship had a counter-weapon that rendered it harmless—

A blindingly bright beam crossed the space from the sling to the behemoth ship. It hit to the side of the shield and would have whizzed past into space if the shield had not been there. Instead, the charge glanced off an invisible barrier that surrounded the ship. For a moment I thought this was it, but then a bright glow spread around the ship. White turned to angry, pulsing red, enveloping the ship before fading slowly.

"All the outside lights have gone out," Deyu said.

She was right. Not that the ship had been well-lit to begin with, but now it was completely dark.

Thayu whispered to me, "Look."

She pointed at the projection, where a shape glowed so brightly that it was hard to make out what it was.

"That's the shield," she said.

The hit from the sling had created a pulsing anpar field full of angry, pulsing energy. As the ship moved, wisps of energy eddied off into space, but this didn't reduce the glow noticeably.

We waited. I barely dared breathe.

Below my feet, the weapons team waited ready to respond with a massive display of fire. Our shield was up as well, which blurred the view on the viewscreens.

Ledaya switched the three-dimensional projection to visible light and enlarged it until a replica of the Aghyrian ship hung in the middle of the room. The outside was still dark.

Sheydu frowned. "I can't imagine that this glancing blow would have killed the ship. They're acting. Drawing out time. They want to destroy the station."

Ledaya was still waiting.

Kando Luczon sat with his eyes closed. His face looked pale and thin. The Aghyrian crew were all unhealthy, if Lilona was to be believed. Was this some sort of macabre suicide mission?

Thayu whispered, "Look at the clock."

"That was a warning shot," came Ezhya's voice through the loud-speakers. "If you do not change course within the count of thirty, we will aim at the centre of the ship and will keep firing until the shield explodes from the heat."

The captain's face remained blank and emotionless.

Bright green numbers started the countdown: twenty-nine . . . twenty-eight . . . twenty-seven . . .

The space station was already over the horizon. It was not particularly well-armed, I thought.

I didn't understand why Ezhya left the Aghyrians in this orbit for so long. If I was him, I would have fired immediately and kept the ship a safe distance from the station. If they killed it now, what was the guarantee that the empty hull or debris wouldn't hit the station? I hoped someone was moving the station to a higher orbit. I hoped that was possible.

Twenty-one . . . twenty . . . nineteen . . .

How many people even lived on the station? I hoped they had been able to evacuate a good proportion of them, but I knew there would barely have been any time.

Fifteen . . . fourteen . . . thirteen . . .

Ledaya sat with his hands on the controls. Watching, ready to spring when the order came.

Twelve . . . eleven . . . ten . . .

I wiped sweat from my upper lip. Lilona hid her face in her hands. A line of lights flashed angry red under the soft skin of her forearm.

Nine . . . eight . . . seven . . .

This was ridiculous. I called out to Kando Luczon, "Come on. You can stop this. They will destroy you. Have you really come here to have your people murdered?"

Six . . . five . . . four . . .

Thayu and Veyada stared at the projection of the ship. The shield glowed as brightly as it had previously, with trailing strands of energy. It was not shedding its energy quickly enough to be able to absorb another hit.

Ledaya made a barely perceptible move with his finger.

Damn it.

Someone yelled, "Action!"

Thayu took in a sharp breath.

Four blinding white spots appeared in the projection: the ship's engines flared with a brief burst of fire. And then another one, longer this time.

Ledaya yelled, "Hold fire!"

More and more people were staring at the projection.

Slowly, the path diverged from the projected trajectory. The ship broke orbit and moved away from the planet.

The captain said behind me, "We'll speak briefly."

29

———————

KANDO LUCZON looked stressed. Hell, everyone looked stressed, with the exception of Tayron, who I had never seen display any emotion whatsoever.

Even Ledaya who was doing his best to hide it, but I spotted him wiping his face and closing his eyes.

"Holy crap," Thayu said. "Can anyone confirm what just happened? Did they just back away?"

"They did," Veyada said.

The Aghyrian ship was still gathering speed, climbing to a higher orbit. The station had come over the curve of the planet and was moving a good distance underneath the ship.

I blew out a heavy breath. "They sure did, but I don't know that I had anything to do with it."

Ledaya in the command chair gestured me over.

I threw the tether magnet and pulled myself to the command module.

Ezhya was on the screen again. "You have the captain still there in one piece?"

"Yes, although I would have loved to have taken a few pieces off him. He says he wants to talk. Briefly."

Ezhya snorted. "Guess who decides the duration of our conversation. Bring him."

A crewmember went to the cargo platform, undid the ties that secured Kando Luczon to the platform. He pulled the captain to the command module by using his tether. He then pushed the captain into the chair and tied his arms and legs. Another crewmember brought a sticky sheet which went over the controls of the bench in front, I guessed so that the captain couldn't see or interfere with them. A third crewmember brought a bigger sheet of flexible material which he bent around the chair, making a little closed-off cubicle. Only when this was all secured did they remove Kando Luczon's blindfold.

He squinted against the light.

On the screen, Ezhya studied him. He said nothing and his face remained blank, but I didn't miss that small jerk of his head, jutting out his chin, a gesture of superiority and utter disdain.

"Why am I here?" Kando Luczon liked to keep people waiting, but sure as hell didn't like to be kept waiting by others.

"I think your all-purpose colonising race is doing pretty well, don't you?" Ezhya's pronouns were absolutely diabolical.

Kando Luczon's nostrils flared. I didn't think he understood the nuances of Coldi pronouns, but the tone of the remark alone was insulting enough.

Ezhya went on. "I think we are doing just fine without help from anyone, least of all you." Coldi: how to utterly demolish someone using nothing other than a choice of pronouns. Ezhya was a master at this. "So. You want a brief meeting. Let's keep it brief: you will piss off." He actually used a rather crude Coldi word, popular in the armed forces. "You will leave and keep out of all space ruled by *gamra*. You will agree to this, or we will shoot you to bits. If you turn up some-where against this agreement, we will shoot you to bits without warning."

"We don't get much of a choice, do we?"

"Nope."

"Well, we better get back to our ship, then."

"There will be transport shortly. No need to slow the ship down. We will match speed and drop you at your ship while you're getting out of here."

I couldn't believe that he was letting them go back to their ship.

"If I may make a suggestion," I said.

Ezhya raised his eyebrows.

"We could use a ship's representative in Barresh," I said. I had no idea if *gamra* would be warm to such an idea, but if necessary, I'd find funds myself.

Kando Luczon gave me a cold look. "Do you think any of us would like to live with you?"

"I think so." I glanced sideways at the platform, where the remaining three hostages sat quietly.

"I think it's important that you have a representative with us, so that we can continue to communicate on the subject of cooperation."

"My advisor is right, as usual. An observer to *gamra* would be good. One only." Ezhya said. He continued to me, "Choose one and return the rest to that floating coffin of theirs. I guess we'll see them turn up somewhere else sooner or later. They need us a lot more than we need them. We can talk when they play by our rules."

I wanted to talk to Ezhya about ideas I had, but there was no opportunity to speak in private. It would have to wait until later, by which time he might well have guessed about the nature of my ideas.

We accompanied the Aghyrians out of the command room back to the shuttle. A couple of uniformed soldiers made sure that we all went in.

Tayron stopped at the door. "Are we all going? I thought someone was going to stay here."

"We will go back via the ship. No one stays on board a military vessel." And certainly *he* would be going back to the ship.

We entered the shuttle and went through the routine of getting into the couches. A few crewmembers helped us. Deyu was also getting deft in zero-g and helped Federza into his couch when both of them had strapped Lilona in.

I let myself be handled by Thayu who was much more handy in zero-g than I was. She clicked the cover shut. Through the little window I could see her climbing into her own couch.

The screens were on and only went dark for the brief period that we left the ship. Then the feed came back on and there was no further blackout, not even when we made a small jump to where the large ship was heading outbound.

The shuttle matched velocity with the ship and let itself be pulled into the dock.

Once again we were in the huge hall and landed on one of the floating pads. Knowing what I knew now, it seemed empty, disused and run-down. Did the Aghyrians have small craft for surface missions? Did they have any people who could fly them?

"So this is where we leave you," I said when we stood at the open door looking into the dark hall.

Kando Luczon never spoke much in any situation, but he had said nothing since leaving the military ship. To be honest, he looked like a walking statue, a robot.

He barely acknowledged us.

So much for a thank you for taking you home.

"The conditions to your peaceful departure will be binding," I said, because I had to say something. "Ezhya Palayi is known for carrying out his threats."

"I shall remember that." Not in a good way, I thought. He held his back straight and his chin in the air.

"Let's go," Tayron said. He turned around to the ship.

Thayu stopped him at the door.

"What?" he said. "You agreed one representative could come back with you."

"Not you." I nodded at Lilona. "We want her."

Lilona burst into tears. "I can't. I'm bound to the ship." She showed us the inside of her arm which had turned into a red welt.

"Can you turn that off or disable it?"

"Can't. Only the captain can do that."

"Then the captain will release you so that you can come with us."

Kando Luczon put his chin in the air. "Being bound to the ship is an honour that many would kill for."

A sudden surge of anger took hold of me. "An honour to expose yourself to danger while the ship jumps, an honour to be treated as a slave? Release her!"

"I selected her as ship's crew."

Sheydu sprang forward, grabbing him by the front of his robe. "He says release her, so you will release her."

"You do *not* touch the captain!" Tayron pulled her arm, but Sheydu hit him aside. He stumbled backwards. He fell and almost slid over the edge of the platform but managed to hold onto Veyada's leg. "Watch out what you're doing!"

The captain shouted and Sheydu shouted, while Deyu ran forward to offer Tayron her hand. She pulled him up easily, despite being much shorter and half his age. Then Tayron shouted at Sheydu and Sheydu shouted back at him and the captain told them all to stop.

A piercing scream stopped all the shouting.

While we were watching Tayron, Lilona had gotten hold of Federza's gun. She had figured how to put it on the narrow beam, low-intensity setting—the one that could be used to cut through things. She had traced a deep cut across her arm. She now pulled a string of nodules from the length of her forearm, covered in blood and tissue. Blood spurted onto the ground. For a moment, she stood still as if she couldn't believe what she had done, and then she crumpled to the ground.

Veyada dropped to his knees, rummaging in his pockets. Finding nothing, he yanked off his shirt and pressed it against Lilona's arm. "Quick. Get the medkit."

Sheydu ran inside the shuttle and came back a moment later with a box which she dumped on the ground and opened it. Veyada rummaged through it, throwing bandages and other items around. Blood was going everywhere.

Federza had also dropped to his knees. He was unwrapping several lengths of bandage, bundling them all into one thick strand.

He lifted up Lilona's arm. He quickly wound the bandage around the upper part of the arm. The blood flow reduced, but not before Federza's trousers and arms had become covered in it.

Veyada opened another package which contained a clear sleeve which he slipped over her arm. "That should keep it stable until we can get her to a hospital." He wiped his face with the bottom of his right arm. "This will need some heavy surgery."

"She'll be all right, won't she?" Federza was gathering the empty wrappers of the bandages. His face was pale and hands trembled. He had blood all over his hands and the left leg of his suit.

"I think so," Veyada said. "No, don't shut the medkit yet. I think I might give her a sedative. We don't want her panicking inside the pod and ripping off the bandages." He rummaged in the kit, finally finding an injector armband which he put around the top of her good arm. He clicked in an ampoule. "There. That should do it. Let's get out of here quickly."

Sheydu and Marin Federza carried Lilona inside, leaving a trail of bloodied footsteps on the ground and the gangplank. The thing Lilona had pulled out still lay there, glistening wetly with blood.

While all this was going on, Tayron and Kando Luczon watched impassively.

"I hope you're happy," I told him. "She would rather kill herself than stay with you."

He said nothing. I met his cold eyes with a sense of disappointment, wanting to shake him out of his stupor, getting him to become angry with me. Or something, anything. I didn't even know what I had expected. He had shown himself to be utterly incapable of feeling or understanding emotions.

Thayu gently pulled me up the gangplank.

"It's a waste of time trying to talk to the arsehole and his understudy," she said when we were inside the craft. "He's nothing but a reason for you to get angry. Don't. He's not worth it. There are much better things to get angry about."

I was still feeling shaky when the craft went through the dock back into space. Sheydu and Federza had put Lilona into one of the antigrav couches and helped me strap in. There was blood everywhere, even on my clothes.

When the lid shut with a click, I leaned back into the soft material, dizzy with fatigue. After spending the past few days on high adrenalin and very little sleep, it was catching up with me big time. No sooner had the craft pulled away than I'd fallen asleep.

30

WE RETURNED to Barresh where people from the hospital waited on the tarmac with a van to take Lilona to the hospital. I knew the woman who leaned against the side of the van. She had once fixed my infected hands. I'd forgotten her name, but remembered that she was good. And she was Aghyrian.

Federza was going with Lilona. I held him back before he got into the van. "Come back to the apartment when you're done at the hospital. You're welcome to stay until you have other accommodation. You left some of your things there, and there is something I'd like to discuss with you."

He promised he'd be there as soon as he could. Raising curiosity was always the best way to secure someone's cooperation.

Ezhya taught me that.

We took the train home. Dirty and smelly as we were, we caught some odd glances from the genteel citizens of the *gamra* island.

I guessed saving civilisation as we knew it was dirty work.

Nicha had heard that we were back and came running down the stairs as soon as we entered the building.

I was the recipient of a very un-Coldi hug, which came with a squeal from the sling at his back.

"How's the little brat been behaving?"

"We've got the night feeds all sorted, and he's starting to like the girls. He likes Reida, too, but don't tell Reida that."

The familiar smell of Eirani's cooking wafted out of the apartment. Evi and Telaris stood at the door. I would have hugged them, too, had that been appropriate.

While we had been away, life had gone on as normal, and most people in Barresh had been oblivious to the battle that had been fought over our section of space. Quite how things were meant to be —because why get people worried about things they could do nothing about?—although it was a little disturbing.

As it turned out, Devlin told me, Delegate Namion had survived the explosion with some moderate, but not life-threatening injuries. He was still in the hospital, his displeasure with the state of affairs evident through hundreds of messages which, according to Devlin, were in my account. At least he had returned control of that account back to me.

The *gamra* court was going to hold a bedside hearing in the hospital, where he would be presented with a full account of evidence that my staff had collected about his strange practices. He would be forced to resign.

We had a late lunch where every member of my staff came into the room, and sat or stood around the table, because there weren't enough chairs to include all the office and domestic staff, Nicha's babysitter and Evi and Telaris. We talked and laughed, and ate cakes and bread and drank tea.

Marin Federza came to the apartment and after having supplied him with a plate of food, we went to my office.

Lilona would be fine, he said. She was going to need surgery and might need bionics to retain full use of her arm, but she was out of danger. An Aghyrian doctor was going to work on her mental state.

He said, "You know what she did to her arm? That's what happened to her mind earlier, when we were in the tunnels and we managed to break her."

He looked exhausted and dirty, his trousers still flecked with Lilona's blood. A wave of nausea washed over me when thinking about how Lilona had pulled that thing out of her arm. That would probably join the gallery of unspeakable memories in my life.

He said he was tired and was about to go to his room when I said, "Having a chat wasn't why I asked you to come here."

"Oh?" He stopped getting up and sat back down.

"Delegate Namion will be deposed because of the material you were able to secure from the Exchange wake and other sources."

Federza nodded. "I guess he was always a placeholder, so that some other people could jostle into the right position."

"Yes, but a placeholder for whom?"

"Well, word goes that it was for you."

"Me?" Seriously, who started all these rumours?

"Yes, since you were absent from that meeting where he was elected."

I snorted. "As I have said to the members of my association, I'm not standing. I would never pass the assembly's scrutiny. I'm not neutral enough. I live in Asto's pockets, they say."

He nodded, glancing at my Domiri earrings. "You're a very curious case. Sometimes you're more Coldi than the Coldi. I don't think I've ever met a non-Coldi person who has such an utter understanding of the Coldi as you do."

"Well . . ." What to say to that? "I could be made to disagree with that."

"Don't bother. No one would believe you."

True. "To get back to our subject, I don't know that Delegate Namion was deliberately set up as interim by anyone in particular. I think he accepted the job knowing that it might be a short tenure. If I were him and I knew what he knew when accepting the position, I would probably have felt the same. The situation remains that we need someone else."

He nodded, deep in thought.

"I wanted to let you know that I am going to nominate you."

His eyes widened. Then he laughed. "I'm the most hated ex-Delegate ever."

"I think you overestimate people's reactions. Especially when court documents start getting released to the public and people can see for themselves how corruption got hold of many in the assembly under the reign of Joyelin Akhtari. When there will be daily reports about what these people did and how they managed to get away with it, your name will come up quite a bit."

"It will. I don't even know if I'd be eligible to stand."

"There is nothing wrong with being called as witness."

He nodded.

"People will feel sympathetic to you."

"I don't want to be given a position out of sympathy."

"No. I'm not going to mention sympathy at all. I think you'll do an evenhanded job."

"Well," he said, and said nothing else for a long time. Didn't reject the offer. He added, "I guess we can only let the assembly decide."

"That, we can. But making sure that our candidates are competent and fair is the first and most important step."

He nodded. "Well. I guess I've been fighting the old guard for long enough. Maybe they'd want me to show them the money."

Clearly warming to the idea. "So that's how it stands and what I will do. I can't guarantee any support, but we can try."

He nodded again. And then he said, "Thank you. For everything." He rose quite suddenly. "I better . . . not take too much of your time. You must be tired."

I was tired, but it would be some time before I could go to bed. "Go back to the main island, if you want. Look after her."

"Thank you," he said again, and then he was gone.

———

Why was I so keen to help Federza, Thayu wanted to know at dinner. All of us were sitting around the big table in the living room and everyone fell quiet when she asked that. "It's like you're fascinated with him. He's not in our association."

"He is not in *this* association, but I think he is in one of mine, in his own way. He believes in doing the right thing, and we should support people who do the right thing."

"Does he do the right thing, though? He could have spoken out much earlier, if he broke with his people," Sheydu said.

"I don't know about that. There are some pretty powerful people pulling the strings in the Aghyrian compound. Probably he relied on their endorsement for some or part of his support, either financial or in some other way that made him dependent on them."

If "blunt" was the cliché descriptor for Coldi people, then the one-word description for the Aghyrians would have to be "manipulative". I could only begin to imagine the web of intrigue and fear that Federza would have been living under.

"Doesn't that then make him more vulnerable as candidate?"

"It would, if we didn't know about it and if he hadn't spoken out about it."

"Well . . ." Sheydu said, and she looked doubtful. "I guess I don't have to vote."

"I think he'll do a better job than either Akhtari and Namion," Veyada said.

And, as it often did, Veyada's opinion settled the matter.

Talk turned to our adventures for the benefit of those who hadn't been there. Nicha had been to the Aghyrian ship, but Reida hadn't; and although he had enjoyed himself at the shooting range with Nicha, the experience paled in comparison to his *zhayma*'s trip to the giant ship.

"It's a piece of floating history," Veyada said. "They like to think that they were so much more superior than we are and that we haven't yet caught up with them, but I think they're wrong about that. I mean —that ship didn't even dampen its wake, broadcasting everything about it to the entire network."

Sheydu nodded. "That thing is a floating coffin."

"I'm more worried about the people they left behind on that other planet," Nicha said. "What have *they* developed?"

"I don't think they'll show up on our doorstep anytime soon," Thayu said. "Having gotten rid of their arsehole captain, why would they?"

No one answered that question.

I looked around the table at my loyal team, happy that we were all safe and all here. I would not have been able to have done any of this without them.

———

The day ended, as so many, in the bath with an activity that was both pleasant and relaxing. Afterwards, we sat on the little underwater bench. I'd gotten out of the water to retrieve two glasses and a bottle of lily bulb liquor from the cupboard against the wall. I'd put the glasses on the edge of the pool and poured while sitting on the under-water bench.

The liquor was sweet and heavy and spread a scent of flowers over the water.

Thayu took her glass from me. She had that expression on her face that said she was ready for serious talk. Since it had proven impossible to talk when she wasn't in the mood for discussing certain things, I seized the occasion. "So, what are we going to tell Menor?"

"I've been thinking," she said, and sipped from her drink. "He is easy and doesn't mind one way or another?"

"No, it's up to us whether or not we use him. Whether or not you want to do this."

She blew out a breath. "I don't."

And she met my eyes.

My heart was hammering. Was this going to be one of those *Thanks, but no thanks* occasions?

"Don't look at me like that."

"Well, I know that you badly want another child, and I can't give you one so . . ." My vision blurred. I had to look away, breathing deeply to keep all those bad feelings at bay.

"So, what? I don't know what you mean. I don't want to use Menor until we have exhausted absolutely all avenues. Talking to Lilona has made me realise that there is a lot more that we don't know, and a lot of things that can possibly be done that we don't yet know about. We have time. I don't need to rush."

All right. I took a deep calming breath, and then another, and downed the contents of my glass in one gulp.

"Hey." She put a warm hand on my arm. "You seem really out-of-sorts whenever this subject comes up. I've avoided it for that reason. You really don't want to use Menor either?"

"It's not about Menor. He's a fine young man, and I'd have no trouble using him. It's that I thought that you didn't want to use him, and that you wanted only a natural child—"

"I do."

"I thought that since I can't give you that, you were . . ." My voice choked up.

"I was what?"

"You were going to leave me." Her beautiful face blurred before my eyes.

Understanding dawned on her face. Then she enveloped me in a strong hug, uttering a little squeak. "Oh. Why didn't you say so? I would have told you that I'd rather forego my right to have another child than leave you. I would never do that."

I hugged her back, relishing the warmth of her against me. "I guess I never said anything because I was too afraid."

"You have nothing to be afraid of."

We sat like that for a while. From deeper in the apartment came the sound of laughter and a baby's squeal. Coldi babies were quick developers, and Ayshada was already starting to show his little personality. "There will be another child in this apartment, one way or another. We'll look into it further. If it's a genuine possibility I don't rule out having my genes upgraded while I'm still alive."

"You make it sound so morbid."

"It *is* kind of morbid. Lilona wasn't even sure it could be done for adults. Anyway, she may know about the technology, but the ship is gone. She doesn't have the equipment and the labs and staff that she might need."

"But they will be back."

I laughed. "In another fifty thousand years' time?" But I knew they wouldn't be that long. I didn't think the Aghyrian ship and crew had the strength for another set of jumps that big. There was no need to go to another galaxy. There were a lot of other worlds full of people they could try to manipulate in this galaxy. Non-*gamra* worlds, where the agreement between Ezhya and Kando Luczon didn't necessarily hold. If the Aghyrians didn't already know about these worlds, they would find out soon. Yes, we would cross paths with them again. Sooner rather than later.

———

The next book in the Ambassador series is *Blue Diamond Sky*. Cory and his team find a message in a bottle on a deserted sand bar in Barresh. The text is in Isla. Who wrote it and where is this person?

Be a champ and get Ambassador 5 direct from the author, in ebook, print or audio.

ABOUT THE AUTHOR

Patty Jansen lives in Sydney, Australia, where she spends most of her time writing Science Fiction and Fantasy.

Her career started in earnest when her story *This Peaceful State of War* placed first in the second quarter of the Writers of the Future contest and was published in their 27th anthology. She has also sold fiction to genre magazines such as Analog Science Fiction and Fact, Redstone SF and Aurealis, before making the move to independent publishing.

Patty has written over fifty novels in both Science Fiction and Fantasy, including the *Icefire Trilogy* and the *Ambassador* series.

pattyjansen.com

BOOKS BY PATTY JANSEN

MORE INFORMATION:

PATTYJANSEN.COM

For a complete list of books, scan the image below with your phone.

www.ingramcontent.com/pod-product-compliance
Lightning Source LLC
Chambersburg PA
CBHW050819190726
48286CB00007B/1919